Owing to circumstances beyond our control,
UltraWord™ has been withdrawn from use at
this time. This book may be read using the
standard BOOK V8.3 imaginotransference
operating system. Our apologies for any
inconvenience.

Council of Genres Ordinance: DOP/0710849

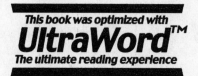

This book was optimized with
UltraWord™
The ultimate reading experience

The Well of Lost Plots

ALSO BY JASPER FFORDE

The Eyre Affair

Lost in a Good Book

THURSDAY NEXT

IN

The Well of Lost Plots

A NOVEL

Jasper Fforde

VIKING

VIKING
Published by the Penguin Group
Penguin Group (USA) Inc., 375 Hudson Street,
New York, New York 10014, U.S.A.
Penguin Books Ltd, 80 Strand, London WC2R ORL, England
Penguin Books Australia Ltd, 250 Camberwell Road, Camberwell,
Victoria 3124, Australia
Penguin Books Canada Ltd, 10 Alcorn Avenue, Toronto, Ontario, Canada M4V 3B2
Penguin Books India (P) Ltd, 11 Community Centre, Panchsheel Park,
New Delhi–110 017, India
Penguin Books (N.Z.) Ltd, Cnr Rosedale and Airborne Roads, Albany,
Auckland, New Zealand
Penguin Books (South Africa) (Pty) Ltd, 24 Sturdee Avenue,
Rosebank, Johannesburg 2196, South Africa

Penguin Books Ltd, Registered Offices:
80 Strand, London WC2R ORL, England

First American edition
Published in 2004 by Viking Penguin, a member of Penguin Group (USA) Inc.

5 7 9 10 8 6

Publisher's Note
This is a work of fiction. Names, characters, places, and incidents either are the
product of the author's imagination or are used fictitiously, and any resemblance to
actual persons, living or dead, business establishments, events, or locales is
entirely coincidental.

LIBRARY OF CONGRESS CATALOGING-IN-PUBLICATION DATA
Fforde, Jasper.
Thursday Next in The well of lost plots : a novel / Jasper Fforde.
p.   cm.
ISBN 0-670-03289-1
1. Next, Thursday (Fictitious character)—Fiction.   2. Characters and characteristics
in literature—Fiction.   3. Women detectives—Great Britain—Fiction.   4. Books
and reading—Fiction.   5. Time travel—Fiction.   6. Libraries—Fiction.
I. Title: Well of lost plots.   II. Title.
PR6106.F67T485 2004
823'.914—dc22   2003062150

This book is printed on acid-free paper. ∞

Printed in the United States of America
Set in Berkeley Medium
Designed by Francesca Belanger

For Mari

who makes the torches burn brighter

Contents

Thursday Next: The Story So Far . . .

Swindon, Wessex, England, circa 1985. SpecOps is the agency responsible for policing areas considered too specialized to be tackled by the regular force, and Thursday Next is attached to the Literary Detectives at SpecOps-27. Following the successful return of Jane Eyre to the novel of the same name, vanquishing master criminal Acheron Hades and bringing peace to the Crimean peninsula, she finds herself a minor celebrity.

On the trail of the seemingly miraculous discovery of the lost Shakespeare play *Cardenio,* she crosses swords with Yorrick Kaine, escapee from fiction and neofascist politician. She also finds herself blackmailed by the vast multinational known as the Goliath Corporation, who want their operative Jack Schitt out of Edgar Allan Poe's "The Raven," in which he was imprisoned. To achieve this they call on Lavoisier, a corrupt member of the time-traveling SpecOps elite, the ChronoGuard, to kill off Thursday's husband. Traveling back thirty-eight years, Lavoisier engineers a fatal accident for the two-year-old Landen, but leaves Thursday's memories of him intact—she finds herself the only person who knows he once lived.

In an attempt to rescue her eradicated husband, she finds a way to enter fiction itself—and discovers that not only is there a policing agency within the BookWorld known as Jurisfiction, but that she has been apprenticed as a trainee agent to Miss Havisham of *Great Expectations*. With her skills at bookjumping growing under Miss Havisham's stern and often unorthodox tuition, Thursday rescues Jack Schitt, only to discover she has been duped. Goliath has no intention of reactualizing her husband and instead wants her to open a door into fiction, something Goliath has decided is a "rich untapped marketplace" for their varied but spectacularly worthless products and services.

Thursday, pregnant with Landen's child and pursued by Goliath and Acheron's little sister, Aornis, an evil genius with a penchant for clothes shopping and memory modification, decides to enter the BookWorld and retire temporarily to the place where all fiction is created: the Well of Lost Plots. Taking refuge in an unpublished book of dubious quality as part of the Character Exchange Program, she *thinks* she will have a quiet time.

Author's Note

To those unfamiliar with the pronunciation of English provincial towns, this is how I pronounce them:

Slough rhymes with *wow* and is *never* pronounced *Sluff*.
Reading is pronounced as in Otis *Redding*.
Goring rhymes with *boring*.
Cheltenham is pronounced *Chelt-num*.
Warwickshire is pronounced *war-rick-shy-er*.
Hobble is a pronounced *limp*.

Mouse your way to my Web site at www.jasperfforde.com

This book has been bundled with special features including "The Making of" documentary, deleted scenes from all three books, outtakes and much more. To access all these free bonus features, log on to www.jasperfforde.com/specialfeatures.html and enter the code word as directed.

"Damn and blast!" yelled Jack. "The Text Sea!"

1.

The Absence of Breakfast

The Well of Lost Plots. To understand the Well you have to have an idea of the layout of the Great Library. The library is where all published fiction is stored so it can be read by the readers in the Outland; there are twenty-six floors, one for each letter of the alphabet. The library is constructed in the layout of a cross with the four corridors radiating from the center point. On all the walls, end after end, shelf after shelf, are *books*. Hundreds, thousands, millions of books. Hardbacks, paperbacks, leatherbound, everything. But the similarity of all these books to the copies we read back home is no more than the similarity a photograph has to its subject; these books are *alive*.

Beneath the Great Library are twenty-six floors of dingy yet industrious subbasements known as the Well of Lost Plots. This is where books are constructed, honed and polished in readiness for a place in the library above—if they make it that far. The failure rate is high. Unpublished books outnumber published by an estimated eight to one.

THURSDAY NEXT,
The Jurisfiction Chronicles

MAKING ONE'S HOME in an unpublished novel wasn't without its compensations. All the boring day-to-day mundanities that we conduct in the real world get in the way of narrative flow and are thus generally avoided. The car didn't need refueling, there were never any wrong numbers, there was always enough hot water, and vacuum cleaner bags came in only two sizes—upright and pull along. There were other more subtle differences, too. For instance, no one ever needed to repeat themselves in case you didn't hear, no one shared the same name, talked at the same time or had a word annoyingly "on the tip of their tongue." Best of all, the bad guy was always someone you knew of, and—Chaucer aside—there wasn't much farting. But there were some downsides. The relative absence of breakfast was the first and most notable difference to my daily timetable. Inside books, dinners are often written about and therefore feature frequently, as do lunches and afternoon tea; probably because they offer more opportunities to further the story.

Breakfast wasn't all that was missing. There was a peculiar lack of cinemas, wallpaper, toilets, colors, books, animals, underwear, smells, haircuts, and strangely enough, minor illnesses. If someone was ill in a book, it was either terminal and dramatically unpleasant or a mild head cold—there wasn't much in between.

I was able to take up residence inside fiction by virtue of a scheme entitled the Character Exchange Program. Due to a spate of bored and disgruntled bookpeople escaping from their novels and becoming what we called PageRunners, the authorities set up the scheme to allow characters a change of scenery. In any year there are close to ten thousand exchanges, few of which result in any major plot or dialogue infringements—the reader rarely suspects anything at all. Since I was from the real world and not actually a character at all, the Bellman and Miss Havisham had agreed to let me live inside the BookWorld in exchange for helping out at Jurisfiction—at least as long as my pregnancy would allow.

The choice of book for my self-enforced exile had not been arbitrary; when Miss Havisham asked me in which novel I would care to reside, I had thought long and hard. *Robinson Crusoe* would have been ideal considering the climate, but there was no one female to exchange with. I could have gone to *Pride and Prejudice,* but I wasn't wild about high collars, bonnets, corsets—and delicate manners. No, to avoid any complications and reduce the possibility of having to move, I had decided to make my home in a book of such dubious and uneven quality that publication and my subsequent enforced ejection was unlikely in the extreme. I found just such a book deep within the Well of Lost

Plots amongst failed attempts at prose and half-finished epics of such dazzling ineptness that they would never see the light of day. The book was a dreary crime thriller set in Reading entitled *Caversham Heights*. I had planned to stay there for only a year, but it didn't work out that way. Plans with me are like De Floss novels—try as you might, you never know *quite* how they are going to turn out.

I read my way into *Caversham Heights*. The air felt warm after the wintry conditions back home, and I found myself standing on a wooden jetty at the edge of a lake. In front of me there was a large and seemingly derelict flying boat of the sort that still plied the coastal routes back home. I had flown on one myself not six months before on the trail of someone claiming to have found some unpublished Burns poetry. But that was another lifetime ago, when I was SpecOps in Swindon, the world I had temporarily left behind.

The ancient flying boat rocked gently in the breeze, tautening the mooring ropes and creaking gently, the water gently slapping against the hull. As I watched the old aircraft, wondering just how long something this decrepit could stay afloat, a well-dressed young woman stepped out of an oval-shaped door in the high-sided hull. She was carrying a suitcase. I had read the novel of *Caversham Heights* so I knew Mary well although she didn't know me.

"Hullo!" she shouted, trotting up and offering me a hand. "I'm Mary. You must be Thursday. My goodness! What's that?"

"A dodo. Her name's Pickwick."

Pickwick plocked and stared at Mary suspiciously.

"Really?" she replied, looking at the bird curiously. "I'm no expert of course but—I *thought* dodoes were extinct."

"Where I come from, they're a bit of a pest."

"Oh?" mused Mary. "I'm not sure I've heard of a book with *live* dodoes in it."

"I'm not a bookperson," I told her, "I'm real."

"Oh!" exclaimed Mary, opening her eyes wide. "An *Outlander*."

She touched me inquisitively with a slender index finger as though I might be made of glass.

"I've never seen someone from the other side before," she announced, clearly relieved to find that I wasn't going to shatter into a thousand pieces. "Tell me, is it true you have to cut your hair on a regular basis? I mean, your hair actually *grows*?"

"Yes"—I smiled—"and my fingernails, too."

"Really?" mused Mary. "I've heard rumors about that but I thought it was just one of those Outlandish legends. I suppose you have to eat, too? To stay alive, I mean, not just when the story calls for it?"

"One of the great pleasures of life," I assured her.

I didn't think I'd tell her about real-world downsides such as tooth decay, incontinence, or old age. Mary lived in a three-year window and neither aged, died, married, had children, got sick or changed in any way. Although appearing resolute and strong-minded, she was only like this because she was *written* that way. For all her qualities, Mary was simply a foil to Jack Spratt, the detective in *Caversham Heights*, the loyal sergeant figure to whom Jack explained things so the readers knew what was going on. She was what writers called an *expositional*, but I'd never be as impolite to say so to her face.

"Is this where I'm going to live?" I was pointing at the shabby flying boat.

"I know what you're thinking." Mary smiled proudly. "Isn't she just the most beautiful thing ever? She's a Sunderland; built in 1943 but last flew in '68. I'm midway converting her to a houseboat, but don't feel shy if you want to help out. Just keep the bilges pumped out, and if you can run the number three engine once a month, I'd be very grateful—the start-up checklist is on the flight deck."

"Well—okay," I muttered.

"Good. I've left a précis of the story taped to the fridge and a rough idea of what you have to say, but don't worry about being word perfect; since we're not published, you can say almost anything you want—within reason, of course."

"Of course." I thought for a moment. "I'm new to the Character Exchange Program. When will I be called to do something?"

"Wyatt is the inbook exchange liaison officer; he'll let you know. Jack might seem gruff to begin with," continued Mary, "but he has a heart of gold. If he asks you to drive his Austin Allegro, make sure you depress the clutch fully before changing gear. He takes his coffee black and the love interest between myself and DC Baker is *strictly* unrequited, is that clear?"

"Very clear," I returned, thankful I would not have to do any love scenes.

"Good. Did they supply you with all the necessary paperwork, IDs, that sort of thing?"

I patted my pocket and she handed me a scrap of paper and a bunch of keys.

"Good. This is my footnoterphone number in case of emergencies, these are the keys to the flying boat and my BMW. If a loser named Arnold calls, tell him I hope he rots in hell. Any questions?"

"I don't think so."

She smiled as a yellow cab with *TransGenre Taxis* painted on the side materialized in front of us. The cabbie looked bored and Mary opened the passenger door.

"Then we're done. You'll like it here. I'll see you in about a year. So long!"

She turned to the cabbie, muttered, "Get me out of this book," and she and the car faded out, leaving me alone on the dusty track.

I sat upon a rickety wooden seat next to a tub of long-dead flowers and let Pickwick out of her bag. She ruffled her feathers indignantly and blinked in the sunlight. I looked across the lake at the sailing dinghies that were little more than brightly colored triangles that tacked backwards and forwards in the distance. Nearer to shore a pair of swans beat their wings furiously and pedaled the water in an attempt to take off, landing almost as soon as they were airborne, throwing up a long streak of spray on the calm waters. It seemed a lot of effort to go a few hundred yards.

I turned my attention to the flying boat. The layers of paint that covered and protected the riveted hull had partly peeled off to reveal the colorful livery of long-forgotten airlines beneath. The Perspex windows had clouded with age, and high in the massive wing untidy cables hung lazily from the oil-stained cowlings of the three empty engine bays, their safe inaccessibility now a haven for nesting birds. Goliath, Aornis, and SpecOps seemed a million miles away—but then, so did Landen. *Landen.* Memories of my husband were never far away. I thought of all the times we had spent together that hadn't actually happened. All the places we hadn't visited, all the things we hadn't done. He might have been eradicated at the age of two, but I still had our memories— just no one to share them with.

I was interrupted from my thoughts by the sound of a motor-cycle approaching. The rider didn't have much control of the vehicle; I was glad that he stopped short of the jetty—his erratic riding might well have led him straight into the lake.

"Hullo!" he said cheerfully, removing his helmet to reveal a youngish man with a dark Mediterranean complexion and deep sunken eyes. "My name's Arnold. I haven't seen you around here before, have I?"

I got up and shook his hand.

"The name's Next. Thursday Next. Character Exchange Program."

"Oh, blast!" he muttered. "Blast and double blast! I suppose that means I've missed her?"

I nodded and he shook his head sadly.

"Did she leave a message for me?"

"Y-es," I said uncertainly. "She said she would, um, see you when she gets back."

"She did?" replied Arnold, brightening up. "That's a good sign. Normally she calls me a loser and tells me to go rot in hell."

"She probably won't be back for a while," I added, trying to make up for not passing on Mary's message properly, "maybe a year—maybe more."

"I see," he murmured, sighing deeply and staring off across

the lake. He caught sight of Pickwick, who was attempting to outstare a strange aquatic bird with a rounded bill.

"What's that?" he asked suddenly.

"I think it's a duck, although I can't be sure—we don't have any where I come from."

"No, the other thing."

"A dodo."[1]

"What's the matter?" asked Arnold.

I was getting a footnoterphone signal; in the BookWorld people generally communicated like this.

"A footnoterphone call," I replied, "but it's not a message—it's like the wireless back home."[2]

Arnold stared at me. "You're not from around here, are you?"

"I'm from the other side of the page. What you call the Outland."[3]

He opened his eyes wide. "You mean—you're *real*?"

"I'm afraid so," I replied, slightly bemused.

"Goodness! Is it true that Outlanders can't say 'red-Buick-blue-Buick' many times quickly?"

"It's true. We call it a tongue twister."

"Fascinating! There's nothing like that *here,* you know. I can say 'The sixth sheikh's sixth sheep's sick' over and over as many times as I want!"

1. ". . . This is WOLP-12 on the Well of Lost Plots' own footnoterphone station, transmitting live on the hour every hour to keep you up-to-date with news in the Fiction Factory . . ."

2. ". . . After the headlines you can hear our weekly documentary show *WellSpeak*, where today we will discuss hiding exposition; following that there will be a *WellNews* special on the launch of the new Book Operating System, UltraWord™, featuring a live studio debate with WordMaster Xavier Libris of Text Grand Central . . ."

3. ". . . here are the main points of the news. Prices of semicolons, plot devices, prologues and inciting incidents continued to fall yesterday, lopping twenty-eight points off the TomJones Index. The Council of Genres has announced the nominations for the 923rd annual BookWorld Awards; Heathcliff is once again to head the Most Troubled Romantic Lead category, for the seventy-eighth year running . . ."

And he did, three times.

"Now you try."

I took a deep breath. "The sixth spleeps sics sleeks . . . sick."

Arnold laughed like a drain. I don't think he'd come across anything quite so funny in his life. I smiled.

"Do it again!"

"No thanks.[4] How do I stop this footnoterphone blabbering inside my skull?"

"Just think *Off* very strongly."

I did, and the footnoterphone stopped.

"Better?"

I nodded.

"You'll get the hang of it."

He thought for a minute, looked up and down the lake in an overtly innocent manner, then said, "Do you want to buy some verbs? Not any of your rubbish, either. Good, strong, healthy regulars—straight from the Text Sea—I have a friend on a scrawltrawler."

I smiled. "I don't think so, Arnold—and I don't think you should ask me—I'm Jurisfiction."

"Oh," said Arnold, looking pale all of a sudden. He bit his lip and gave such an imploring look that I almost laughed.

"Don't sweat," I told him, "I won't report it."

He sighed a deep sigh of relief, muttered his thanks, re-mounted his motorbike and drove off in a jerky fashion, narrowly missing the mailboxes at the top of the track.

The interior of the flying boat was lighter and more airy than I had imagined, but it smelt a bit musty. Mary was mistaken; she had not been halfway through the craft's conversion—it was more like one-tenth. The walls were half-paneled with pine tongue-

---

4. ". . . A new epic poem is to be constructed for the first time in eighty-seven years. Title and subject to be announced, but pundits reckon that it's a pointless exercise: skills have all but died out. Next week will also see the launch of a new shopping chain offering off-the-peg narrative requisites. It will be called *Prêt-à-Écrire* . . ."

and-groove, and rock-wool insulation stuck out untidily along with unused electrical cables. There was room for two floors within the boat's cavernous hull, the downstairs a large, open-plan living room with a couple of old sofas pointing towards a television set. I tried to switch it on but it was dead—there was no TV in the BookWorld unless called for in the narrative. Much of what I could see around me were merely props, necessary for the chapter in which Jack Spratt visits the Sunderland to discuss the case. On the mantelpiece above a small wood-burning stove were pictures of Mary from her days at the police training college, and another from when she was promoted to detective sergeant.

I opened a door that led into a small kitchenette. Attached to the fridge was the précis of *Caversham Heights*. I flicked through it. The sequence of events was pretty much as I remembered from my first reading in the Well, although it seemed that Mary had overstated her role in some of the puzzle-solving areas. I put the précis down, found a bowl and filled it with water for Pickwick, took her egg from my bag and laid it on the sofa, where she quickly set about turning it over and tapping it gently with her beak. I went forward and discovered a bedroom where the nose turret would have been and climbed a narrow aluminum ladder to the flight deck directly above. This was the best view in the house, the large greenhouselike Perspex windows affording a vista of the lake. The massive control wheels were set in front of two comfortable chairs, and facing them and ahead of a tangled mass of engine control levers was a complex panel of broken and faded instruments. To my right I could see the one remaining engine, looking forlorn, the propeller blades streaked with bird droppings.

Behind the pilots' seats, where the flight engineer would have sat, there was a desk with reading lamp, footnoterphone and typewriter. On the bookshelf were mainly magazines of a police nature and lots of forensic textbooks. I walked through a narrow doorway and found a pleasant bedroom. The headroom was not overgenerous, but it was cozy and dry and was paneled in pine with a porthole above the double bed. Behind the bedroom was a storeroom, a hot-water boiler, stacks of wood and a spiral staircase. I was just about to go downstairs when I heard someone speak from the living room below.

"What do you think that is?"

The voice had an empty ring to it and was neuter in its inflection—I couldn't tell if it was male or female.

I stopped and instinctively pulled my automatic from my shoulder holster. Mary lived alone—or so it had said in the book. As I moved slowly downstairs, I heard another voice answer the first: "I think it's a bird of some sort."

The second voice was no more distinctive than the first, and indeed, if the second voice had not been *answering* the first, I might have thought they belonged to the same person.

As I rounded the staircase, I saw two figures standing in the middle of the room staring at Pickwick, who stared back, courageously protecting her egg from behind a sofa.

"Hey!" I said, pointing my gun in their direction. "Hold it right there!"

The two figures looked up and stared at me without expression from features that were as insipid and muted as their voices. Because of their equal blandness it was impossible to tell them apart. Their arms hung limply by their sides, exhibiting no body language. They might have been angry or curious or worried or elated—but I couldn't tell.

"Who are you?" I asked.

"We are nobody," replied the one on the left.

"Everyone is *someone*," I replied.

"Not altogether correct," said the one on the right. "We have a code number but nothing more. I am TSI-1404912-A and this is TSI-1404912-C."

"What happened to B?"

"Taken by a grammasite last Tuesday."

I lowered my gun. Miss Havisham had told me about Generics. They were created here in the Well to populate the books that were to be written. At the point of creation they were simply a human canvas without paint—blank like a coin, ready to be stamped with individualism. They had no history, no conflicts, no foibles—nothing that might make them either readable or interesting in any way. It was up to various institutions to teach them to be useful members of fiction. They were graded, too. A to D, one through ten. Any that were D-graded were like worker bees in crowds and busy streets. Small speaking parts were C-grades; B-grades usually made up the bulk of featured but not *leading* characters. These parts usually—but not always—went to the A-grades, handpicked for their skills at character projection and multidimensionality. Huckleberry Finn, Tess and Anna Karenina were all A-grades, but then so were Mr. Hyde, Hannibal Lecter and Professor Moriarty. I looked at the ungraded Generics again. Murderers or heroes? It was impossible to tell how they would turn out. Still, at this stage of their development they would be harmless. I reholstered my automatic.

"You're Generics, right?"

"Indeed," they said in unison.

"What are you doing here?"

"You remember the craze for minimalism?" asked the one on the right.

"Yes?" I replied, moving closer to stare at their blank faces curiously. There was a lot about the Well that I was going to have to get used to. They were harmless enough—but decidedly creepy. Pickwick was still hiding behind the sofa.

"It was caused by the 1982 character shortage," said the one on the left. "Vikram Seth is planning a large book in the next few years and I don't think the Well wants to be caught out again—we're being manufactured and then sent to stay in unpublished novels until we are called into service."

"Sort of stockpiled, you mean?"

"I'd prefer the word *billeted*," replied the one on the left, the slight indignation indicating that it wouldn't be without a personality forever.

"How long have you been here?"

"Two months," replied the one on the right. "We are awaiting placement at St. Tabularasa's Generic College for basic character training. I live in the spare bedroom in the tail."

"So do I," added the one on the left. "Likewise."

I paused for a moment. "O-kay. Since we all have to live together, I had better give you names. You," I said, pointing a finger at the one on the right, "are henceforth called *ibb*. You"—I pointed to the other—"are called *obb*."

I pointed at them again in case they had missed it as neither made any sign of comprehending what I'd said—or even hearing it.

"*You* are ibb, and *you* are obb."

I paused. Something didn't sound right about their names but I couldn't place it.

"ibb," I said to myself, then: "obb. ibb. ibb-obb. Does that sound strange to you?"

"No capitals," said obb. "We don't get capitalized until we start school—we didn't expect a name so soon, either. Can we keep it?"

"It's a gift from me," I told them.

"I am ibb," said ibb, as if to make the point.

"And I am obb," said obb.

"And I'm Thursday," I told them, offering my hand. They shook it in turn slowly and without emotion. I could see that this pair weren't going to be a huge bundle of fun.

"And that's Pickwick."

They looked at Pickwick, who plocked quietly, came out from behind the sofa, settled herself on her egg and pretended to go to sleep.

"Well," I announced, clapping my hands together, "does anyone know how to cook? I'm not very good at it and if you don't want to eat beans on toast for the next year, you had better start to learn. I'm standing in for Mary, and if you don't get in my way, I won't get in yours. I go to bed late and wake up early. I have a husband who doesn't exist and I'm going to have a baby later this year so I might get a little cranky—and overweight. Any questions?"

"Yes," said the one on the left. "Which one of us is obb, did you say?"

I unpacked my few things in the small room behind the flight deck. I had sketched a picture of Landen from memory and I placed it on the bedside table, staring at it for a moment. I missed him dreadfully and wondered, for the umpteenth time, whether perhaps I shouldn't be here hiding, but out *there,* in my own world, trying to get him back. Trouble was, I'd tried that and made a complete pig's ear of it—if it hadn't have been for Miss Havisham's timely rescue, I would still be locked up in a Goliath vault somewhere. With our child growing within me I had decided that flight was not a coward's option but a sensible one—I would stay here until the baby was born. I could then plan my return, and following that, Landen's.

I went downstairs and explained to obb the rudiments of cooking, which were as alien to it as having a name. Fortunately I found an old copy of *Mrs. Beeton's Complete Housekeeper,* which I told obb to study, half-jokingly, as research. Three hours later it had roasted a perfect leg of lamb with all the trimmings. I had discovered one thing about Generics already: dull and uninteresting they may be—but they learn fast.

2.

Inside *Caversham Heights*

Book/YGIO/1204961/: **Title:** *Caversham Heights*. UK, 1976, 90,000 words. **Genre:** Detective fiction. **Book Operating System:** BOOK V7.2. **Grammasite Infestation:** 1 (one) nesting pair of Parenthiums (protected). **Plot:** Routine detective thriller with stereotypical detective Jack Spratt. Set in Reading (England), the plot (such as it is) revolves around a drug czar hoping to muscle in on Reading's seedy underworld. Routine and unremarkable, *Caversham Heights* represents all the worst aspects of amateur writing. Flat characters, unconvincing police work and a pace so slow that snails pass it in the night. **Recommendation:** Unpublishable. Suggest book to be broken up for salvage at soonest available opportunity. **Current Status:** Awaiting Council of Genres Book Inspectorate's report before ordering demolition.

Library Subbasement Gazetteer,
1982, volume CLXI

I DISCUSSED THE RUDIMENTS of breakfast with ibb and obb the following morning. I told them that cereal traditionally came *before* the bacon and eggs, but that toast and coffee had no fixed place within the meal; they had problems with the fact that marmalade was almost exclusively the preserve of breakfast, and I was just trying to explain the technical possibilities of dippy egg fingers when a copy of *The Toad* dropped on the mat. The only news story was about some sort of drug-related gang warfare in Reading. It was part of the plot in *Caversham Heights* and reminded me that sooner or later—and quite possibly sooner—I would be expected to take on the mantle of Mary as part of the Character Exchange Program. I had another careful read of the précis, which gave me a good idea of the plot chapter by chapter, but no precise dialogue or indication as to what I should be doing, or when. I didn't have to wonder very long as a knock at the door revealed an untidy man wearing a hat named Wyatt.

"Sorry," he said sheepishly, apologizing for the misrelated grammatical construction almost immediately, "Wyatt is *my* name, not the hat's."

"I kind of figured that," I replied.

Wooden and worn with use, he was holding a clipboard.

"Oh, bother!" he said in the manner of someone who had just referred to George Eliot as "he" in a room full of English professors. "I've done it again!"

"Really, I don't mind," I repeated. "What can I do for you?"

"You're very kind. As a Character Exchange Program member, I would like to ask you to get yourself into Reading." He stopped and his shoulders sagged. "No, I'm *not* the Character Exchange Program member—you are. And *you* need to get into Reading."

"Sure. Do you have an address for me?"

Dog-eared and grubby, he handed me a note from his clipboard.

"Don't worry," I said before he could apologize again, "I understand."

His condition was almost certainly permanent, and since I didn't seem to care that much, he regained some confidence.

"Despite the ten-year demolition order hanging over us," he continued, "you should try and give it your best. The last Character Exchanger didn't take it seriously at all. Had to send him dusty and covered in asphalt on the road out of here."

He raised an eyebrow quizzically.

"I won't let you down," I assured him.

He thanked me, and small, brown and furry, the man with the hat named Wyatt raised it and vanished.

I took Mary's car and drove into Reading across the M4, which seemed as busy as it was back home; I used the same road myself when traveling between Swindon and London. Only when I was approaching the junction at the top of Burghfield road did I realize there were, at most, only a half dozen or so different vehicles on the roads. The vehicle that first drew my attention to this strange phenomenon was a large, white truck with *Dr. Spongg Footcare Products* painted on the side. I saw three in under a minute, all with an identical driver dressed in a blue boilersuit and flat cap. The next most obvious vehicle was a red VW Beetle driven by a young lady, then a battered blue Morris Marina with an elderly man at the wheel. By the time I had drawn up outside the scene of *Caversham Heights'* first murder, I had counted forty-three white trucks, twenty-two red Beetles and sixteen identically battered Morris Marinas, not to mention several green Ford Escorts and a brace of white Chevrolets. It was obviously a limitation within the text and nothing more, so I hurriedly parked, read Mary's notes again to make sure I knew what I had to do, took a deep breath and walked across to the area that had been taped off. A few uniformed police officers were milling around. I showed my pass and ducked under the *Police: Do Not Cross* tape.

The yard was shaped as an oblong, fifteen feet wide and about twenty feet long, surrounded by a high redbrick wall with crumbling mortar. A large, white SOCO tent was over the scene, and a forensic pathologist, dictating notes into a tape recorder, was kneeling next to a well-described corpse.

"Hullo!" said a jovial voice close by. I turned to see a large man in a mackintosh grinning at me.

"Detective Sergeant Mary," I told him obediently. "Transferred here from Basingstoke."

"You don't have to worry about all that *yet*." He smiled. "The story is with Jack at the moment—he's meeting Officer Tibbit on the street outside. My name's DCI Briggs and I'm your friendly yet long-suffering boss in this little caper. Crusty and prone to outbursts of temper yet secretly supportive, I will have to suspend Jack at least once before the story is over."

"How do you do?" I spluttered.

"Excellent!" said Briggs, shaking my hand gratefully. "Mary told me you're with Jurisfiction. Is that true?"

"Yes."

"Any news about when the Council of Genres Book Inspectorate will be in?" asked Briggs. "It would be a help to know. You've heard about the demolition order, I take it?"

"Council of Genres?" I echoed, trying not to make my ignorance show. "I'm sorry. I've not spent that much time in the BookWorld."

"An Outlander?" replied Briggs, eyes wide in wonderment. "Here, in *Caversham Heights*?"

"Yes, I'm—"

"Tell me, what do waves look like when they crash on the shore?"

"Who's an Outlander?" echoed the pathologist, a middle-aged Indian woman who suddenly leapt to her feet and stared at me intently. "You?"

"Y-es," I admitted.

"I'm Dr. Singh," explained the pathologist, shaking my hand vigorously. "I'm matter-of-fact, apparently without humor, like cats and people who like cats, don't suffer fools, yet on occasion I do exhibit a certain warmth. Tell me, do you think I'm anything like a *real* pathologist?"

"Of course," I answered, trying to think of her brief appearances in the book.

"You see," she went on with a slightly melancholic air, "I've never seen a *real* pathologist and I'm really not sure what I'm meant to do."

"You're doing fine," I assured her.

"What about me?" asked Briggs. "Do you think I need to develop more as a character? Am I like all those *real* people you rub shoulders with, or am I a bit one-dimensional?"

"Well—"

"I knew it!" he cried unhappily. "It's the hair, isn't it? Do you think it should be shorter? Longer? What about having a bizarre character trait? I've been learning the trombone—that would be unusual, yes?"

"Someone said there was an Outlander in the book!" interrupted a uniformed officer, one of a pair who had just walked into the yard. "I'm Unnamed Police Officer No. 1; this is my colleague, Unnamed Police Officer No. 2. Can I ask a question about the Outland?"

"Sure."

"What's the point of alphabet soup?"

"I don't know."

"Are you sure you're from the Outland?" he asked suspiciously. "Then tell me this: Why is there no singular for *scampi*?"

"I'm not sure."

"You're *not* from the Outland," said Unnamed Police Officer No. 1 sadly. "You should be ashamed of yourself, lying and raising our hopes like that!"

"Very well," I replied, covering my eyes, "I'll prove it to you. Speak to me in turn but leave off your speech designators."

"Okay," said Unnamed Police Officer No. 1. "Who is this talking?"

"And who is this?" added Dr. Singh.

"I said leave *off* your speech designators. Try again."

"It's harder than you think," sighed Unnamed Police Officer No. 1. "Okay, here goes."

There was a pause.

"Which one of us is talking now?"

"And who am I?"

"Mrs. Singh first, Unnamed Police Officer No. 1 second. Was I correct?"

"Amazing!" murmured Mrs. Singh. "How do you do that?"

"I can recognize your voices. I have a sense of smell, too."

"No kidding? Do you know anyone in publishing?"

"None who would help. My husband is, or was, an author,

but his contacts wouldn't know me from Eve at present. I'm a SpecOps officer; I don't have much to do with contemporary fiction."

"SpecOps?" queried UPO No. 2. "What's that?"

"We're going to be scrapped, you know," interrupted Briggs, "unless we can get a publisher."

"We could be broken down into *words*," added UPO No. 1 in a hushed tone, "cast into the Text Sea; and I have a wife and two kids—or at least, in my backstory I do."

"I can't help you," I told them, "I'm not even—"

"Places, please!" yelled Briggs so suddenly I jumped.

The pathologist and the two unnamed officers both hurried back to their places and awaited Jack, whom I could hear talking to someone in the house.

"Good luck," murmured Briggs from the side of his mouth as he motioned me to sit on a low wall. "I'll prompt you if you dry."

"Thanks."

DCI Briggs was sitting on a low wall with a plainclothes policewoman who busied herself taking notes and did not look up. Briggs stood as Jack entered and looked at his watch in an unsubtle way. Jack answered the unasked question in the defensive, which he soon realized was a mistake.

"I'm sorry, sir, I came here as quick as I could."

Briggs grunted and waved a hand in the direction of the corpse.

"It looks like he died from gunshot wounds," he said grimly. "Discovered dead at eight forty-seven this morning."

"Anything else I need to know?" asked Spratt.

"A couple of points. First, the deceased is the nephew of crime boss Angel DeFablio, so I wanted someone good with the press in case the media decide to have a bonanza. Second, I'm giving you this job as a favor. You're not exactly first seed with the seventh floor at the moment. There are some people who want to see you take a fall—and I don't want that to happen."

"Is there a third point?"

"No one else is available."

"I preferred it when there were only two."

"Listen, Jack," Briggs went on. "You're a good officer, if a little sprung-loaded at times, and I want you on my team without any mishaps."

"Is this where I say thank you?"

"You do. Mop it up nice and neat and give me an initial report as soon as you can. Okay?"

Briggs nodded in the direction of the young lady who had been waiting patiently.

"Jack, I want you to meet Thurs—I mean, DS Mary Jones."

"Hello," said Jack.

"Pleased to meet you, sir," said the young woman.

"And you. Who are you working with?"

"Next—I mean *Jones* is your new detective sergeant," said Briggs, beginning to sweat for some inexplicable reason. "Transferred with an A-one record from Swindon."

"Basingstoke," corrected Mary.

"Sorry. *Basingstoke.*"

"No offense to DS Jones, sir, but I was hoping for Butcher, Spooner or—"

"Not possible, Jack," said Briggs in the tone of voice that made arguing useless. "Well, I'm off. I'll leave you here with, er—"

"Jones."

"Yes, Jones, so you can get acquainted. Remember, I need that report as soon as possible. Got it?"

Jack did indeed get it and Briggs departed.

He shivered in the cold and looked at the young DS again.

"Mary Jones, eh?"

"Yes, sir."

"What have you found out so far?"

She dug in her pocket for a notebook, couldn't find it, so counted the points off on her fingers instead.

"Deceased's name is Sonny DeFablio."

There was a pause. Jack didn't say anything, so Jones, now slightly startled, continued as though he had.

"Time of death? Too early to tell. Probably three A.M. last night, give or take an hour. We'll know more when we get the corpse. Gun? We'll know when . . ."

". . . Jack, are you okay?"

He had sat down wearily and was staring at the ground, head in hands.

I looked around, but both Dr. Singh, her assistants and the unnamed officers were busily getting on with their parts, unwilling, it seemed, to get embroiled—or perhaps they were just embarrassed.

"I can't do this anymore," muttered Jack.

"Sir," I persisted, trying to ad-lib, "do you want to see the body or can we remove it?"

"What's the use?" sobbed the crushed protagonist. "No one is reading us; it doesn't matter."

I placed my hand on his shoulder.

"I've *tried* to make it more interesting," he sobbed, "but nothing seems to work. My wife won't speak to me, my job's on the line, drugs are flooding into Reading and if I don't make the narrative even remotely readable, then we all get demolished and there's nothing left at all except an empty hole on the bookshelf and the memory of a might-have-been in the head of the author."

"Your wife only left you because *all* loner, maverick detectives have domestic problems," I explained. "I'm sure she loves you really."

"No, no, she doesn't," he sobbed again. "All is lost. Don't you see? It's customary for detectives to drive unusual cars and I had a wonderful 1924 Delage-Talbot Supersport. The idea was stolen and replaced with that dreadful Austin Allegro. If any *scenes* get deleted, we'll really be stuffed."

He paused and looked up at me. "What's your name?"

"Thursday Next."

He perked up suddenly. "Thursday Next the Outlander Jurisfiction agent apprenticed to Miss Havisham Thursday Next?"

I nodded. News travels fast in the Well.

An excited gleam came into his eye. "I read about you in *The Word*. Tell me, would you have any way of finding out when the Book Inspectorate are due to read our story? I've lined up seven three-dimensional B-2 freelancers to come in and give the book a bit of an edge—just for an hour or so. With their help we might be able to hang on to it; all I need to know is the *when*."

"I'm sorry, Mr. Spratt," I sighed, "I'm new to all this; what exactly *is* the Council of Genres?"

"They look after fictional legislature, dramatic conventions, mainly—a representative from every genre sits on the Council— it is *they* who decide the conventions of storytelling, and it is *they*, through the Book Inspectorate, who decide whether an unpublished book is to be kept—or demolished."

"Oh," I replied, realizing that the BookWorld was governed by almost as many rules and regulations as my own, "then I can't help you."

"What about Text Grand Central? Do you know anyone there?"

TGC I *had* heard of: amongst other things, they monitored the books in the Great Library and passed any textual problems on to us at Jurisfiction, who were purely a policing agency—but I knew no more than that. I shook my head again.

"Blast!" he muttered, staring at the ground. "I've applied to the C of G for a cross-genre makeover, but you might as well try and speak to the Great Panjandrum himself."

"Why don't you change the book from *within*?"

"Change without permission?" he replied, shocked at my suggestion. "That would mean rebellion. I want to get the C of G's attention, but not like that—we'd be crushed in less than a chapter!"

"But if the inspectorate haven't been round yet," I said slowly, "then how would they even know anything had changed?"

He thought about this for a moment. "Easier said than done—if I start to fool with the narrative, it might all collapse like a pack of cards!"

"Then start small, change *yourself* first. If that works, you can try to bend the plot slightly."

"Y-esss," said Jack slowly, "what did you have in mind?"

"Give up the booze."

"How did you know about my drink problem?"

"All maverick, loner detectives with domestic strife have drinking problems. Give up the liquor and go home to your wife."

"That's not how I've been written," replied Jack slowly. "I just can't do it—it would be going against type—the readers—!"

"Jack, there are no readers. And if you don't at least try what I suggest, there *never* will be any readers—or any Jack Spratt. But if things go well, you might even be in . . . a sequel."

"A sequel?" repeated Jack with a sort of dreamy look in his eyes. "You mean—a Jack Spratt *series*?"

"Who knows"—I shrugged—"maybe even one day—a boxed set."

His eyes gleamed and he stood up. "A boxed set," he whispered, staring into the middle distance. "It's up to me, isn't it?" he said in a slow voice.

"Yes. Change yourself, change the book—and soon, before it's too late—make the novel into something the Book Inspectorate will *want* to read."

"Okay," he said at last, "beginning with the next chapter. Instead of arguing with Briggs about letting a suspect go without charging them, I'll take my ex-wife out to lunch."

"No."

"No?"

"No," I affirmed. "Not tomorrow or next chapter or even next page or paragraph—you're going to change *now*."

"We can't! There are at least nine more pages while you and I discuss the state of the body with Dr. Singh and go through all that boring forensic stuff."

"Leave it to me. We'll jump back a paragraph or two. Ready?"

He nodded and we moved to the top of the previous page, just as Briggs was leaving.

Jack did indeed get it and Briggs departed.

He shivered in the cold and looked at the young DS again.

"Mary Jones, eh?"

"Yes, sir."

"What have you found out so far?"

She dug in her pocket for a notebook, couldn't find it, so counted the points off on her fingers instead.

"Deceased's name is Sonny DeFablio."

"What else?"

"Your wife phoned."

"She . . . did?"

"Yes. Said it was important."

"I'll drop by this evening."

"She said it was *very* urgent," stressed Jones.

"Hold the fort for me, would you?"

"Certainly, sir."

Jack walked from the crime scene leaving Jones with Dr. Singh.

"Right," said Mary. "What have we got?"

We ran the scene together, Dr. Singh telling me all the information that she was more used to relating to Jack. She went into a huge amount of detail regarding the time of death and a more-than-graphic explanation of how she thought it had happened. Ballistics, trajectory, blood-splatter patterns, you name it. I was really quite glad when she finished and the chapter moved off to Jack's improvised meeting with his ex-wife.

As soon as we were done, Dr. Singh turned to me and said in an anxious tone, "I hope you know what you're doing."

"Not a clue."

"Me neither," replied the quasi pathologist. "You know that

long speech I made just now about postmortem bruising, angles of bullet entry and discoloration of body tissues?"

"Yes?"

She leaned closer. "Didn't understand a word. Eight pages of technical dialogue and haven't the foggiest what I'm talking about. I only trained at Generic college as a mother figure in domestic potboilers. If I'd known I was to be drafted to *this*, I would have spent a few hours in a Cornwell. Do you have any clues as to what I'm actually meant to do?"

I rummaged in her bag and brought out a large thermometer. "Try this."

"What do I do with it?"

I pointed.

"You're *kidding* me," replied Dr. Singh, aghast.

3.

Three Witches, Multiple Choice and Sarcasm

Jurisfiction is the name given to the policing agency that works *inside* books. Under a remit from the Council of Genres and working with the intelligence-gathering capabilities of Text Grand Central, the Prose Resource Operatives at Jurisfiction comprise a mixed bag of characters, most drawn from the ranks of fiction but some, like Harris Tweed and myself, from the real world. Problems in fiction are noticed by "spotters" employed at Text Grand Central, and from there relayed to the Bellman, a ten-yearly elected figure who runs Jurisfiction under strict guidelines laid down by the Council of Genres. Jurisfiction has its own code of conduct, technical department, canteen and resident washerwoman.

THURSDAY NEXT,
The Jurisfiction Chronicles

DR. SINGH DIDN'T waste the opportunity, and she gathered together several other trainee pathologists she knew from the Well. They all sat spellbound as I recounted the limited information I possessed. Exhausted, I managed to escape four hours later. It was evening when I finally got home. I opened the door to the flying boat and kicked off my shoes. Pickwick rushed up to greet me and tugged excitedly at my trouser leg. I followed her through to the living room and then had to wait while she remembered where she had left her egg. We finally found it rolled behind the hi-fi and I congratulated her, despite there being no change in its appearance.

I returned to the kitchen. ibb and obb had been studying *Mrs. Beeton's* all day, and ibb was attempting steak diane with french fries. Landen used to cook that for me and I suddenly felt lonesome and small, so far from home I might well be on Pluto. obb was making the final touches to a fully decorated four-tier wedding cake.

"Hello, ibb," I said, "how's it going?"

"How's what going?" replied the Generic in that annoying literal way that they spoke. "And I'm obb."

"Sorry—obb."

"Why are you sorry? Have you done something?"

"Never mind."

I sat down at the table and opened a package that had arrived. It was from Miss Havisham and contained the Jurisfiction Standard Entrance Exam. I had joined Jurisfiction almost by accident—I had wanted to get Landen out of "The Raven" and getting involved with the agency seemed to be the best way to learn. But Jurisfiction had grown on me and I now felt strongly about maintaining the solidity of the written word. It was the same job I had undertaken at SpecOps, just from the other side. But it struck me that, on this occasion, Miss Havisham was wrong—I was not yet ready for full membership.

The hefty tome consisted of five hundred questions, nearly all of them multiple choice. I noticed that the exam was self-invigilating; as soon as I opened the book a clock in the top left-hand corner started to count down from two hours. The questions were mostly about literature, which I had no problem with. Jurisfiction law was trickier and I would probably need to consult with Miss Havisham. I made a start and ten minutes later was pondering question forty-six: *Which of the following poets never used the outlawed word* majestic *in their work?* when there was a knock at the door accompanied by a peal of thunder.

I closed the exam book and opened the door. On the jetty were three ugly, old crones dressed in filthy rags. They had bony features, rough and warty skin, and they launched into a well-rehearsed act as soon as the door opened.

"When shall we three meet again?" said the first witch. "In Thurber, Wodehouse, or in Greene?"

"When the hurly-burly's done," added the second, "when the story's thought and spun!"

There was a pause until the second witch nudged the third.

"That will be Eyre the set of sun," she said quickly.

"Where the place?"

"Within the text."

"There to meet with MsNext!"

They stopped talking and I stared, unsure of what I was meant to do.

"Thank you very much," I replied, but the first witch snorted disparagingly and wedged her foot in the door as I tried to close it.

"Prophecies, kind lady?" she asked as the other two cackled hideously.

"I really don't think so," I answered, pushing her foot away, "perhaps another time."

"*All hail, MsNext! Hail to thee, citizen of Swindon!*"

"Really, I'm sorry—and I'm out of change."

"*All hail, MsNext, hail to thee, full Jurisfiction agent, thou shalt be!*"

"If you don't go," I began, starting to get annoyed, "I'll—"

"*All hail, MsNext, thou shalt be Bellman thereafter!*"

"Sure I will. Go on, clear off, you imperfect speakers—bother someone else with your nonsense!"

"A shilling!" said the first. "And we shall tell you more—or less, as you please."

I closed the door despite their grumbling and went back to my multiple choice. I'd only answered question forty-nine: *Which of the following is not a gerund?* when there was another knock at the door.

"Blast!" I muttered, getting up and striking my ankle on the table leg. It was the three witches again.

"I thought I told you—"

"Sixpence, then," said the chief hag, putting out a bony hand.

"No," I replied firmly, rubbing my ankle, "I *never* buy anything at the door."

They all started up then: *"Thrice to thine and thrice to mine, and thrice again, to make up—"*

I shut the door again. I wasn't superstitious and had far more important things to worry about. I had just sat down again, sipped at my tea and answered the next question: *Who wrote* Toad of Toad Hall? when there was another rap at the door.

"Right," I said to myself, marching across the room, "I've had it with you three."

I pulled open the door and said, "Listen here, hag, I'm really not interested, nor ever will be in your . . . Oh."

I stared. Granny Next. If it had been Admiral Lord Nelson himself I don't think I could have been more surprised.

"Gran!?!" I exclaimed. "What on earth are you doing here?"

She was dressed in her usual outfit of spectacular blue gingham, from her dress to her overcoat and even her hat, shoes and bag.

I hugged her. She smelt of Bodmin for Women. She hugged me in return in that sort of fragile way that very elderly people do. And she *was* elderly—108, at the last count.

"I have come to look after you, young Thursday," she announced.

"Er—thank you, Gran," I replied, wondering quite how she had got here.

"You're going to have a baby and need attending to," she added grandly. "My suitcase is on the jetty and you're going to have to pay the taxi."

"Of course," I muttered, going outside and finding a yellow TransGenre Taxi.

"How much?" I asked the cabby.

"Seventeen and six."

"Oh, yes?" I replied sarcastically. "Took the long way round?"

"Trips to Horror, Bunyan and the Well cost double," said the cabbie. "Pay up or I'll make sure Jurisfiction hears about it. I had that Heathcliff in the back of my cab once."

"Really?" I replied, handing him a pound.

He patted his pockets. "Sorry, have you got anything smaller? I don't carry much change."

"Keep it," I told him as his footnoterphone muttered something about a party of ten wanting to get out of Florence in *The Decameron*. I got a receipt and he melted from view. I picked up Gran's suitcase and hauled it into the Sunderland.

"This is ibb and obb," I explained. "Generics billeted with me. The one on the left is ibb."

"I'm obb."

"Sorry. *That's* ibb and *that's* obb. This is my grandmother."

"Hello," said Granny Next, gazing at my two houseguests.

"You're very old," observed ibb.

"One hundred and eight," announced Gran proudly. "Do you two do anything but stare?"

"Not really," said ibb.

"Plock," said Pickwick, who had popped her head round the door, ruffled her feathers excitedly and rushed up to greet Gran, who always seemed to have a few spare marshmallows about her.

"What's it like being old?" asked ibb, who was peering closely at the soft, pink folds in Gran's skin.

"Death's adolescence," replied Gran. "But you know the worst part?"

ibb and obb shook their heads.

"I'm going to miss my funeral by three days."

"Gran!" I scolded. "You'll confuse them—they tend to take things literally."

It was too late.

"Miss your own funeral?" muttered ibb, thinking hard. "How is that possible?"

"Think about it, ibb," said obb. "If she lived three days longer, she'd be able to *speak* at her own funeral—get it?"

"Of course," said ibb, "stupid of me."

And they went into the kitchen, talking about Mrs. Beeton's book and the best way to deal with amorous liaisons between the scullery maid and the bootboy—it must have been an old edition.

"When's supper?" asked Gran, looking disdainfully at the interior of the flying boat. "I'm absolutely famished—but nothing tougher than suet, mind. The gnashers aren't what they were."

I delicately helped her out of her gingham coat and sat her down at the table. Steak diane would be like eating railway sleepers to her, so I started to make an omelette.

"Now, Gran," I said, cracking some eggs into a bowl, "I want you to tell me what you're doing here."

"I need to be here to remind you of things you might forget, young Thursday."

"Such as what?"

"Such as Landen. They eradicated my husband, too, and the one thing I needed was someone to help me through it, so that's what I'm here to do for you."

"I'm not going to forget him, Gran!"

"Yes," she agreed in a slightly peculiar way, "I'm here to make sure of it."

"That's the *why*," I persisted, "but what about the *how*?"

"I, too, used to do the occasional job for Jurisfiction in the old days. A long time ago, mind, but it was just one of many jobs that I did in my life—and not the strangest, either."

"What *was*?" I asked, knowing in my heart that I shouldn't really be asking.

"Well, I was God Emperor of the Universe, once," she answered in the same manner to which she might have admitted to going to the pictures, "and being a man for twenty-four hours was pretty weird."

"Yes, I expect it was."

ibb laid the table and we sat down to eat ten minutes later. As Gran sucked on her omelette I tried to make conversation with ibb and obb. The trouble was, neither of them had the requisite powers of social communication to assimilate anything from speech other than the bald facts it contained. I tried a joke I had heard from Bowden, my partner at SpecOps, about an octopus and a set of bagpipes. But when I delivered the punch line, they both stared at me.

"Why would the bagpipes be dressed in pajamas?" asked ibb.

"It wasn't," I replied, "it was the tartan. That's just what the octopus *thought* they were."

"I see," said obb, not seeing at all. "Would you mind going over it again?"

"That's it," I said resolutely, "you're going to have a personality if it kills me."

"Kill you?" inquired ibb in all seriousness. "Why would it kill you?"

I thought carefully. There had to be *somewhere* to begin. I clicked my fingers.

"Sarcasm," I said. "We'll start with that."

They both looked at me blankly.

"Well," I began, "sarcasm is closely related to irony and implies a twofold view—a literal meaning, yet a wholly *different* intention from what is said. For instance, if you were lying to me about who ate all the anchovies I left in the cupboard, and you *had* eaten them, you might say, 'It wasn't me,' and I would say, '*Sure* it wasn't,' meaning I'm sure it *was* but in an ironic or sarcastic manner."

"What's an anchovy?" asked ibb.

"A small and very salty fish."

"I see," replied ibb. "Does sarcasm work with other things or is it only fish?"

"No, the stolen anchovies was only by way of an example. Now you try."

"An anchovy?"

"No, you try some sarcasm."

They continued to look at me blankly.

I sighed. "Like trying to nail jelly to the wall," I muttered under my breath.

"Plock," said Pickwick in her sleep as she gently keeled over. "Plocketty-plock."

"Sarcasm is better explained through humor," put in Gran, who had been watching my efforts with interest. "You know that Pickwick isn't too clever?"

Pickwick stirred in her sleep where she had fallen, resting on her head with her claws in the air.

"Yes, we know that," replied ibb and obb, who were nothing if not observant.

"Well, if I were to say that it is easier to get yeast to perform tricks than Pickwick, I'm using mild sarcasm to make a joke."

"Yeast?" queried ibb. "But yeast has no intelligence."

"Exactly," replied Gran. "So I am making a sarcastic observation that Pickwick has less brainpower than yeast. You try."

The Generic thought long and hard.

"So," said ibb slowly, "how about . . . Pickwick is so clever she sits on the TV and stares at the sofa?"

"It's a start," said Gran.

"And," added ibb, gaining confidence by the second, "if Pickwick went on *Mastermind*, she'd do best to choose 'dodo eggs' as her specialist subject."

obb was getting the hang of it, too. "If a thought crossed her mind, it would be the shortest journey on record."

"Pickwick has a brother at Oxford. In a jar."

"All right, that's enough sarcasm," I said quickly. "I know Pickwick won't win 'Brain of BookWorld' but she's a loyal companion."

I looked across at Pickwick, who slid off the sofa and landed with a thump on the floor. She woke up and started plocking loudly at the sofa, coffee table, rug—in fact, anything close by— before calming down, climbing on top of her egg and falling asleep again.

"You did well, guys," I said. "Another time we'll tackle subtext."

ibb and obb went to their room soon afterwards, discussing how sarcasm was related to irony, and whether irony itself could be generated in laboratory conditions. Gran and I chatted about home. Mother was very well, it seemed, and Joffy and Wilbur and Orville were as mad as ever. Gran, conscious of my dealings with Yorrick Kaine in the past, reported that Kaine had returned soon after the episode with the Glatisant at Volescamper Towers, lost his seat in the House and been back at the helm of his newspaper and publishing company soon after. I knew he was fictional and a danger to my world but couldn't see what to do about it from here. We talked into the night about the BookWorld, Landen, eradications and having children. Gran had had three herself so gleefully told me all the stuff they don't tell you when you sign on the dotted line.

"Think of swollen ankles as trophies," she said, somewhat unhelpfully.

That night I put Gran in my room and slept in the bedroom under the flight deck. I washed, undressed and climbed into bed, weary after the day's work. I lay there, staring at the pattern of reflected light dancing on the ceiling and thought of my father, Emma Hamilton, Jack Spratt, Dream Topping and babies. I was meant to be here resting but the demolition problem of *Caversham Heights*, my adopted home, couldn't be ignored—I could have moved but I liked it here, and besides, I had done enough running away already. The arrival of Gran had been strange, but since much was odd here in the Well, weird had become commonplace. If things carried on like this, the dull and meaningless would become items of spectacular interest.

4.

Landen Parke-Laine

They say that no one really dies until you forget them, and in Landen's case it was especially true. Since Landen had been eradicated, I had discovered that I could bring him back to life in my memories and my dreams, and I had begun to look forward to falling asleep and returning to treasured moments that we could share, albeit only fleetingly.

Landen had lost a leg to a land mine and his best friend to a military blunder. The friend had been my brother Anton—and Landen had testified against him at the hearing that followed the disastrous "Charge of the Light Armored Brigade" in 1973. My brother was blamed for the debacle, Landen was honorably discharged and I was awarded the Crimea Star for gallantry. We didn't speak for ten years, and we were married two months ago. Some people say it was an unorthodox romance—but I never noticed myself.

THURSDAY NEXT,
The Jurisfiction Chronicles

THAT NIGHT, I went to the Crimea again. Not, you might think, the most obvious port of call in my sleep. The peninsula had been a constant source of anguish in my waking hours: a time of stress, of pain, and violent death. But the Crimea was where I'd met Landen, and where we'd fallen in love. The memories were more dear to me now because they had never happened, and for this reason the Crimea's sometimes painful recollections came back to me. I relaxed and was transported in the arms of Morpheus to the Black Sea peninsula, twelve years before.

No shots had been fired for ten years when I arrived on the

peninsula in the May of 1973, although the conflict had been going for 120 years. I was attached to the Third Wessex Tank Light Armored Brigade as a driver—I was twenty-three years old and drove thirteen tons of armored vehicle under the command of Major Phelps, who was later to lose his lower arm and his mind during a badly timed charge into the massed Russian artillery. In my youthful naïveté, I had thought the Crimea was fun—a notion that was soon to change.

"Report to the vehicle pool at fourteen hundred hours," I was told one morning by our sergeant, a kindly yet brusque man by the name of Tozer. He would survive the charge but be lost in a training accident eight years later. I was at his funeral. He was a good man.

"Any idea what I'll be doing, Sarge?" I asked.

Sergeant Tozer shrugged. "Special duties. I was told to allocate someone intelligent—but they weren't available, so you'll have to do."

I laughed. "Thanks, Sarge."

I dreamed this scene more often these days and the reason was clear—it was the first time Landen and I spent any time together. My brother Anton was also serving out here and he had introduced us a few weeks before—but Anton did that a lot. Today I was to drive Landen in an armored scout car to an observation post overlooking a valley in which a buildup of Imperial Russian artillery had been reported. We referred to the incident as "our first date."

I arrived for duty and was told to sign for a Dingo scout car, a small, two-person armored vehicle with enough power to get out of trouble quickly—or into it, depending on one's level of competency. I duly picked up the scout car and waited for nearly an hour, standing in a tent with a lot of other drivers, talking and laughing, drinking tea and telling unlikely stories. It was a chilly day but I was glad I was doing this instead of daily orders, which generally meant cleaning up the camp and other tedious tasks.

"Corporal Next?" said an officer who poked his head into the tent. "Drop the tea—we're off!"

He wasn't handsome but he was *intriguing,* and unlike many of the officers, he seemed to have a certain relaxed manner about him.

I jumped to my feet. "Good morning, sir," I said, unsure of whether he remembered me. I needn't have worried. I didn't know it yet, but he had specifically asked Sergeant Tozer for me. He was intrigued, too, but fraternizing on active duty was a subtle art. The penalties could be severe.

I led him to where the Dingo was parked and climbed in. I pressed the starter and the engine rumbled to life. Landen lowered himself into the commander's seat.

"Seen Anton recently?" he asked.

"He's up the coast for a few weeks," I told him.

"Ah, you made me fifty pounds when you won the ladies' boxing last weekend. I'm very grateful."

I smiled and thanked him but he wasn't paying me any attention—he was busy studying a map.

"We're going here, Corporal."

I studied the chart. It was the closest to the front lines I'd ever been. To my shame, I found the perceived danger somewhat intoxicating. Landen sensed it.

"It's not as wildly exciting as you might think, Next. I've been up there twenty times and was only shelled once."

"What was it like?"

"Disagreeably noisy. Take the road to Balaklava—I'll tell you when to turn right."

So we bumped off up the road, past a scene of such rural tranquillity that it was hard to imagine that two armies were facing each other not ten miles away with enough firepower to lay the whole peninsula to waste.

"Ever seen a Russian?" he asked as we passed military trucks supporting the frontline artillery batteries; their sole job was to lob a few shells towards the Russians—just to show we were still about.

"Never, sir."

"They look just like you and me, you know."

"You mean they don't wear big furry hats and have snow on their shoulders?"

The sarcasm wasn't wasted.

"Sorry," he said, "I didn't mean to patronize. How long have you been out here?"

"Two weeks."

"I've been here two *years*, but it might as well be two weeks. Take a right at the farmhouse just ahead."

I slowed down and cranked the wheel round to enter the dusty farm track. The springs on a Dingo are quite hard—it was a jarring ride along the track, which passed empty farm buildings, all bearing the scars of long-past battles. Old and rusting armor and other war debris was lying abandoned in the countryside, reminders of just how long this static war had been going on. Rumor had it that in the middle of no-man's-land there were still artillery pieces dating from the nineteenth century. We stopped at a checkpoint, Landen showed his pass and we drove on, a soldier joining us up top "as a precaution." He had a second ammunition clip taped to the first in his weapon—always a sign of someone who expected trouble—and a dagger in his boot. He had only fourteen words and twenty-one minutes left before he was to die amongst a small spinney of trees that in happier times might have been a good place for a picnic. The bullet would enter below his left shoulder blade, deflect against his spine, go straight through his heart and exit three inches below his armpit, where it would lodge in the fuel gauge of the Dingo. He would die instantly and eighteen months later I would relate what had happened to his parents. His mother would cry and his father would thank me with a dry throat. But the soldier didn't know that. These were my memories, not his.

"Russian spotter plane!" hissed the doomed soldier.

Landen ordered me back to the trees. The soldier had eleven words left. He would be the first person I saw killed in the conflict but by no means the last. As a civvy you are protected from such unpleasantries, but in the forces it is commonplace—and you never get used to it.

I pulled the wheel over hard and doubled back towards the spinney as fast as I could. We halted under the protective cover of the trees and watched the small observation plane from the dappled shade. We didn't know it at the time, but an advance party of Russian commandos were pushing towards the lines in our direction. The observation post we were heading for had been overrun half an hour previously, and the commandos were being supported by the spotter plane we had seen—and behind them, twenty Russian battle tanks with infantry in support. The attack was to fail, of course, but only by virtue of the VHF wireless set carried in the Dingo. I would drive us out of there and Landen would call in an airstrike. That was the way it had happened. That's the way it had *always* happened. Brought together in the white heat and fear of combat. But as we sat beneath the cover of the birch trees, huddled down in the scout car, the only sound the gentle thrum of the Dingo's engine, we knew nothing—and were only concerned that the spotter plane that wheeled above us would delay our arrival at the OP.

"What's it doing?" whispered Landen, shielding his eyes to get a better look.

"Looks like a Yak-12," replied the soldier.

Six words left and under a minute. I had been looking up with them but now glanced out of the hatch at the front of the scout car. My heart missed a beat as I saw a Russian run and jump into a natural hollow a hundred yards in front of the Dingo.

"Russki!" I gasped. "Hundred yards, twelve o'clock!"

I reached up to close the viewing hatch but Landen grabbed my wrist.

"Not yet!" he whispered. "Put her in gear."

I did as I was told as Landen and the soldier twisted around to look.

"What have you got?" hissed Landen.

"Five, maybe six," the soldier whispered back, "heading this way."

"Me, too," muttered Landen. "Go, Corporal, go!"

I revved the engine, dropped the clutch and the Dingo lunged forward. Almost instantaneously there was a rasp of machine-gun fire as the Russians opened up. To them, we were a surprise ruined. I heard the closer rattle of gunfire as our soldier replied along with the sporadic crack of a pistol that I knew was Landen. I didn't close the steel viewing hatch; I needed to be able to see as much as I could. The scout car bounced across the track and swerved before gathering speed with the metallic *spang* of small-arms fire hitting the armor plate. I felt a weight slump against my back and a bloodied arm fell into my vision.

"Keep going!" shouted the soldier. "And don't stop until I say!"

He let go another burst of fire, took out the spent clip, knocked the new magazine on his helmet, reloaded and fired again.

"That wasn't how it happened—!" I muttered aloud, the soldier having gone way over his allotted time and word count. I looked at the bloodied hand that had fallen against me. A feeling of dread began to gnaw slowly inside me—the fuel gauge was still intact—shouldn't it have been shattered when the soldier was shot? Then I realized. The soldier had survived and the *officer* was dead.

I sat bolt upright in the bed, covered in sweat and breathing hard. The strength of the memories had lessened with the years, but here was something new, something unexpected. I replayed the images in my head, watching the bloodstained hand fall again and again. It all felt so horribly real. But there was something, just there outside my grasp, something that I should know but didn't—a loss that I couldn't explain, an absence of some sort I couldn't place—

"Landen," said a soft voice in the darkness, "his name was *Landen.*"

"Landen—!" I cried. "Yes, yes, his name was Landen."

"And he didn't die in the Crimea. The soldier did."

"No, no, I just remembered him dying!"

"You remembered *wrong.*"

It was Gran, sitting beside me in her gingham nightie. She held my hand tightly and gazed at me through her spectacles, her gray hair adrift and hanging down in wispy strands. And with her words, I began to remember. Landen *had* survived—he must have done in order to call up the airstrike. But even now, awake, I could remember him lying dead beside me. It didn't make sense.

"He didn't die?"

"No."

I picked up the picture I had sketched of him from the bed-side table.

"Did I ever see him again?" I asked, studying the unfamiliar face.

"Oh, yes," replied Gran. "Lots and lots. In fact, you married him."

"I did, didn't I?" I cried, tears coming to my eyes as the memories returned. "At the Blessed Lady of the Lobster in Swindon! Were you there?"

"Yes, wouldn't have missed it for the world."

I was still confused. "What happened to him? Why isn't he with me now?"

"He was eradicated," replied Gran in a low voice, "by Lavoisier—and Goliath."

"I remember," I answered, the darkness in my mind made light as a curtain seemed to draw back and everything that had happened flooded in. "Jack Schitt. Goliath. They eradicated Landen to blackmail me. But I failed. I didn't get him back—and that's why I'm here." I stopped. "But, but, how could I possibly forget him? I was only thinking about him yesterday! What's happening to me?"

"It's Aornis, my dear," explained Gran, "she is a mnemonomorph. A memory-changer. Remember the trouble you had with her back home?"

I did, now she mentioned it. Gran's prompting broke the delicate veil of forgetfulness that cloaked Aornis's presence in my mind—and everything about Hades's little sister returned to me as though no longer hidden from my conscious memory. Aornis, who had sworn revenge for her brother's death at my hands; Aornis, who could manipulate memories as she chose; Aornis, who had nearly brought about a gooey Dream Topping global Armageddon. But Aornis wasn't from here. She lived in—

"—the *real* world," I murmured out loud. "How can she be here, inside fiction? In *Caversham Heights* of all places?"

"She isn't," replied Gran. "Aornis is only in your mind. It isn't all of her, either—simply a mindworm—a sort of mental virus. She is resourceful, adaptable and spiteful; I know of no one else who can have an independent life within someone else's memory."

"So how do I get rid of her?"

"I have some experience of mnemonomorphs from my youth, but some things you have to defeat on your own. Stay on your toes and we will speak often and at length."

"Then this isn't over yet?"

"No," replied Gran sadly, shaking her head. "I wish it were. Be prepared for a shock, young Thursday—tell me Landen's name in full."

"Don't be ridiculous!" I scoffed. "It's Landen Parke—"

I stopped as a cold fear welled up inside my chest. Surely I could remember my own husband's name? But try as I might, I could not. I looked at Gran.

"Yes, I do know," she replied, "but I'm not going to tell you. When you remember, you will know you have won."

5.

The Well of Lost Plots

Footnoterphone: Although the idea of using footnotes as a communication medium was suggested by Dr. Faustus as far back as 1622, it wasn't until 1856 that the first practical footnoterphone was demonstrated. By 1895 an experimental version was built into *Hard Times*, and within the next three years most of Dickens was connected. The system was expanded rapidly, culminating in the first transgenre trunk line, opened with much fanfare in 1915 between Human Drama and Crime. The network has been expanded and improved ever since, but just recently the advent of mass junkfootnoterphones and the deregulation of news and entertainment channels has almost clogged the system. A mobilefootnoterphone network was introduced in 1985.

CAT FORMERLY KNOWN AS CHESHIRE,
Guide to the Great Library

GRAN HAD GOT up early to make my breakfast and I found her asleep in the armchair with the kettle almost molten on the stove and Pickwick firmly ensnared in Gran's knitting. I made some coffee and cooked myself breakfast despite feeling nauseated. ibb and obb wandered in a little later and told me they had "slept like dead people" and were so hungry they could "eat a horse between two mattresses." They were just tucking into my breakfast when there was a rap at the door. It was Akrid Snell, one-half of the Perkins & Snell series of detective fiction. He was about forty, dressed in a sharp fawn suit with a matching fedora, and wore a luxuriant red mustache. He was one of Jurisfiction's lawyers and had been appointed to represent me; I was still facing a charge of Fiction Infraction after I changed the ending of *Jane Eyre*.

"Hello!" he said. "Welcome to the BookWorld!"

"Thank you. Are you well?"

"Just dandy! I got Oedipus off the incest charge—technicality, of course—he didn't know it was his mother at the time."

"Of course. And Fagin?"

"Still due to hang, I'm afraid," he said more sadly. "The Gryphon is onto it—he'll find a way out, I'm sure."

He was looking around the shabby flying boat as he spoke.

"Well!" he said at last. "You do make some odd decisions. I've heard the latest Daphne Farquitt novel is being built just down the shelf—it's set in the eighteenth century and would be a lot more comfortable than this. Did you see the review of my latest book?"

He meant the book he was featured in, of course—Snell was fictional from the soles of his brogues to the crown of his fedora—and like most fictioneers, a little sensitive about it. I had read the review of *Wax Lyrical for Death* and it was pretty scathing; tact was of the essence in situations like these.

"No, I think I must have missed it."

"Oh! Well, it was really—really quite good, actually. I was glowingly praised as 'Snell is . . . very good . . . *well rounded* is . . . the phrase I would use,' and the book itself was described as 'surely the biggest piece of . . . 1986.' There's talk of a boxed set, too. Listen, I wanted to tell you that your Fiction Infraction trial will probably be next week. I tried to get another postponement but Hopkins is nothing if not tenacious; place and time to be decided upon."

"Should I be worried?" I asked, thinking about the last time I'd faced a court here in the BookWorld. It had been in Kafka's *The Trial* and it turned out predictably unpredictable.

"Not really," admitted Snell. "Our 'strong readership approval' defense should count for something—after all, you did actually do it, so just plain lying might not help so much after all.

Listen," he went on without stopping for breath, "Miss Havisham asked me to introduce you to the wonders of the Well—she would have been here this morning but she's on a grammasite extermination course."

"We saw a grammasite in *Great Expectations*."

"So I heard. You can never be too careful as far as grammasites are concerned." He looked at ibb and obb, who were just finishing off my bacon and eggs. "Is this breakfast?"

I nodded.

"Fascinating! I've always wondered what a breakfast looked like. In our books we have twenty-three dinners, twelve lunches and eighteen afternoon teas—but no breakfasts." He paused for a moment. "And why is orange jam called marmalade, do you suppose?"

I told him I didn't know and passed him a mug of coffee.

"Do you have any Generics living in your books?" I asked.

"A half dozen or so at any one time," he replied, spooning in some sugar and staring at ibb and obb, who, true to form, stared back. "Boring bunch until they develop a personality, then they can be quite fun. Trouble is, they have an annoying habit of assimilating themselves into a strong leading character, and it can spread amongst them like a rash. They used to be billeted en masse, but that all changed after we lodged six thousand Generics inside *Rebecca*. In under a month all but eight had become Mrs. Danvers. Listen, I don't suppose I could interest you in a couple of housekeepers, could I?"

"I don't think so," I replied, recalling Mrs. Danvers's slightly abrasive personality.

"Don't blame you," replied Snell with a laugh.

"So now it's only limited numbers per novel?"

"You learn fast. We had a similar problem with Merlins. We've had aged-male-bearded-wizard-mentor types coming out of our ears for years." He leaned closer. "Do you know how many Merlins the Well of Lost Plots has placed over the past fifty years?"

"Tell me."

"Nine thousand!" he breathed. "We even altered plotlines to include older male mentor figures! Do you think that was wrong?"

"I'm not sure," I said, slightly confused.

"At least the Merlin type is a popular character. Stick a new hat on him and he can appear pretty much anywhere. Try getting rid of thousands of Mrs. Danvers. There isn't a huge demand for creepy fifty-something housekeepers; even buy-two-get-one-free deals didn't help—we use them on anti-mispeling duty, you know. A sort of army."

"What's it like?" I asked.

"How do you mean?"

"Being fictional."

"Ah!" replied Snell slowly. "Yes—fictional."

I realized too late that I had gone too far—it was how I imagined a dog would feel if you brought up the question of distemper in polite conversation.

"I forgive your inquisitiveness, Miss Next, and since you are an Outlander, I will take no offense. If I were you, I shouldn't inquire too deeply about the past of fictioneers. We all aspire to be ourselves, an original character in a litany of fiction so vast that we know we cannot. After basic training at St. Tabularasa's, I progressed to the Dupin school for detectives; I went on field trips around the works of Hammett, Chandler and Sayers before attending a postgraduate course at the Agatha Christie finishing school. I would have liked to be an original, but I was born seventy years too late for that."

He stopped and paused for reflection. I was sorry to have raised the point. It can't be easy, being an amalgamation of all that has been written before.

"Right!" he said, finishing his coffee. "That's enough about me. Ready?"

I nodded.

"Then let's go."

So, taking my hand, he transported us both out of *Caversham Heights* and into the endless corridors of the Well of Lost Plots.

The Well was similar to the library as regards the fabric of the building—dark wood, thick carpet, tons of shelves—but here the similarity ended. Firstly, it was *noisy*. Tradesmen, artisans, technicians and Generics all walked about the broad corridors appearing and vanishing as they moved from book to book, building, changing and deleting to the author's wishes. Crates and packing cases lay scattered about the corridors, and people ate, slept and conducted their business in shops and small houses built in the manner of an untidy shantytown. Advertising billboards and posters were everywhere, promoting some form of goods or services unique to the business of writing.[1]

"I think I'm picking up junkfootnoterphone messages, Snell," I said above the hubbub. "Should I be worried?"

"You get them all the time down here. Ignore them—and never pass on chain footnotes."[2]

We were accosted by a stout man wearing a sandwich board advertising bespoke plot devices "for the discerning wordsmith."

"No, thank you," yelled Snell, taking me by the arm and walking us to a quieter spot between Dr. Forthright's Chapter Ending Emporium and The Premier Mentor School.

"There are twenty-six floors down here in the Well," he told me, waving a hand towards the bustling crowd. "Most of them are chaotic factories of fictional prose like this one, but the twenty-sixth subbasement has an entrance to the Text Sea—we'll go down there and see them off-loading the scrawltrawlers one evening."

"What do they unload?"

---

1. "... Visit Aaron's Assorted Alliteration Annex, the superior sellers of stressed-syllable or similar-sounding speech sequences since the sixteenth century. Stop soon and see us situated on floor sixteen, shelf six seventy-six..."

2. "... Visit Bill's Dictionorium for every word you'll ever need! From *be* to *antidisestablishmentarianism*, we have words to suit all your plotting needs—floor twelve, shelf seventy-eight..."

"Words"—Snell smiled—"words, words and more words. The building blocks of fiction, the DNA of story."

"But I don't *see* any books being written," I observed, looking around.

He chuckled. "You Outlanders! Books may *look* like nothing more than words on a page, but they are actually an infinitely complex imaginotransference technology that translates odd, inky squiggles into pictures inside your head. Vast storycode engines at Text Grand Central throughput the images to the readers as they scan the text in the Outland. We're currently using Book Operating System V8.3—not for long, though—Text Grand Central want to upgrade the system."

"Someone mentioned UltraWord™ on the news last night," I observed.

"Fancy-pants name. It's BOOK V9 to me and you. Word-Master Libris should be giving us a presentation shortly. Ultra-Word™ is being tested as we speak—if it's as good as they say it is, books will never be the same again!"

"Well," I sighed, trying to get my head around this idea, "I had always thought novels were just, well, *written*."

"*Write* is only the word we use to describe the recording process," replied Snell as we walked along. "The Well of Lost Plots is where we interface the writer's imagination with the characters and plots so that it will make sense in the reader's mind. After all, reading is arguably a far more creative and imaginative process than writing; when the reader creates emotion in their head, or the colors of the sky during the setting sun, or the smell of a warm summer's breeze on their face, they should reserve as much praise for themselves as they do for the writer—perhaps more."

This was a new approach; I mulled the idea around in my head.

"Really?" I replied, slightly doubtfully.

"Of course!" Snell laughed. "*Surf pounding the shingle* wouldn't mean diddly unless you'd seen the waves cascade onto the foreshore, or felt the breakers tremble the beach beneath your feet, now would it?"

"I suppose not."

"Books"—Snell smiled—"are a kind of magic."

I thought about this for a moment and looked around at the chaotic fiction factory. My husband *was* or *is* a novelist—I had always wanted to know what went on inside his head, and this, I figured, was about the nearest I'd ever get.[3] We walked on, past a shop called A Minute Passed. It sold descriptive devices for marking the passage of time—this week they had a special on seasonal changes.

"What happens to the books which are unpublished?" I asked, wondering whether the characters in *Caversham Heights* really had so much to worry about.

"The failure rate is pretty high," admitted Snell, "and not just for reasons of dubious merit. *Bunyan's Bootscraper* by John McSquurd is one of the best books ever written, but it's never been out of the author's hands. Most of the dross, rejects or otherwise unpublished just languish down here in the Well until they are broken up for salvage. Others are so bad they are just demolished—the words are pulled from the pages and tossed into the Text Sea."

"All the characters are just recycled like waste cardboard or something?"

Snell paused and coughed politely. "I shouldn't waste too much sympathy on the one-dimensionals, Thursday. You'll run yourself ragged and there really isn't the time or resources to recharacterize them into anything more interesting."

"Mr. Snell, sir?"

It was a young man in an expensive suit, and he carried what

3. ". . . Soon to be launched: UltraWord™—the ultimate reading experience. For *free* information on the very latest Book Operating System and how its new and improved features will enhance your new book, call Text Grand Central on freefootnoterphone/ultraword . . ."

looked like a very stained pillowcase with something heavy in it about the size of a melon.

"Hello, Alfred!" said Snell, shaking the man's hand. "Thursday, this is Garcia—he has been supplying the Perkins and Snell series of books with intriguing plot devices for over ten years. Remember the unidentified torso found floating in the Humber in *Dead Among the Living*? Or the twenty-year-old corpse discovered with the bag of money bricked up in the spare room in *Requiem for a Safecracker*?"

"Of course!" I said, shaking the technician's hand. "Good, intriguing page-turning stuff. How do you do?"

"Well, thank you," replied Garcia, turning back to Snell after smiling politely. "I understand the next Perkins and Snell novel is in the pipeline and I have a little something that might interest you."

He held the bag open and we looked inside. It was a head. Or more importantly, a *severed* head.

"A head in a bag?" queried Snell with a frown, looking closer.

"Indeed," murmured Garcia proudly, "but not *any* old head in a bag. This one has an intriguing tattoo on the nape of the neck. You can discover it in a skip, outside your office, in a deceased suspect's deep freeze—the possibilities are endless."

Snell's eyes flashed excitely. It was the sort of thing his next book needed after the critical savaging of *Wax Lyrical for Death*.

"How much?" he asked.

"Three hundred," ventured Garcia.

"Three hundred?!" exclaimed Snell. "I could buy a dozen head-in-a-bag plot devices with that and still have change for a missing Nazi gold consignment."

"No one's using the old 'missing Nazi gold consignment' plot device anymore." Garcia laughed. "If you don't want the head you can pass—I can sell heads pretty much anywhere I like. I just came to you first because we've done business before and I like you."

Snell thought for a moment. "A hundred and fifty."

"Two hundred."

"One seventy-five."

"Two hundred and I'll throw in a case of mistaken identity, a pretty female double agent and a missing microfilm."

"Done!"

"Pleasure doing business with you," said Garcia as he handed over the head and took the money in return. "Give my regards to Mr. Perkins, won't you?"

He smiled, shook hands with us both and departed.

"Oh, boy!" exclaimed Snell, excited as a kid with a new bicycle. "Wait until Perkins sees this! Where do you think we should find it?"

I thought in all honesty that "head in a bag" plot devices were a bit lame, but being too polite to say so, I said instead, "I liked the deep-freezer idea, myself."

"Me, too!" Snell enthused as we passed a small shop whose painted headboard read: *Backstories built to order. No job too difficult. Painful childhoods a specialty.*

"Backstories?"

"Sure. Every character worth their salt has a backstory. Come on in and have a look."

We stooped and entered the low doorway. The interior was a workshop, small and smoky. A workbench in the middle of the room was liberally piled with glass retorts, test tubes and other chemical apparatus; the walls, I noticed, were lined with shelves that held tightly stoppered bottles containing small amounts of colorful liquids, all with labels describing varying styles of backstory, from one named *Idyllic childhood* to another entitled *Valiant war record.*

"This one's nearly empty," I observed, pointing to a large bottle with *Misguided feelings of guilt over the death of a loved one/partner ten years previously* written on the label.

"Yes," said a small man in a corduroy suit so lumpy it looked as though the tailor were still inside doing alterations, "that one's been quite popular recently. Some are hardly used at all. Look above you."

I looked up at the full bottles gathering dust on the shelves above. One was labeled *Studied squid in Sri Lanka* and another, *Apprentice Welsh mole catcher.*

"So what can I do for you?" inquired the backstoryist, gazing at us happily and rubbing his hands. "Something for the lady? Ill treatment at the hands of sadistic stepsisters? Traumatic incident with a wild animal? No? We've got a deal this week on unhappy love affairs; buy one and you get a younger brother with a drug problem at no extra charge."

Snell showed the merchant his Jurisfiction badge.

"Business call, Mr. Grnksghty—this is apprentice Next."

"Ah!" he said, deflating slightly. "The law."

"Mr. Grnksghty here used to write backstories for the Brontës and Thomas Hardy," explained Snell, placing his bag on the floor and sitting on a table edge.

"Ah, yes!" replied the man, gazing at me from over the top of a pair of half-moon spectacles. "But that was a long time ago. Charlotte Brontë, now she *was* a writer. A lot of good work for her, some of it barely used—"

"Yes, speaking," interrupted Snell, staring vacantly at the array of glassware on the table. "I'm with Thursday down in the Well. . . . What's up?"

He noticed us both staring at him and explained, "Footnoterphone. It's Miss Havisham."

"It's so rude," muttered Mr. Grnksghty. "Why can't he go outside if he wants to talk on one of those things?"

"It's probably nothing but I'll go and have a look," said Snell, staring into space. He turned to look at us, saw Mr. Grnksghty glaring at him and waved absently before going outside the shop, still talking.

"Where were we, young lady?"

"You were talking about Charlotte Brontë ordering backstories and then not using them?"

"Oh, yes." The man smiled, delicately turning a tap on the apparatus and watching a small drip of an oily colored liquid fall into a flask. "I made the most wonderful backstory for both Edward and Bertha Rochester, but do you know she only used a very small part of it?"

"That must have been very disappointing."

"It was," he sighed. "I am an artist, not a technician. But it didn't matter. I sold it lock, stock and barrel a few years back to *The Wide Sargasso Sea*. Harry Flashman from *Tom Brown's School-days* went the same way. I had Mr. Pickwick's backstory for years but couldn't make a sale—I donated it to the Jurisfiction museum."

"What do you make a backstory out of, Mr. Grnksghty?"

"Treacle, mainly," he replied, shaking the flask and watching the oily substance change to a gas, "and memories. *Lots* of memories. In fact, the treacle is really only there as a binding agent. Tell me, what do you think of this upgrade to UltraWord™?"

"I have yet to hear about it properly," I admitted.

"I particularly like the idea of ReadZip™," mused the small man, adding a drop of red liquid and watching the result with great interest. "They say they will be able to crush *War and Peace* into eighty-six words and still retain the scope and grandeur of the original."

"Seeing is believing."

"Not down here," Mr. Grnksghty corrected me. "Down here, *reading* is believing."

There was a pause as I took this in.

"Mr. Grnksghty?"

"Yes?"

"How do you pronounce your name?"

At that moment Snell strolled back in.

"That was Miss Havisham," he announced, retrieving his head. "Thank you for your time, Mr. Grnksghty—come on, we're off."

Snell led me down the corridor past more shops and traders until we arrived at the bronze-and-wood elevators. The doors opened and several small street urchins ran out holding cleft sticks with a small scrap of paper wedged in them.

"Ideas on their way to the books-in-progress," explained Snell as we stepped into the elevator. "Trading must have just started. You'll find the Idea Sales and Loan department on the seventeenth floor."

The ornate elevator plunged rapidly downwards.

"Are you still being bothered by junkfootnoterphones?"

"A little."[4]

"You'll get used to ignoring them."

The bell sounded and the elevator doors slid open, bringing with it a chill wind. It was darker than the floor we had just visited and several disreputable-looking characters stared at us from the shadows. I moved to get out but Snell stopped me. He looked about and whispered, "This is the twenty-second subbasement. The roughest place in the Well. A haven for cutthroats, bounty hunters, murderers, thieves, cheats, shape-shifters, scene-stealers, brigands and plagiarists."

"We don't tolerate these sort of places back home," I murmured.

"We *encourage* them here," explained Snell. "Fiction wouldn't be much fun without its fair share of scoundrels, and they have to live somewhere."

I could feel the menace as soon as we stepped from the elevator. Low mutters were exchanged amongst several hooded figures who stood close by, their faces obscured by the shadows, their hands bony and white. We walked past two large cats with eyes that seemed to dance with fire; they stared at us hungrily and licked their lips.

"Dinner," said one, looking us both up and down. "Shall we eat them together or one by one?"

4. ". . . Honest John's Prefeatured Character salesroom for all your character needs! Honest John has Generics grade A-6 to D-9. Top bargains this week: Mrs. Danvers, choice of three, unused. +++Lady of Shallot cloned for unfinished remake; healthy A-6 in good condition. +++Group of unruly C-5s suitable for any crowd scene—call for details. Listen to our full listings by polling on footnoterphone/honestjohn . . ."

"One by one," said the second cat, who was slightly bigger and a good deal more fearsome, "but we better wait until Big Martin gets here."

"Oh, yeah," said the first cat, retracting his claws quickly, "so we'd better."

Snell had ignored the two cats completely; he glanced at his watch and said, "We're going to the Slaughtered Lamb to visit a contact of mine. Someone has been cobbling together plot devices from half-damaged units that should have been condemned. It's not only illegal—it's dangerous. The last thing anyone needs is a 'Do we cut the red wire or the blue wire?' plot device going off an hour too early and ruining the suspense—how many stories have you read where the bomb is defused with an hour to go?"

"Not many, I suppose."

"You suppose right. We're here."

The gloomy interior was shabby and smelt of beer. Three ceiling fans stirred the smoke-filled atmosphere, and a band was playing a melancholy tune in one corner. The dark walls were spaced with individual booths where somberness was an abundant commodity; the bar in the center seemed to be the lightest place in the room and gathered there, like moths to a light, were an odd collection of people and creatures, all chatting and talking in low voices. The atmosphere in the room was so thick with dramatic clichés you could have cut it with a knife.

"See over there?" said Snell, indicating two men who were deep in conversation.

"Yes?"

"Mr. Hyde talking to Blofeld. In the next booth are Von Stalhein and Wackford Squeers. The tall guy in the cloak is Emperor Zhark, tyrannical ruler of the known galaxy and star of the Zharkian Empire series of SF books. The one with the spines is Mrs. Tiggy-winkle—they'll be on a training assignment, just like us."

"Mrs. Tiggy-winkle is an apprentice?" I asked incredulously, staring at the large hedgehog who was holding a basket of laundry and sipping delicately at a sherry.

"No; Zhark is the apprentice—Tiggy's a full agent. She deals with children's fiction, runs the Hedgepigs Society—and does our washing."

"Hedgepigs Society?" I echoed. "What does *that* do?"

"They advance hedgehogs in all branches of literature. Mrs. Tiggy-winkle was the first to get star billing and she's used her position to further the lot of her species; she's got references into Kipling, Carroll, Aesop and four mentions in Shakespeare. She's also good with really stubborn stains—and never singes the cuffs."

"*Tempest, Midsummer Night's Dream, Macbeth,*" I muttered, counting them off on my fingers. "Where's the fourth?"

"*Henry VI*, part one, act four, scene one: 'Hedge-born Swaine.' "

"I always thought that was an insult, not a hedgehog. *Swaine* can be a *country lad* just as easily as a *pig*—perhaps more so."

"Well," sighed Snell, "we've given her the benefit of the doubt—it helps with the indignity of being used as a croquet ball in *Alice*. Don't mention Tolstoy or Berlin when she's about, either—conversation with Tiggy is easier when you avoid talk of theoretical sociological divisions and stick to the question of washing temperatures for woolens."

"I'll remember that," I murmured. "The bar doesn't look so bad with all those pot plants scattered around, does it?"

Snell sighed audibly. "They're Triffids, Thursday. The big blobby thing practicing golf swings with the Jabberwock is a Krell, and that rhino over there is Rataxis. Arrest anyone who tries to sell you soma tablets, don't buy any Bottle Imps no matter how good the bargain and above all *don't look at Medusa*. If Big Martin or the Questing Beast turn up, run like hell. Get me a drink and I'll see you back here in five minutes."

"Right."

He departed into the gloom and I was left feeling a bit ill at ease. I made my way to the bar and ordered two drinks. On the other side of the bar a third cat had joined the two I had previously seen. The newcomer pointed to me but the others shook their heads and whispered something in his ear. I turned the other way and jumped in surprise as I came face-to-face with a curious creature that looked as though it had escaped from a bad science fiction novel—it was all tentacles and eyes. A smile may have flicked across my face because the creature said in a harsh tone:

"What's the problem, never seen a Thraal before?"

I didn't understand; it sounded like a form of Courier bold, but I wasn't sure so said nothing, hoping to brazen it out.

"Hey!" it said. "I'm talking to you, two-eyes."

The altercation had attracted another man, who looked like the product of some bizarre genetic experiment gone hopelessly wrong.

"He says he doesn't like you."

"I'm sorry."

"I don't like you, either," said the man in a threatening tone, adding, as if I needed proof, "I have the death sentence in seven genres."

"I'm sorry to hear that," I assured him, but this didn't seem to work.

"You're the one who'll be sorry!"

"Come, come, Nigel," said a voice I recognized. "Let me buy you a drink."

This wasn't to the genetic experiment's liking for he moved quickly to his weapon; there was a sudden blur of movement and in an instant I had my automatic pressed hard against his head—Nigel's gun was still in his shoulder holster. The bar went quiet.

"You're quick, girlie," said Nigel. "I respect that."

"She's with me," said the newcomer. "Let's all just calm down."

I lowered my gun and replaced the safety. Nigel nodded respectfully and returned to his place at the bar with the odd-looking alien.

"Are you all right?"

It was Harris Tweed. He was a fellow Jurisfiction agent and

Outlander, just like me. The last time I had seen him was three days ago in Lord Volescamper's library, when we had flushed out the renegade fictioneer Yorrick Kaine after he had invoked the Questing Beast to destroy us. Tweed had been carried off by the exuberant bark of a bookhound and I had not seen him since.

"Thanks for that, Tweed," I said. "What did the alien thing want?"

"He was a Thraal, Thursday—speaking in **Courier bold**, the traditional language of the Well. Thraals are not only all eyes and tentacles, but mostly mouth, too—he'd not have harmed you. Nigel, on the other hand, has been known to go a step too far on occasion—what are you doing alone in the twenty-second subbasement anyway?"

"I'm not alone. Havisham's busy so Snell's showing me around."

"Ah," replied Tweed, looking about, "does this mean you're taking your entrance exams?"

"Third of the way through the written already. Did you track down Kaine?"

"No. We went all the way to London, where we lost the scent. Bookhounds don't work so well in the Outland, and besides—we have to get special permission to pursue PageRunners into the real world."

"What does the Bellman say about that?"

"He's for it, of course," replied Tweed, "but the launch of UltraWord™ has dominated the Council of Genres' discussion time. We'll get round to Kaine in due course."

I was glad of this; Kaine wasn't only an escapee from fiction but a dangerous right-wing politician back home. I would be only too happy to see him back inside whatever book he'd escaped from—permanently.

At that moment Snell returned and nodded a greeting to Tweed, who returned it politely.

"Good morning, Mr. Tweed," said Snell, "will you join us for a drink?"

"Sadly, I cannot," replied Tweed. "I'll see you tomorrow morning at roll call, yes?"

"Odd sort of fellow," remarked Snell as soon as Tweed had left. "What was he doing here?"

I handed Snell his drink and we sat down in an empty booth. It was near the three cats and they stared at us hungrily while consulting a large recipe book.

"I had a bit of trouble at the bar and Tweed stepped in to help."

"Good thing, too. Ever see one of these?"

He rolled a small globe across the table and I picked it up. It was a little like a Christmas decoration but a lot more sturdy. A small legend complete with a bar code and ID number was printed on the side.

" 'Suddenly, a Shot Rang Out! FAD/167945,' " I read aloud. "What does it mean?"

"It's a stolen freeze-dried plot device. Crack it open and *pow!*—the story goes off at a tangent."

"How do we know it's stolen?"

"It doesn't have a Council of Genres seal of approval. Without one, these things are worthless. Log it as evidence when you get back to the office."

He took a sip of his drink, coughed and stared into the glass. "W-what is this?"

"I'm not sure but mine is just as bad."

"Not possible. Hello, Emperor, have you met Thursday Next? Thursday, this is Emperor Zhark."

A tall man swathed in a high-collared cloak was standing next to our table. He had a pale complexion, high cheekbones and a small and precise goatee. He looked at me with cold, dark eyes and raised an eyebrow imperiously.

"Greetings," he intoned indifferently. "You must send my regards to Miss Havisham. Snell, how is my defense looking?"

"Not too good, Your Mercilessness," he replied. "Annihilating all the planets in the Cygnus cluster might not have been a very good move."

"It's those bloody Rambosians," Zhark said angrily. "They threatened my empire. If I didn't destroy entire star systems, no one would have any respect for me; it's for the good of galactic peace, you know—*stability*, and anyway, what's the point in possessing a devastatingly destructive death ray if you can't use it?"

"Well, I should keep that to yourself. Can't you claim you were cleaning it when it went off or something?"

"I suppose," said Zhark grudgingly. "Is there a head in that bag?"

"Yes, do you want to have a look?"

"No, thanks. Special offer, yes?"

"What?"

"Special offer. You know, clearance sale. How much did you pay for it?"

"Only a . . . hundred," Snell said, glancing at me. "Less than that, actually."

"You were done." Zhark laughed. "They're forty a half dozen at CrimeScene, Inc.—with double stamps, too."

Snell's face flushed with anger and he jumped up.

"The little scumbag!" he spat. "I'll have *him* in a bag when I see him again!" He turned to me. "Will you be all right getting out on your own?"

"Sure."

"Good," he replied through gritted teeth. "See you later!"

"Hold it!" I said, but it was too late. He had vanished.

"Problems?" asked Zhark.

"No," I replied slowly, holding up the dirty pillowcase, "he just forgot his head—and careful, Emperor, there's a Triffid creeping up behind you."

Zhark turned to face the Triffid, who stopped, thought better of an attack and rejoined his friends, who were cooling their roots at the bar.

Zhark departed and I looked around. At the next table a *fourth* cat had joined the other three. It was bigger than the others and considerably more battle-scarred—it had only one eye and both ears had large bites taken out of them. They all licked their lips as the newest cat said in a low voice, "Shall we eat her?"

"Not yet," replied the first cat, "we're waiting for Big Martin."

They returned to their drinks but never took their eyes off me. I could imagine how a mouse felt. After ten minutes I decided that I was not going to be intimidated by outsize house pets and got up to leave, taking Snell's head with me. The cats got up and followed me out, down the dingy corridor. Here the shops sold weapons, dastardly plans for world domination and fresh ideas for murder, revenge, extortion and other general mayhem. Generics, I noticed, could be trained in the dark art of being an accomplished evildoer as easily as any other profession. The cats yowled excitedly and I quickened my step only to stumble into a clearing amidst the shantytown of wooden buildings. The reason for the clearing was obvious. Sitting atop an old packing case was another cat. But this one was different. No oversize house cat, this beast was four times the size of a tiger and it stared at me with ill-disguised malevolence. Its claws were extended and fangs at the ready, glistening slightly with hungry anticipation. I stopped and looked behind me to where the four other cats had lined up and were staring at me expectantly, tails gently lashing the air. A quick glance around the corridor proved that there was no one near who might offer me any assistance; indeed, most of the bystanders seemed to be getting ready for something of a show.

I pulled out my automatic as one of the cats bounded up to the newcomer and said, "Can we eat her now, please?"

The large cat placed one of its claws in the packing case and drew it through the wood like a razor-sharp chisel cutting through soft clay; it stared at me with huge green eyes and said in a deep, rumbling voice:

"Shouldn't we wait until Big Martin gets here?"

"Yes," sighed the smaller cat with a strong air of disappointment, "perhaps we should."

Suddenly, the big cat pricked up his ears and jumped from his box into the shadows; I pointed my gun but it wasn't attacking—

the overgrown tiger was departing in a panic. The other cats quickly left the scene and pretty soon the bystanders had gone, too. Within a few moments I was completely alone in the corridor, with nothing to keep me company but the rapid thumping of my own heart, and a head in a bag.

6.

Night of the Grammasites

Grammasite: Generic term for a parasitic life-form that lives inside books and feeds on grammar. Technically known as Gerunds or Ingers, they were an early attempt to transform nouns (which were plentiful) into verbs (which at the time were not) by simply attaching an *ing*. A dismal failure at verb resource management, they escaped from captivity and now roam freely in the subbasements. Although they are thankfully quite rare in the library itself, isolated pockets of grammasites are still found from time to time and dealt with mercilessly.

CAT FORMERLY KNOWN AS CHESHIRE,
Guide to the Great Library

I TURNED AND WALKED quickly towards the elevators, a strong feeling of impending oddness raising the hair on the back of my neck. I pressed the call button but nothing happened. I quickly dashed across the corridor and tried the second bank of elevators, but with no more success. I was just thinking of running to the stairwell when I heard a noise. It was a distant, low moan that was quite unlike any other sort of low moan that I had ever heard, nor would ever want to hear again. I put down the head in a bag as my palms grew sweaty, and although I *told* myself I was calm, I pressed the call button several more times and reached for my automatic as a shape hove into view from the depths of the corridor. It was flying close to the bookshelves and was something like a bat, something like a lizard and something like a vulture. It was covered in patchy gray fur and wearing stripy socks and a brightly colored waistcoat of questionable taste. I had seen this sort of thing before; it was a grammasite, and although dissimilar to the adjectivore I had seen in *Great Expectations*, I imagined it could do just as much harm—it was little wonder that the residents of the Well had locked themselves away. The grammasite swept past in a flash without noticing me and was soon gone with a rumble like distant artillery. I relaxed slightly, expecting to see the Well spring back into life, but nothing stirred. Far away in the distance, beyond the Slaughtered Lamb, an excited burble reached my straining ears. I pressed the call button again as the noise grew louder and a slight breeze drafted against my face, like the oily zephyr that precedes an underground train. I shuddered. Where I came from, a Browning automatic spoke volumes, but how it would work on a grammar-sucking parasite, I had no idea—and I didn't think this would be a good time to find out. I was preparing myself to run when there was a melodious *bing*, the call button light came on and one of the elevator pointers started to move slowly towards my floor. I ran across and leaned with my back against the doors, releasing the safety on my automatic as the wind and noise increased. By the time the elevator was four floors away, the first grammasites had arrived. They looked around the corridor as they flew, sniffing at books with their long snouts and giving off excited squeaks. This was the advance guard. A few seconds later the main flock arrived with a deafening roar. One or two of them poked at books until they fell off the shelves, while other grammasites fell upon the unfinished manuscripts with an excited cry. There was a scuffle as a character burst from a page, only to be impaled by a grammasite, who reduced the unfortunate wretch to a few explanatory phrases, which were then eaten by scavengers waiting on the sidelines. I had seen enough. I opened fire and got three of them straightaway, who were devoured in turn by the same scavengers—clearly there was little honor or sense of loss amongst grammasites; their compatriots merely shuffled into the gaps left by their fallen comrades. I picked off two who were scrabbling at the bookcases attempting to dislodge more books and then turned away to reload. As I did, another eerie silence filled the corridor. I released the slide on my automatic and looked up. About a hundred or so grammasites were staring at me with their small black eyes, and it wasn't a look that I'd describe as anywhere near friendly. I sighed. What a way to go. I could see my headstone now:

Thursday Next
1950–1986
SpecOps agent & beloved wife
to someone who doesn't exist
*Died for no adequately explained reason
in an abstract place by an abstract foe.*

I raised my gun and the grammasites shuffled slightly, as though deciding amongst themselves who would be sacrificed for them to overpower me. I pointed the gun at whichever one started to move, hoping to postpone the inevitable. The one who seemed to be the leader—he had the brightest-colored waistcoat, I noted—took a step forward and I pointed my gun at him as another grammasite seized the opportunity and made a sudden leap towards me, its sharpened beak heading straight for my chest. I whirled around in time to see its small black eyes twinkle with a thousand well-digested verbs when a hand on my shoulder pulled me roughly backwards into the elevator. The grammasite, carried on by its own momentum, buried its beak into the wood surround. I reached to thump the close button, but my wrist was deftly caught by my as yet unseen savior.

"We *never* run from grammasites."

It was a scolding tone of voice that I knew only too well. Miss Havisham. Dressed in her rotting wedding dress and veil, she stared at me with despair. I think I was one of the worst apprentices she had ever trained—or that was the way she made me feel, at any rate.

"We have nothing to fear except fear itself," she intoned, whipping out her pocket derringer and dispatching two grammasites who made a rush at the elevator's open door. "I seem to spend my waking hours extricating you from the soup, my girl!"

The grammasites were slowly advancing on us; they were now at least three hundred strong and others were joining them. We were heavily outnumbered.

"I'm sorry," I replied quickly, curtsying just in case as I loosed off another shot, "but don't you think we should be departing?"

"I fear only the Questing Beast," announced Havisham imperiously. "The Questing Beast, Big Martin . . . and semolina."

She shot another grammasite with a particularly fruity waistcoat and carried on talking. "If you had troubled to do some homework, you would know that these are Verbisoids and probably the easiest grammasite to vanquish of them all."

And almost without pausing for breath, Miss Havisham launched into a croaky and out-of-tune rendition of William Blake's "Jerusalem." The grammasites stopped abruptly and stared at one another. By the time I had joined her at the "holy Lamb of God" line, they had begun to back away in fright. We sang louder, Miss Havisham and I, and by "dark Satanic mills" they had started to take flight; by the time we had got to "Bring me my chariot of fire," they had departed completely.

"Quick!" said Miss Havisham. "Grab the waistcoats—there's a bounty on each one."

We stripped the waistcoats from the fallen grammasites; it was not a pleasant job—the corpses smelt so strongly of ink that it made me cough. The carcasses would be taken away by a verminator, who would boil down the bodies and distill off any verbs he could. In the Well, nothing is wasted.

"What were the smaller ones?"

"I forget," replied Havisham, gathering up the waistcoats. "Here, you're going to need this. Study it well if you want to pass your exams."

She handed me my TravelBook, the one that Goliath had taken. Within its pages were almost all the tips and equipment I needed for travel within the BookWorld.

"How did you manage that?"

Miss Havisham didn't answer. She was a bit like a strict parent, your worst teacher and a newly appointed South American dictator all rolled into one—which wasn't to say I didn't like her or respect her. It was just that I felt I was still nine whenever she spoke to me.

"Why do grammasites wear stripy socks?" I ventured, tying up the waistcoats with some string that Havisham had given me.

"Probably because spotted ones are out of fashion," she replied with a shrug, reloading her pistol. "What's in the bag?"

"Oh, some, er, shopping of Snell's."

I tried to change the subject. I didn't suppose carrying around unlicensed plot devices was something Havisham would approve of—even if they were Snell's.

"So why did we, um, sing 'Jerusalem' to get rid of them?"

"As I said, those grammasites were Verbisoids," she replied without looking up, "and a Verbisoid, in common with many language students, hates and fears *irregular* verbs—they far prefer consuming regular verbs with the *ed* word ending. Strong irregulars such as *to sing* with their internal vowel changes—we will *sing*—we *sang*—we have *sung*—tend to scramble their tiny minds."

"*Any* irregular verb frightens them off?" I asked with interest.

"Pretty much; but some irregulars are more easy to demonstrate than others—we could *cut,* I suppose, or even *be,* but then the proceedings change into something akin to a desperate game of charades—far easier to just sing and have done with it."

"What about if we were *to go*?" I ventured, thinking practically for once. "There can't be anything more irregular than *go, went, gone,* can there?"

"Because," replied Miss Havisham, her patience eroding by the second, "they might misconstrue it as *walked*—note the *ed* ending?"

"Not if we *ran,*" I added, not wanting to let this go. "That's irregular, too."

Miss Havisham stared at me icily. "Of course we could. But *ran* might be seen in the eyes of a hungry Verbisoid to be either trott*ed*, gallop*ed*, rac*ed*, rush*ed*, hurri*ed*, hasten*ed*, sprint*ed* and even depart*ed*."

"Ah," I said, realizing that trying to catch Miss Havisham out was about as likely as nailing Banquo's ghost to a coffee table, "yes, it might, mightn't it?"

"Look," said Miss Havisham, softening slightly, "if running away killed grammasites, there wouldn't be a single one left. Stick to 'Jerusalem' and you won't go far wrong—just don't try it with adjectivores or the parataxis; they'd probably join in—and then eat you."

She snorted, picked up the bundle of waistcoats and pulled me towards the elevator, which had just reopened. It was clear that the twenty-second subbasement wasn't a place she liked to be. I couldn't say I blamed her.

She relaxed visibly as we rose from the subbasements and into the more ordered nature of the library itself. We weren't alone in the elevator. With us was a large Painted Jaguar and her son, who had a paddy-paw full of prickles and was complaining bitterly that he had been tricked by a hedgehog and a tortoise, who had both escaped. The Mother Jaguar shook her head sadly and looked at us both with an exasperated air before addressing her son:

"Son, son," she said, ever so many times, graciously waving her tail, "what have you been doing that you shouldn't have?"

"So," said Miss Havisham as the elevator moved off, "how are you getting along in that frightful *Caversham Heights* book?"

"Well, thank you, Miss Havisham," I muttered, "the characters in it are worried that their book will be demolished from under their feet."

"With good reason I expect. Hundreds of books like *Heights* are demolished every day. If you stopped to waste any sympathy, you'd go nuts—so don't. It's man eat man in the Well. I'd keep yourself to yourself and don't make too many friends—they have a habit of dying just when you get to like them. It always happens that way. It's a narrative thing."

"*Heights* isn't a bad place to live," I ventured, hoping to elicit a bit of compassion.

"Doubtless," she murmured, staring at the floor indicator. "I remember when I was in the Well, when they were building *Great Expectations*. I thought I was the luckiest girl in the world when they told me I would be working with Charles Dickens. Top of my class at Generic College and, without seeming immodest, something of a beauty. I thought I would make an admirable young Estella—both refined and beautiful, haughty and proud, yet ultimately overcoming the overbearing crabbiness of her cantankerous benefactor to find true love."

"So . . . what happened?"

"I wasn't tall enough."

"Tall enough? For a book? Isn't that like having the wrong hair color for the wireless?"

"They gave the part to a little strumpet who was on salvage from a demolished Thackeray. Little cow. It's no wonder I treat her so rotten—the part should have been mine!"

She fell into silence.

"Let me get this straight," said the Painted Jaguar, who was having a bit of trouble telling the difference between a hedgehog and a tortoise. "If it's slow and solid, I drop him in the water and then scoop him out of his shell—"

"Son, son!" said his mother, ever so many times, graciously waving her tail. "Now attend to me and remember what I say. A hedgehog curls himself up into a ball and his prickles stick out every way—"

"Did you get the Jurisfiction exam papers I sent you?" asked Miss Havisham. "I've got your practical booked for the day after tomorrow."

"Oh!" I said with quite the wrong tone in my voice.

"Problems?" she asked, eyeing me suspiciously.

"No, ma'am—I just feel a bit unprepared—I think I might make a pig's ear of it."

"I disagree. I *know* you'll make a pig's ear of it. But wheels within wheels—all I ask is you don't make a fool of yourself or lose your life. Now that *would* be awkward."

"So," said the Painted Jaguar, rubbing his head, "if it can roll itself into a ball it must be a tortoise and—"

"*Ahhh!*" cried the Mother Jaguar, lashing her tail angrily. "*Completely* wrong. Miss Havisham, what am I to do with this boy?"

"I have no idea," she replied. "All men are dolts, from where I'm standing."

The Painted Jaguar looked crestfallen and stared at the floor.

"Can I make a suggestion?" I asked.

"Anything!" replied the Mother Jaguar.

"If you make a rhyme out of it, he *might* be able to remember."

The Mother Jaguar sighed. "It won't help. Yesterday he forgot he was a Painted Jaguar. He makes my spots ache, really he does."

"How about this?" I said, making up a rhyme on the spot:

> Can't curl, but can swim—
> Slow-Solid, that's him!
> Curls up, but can't swim—
> Stickly-Prickly, that's him!

The Mother Jaguar stopped lashing her tail and asked me to write it down. She was still trying to get her son to remember it when the elevator doors opened on the fifth floor and we got out.

"I thought we were going to the Jurisfiction offices," I said as we walked along the corridors of the Great Library, the wooden shelves groaning under the weight of the collected imaginative outpourings of nearly two millennia.

"The next roll call is tomorrow," Miss Havisham replied, stopping at a shelf and dropping the grammasite's waistcoats into a heap before picking out a roughly bound manuscript, "and I told Perkins you'd help him feed the Minotaur."

"You did?" I asked slightly apprehensively.

"Of course. Fictionalzoology is a fascinating subject and believe me, it's an area in which you should know more."

She handed me the book, which, I noticed, was handwritten.

"It's code-word protected," announced Havisham. "Mumble *sapphire* before you read yourself in." She gathered up the waistcoats again. "I'll pick you up in about an hour. Perkins will be waiting for you on the other side. Please pay attention and don't let him talk you into looking after any rabbits. Don't forget the password—you'll not get in or out without it."

"Sapphire," I repeated.

"Very good," she said, and vanished.

I placed the book on one of the reading desks and sat down. The marble busts of writers that dotted the library seemed to glare at me, and I was just about to start reading when I noticed, high up on the shelf opposite, an ethereal form that was coalescing, wraithlike, in front of my eyes. At home this might be considered a matter of great pith and moment, but here it was merely the Cheshire Cat making one of his celebrated appearances.

"Hullo!" he said as soon as his mouth had appeared. "How are you getting along?"

The Cheshire Cat was the librarian and the first person I had met in the BookWorld. With a penchant for non sequiturs and obtuse comments, it was hard not to like him.

"I'm not sure," I replied. "I was attacked by grammasites, threatened by Big Martin's friends and a Thraal. I've got two Generics billeted with me, the characters in *Caversham Heights* think I can save their book and right now I have to give the Minotaur his breakfast."

"Nothing remarkable *there*. Anything else?"

"How long have you got?"[1]

I tapped my ears.

---

1. "Vera Tushkevitch! Can you hear me?"

"Yes, I'm here. No need to shout. You will deafen me, I'm sure!"

"I don't trust these strange footnoterphone devices. I'm sure I'll catch some nasty proletarian disease. Where did we last meet? At that party with the Schuetzburgs? The one where they served Apples Benedict?"

"No, Sofya, my husband and I were not invited. He voted against Count Schuetzburg at the last election."

"Then it must have been at Bolshaia Marskaia with Princess Betsys. Whatever did happen to that Karenin girl, have you any idea?"

"Anna? Yes, indeed—but you must not tell a soul! Alexey Vronsky was smitten by her from the moment he saw her at the station."

"The station? Which station?"

"Problems?"

"I can hear two Russians gossiping, right here inside my head."

"Probably a crossed footnoterphone line," replied the Cat.

He jumped down, pressed his head against mine and listened intently.

"Can you hear them?" I asked after a bit.

"Not at all," replied the Cat, "but you do have *very* warm ears. Do you like Chinese food?"

"Yes, please." I hadn't eaten for a while.

"Me, too," mused the Cat. "Shame there isn't any. What's in the bag?"

"Something of Snell's."

"Ah. What do you think of this UltraWord™ lark?"

"I'm really not sure," I replied, truthfully enough. "How about you?"

"How about me what?"

"What do you think of the new operating system?"

"When it comes in, I shall give it my fullest attention," he said ambiguously, adding, "It's a laugh, isn't it?"

"What is?"

"That noise you make at the back of your throat when you hear something funny. Let me know if you need anything. Bye."

And he slowly faded out, from the tip of his tail to the tip of his nose. His grin, as usual, stayed for some time after the rest of him had gone.

I turned back to the book, murmured, "Sapphire," and read the first paragraph aloud.

"St. Petersburg; you remember when a guard fell beneath the train and was crushed?"

"Anna and Vronsky met *there*? How terribly unsophisticated!"

"There is more, my dear Sofya. Wait—the doorbell! I must leave you; not a word to anyone and I will call again soon!"

7.

Feeding the Minotaur

Name and Operator's Number: Perkins, David "Pinky." AGD136-323
Address: c/o Perkins & Snell Detective Series
Induction Date: September 1957
Notes: Perkins joined the service and has shown exemplary conduct throughout his service career. After signing up for a twenty-year tour of duty, he extended that to another tour in 1977. After five years heading the mispeling Protection Squad, he was transferred to grammasite inspection and eradication and in 1981 took over leadership of the grammasite research facility.

ENTRY FROM JURISFICTION SERVICE RECORD (ABRIDGED)

I FOUND MYSELF IN a large meadow next to a babbling brook. Willows and larches hung over the crystal clear waters while mature oaks punctuated the land. It was warm and dry and quite delightful—like a perfect summer's day in England, in fact, and I suddenly felt quite homesick.

"I used to look at the view a lot," said a voice close at hand. "Don't seem to have the time, these days."

I turned to see a tall and laconic man leaning against a silver birch, holding a copy of the Jurisfiction trade paper, *Movable Type*. I recognized him although we had never been introduced. It was Perkins, who partnered Snell at Jurisfiction, much as they did in the Perkins & Snell series of detective novels.

"Hello," he said, proffering a hand and smiling broadly, "put it there. Perkins is the name. Akrid tells me you sorted Hopkins out good and proper."

"Thank you. Akrid's very kind, but it isn't over yet."

He cast an arm towards the horizon. "What do you think?"

I looked at the view. High, snowcapped mountains rose in the distance above a green and verdant plain. At the foot of the hills were forests, and a large river wended its way through the valley.

"Beautiful."

"We bought it from the fantasy division of the Well of Lost Plots. It's a complete world in itself, written for a sword-and-sorcery novel entitled *The Sword of the Zenobians*. Beyond the mountains are icy wastes, deep fjords and relics of long-forgotten civilizations, castles, that sort of stuff. It was auctioned off when the book was abandoned. There were no characters or events written in, which was a shame—considering the work he did on the world itself, this might have been a bestseller. Still, the Outland's loss is our gain. We use it to keep grammasites and other weird beasts who for one reason or another can't live safely within their own books."

"Sanctuary?"

"Yes—and also for study and containment—hence the password."

"There seem to be an awful lot of rabbits," I observed, looking around.

"Ah, yes," replied Perkins, crossing a stone-arched bridge that spanned the small stream, "we never did get the lid on reproduction within *Watership Down*—if left to their own devices, the book would be so full of dandelion-munching lagomorphs that every other word would be *rabbit* within a year. Still, Lennie enjoys it here when he has some time off."

We walked up a path towards a ruined castle. Grass covered the mounds of masonry that had collapsed from the curtain wall, and the wood of the drawbridge had rotted and fallen into a moat now dry and full of brambles. Above us, what appeared to be ravens circled the highest of the remaining towers.

"Not birds," said Perkins, handing me a pair of binoculars. "Have a look."

I peered up at the circling creatures who were soaring on large wings of stretched skin. "Parenthiums?"

"Very good. I have six breeding pairs here—purely for research, I hasten to add. Most books can easily support forty or so with no ill effects—it's just when the numbers get out of hand that we have to take action. A swarm of grammasites can be pretty devastating."

"I know, I was almost—"

"Watch out!"

He pushed me aside as a lump of excrement splattered on the ground near where I had been standing. I looked up at the battlements and saw a man-beast covered in coarse, dark hair who glared down at us and made a strangled cry in the back of his throat.

"Yahoos," explained Perkins with disdain. "They're not terribly well behaved and *quite* beyond training."

"From *Gulliver's Travels*?"

"Bingo. When truly original works like Jonathan Swift's are made into new books, characters are often duplicated for evaluation and consultative purposes. Characters can be retrained, but *creatures* usually end up here. Yahoos are not exactly a favorite of mine but they're harmless enough, so the best thing to do is ignore them."

We walked quickly under the keep to avoid any other possible missiles and entered the inner bailey, where a pair of centaurs were grazing peacefully. They looked up at us, smiled, waved and carried on eating. I noticed that one of them was listening to a Walkman.

"You have centaurs here?"

"And satyrs, troglodytes, chimeras, elves, fairies, dryads, sirens, Martians, leprechauns, goblins, harpies, aliens, daleks, trolls—you name it." Perkins smiled. "A large proportion of unpublished novels are in the fantasy genre, and most of them feature mythical beasts. Whenever one of those books gets demolished, I can usually be found down at the salvage yard. It would be a shame to reduce them to text, now wouldn't it?"

"Do you have unicorns?"

"Yes," sighed Perkins, "sackloads. More than I know what to do with. I wish potential writers would be more responsible with their creations. I can understand children writing about them, but adults should know better. Every unicorn in every demolished story ends up here. I had this idea for a bumper sticker: 'A unicorn isn't for page twenty-seven, it's for eternity.' What do you think?"

"I think you won't be able to stop people writing about them. How about taking the horn off and seeking placement in pony books?"

"I'll pretend I didn't hear that," replied Perkins stonily, adding, "We have dragons, too. We can hear them sometimes, at night when the wind is in the right direction. When—or *if*—Pellinore captures the Questing Beast, it will come to live here. Somewhere a long way away, I hope. Careful—don't tread in the Orc shit. You're an Outlander, aren't you?"

"Born and bred."

"Has anyone realized that platypuses and sea horses are fictional?"

"Are they?"

"Of course—you don't think anything that weird could have evolved by chance, do you? By the way, how do you like Miss Havisham?"

"I like her a great deal."

"So do we all. I think she quite likes us, too, but she'd never admit it."

We had arrived at the inner keep and Perkins pushed open the door. Inside was his office and laboratory. One wall was covered with glass jars filled with odd creatures of all shapes and sizes, and on the table was a partially dissected grammasite. Within its gut were words being digested into letters.

"I'm not really sure how they do it," said Perkins, prodding at the carcass with a spoon. "Have you met Mathias?"

I looked around but could see nothing but a large chestnut horse whose flanks shone in the light. The horse looked at me and I looked at the horse, then past the horse—but no one else was in the room. The penny dropped.

"Good morning, Mathias," I said as politely as I could. "I'm Thursday Next."

Perkins laughed out loud and the horse brayed and replied in a deep voice, "Delighted to make your acquaintance, madam. Permit me to join you in a few moments?"

I agreed and the horse returned to what I now saw were some complicated notes it was writing in a ledger open on the floor. Every now and then it paused and dipped the quill that was attached to its hoof into an inkpot and wrote in a large copperplate script.

"A Houyhnhnm?" I asked. "Also from *Gulliver's Travels*?"

Perkins nodded. "Mathias, his mare and the two Yahoos were all used as consultants for Pierre Boulle's 1963 remake: *La planète des singes*."

"Louis Aragon once said," announced Mathias from the other side of the room, "that the function of geniuses was to furnish cretins with ideas twenty years on."

"I hardly think that Boulle was a cretin, Mathias," said Perkins, "and anyway, it's always the same with you, isn't it? 'Voltaire said this,' 'Baudelaire said that.' Sometimes I think that you just, just—"

He stopped, trying to think of the right words.

"Was it da Vinci who said," suggested the horse helpfully, "that anyone who quotes authors in discussion is using their memory, not their intellect?"

"Exactly," replied the frustrated Perkins, "what I was about to say."

"*Tempora mutantur, et nos mutamur in illis,*" murmured the horse, staring at the ceiling in thought.

"The only thing *that* proves is how pretentious you are," muttered Perkins. "It's always the same when we have visitors, isn't it?"

"Someone has to raise the tone in this miserable backwater," replied Mathias, "and if you call me a 'pseudo-erudite ungulate' again, I shall bite you painfully on the buttock."

Perkins and the horse glared at one another.

"You said there was a pair of Houyhnhnms?" I asked, trying to defuse the situation.

"My partner, my love, my mare," explained the horse, "is currently at Oxford, *your* Oxford—studying political science at All Souls."

"Don't they notice?" I asked. "A horse, at Oxford?"

"You'd be surprised how unobservant some of the professors are," replied Perkins. "Napoleon the pig studied Marxism at Nuffield. Got a first, too. This way. I keep the Minotaur in the dungeons. You are fully conversant with the legend?"

"Of course," I replied. "It's the half-man, half-bull offspring of King Minos' wife, Pasiphaë."

"Spot on." Perkins chuckled. "The tabloids had a field day: 'Cretan Queen in Bull Love-Child Shock.' We built a copy of the labyrinth to hold it, but the Monsters' Humane Society insisted two officials inspect it first."

"And?"

"That was over twelve years ago; I think they're still in it. I keep the Minotaur in here."

He opened a door that led into a vaulted room below the old hall. It was dark and smelt of rotten bones and sweat.

"Er, you do keep it locked up?" I asked as my eyes struggled to see in the semidark.

"Of course!" he replied, nodding towards a large key hanging from a hook. "What do you think I am, an idiot?"

As my eyes became accustomed to the gloom, I could see that the back half of the vault was caged off with rusty iron bars. A door in the center was secured with a ridiculously large padlock.

"Don't get too near," warned Perkins as he took a steel bowl down from a shelf. "I've been feeding him on yogurt for almost five years, and to be truthful he's getting a bit bored."

"Yogurt?"

"With some bran mixed in. Feeding him on Grecian virgins was too expensive."

"Wasn't he slain by Theseus?" I asked, as a dark shape started moving at the back of the vault accompanied by a low growling noise. Even with the bars I really wasn't happy to be there.

"Usually," replied Perkins, ladling out some yogurt, "but mischievous Generics took him out of a copy of Graves's *The Greek Myths* in 1944 and dropped him in Stalingrad. A sharp-eyed Jurisfiction agent figured out what was going on and we took him out—he's been here ever since."

Perkins filled the steel bowl with yogurt, mixed in some bran from a large dustbin and then placed the bowl on the floor a good five feet from the bars. He pushed the dish the remainder of the way with the handle of a floor mop.

As we watched, the Minotaur appeared from the dark recesses of the cage and I felt the hair bristle on the back of my neck. His large and muscular body was streaked with dirt, and sharpened horns sprouted from his bull-like head. He moved with the low gait of an ape, using his forelegs to steady himself. As I watched, he put out two clawed hands to retrieve the bowl, then slunk off to a dark corner. I caught a glimpse of his fangs in the dim light, and a pair of deep yellow eyes that glared at me with hungry malevolence.

"I'm thinking of calling him Norman," murmured Perkins. "Come on, I want to show you something."

We left the dark and fetid area beneath the old hall and walked back into the laboratory, where Perkins opened a large leatherbound book that was sitting on the table.

"This is the Jurisfiction bestiary," he explained, turning the page to reveal a picture of the grammasite we had encountered in *Great Expectations*.

"An adjectivore," I murmured.

"Very good. Fairly common in the Well but under control in fiction generally."

He turned a page to reveal a sort of angler fish, but instead of a light dangling on a wand sticking out of its head, it had the indefinite article.

"Nounfish," explained Perkins. "They swim the outer banks of the Text Sea, hoping to attract and devour stray nouns eager to start an embryonic sentence."

He turned the page to reveal a picture of a small maggot.

"A bookworm?" I suggested, having seen these before at my uncle Mycroft's workshop.

"Indeed. Not strictly a pest and actually quite necessary to the existence of the BookWorld. They take words and expel alternate meanings like a hot radiator. I think earthworms are the nearest equivalent in the Outland. They aerate the soil, yes?"

I nodded.

"Bookworms do the same job down here. Without them, words would have one meaning, and meanings would have one word. They live in thesauri but their benefit is felt throughout fiction."

"So why are they considered a pest?"

"Useful, but not without their drawbacks. Get too many bookworms in your novel and the language becomes almost unbearably flowery."

"I've read books like that," I confessed.

He turned the page and I recognized the grammasites that had swarmed through the Well earlier.

"Verbisoid," he said with a sigh, "to be destroyed without mercy. Once the Verbisoid extracts the verb from a sentence, it generally collapses; do that once too often and the whole narrative falls apart like a bread roll in a rainstorm."

"Why do they wear waistcoats and stripy socks?"

"To keep warm, I should imagine."

"Ah. What about the mispeling vyrus?"

"*Speltificarious molesworthian,*" murmured Perkins, moving to where a pile of dictionaries were stacked up around a small glass jar. He picked out the container and showed it to me. A thin purple haze seemed to wisp around inside; it reminded me of one of Spike's SEBs.

"This is the larst of the vyrus," explained Perkins. "We had to distroy the wrist. Wotch this."

He picked up a letter opener and delicately brought it towards the vyrus. As I watched, the opener started to twist and change shape until it looked more like a miniature sheaf of papers—an operetta, complete with libretto and score. I think it was *The Pirates of Penzance*, but I couldn't be sure.

"The vyrus works on a subtextual level and disstorts the *meaning* of a wurd," explained Perkins, removing the operetta, which morphed back to its previous state. "The mispeling arises as a consekwence of this."

He replaced the jar back in the dictosafe.

"So the mispeling itself is really only a symptom of sense distortion?"

"Exactly so. The vyrus was rampant before Agent Johnson's *Dictionary* in 1744," added Perkins. "*Lavinia-Webster* and the *Oxford English Dictionary* keep it all in check, but we have to be careful. We used to contain any outbreak and off-load it in the *Molesworth* series, where no one ever notices. These days we destroy any new vyrus with a battery of dictionaries we keep on the seventeenth floor of the Great Library. But we can't be too careful. *Every* mispeling you come across has to be reported to the Cat on a form S-12."

There was the raucous blast of a car horn from outside.

"Time's up!" Perkins smiled. "That will be Miss Havisham."

Miss Havisham was not on her own. She was sitting in a vast automobile, the bonnet of which stretched ten feet in front of her. The large-spoked and unguarded wheels carried tires that looked woefully skinny and inadequate; eight huge exhaust pipes sprouted from either side of the bonnet, joined into one and stretched the length of the body. The tail of the car was pointed, like a boat, and just forward of the rear wheels two huge drive sprockets carried the power to the rear axle on large chains. It was a fearsome beast. It was the twenty-seven-liter Higham Special.

8.

Ton-Sixty on the A419

The wealthy son of a Polish count and an American mother, Louis Zborowski lived at Higham Place near Canterbury, where he built three aero-engined cars, all called Chitty Bang Bang. But there was a fourth: the Higham Special, a car he and Clive Gallop had engineered by squeezing a twenty-seven-liter aero-engine into a Rubery Owen chassis and mating it with a Benz gearbox. At the time of Zborowski's death at Monza behind the wheel of a Mercedes, the Special had been lapping Brooklands at 116 mph—but her potential was as yet unproved. After a brief stint with a lady owner whose identity has not been revealed, the Special was sold to Parry Thomas, who with careful modifications of his own pushed the land speed record up to 170.624 mph at Pendine sands, south Wales, in 1926.

THE VERY REVEREND MR. TOREDLYNE,
The Land Speed Record

HAS SHE BEEN boring you, Mr. Perkins?" called out Havisham.

"Not at all," replied Perkins, giving me a wink, "she has been a most attentive student."

"Humph," muttered Havisham. "Hope springs eternal. Get in, girl, we're off!"

I paused. I had been driven by Miss Havisham once before, and that was in a car that I thought relatively safe. This beast of an automobile looked as though it could kill you twice before even reaching second gear.

"What are you waiting for, girl?" said Havisham impatiently.

"If I let the Special idle any longer, we'll coke up the plugs. Besides, I'll need all the fuel to do the run."

"The run?"

"Don't worry!" shouted Miss Havisham as she revved the engine. The car lurched sideways with the torque, and a throaty growl filled the air. "You won't be aboard when I do—you're needed for other duties."

I took a deep breath and climbed into the small two-seater body. It looked newly converted and was little more than a racing car with a few frills tacked on to make it roadworthy. Miss Havisham depressed the clutch and wrestled with the gearshift for a moment. The large sprockets took up the power with a slight tug; it felt like a Thoroughbred racehorse that had just got the scent of a steeplechase.

"Where are we going?" I asked.

"Home!" answered Miss Havisham as she moved the hand throttle. The car leaped forward across the grassy courtyard and gathered speed.

"To *Great Expectations*?" I asked as Miss Havisham steered in a broad circuit, fiddling with the levers in the center of the massive steering wheel.

"Not my home," she retorted, "yours!"

With another deep growl and a lurch the car accelerated rapidly forward—but to where I was not sure. In front of us lay the broken drawbridge and stout stone walls of the castle.

"Fear not!" yelled Havisham above the roar of the engine. "I'll read us into the Outland as easy as blinking!"

We gathered speed. I expected us to jump straightaway, but we didn't. We carried on towards the heavy castle wall at a speed not wholly compatible with survival.

"Miss Havisham?" I asked, my voice tinged with fear.

"I'm just trying to think of the best words to get us there, girl!" she replied cheerfully.

"Stop!" I yelled as the point of no return came and went in a flash.

"Let me see . . . ," muttered Havisham, thinking hard, the accelerator still wide open.

I covered my eyes. The car was running too fast to jump out and a collision seemed inevitable. I grasped the side of the car's body and tensed as Miss Havisham took herself, me and two tons of automobile through the barriers of fiction and into the real world. *My* world.

I opened my eyes again. Miss Havisham was studying a road map as the Higham Special swerved down the middle of the road. I grabbed the steering wheel as a milk-float swerved into the hedge.

"I won't use the M4 in case the C of G get wind of it," she said, looking around. "We'll use the A419—are we anywhere close?"

I recognized where we were instantly. Just north of Swindon outside a small town called Highworth.

"Continue round the roundabout and up the hill into the town," I told her, adding, "but it's *not* your right of way, remember."

It was too late. To Miss Havisham, her way *was* the right way. The first car braked in time but the one behind it was not so lucky—it drove into the rear of the first with a crunch. I held on tightly as Miss Havisham accelerated rapidly away up the hill into Highworth. I was pressed into my seat, and for a single moment, perched above two tons of bellowing machinery, I suddenly realized why Havisham liked this sort of thing—it was, in a word, *exhilarating*.

"I've only borrowed the Special from the count," she explained. "Parry Thomas will take delivery of it next week and aim to lift the speed record for himself. I've been working on a new mix of fuels; the A419 is straight and smooth—I should be able to do at least a ton-eighty on *that*."

"Turn right onto the B4019 at the Jesmond," I told her, "*after* the lights turn to greeeeeeen."

The truck missed us by about six inches.

"What's that?"

84

"Nothing."

"You know, Thursday, you should really loosen up and learn to enjoy life more—you can be such an old stick-in-the-mud."

I lapsed into silence.

"And don't sulk," added Miss Havisham. "If there's something I can't abide, it's a sulky apprentice."

We bowled down the road, nearly losing it on an S-bend, until miraculously we reached the main Swindon-Cirencester road. It was a no right turn but we did anyway, to a chorus of screeching tires and angry car horns. Havisham accelerated off, and we had just approached the top of the hill when we came across a large *Diversion* sign blocking the road. Havisham thumped the steering wheel angrily.

"I don't believe it!" she bellowed.

"Road closed?" I queried, trying to hide my relief. "Good—I mean, good-*ness* gracious, what a shame—another time, eh?"

Havisham clunked the Special into first gear and we moved off round the sign and motored down the hill.

"It's *him,* I can sense it!" she growled. "Trying to steal the speed record from under my very nose!"

"Who?"

As if in answer, another racing car shot past us with a loud *poop poop!*

"*Him,*" muttered Havisham as we pulled off the road next to a speed camera. "A driver so bad he is a menace to himself and every sentient being on the highways."

He must have been truly frightful for Havisham to notice. A few minutes later the other car returned and pulled up alongside.

"What ho, Havisham!" said the driver, taking the goggles from his bulging eyes and grinning broadly. "Still using Count 'Snail' Zborowski's old slowpoke Special, eh?"

"Good afternoon, Mr. Toad," said Havisham. "Does the Bellman know you're in the Outland?"

"Of course not!" yelled Mr. Toad, laughing. "And you're not going to tell him, old girl, because you're not meant to be here either!"

Havisham was silent and looked ahead, trying to ignore him.

"Is that a Liberty aero-engine under there?" asked Mr. Toad, pointing at the Special's bonnet, which trembled and shook as the vast engine idled roughly to itself.

"Perhaps," replied Havisham.

"Ha!" replied Toad with an infectious smile. "I had a Rolls-Royce Merlin shoehorned into this old banger!"

I watched Miss Havisham with interest. She stared ahead but her eye twitched slightly when Mr. Toad revved his car's engine. In the end, she could resist it no more and her curiosity got the better of her disdain.

"How does it go?" she asked, eyes gleaming.

"Like a rocket!" replied Mr. Toad, jumping up and down in his excitement. "Over a thousand horses to the back axle—makes your Higham Special look like a motor-mower!"

"We'll see about *that*," replied Havisham, narrowing her eyes. "Usual place, usual time, usual bet?"

"You're on!" Mr. Toad revved his car, pulled down his goggles and vanished in a cloud of rubber smoke. The *poop poop* of his horn lingered on as an echo some seconds after he had gone.

"Slimy reptile," muttered Havisham.

"Strictly speaking, he's neither," I retorted. "More like a dry-skinned, land-based amphibian."

It felt safe to be impertinent because I knew she wasn't listening.

"He's caused more accidents than you've had hot dinners."

"And you're going to race him?" I asked slightly nervously.

"And beat him, too, what's more." She handed me a pair of bolt cutters.

"What do you want me to do?"

"Open up the speed camera and get the film out once I've done my run."

She donned a pair of goggles and was gone in a howl of engine noise and screeching of tires. I looked nervously around as she and the car hurtled off into the distance, the roar of the engine fading into a hum, occasionally punctuated by muffled cracks from the exhaust. I looked around. The sun was out and I could see at least three airships droning across the sky; I wondered what was going on at SpecOps. I had written a note to Victor telling him I had to be away for a year or more and tendered my resignation. Suddenly I was shaken from my daydream by something else. Something dark and just out of sight. Something I should have done or something I'd forgotten. I shivered and then it clicked. Last night. Gran. Aornis's mindworm. What had she been unraveling in my mind? I sighed as the pieces slowly started to merge together in my head. Gran had told me to run the facts over and over to renew the familiar memories that Aornis was trying to delete. But how do you start trying to find out what it is you've forgotten? I concentrated. . . . Landen. I hadn't thought about him all day and that was unusual. I could remember where we met and what had happened to him—no problem there. Anything else? His full name. Damn and blast! Landen Parke-*something*. Did it begin with a *B*? I couldn't remember. I sighed and placed my hand on where I imagined our baby to be, now the size of a half crown. I remembered enough to know I loved him, and I missed him dreadfully—which was a good sign, I supposed. I thought of Lavoisier's perfidy and the Schitt brothers and started to feel rage building inside me. I closed my eyes and tried to relax. There was a phone box by the side of the road, and on impulse I called my mother.

"Hi, Mum, it's Thursday."

"Thursday!" she screamed excitedly. "Hang on—the stove's on fire."

"The stove?"

"Well, the kitchen really—wait a mo!"

There was a crashing noise and she came back on the line a few seconds later.

"Out now. Darling! Are you okay?"

"I'm fine, Mum."

"And the baby?"

"Fine, too. How are things with you?"

"Frightful! Goliath and SpecOps have been camping outside

since the moment you left, and Emma Hamilton is living in the spare room and eats like a horse."

There was an angry growl and a loud whooshing noise as Havisham swept past in little more than a blur. Two flashes from the speed camera went off in quick succession, and there were several more loud bangs as Havisham rolled off the throttle.

"What was that noise?" asked my mother.

"You'd never believe me if I told you. My, er, *husband* hasn't been round looking for me, has he?"

"I'm afraid not, sweetheart," she said in her most understanding voice. She knew about Landen and understood better than most—her own husband, my father, had been eradicated himself seventeen years previously. "Why don't you come round and talk. The Eradications Anonymous meeting is at eight this evening; you'll be among friends there."

"I don't think so, Mum."

"Are you eating regularly?"

"Yes, Mum."

"I managed to get DH-82 to do a few tricks."

DH-82 was her rescue thylacine. Training a usually unbelievably torpid thylacine to do anything except eat or sleep on command was almost front-page news.

"That's good. Listen, I just called to say I missed you and not to worry about me—"

"I'm going to try another run!" shouted Miss Havisham, who had drawn up. I waved to her and she drove off.

"Are you keeping Pickwick's egg warm?"

I told Mum that this was Pickwick's job, that I would call again and hung up. I thought of ringing Bowden but decided on the face of it that this was probably not a good idea. Mum's phone was bound to have been tapped and I had given them enough already. I walked back to the road and watched as a small gray dot grew larger and larger until it swept past with a strident bellow. The speed camera flashed again and a belch of flame erupted from the exhaust pipe. It took Miss Havisham about a mile to slow down, so I sat on a wall and waited patiently for her to return. A small four-seater airship had appeared no more than half a mile away. It appeared to be a SpecOps traffic patrol and I couldn't risk them finding out who I was. I looked urgently towards where Havisham was motoring slowly back to me.

"Come on," I muttered under my breath, "put some speed on, for goodness' sake."

Havisham pulled up and shook her head sadly. "Mixture's too rich. Take the film out of the speed camera, will you?"

I pointed out the airship heading our way. It was approaching quite fast—for an airship.

Miss Havisham looked over at it, grunted and jumped down to open the huge bonnet and peer inside. I cut off the padlock, pulled the speed camera down and rewound the film as quickly as I could.

"Halt!" barked the PA system on the airship when it was within a few hundred yards. "You are both under arrest. Wait by your vehicle."

"We've got to go," I said, this time more urgently.

"Poppycock!" replied Miss Havisham.

"Place you hands on the bonnet of the car!" yelled the PA as the airship droned past at treetop level. "You have been warned!"

"Miss Havisham, if they find out who I am, I could be in a lot of trouble!"

"*Nonsense,* girl. Why would they want someone as inconsequential as you?"

The airship swung round with the vectored engines in reverse; once they started asking questions, I'd be answering them for a long time.

"We have to go, Miss Havisham!"

She sensed the urgency in my voice and beckoned for me to get in the car. Within a moment we were away from that place, car and all, back to the lobby of the Great Library.

"You're not so popular in the Outland, then?" Havisham asked, turning off the engine, which spluttered and shook to a halt, the sudden quiet a welcome break.

89

"You could say that."

"Broken the law?"

"Not really."

She stared at me for a moment. "I thought it a bit odd that Goliath had you trapped in their deepest and most secure subbasement. Do you have the film from the speed camera?"

I handed it over.

"I'll get double prints," she mused. "Thanks for your help. See you at roll call tomorrow—don't be late!"

I waited until she had gone, then retraced my steps to the library where I had left Snell's head-in-a-bag plot device and made my way home. I didn't jump direct; I took the elevator. Book-jumping might be a quick way to get around, but it was also kind of knackering.

9.

Apples Benedict, a Hedgehog and Commander Bradshaw

ImaginoTransferenceRecordingDevice: A machine used to write books in the Well, the ITRD resembles a large horn (typically eight feet across and made of brass) attached to a polished mahogany mixing board a little like a church organ but with many more stops and levers. As the story is enacted in front of the *collecting horn*, the actions, dialogue, humor, pathos, etc., are collected, mixed and transmitted as raw data to Text Grand Central, where the wordsmiths hammer it into readable storycode. Once done, it is beamed direct to the author's pen or typewriter, and from there through a live footnoterphone link back to the Well as plain text. The page is read, and if all is well, it is added to the manuscript and the characters move on. The beauty of the system is that authors never suspect a thing—they think *they* do all the work.

COMMANDER TRAFFORD BRADSHAW, CBE,
Bradshaw's Guide to the BookWorld

I'M HOME!" I yelled as I walked through the door. Pickwick plocked happily up to me, realized I didn't have any marshmallows and then left in a huff, only to return with the gift of a piece of paper she had found in the wastepaper basket. I thanked her profusely and she went back to her egg.

"Hello," said ibb, who had been experimenting, Beeton-like, in the kitchen. "What's in the bag?"

"You don't want to know."

"Hmm," replied ibb thoughtfully, "since I wouldn't have asked if I *didn't* want to know, your response must be another way of saying, 'I'm not going to tell you, so sod off.' Is that correct?"

"More or less," I replied, placing the bag in the broom cupboard. "Is Gran around?"

"I don't think so."

obb walked in a little later, reading a textbook entitled *Personalities for Beginners*.

"Hello, Thursday," it said. "A hedgehog and a tortoise came round to see you this afternoon."

"What did they want?"

"They didn't say."

"And Gran?"

"In the Outland. She said not to wait up for her. You look very tired; are you okay?"

It was true, I *was* tired, but I wasn't sure why. Stress? It's not every day that you have to fight swarms of grammasites and deal with Havisham's driving, Yahoos, Thraals, Big Martin's friends or head-in-a-bag plot devices. Maybe it was just the baby playing silly buggers with my hormones.

"What's for supper?" I asked, slumping in a chair and closing my eyes.

"I've been experimenting with alternative recipes," said ibb, "so we're having Apples Benedict."

"*Apples* Benedict?"

"Yes; it's like Eggs Benedict but with—"

"I get the picture. Anything else?"

"Of course. You could try Turnips à l'Orange or Macaroni Custard; for pudding I've made Anchovy Trifle and Herring Fool. What will you have?"

"Beans on toast."

I sighed. It was like being back home at mother's.

I didn't dream that night. Landen was absent, but then so, too, was . . . was . . . what's-her-name. I slept soundly and missed the alarm. I woke up feeling terrible and just lay flat on my back, breathing deeply and trying to push away the clouds of nausea. There was a rap at the door.

"ibb!" I yelled. "Can you get that?"

My head throbbed but there was no answer. I glanced at the clock; it was nearly nine and both of them would be out at St. Tabularasa's practicing whimsical asides or something. I hauled myself out of bed, steadied myself for a moment, wrapped myself in a dressing gown and went downstairs. No one was there when I opened the door. I was just closing it when a small voice said:

"We're down here."

It was a hedgehog and a tortoise. But the hedgehog wasn't like Mrs. Tiggy-winkle, who was as tall as me; this hedgehog and tortoise were just the size they should have been.

"Thursday Next?" said the hedgehog.

"Yes. What can I do for you?"

"You can stop poking your nose in where it's not wanted," said the hedgehog haughtily, "that's what you can do."

"I don't understand."

"Painted Jaguar?" suggested the tortoise. "*Can't curl, can swim*. Ring any bells, smart aleck?"

"Oh! You must be Stickly-Prickly and Slow-Solid."

"The same. And that little mnemonic you so *kindly* gave to the Painted Jaguar is going to cause us a few problems—the dopey feline will never forget *that* in a month of Sundays."

I sighed. Living in the BookWorld was a great deal more complicated than I had imagined.

"Well, why don't you learn to swim or something?"

"Who, me?" said Stickly-Prickly. "Don't be absurd; whoever heard of a hedgehog swimming?"

"And you could learn to curl," I added to Slow-Solid.

"Curl?" replied the tortoise indignantly. "I don't think so, thank you very much."

"Give it a go," I persisted. "Unlace your backplates a little and try and touch your toes."

There was a pause. The hedgehog and the tortoise looked at one another and giggled.

"Won't Painted Jaguar be surprised!" they chortled, thanked me and left.

I closed the door, sat down and looked in the fridge, shrugged and ate a large portion of Apples Benedict before having a long and relaxing shower.

The corridors of the Well were as busy as the day before. Traders bustled with buyers, deals were done, orders taken, bargains struck. Every now and then I saw characters fading in and out as their trade took them from book to book. I looked at the shopfronts as I walked past, trying to guess how they did what they did. There were holesmiths, grammatacists, pacesetters, moodmongers, paginators—you name it.[1]

It was the junkfootnoterphones starting up again. I tried to shut it out but only succeeded in lowering the volume. As I walked along, I noticed a familiar figure amongst the traders and plot speculators. He was dressed in his usual African-explorer garb: safari jacket, pith helmet, shorts, stout boots and a revolver in a leather holster. It was Commander Bradshaw, star of thirty-four thrilling adventure stories for boys available in hardback at 7/6 each. Out of print since the thirties, Bradshaw entertained himself in his retirement by being something of an éminence grise at Jurisfiction. He had seen and done it all—or claimed he had.

"A hundred!" he exclaimed bitterly as I drew closer. "Is that the best you can offer?"

The Action Sequence trader he was talking to shrugged. "We don't get much call for lion attacks these days."

"But it's terrifying, man, terrifying!" exclaimed Bradshaw.

---

1. ". . . Special on at St. Tabularasa's Generic College—superior-quality Blocking Characters available now for instant location to your novel. From forbidding fathers to 'by the book' superior police officers, our high-quality Blockers will guarantee conflict from the simplest protagonist! Call freefootnoterphone/St.Tabularasa's for more details . . ."

"Real hot-breath-down-the-back-of-your-neck stuff. Brighten up contemporary romantic fiction no end, I should wager—make a change from parties and frocks, what?"

"A hundred and twenty, then. Take it or leave it."

"Bloodsucker!" mumbled Bradshaw, taking the money and handing over a small glass globe with the lion attack, I presumed, safely freeze-dried within. He turned away from the trader and caught me looking at him. He quickly hid the cash and raised his pith helmet politely.

"Good morning!"

"Good morning," I replied.

He waved a finger at me. "It's Havisham's apprentice, isn't it? What was your name again?"

"Thursday Next."

"Is it, by gum! Well, I never."

He was, I noticed, a good foot taller than the last time we had met. He now almost came up to my shoulder.

"You're much—" I began, then checked myself.

"Taller?" he guessed. "Quite correct, girlie. Appreciate a woman who isn't trammeled by the conventions of good manners. Melanie—that's the wife, you know—she's pretty rude, too. 'Trafford,' she says—that's my name, Trafford—'Trafford,' she said, 'you are a worthless heap of elephant dung.' Well, this was from out the blue—I had just returned home after a harrowing adventure in Central Africa where I was captured and nearly roasted on a spit. The sacred emerald of the Umpopo had been stolen by two Swedish prospectors and—"

"Commander Bradshaw," I interrupted, desperate to stop him from recounting one of his highly unlikely and overtly jingoistic adventures, "have you seen Miss Havisham this morning?"

"Quite right to interrupt me," he said cheerfully, "appreciate a woman who knows when to subtly tell a boring old fart to button his lip. You and Mrs. Bradshaw have a lot in common. You must meet up someday."

We walked down the busy corridor.[2]

I tapped my ears.

"Problems?" inquired Bradshaw.

"Yes, I've got two gossiping Russians inside my head again."

"Crossed line? Infernal contraptions. Have a word with Plum at JurisTech if it persists. I say," he went on, lowering his voice and looking round furtively, "you won't tell anyone about that lion-attack sale, will you? If the story gets around that old Bradshaw is cashing in his Action Sequences, I'll never hear the last of it."

"I won't say a word," I assured him as we avoided a trader trying to sell us surplus B-3 Darcy clones, "but do many people try and sell off parts of their own books?"

"Oh, yes. But only if they are out of print and can spare it. Trouble is, I'm a bit strapped for the old moola. What with the

---

2. "Vera? Is that you? What a day! All noise and rain. Do please carry on about Anna!"

"Well, Anna danced with Vronsky at the ball that night; he became her shadow and very much more!"

"No! Alexey Vronsky and Anna—an *affair*! What about her husband? Surely he found out?"

"Eventually, yes. I think Anna told him, but not until she was with child, Vronsky's child. There was to be no hiding *that*."

"What did he say?"

"Believe it or not, he forgave them both! Insisted that they remain married and attempted to continue as if nothing had happened."

"I always did think that man was a fool. What happened next?"

"Vronsky shot himself, claiming he could not bear to be apart. Melodramatic is *not* the word for it!"

"It reads like a cheap novelette! Did he die?"

"No; merely wounded. It gets worse. Karenin realized that to save Anna he *himself* must take the disgrace and admit that he had been unfaithful so that Anna was not ruined and could marry Vronsky."

"So Karenin let them go? He didn't ban her from ever seeing her lover again? Didn't horsewhip either of them or sell his story to *The Mole*? It strikes me Karenin himself may have had some totty on the side, too. Wait! My husband calls me—stay tuned, farewell for now, my dear Vera!"

BookWorld Awards coming up and Mrs. Bradshaw a bit shy in public, I thought a new dress might be just the ticket—and the cost of clothes are pretty steep down here, y'know."

"It's the same in the Outland."

"Is it, by George?" he guffawed. "The Well always reminds me of the market in Nairobi; how about you?"

"There seems to be an awful lot of bureaucracy. I would have thought a fiction factory would be, by definition, a lot more free and relaxed."

"If you think this is bad, you ought to visit nonfiction. Over there, the rules governing the correct use of a semicolon alone run to several volumes. *Anything* devised by man has bureaucracy, corruption and error hardwired at inception, m'girl. I'm surprised you hadn't figured that out yet. What do you think of the Well?"

"I'm still a bit new to it."

"Really? Let me help you out."

He stopped and looked around for a moment, then pointed out a man in his early twenties who was walking towards us. He was dressed in a long riding jacket and carried a battered leather suitcase emblazoned with the names of books and plays he had visited in his trade.

"Yes?"

"He's an artisan—a *holesmith*."

"He's a plasterer?"

"No; he fills *narrative* holes—plot and expositional anomalies—bloopholes. If a writer said something like 'The daffodils bloomed in summer' or 'They checked the ballistics report on the shotgun,' then artisans like him are there to sort it out. It's one of the final stages of construction just before the grammatacists, echolocators and spellcheckers move in to smooth everything over."

The young man had drawn level with us by this time.

"Hello, Mr. Starboard," said Bradshaw to the holesmith, who gave a wan smile of recognition.

"Commander Bradshaw," he muttered slightly hesitantly, "what a truly delightful honor it is to meet you again, sir. Mrs. Bradshaw quite well?"

97

"Quite well, thank you. This is Miss Next—new at the department. I'm showing her the ropes."

The holesmith shook my hand and made welcoming noises.

"I closed a hole in *Great Expectations* the other day," I told him. "Was that one of your books?"

"Goodness me, no!" exclaimed the young man, smiling for the first time. "Holestitching has come a long way since Dickens. You won't find a holesmith worth his thread trying the old 'door opens and in comes the missing aunt/father/business associate/friend, et cetera,' all ready to explain where they've been since mysteriously dropping out of the narrative two hundred pages previously. The methodology we choose these days is to just go back and patch the hole, or more simply, to *camouflage* it."

"I see."

"Indeed," carried on the young man, becoming more flamboyant in the light of my perceived interest, "I'm working on a system that hides holes by *highlighting* them to the reader, that just says, 'Ho! I'm a hole, don't think about it!' but it's a little cutting-edge. I think," added the young man airily, "that you will not find a more experienced holesmith anywhere in the Well; I've been doing it for more than forty years."

"When did you start?" I asked, looking at the youth curiously. "As a baby?"

The young man aged, grayed and sagged before my eyes until he was in his seventies and then announced, arms outstretched and with a flourish:

"Da-daaaa!"

"No one likes a show-off, Llyster," said Bradshaw, looking at his watch. "I don't want to hurry you, Tuesday, old girl, but we should be getting over to Norland Park for the roll call."

He gallantly offered me an elbow to hold and I hooked my arm in his.

"Thank you, Commander."

"Stouter than stout!" Bradshaw said, laughing, and read us both into *Sense and Sensibility*.

10.

Jurisfiction Session No. 40319

JurisTech: Popular contraction of Jurisfiction Technological Division. This R&D company works exclusively for Jurisfiction and is financed by the Council of Genres through Text Grand Central. Due to the often rigorous and specialized tasks undertaken by Prose Resource Operatives, JurisTech is permitted to build gadgets deemed outside the usual laws of physics—the only department (aside from the SF genre) licensed to do so. The standard item in a PRO's manifest is the TravelBook (qv), which itself contains other JurisTech designs like the Martin-Bacon Eject-O-Hat, Punctuation Repair Kit and textual sieves of various porosity, to name but a few.

CAT FORMERLY KNOWN AS CHESHIRE,
Guide to the Great Library

THE OFFICES OF Jurisfiction were situated at Norland Park, the house of the Dashwoods in *Sense and Sensibility*. The family kindly lent the ballroom to Jurisfiction on the unspoken condition that Jane Austen books would be an area of special protection.

Norland Park was located within a broad expanse of softly undulating grassland set about with ancient oaks. The evening was drawing on, as it generally did, when we arrived, and wood pigeons cooed from the dovecote. The grass felt warm and comfortable like a heavily underlaid carpet, and the delicate scent of pine needles filled the air.

But all was not perfect in this garden of nineteenth-century prose; as we approached the house, there seemed to be some sort of commotion. A demonstration, in fact—the sort of thing I was used to seeing at home. But this wasn't a rally about the price of cheese or whether the Whig party were dangerously right-wing and anti-Welsh, nor of whether Goliath had the right to force legislation compelling everyone to eat SmileyBurger at least twice a week. No, this demonstration was one you would expect to find only in the world of fiction.

The Bellman, elected head of Jurisfiction and dressed in his usual garb of a town crier, was angrily tingling his bell to try to persuade the crowd to calm down.

"Not *again*," muttered Bradshaw as we walked up. "I wonder what the Orals want this time?"

I was unfamiliar with the term *Orals,* and since I didn't want to appear foolish, I tried to make sense of the crowd on my own. The person nearest to me was a shepherdess, although that was only a guess on my part as she didn't have any sheep—only a large crook. A boy dressed in blue with a horn was standing next to her discussing the falling price of lamb, and next to them was a very old woman with a small dog who whined, pretended to be dead, smoked a pipe and performed various other tricks in quick succession. Standing next to her was a small man in a long nightdress and bed hat who yawned loudly. Perhaps I was being slow, but it was only when I saw a large egg with arms and legs that I realized who they were.

"They're all nursery rhyme characters!" I exclaimed.

"They're a pain in the whatsit, that's what they are," murmured Bradshaw as a small boy jumped from the crowd, grabbed a pig and made a dash for it. Bo-peep hooked his ankle with her crook, and the boy sprawled headlong on the grass. The pig rolled into a flower bed with a startled oink and then beat a hurried escape as a large man started to give the boy six of the best.

". . . all we want is the same rights as any other character in the BookWorld," said Humpty-Dumpty, his ovoid face a deep crimson. "Just because we have a duty to children and the oral tradition doesn't mean we can be taken advantage of."

The crowd murmured and grunted their agreement. Humpty-

Dumpty continued as I stared at him, wondering whether his belt was actually a cravat, as it was impossible to tell which was his neck and which was his waist.

". . . we have a petition signed by over a thousand Orals who couldn't make it today," said the large egg, waving a wad of papers amidst shouts from the crowd.

"We're not joking this time, Mr. Bellman," added a baker who was standing in a wooden tub with a butcher and a candlestick maker. "We are quite willing to withdraw our rhymes if our terms are not met."

There was a chorus of approval from the assembled characters.

"It was fine before they were unionized," Bradshaw whispered in my ear. "Come on, let's take the back door."

We walked around to the side of the house, our feet crunching on the gravel chippings.

"Why can't characters from the oral tradition be a part of the Character Exchange Program?" I asked.

"Who'd cover for them?" snorted Bradshaw. "You?"

"Couldn't we train up Generics as sort of, well, 'character locums'?"

"Best to leave industrial relations to the people with the facts at their fingertips. We can barely keep pace with the volume of new material as it is. I shouldn't worry about Mr. Dumpty; he's been agitating for centuries. It's not our fault he and his badly rhyming friends are still looked after by the old OralTradPlus agreement— Good heavens, Miss Dashwood! Does your mother know that you smoke?"

It was Marianne Dashwood and she had been puffing away at a small cigarette as we rounded the corner. She quickly threw the butt away and held her breath for as long as possible before coughing and letting out a large cloud of smoke.

"Commander!" she wheezed, eyes watering. "Promise you won't tell!"

"My lips are sealed," replied Bradshaw sternly, "just this once."

Marianne breathed a sigh of relief and turned to me. "Miss

Next!" she enthused. "Welcome back to our little book. I trust you are well?"

"Quite well," I assured her, passing her the Marmite, Minto-las and AA batteries I had promised her from my last visit. "Will you make sure these get to your sister and mother?"

She clapped her hands with joy and took the gifts excitedly. "You are a darling!" she said happily. "What can I do to re-pay you?"

"Don't let Lola Vavoom play you in the movie."

"Out of my hands," she replied unhappily, "but if you need a favor, I'm here!"

We made our way up the servants' staircase and into the hall above where a much bedraggled Bellman was walking towards us, shaking his head and holding the employment demands that Humpty-Dumpty had thrust into his hands.

"Those Orals get more and more militant every day," he gasped. "They are planning a forty-eight-hour walkout tomorrow."

"What effect will that have?" I asked.

"I should have thought that would be obvious," chided the Bellman. "Nursery rhymes will be unavailable for recall. In the Outland there will be a lot of people thinking they have bad memories. It won't do the slightest bit of good—a storybook is usually in reach wherever a nursery rhyme is told."

"Ah," I said.

"The biggest problem," added the Bellman, mopping his brow, "is that if we give in to the nursery rhymsters, everyone *else* will want to renegotiate their agreements—from the poeticals all the way through to nursery stories and even characters in jokes. Sometimes I'm glad I'm up for retirement—then someone like you can take over, Commander Bradshaw!"

"Not me!" he said grimly. "I wouldn't be the Bellman again for all the *T*'s in *Little Tim Tottle's twin sisters take time tittle-tattling in a tuttle-tuttle tree—twice.*"

The Bellman laughed and we entered the ballroom of Norland Park.

"Have you heard?" said a young man who approached us with no small measure of urgency in his voice. "The Red Queen had to have her leg amputated. Arterial thrombosis, the doctor told me."

"Really?" I said. "When?"

"Last week. And that's not all." He lowered his voice. *"The Bellman has gassed himself!"*

"But we were just talking to him," I replied.

"Oh," said the young man, thinking hard. "I meant *Perkins* has gassed himself."

Miss Havisham joined us.

"Billy!" she said in a scolding tone. "That's quite enough of that. Buzz off before I box your ears!"

The young man looked deflated for a moment, then pulled himself up, announced haughtily that he had been asked to write additional dialogue for John Steinbeck and strode off. Miss Havisham shook her head sadly.

"If he ever says 'good morning,' " she said, "don't believe him. All well, Trafford?"

"Top-notch, Estella, old girl, top-notch. I bumped into Tuesday here in the Well."

"Not selling parts of your book, were you?" she asked mischievously.

"Good heavens, no!" replied Bradshaw, feigning shock and surprise. "Goodness me," he added, staring into the room for some form of escape, "I must just speak to the Warrington Unitary—I mean the authority of Cat—wait—I mean, the Cat formerly known as Cheshire. Good day!"

And tipping his pith helmet politely, he was gone.

"Bradshaw, Bradshaw," sighed Miss Havisham, shaking her head sadly. "If he flogs one more inciting incident from *Bradshaw Defies the Kaiser*, it will have so many holes we could use it as a colander."

"He needed the money to buy a dress for Mrs. Bradshaw," I explained.

"Have you met her yet?"

"Not yet."

"When you do, don't stare, will you? It's very rude."

"Why would I—"

"Come along! Almost time for roll call!"

The ballroom of Norland Park had long since been used for nothing but Jurisfiction business. The floor space was covered with tables and filing cabinets, and the many desks were piled high with files tied up with ribbon. There was a table to one side with food upon it, and waiting for us—or the Bellman, at least—were the staff at Jurisfiction. About thirty operatives were on the active list, and since up to ten of them were busy on assignment and five or so active in their own books, there were never more than fifteen people in the office at any one time. Vernham Deane gave me a cheery wave as we entered. He was the resident cad and philanderer in a Daphne Farquitt novel entitled *The Squire of High Potternews*, but you would never know to talk to him—he had always been polite and courteous to me. Next to him was Harris Tweed, who had intervened back at the Slaughtered Lamb only the day before.

"Miss Havisham!" he exclaimed, walking over and handing us both a plain envelope. "I've got your bounty for those grammasites you killed; I split it equally, yes?"

He winked at me, then left before Havisham could say anything.

"Thursday!" said Akrid Snell, who had approached from another quarter. "Sorry to dash off like that yesterday—hello, Miss Havisham—I heard you got swarmed by a few grammasites; no one's ever shot six Verbisoids at one go before!"

"Piece of cake," I replied. "And, Akrid, I've still got that, er, thing you bought."

"Thing? What thing?"

"You remember," I urged, knowing that trying to influence his own narrative was strictly forbidden, "the *thing*. In a bag. You know."

"Oh! Ah . . . ah, yes," he said, finally realizing what I was talking about. "The *thing* thing. I'll pick it up after work, yes?"

"Snell insider-trading again?" asked Havisham quietly as soon as he had left.

"I'm afraid so."

"I'd do the same if my book was as bad as his."

I looked around to see who else had turned up. Sir John Falstaff was there, as was King Pellinore, Deane, Lady Cavendish, Mrs. Tiggy-winkle with Emperor Zhark in attendance, Gully Foyle, and Perkins.

"Who are they?" I asked Havisham, pointing to two agents I didn't recognize.

"The one on the left holding the pumpkin is Ichabod Crane. Beatrice is the other. A bit loud for my liking, but good at her job."

I thanked her and looked around for the Red Queen, whose open hostility to Havisham was Jurisfiction's least-well-kept secret; she was nowhere to be seen.

"Hail, Miss Next!" rumbled Falstaff, waddling up and staring at me unsteadily from within a cloud of alcohol fumes. He had drunk, stolen and womanized throughout *Henry IV* parts I and II, then inveigled himself into *Merry Wives of Windsor*. Some saw him as a likable rogue; I saw him as just plain revolting—although he *was* the blueprint of likable debauchers in fiction everywhere, so I thought I should try to cut him a bit of slack.

"Good morning, Sir John," I said, trying to be polite.

"Good morning to *you,* sweet maid," he exclaimed happily. "Do you ride?"

"A little."

"Then perhaps you might like to take a ride up and down the length of my merry England? I could take you places and show you things—"

"I must politely decline, Sir John."

He laughed noisily in my face. I felt a flush of anger rise within me, but luckily the Bellman, unwilling to waste any more time, had stepped up to his small dais and tingled his bell.

"Sorry to keep you all waiting," he muttered. "As you have seen, things are a little fraught outside. But I am delighted to see so many of you here. Is there anyone still to come?"

"Shall we wait for Godot?" inquired Deane.

"Anyone know where he is?" asked the Bellman. "Beatrice, weren't you working with him?"

"Not I," replied the young woman. "You might inquire this of Benedict if he troubles to attend, but you would as well speak to a goat."

"The sweet lady's tongue does abuse to our ears," said Benedict, who had been seated out of our view but now rose to glare at Beatrice. "Were the fountain of your mind clear again, that I might water an ass at it."

"Ah!" retorted Beatrice with a laugh. "Look, he's winding up the watch of his wit; by and by it will strike!"

"Dear Beatrice," returned Benedict, bowing low, "I was looking for a fool when I found you."

"You, Benedict? Who has not so much brain as earwax?"

He thought hard for a moment. "Methink'st thou art a general offense and every man should beat thee, fair Beatrice."

They narrowed their eyes at each other and then smiled with polite enmity.

"All right, all right," interrupted the Bellman, "calm down, you two. Do you know where Agent Godot is or not?"

Beatrice answered that she didn't.

"Then," announced the Bellman, "we'll get on. Jurisfiction meeting number 40319 is now in session."

He tingled his bell again, coughed and consulted his clipboard.

"Item one. Our congratulations go to Deane and Lady Cavendish for foiling the bowdlerisers in Chaucer."

There were a few words of encouragement and backslapping.

"There has been damage done but it's got no worse, so let's just try and keep an eye out in the future. Item two."

He put down his clipboard and leaned on the lectern.

"Remember that craze a few years back in the BookWorld for sending chain letters? Receive a letter and send one on to ten friends? Well, someone has been overenthusiastic with the letter *U*—I've got a report here from the Text Sea Environmental Protection Agency saying that reserves of the letter *U* have reached dangerously low levels—we need to decrease consumption until stocks are brought back up. Any suggestions?"

"How about using a lower-case *n* upside down?" said Benedict.

"We tried that with *M* and *W* during the great *M* Migration of '62; it never worked."

"How about *respelling* what, what?" suggested King Pellinore, stroking his large white mustache. "Any word with the *our* ending could be spelt *or*, don'tchaknow."

"Like *neighbor* instead of *neighbour*?"

"It's a good idea," put in Snell. "*Labor, valor, flavor, harbor*—there must be hundreds. If we confine it to one geographical area, we can claim it as a local spelling idiosyncrasy."

"Hmm," said the Bellman, thinking hard, "do you know, it just might work."

He looked at his clipboard again. "Item three—Tweed, are you here?"

Harris Tweed signaled from where he was standing.

"Good," continued the Bellman. "I understand you were pursuing a PageRunner who had taken up residence in the Outland?"

Tweed glanced at me and stood up.

"Fellow by the name of Yorrick Kaine. He's something of a big cheese in the Outland—runs Kaine Publishing and has set himself up as head of his own political party—"

"Yes, yes," said the Bellman impatiently, "and he stole *Cardenio,* I know. But the point is, where is he now?"

"He went back to the Outland, where I lost him," replied Tweed.

"The Council of Genres are not keen to sanction any work in the real world," said the Bellman slowly, "it's too risky. We don't even know which book Kaine is from—and since he's not doing anything against us at present, I think he should stay in the Outland."

"But Kaine is a real danger to *our* world," I exclaimed.

Considering Kaine's righter-than-right politics, this was a fresh limit to the word *understatement*.

"He has stolen from the Great Library once," I continued. "How can we suppose he won't do the same again? Don't we have a duty to the readers to protect them from fictionauts hell-bent on—"

"Ms. Next," interrupted the Bellman, "I understand what you are saying, but I am *not* going to sanction an operation in the Outland. I'm sorry, but that is how it is going to be. He goes on the PageRunners' register and we'll set up textual sieves on every floor of the library in case he plans to come back. Out there you may do as you please; here you do as we tell you. Is that clear?"

I grew hot and angry but Miss Havisham squeezed my arm, so I remained quiet.

"Good," carried on the Bellman, consulting his clipboard. "Item four. Text Grand Central have reported several attempted incursions from the Outland. Nothing serious, but enough to generate a few ripples in the Ficto-Outland barrier. Miss Havisham, didn't you report that an Outlander company was doing some research into entering fiction?"

It was true. Goliath had been attempting entry into the Book-World for many years but with little success; all they had managed to do was extract a stodgy gunge from volumes one to eight of *The World of Cheese*. Uncle Mycroft had sought refuge in the Sherlock Holmes series to avoid them.

"It was called the *Something* Company," replied Havisham thoughtfully.

"Goliath," I told her. "It's called the *Goliath* Corporation."

"Goliath. That was it. I had a look round while I was retrieving Miss Next's TravelBook."

"Do you think their technology is that far advanced?" asked the Bellman.

"No. They're still a long way away. They'd been trying to send an unmanned probe into *The Listeners,* but from what I saw, with little success."

"Okay," replied the Bellman, "we'll keep an eye on them. What was their name again?"

"Goliath," I said.

He made a note.

"Item five. All of the punctuation has been stolen from the final chapter of *Ulysses*. Probably about five hundred assorted full stops, commas, apostrophes and colons." He paused for a moment. "Vern, weren't you doing some work on this?"

"Indeed," replied the squire, stepping forward and opening a notebook, "we noticed the theft two days ago. To take so much punctuation in one hit initially sounds audacious, but perhaps the thief thought no one would notice as most readers never get that far into *Ulysses*—you will recall the theft of chapter sixty-two from *Moby-Dick*, where no one noticed? Well, this theft *was* noted, but initial reports show that readers are regarding the lack of punctuation as not a cataclysmic error but the mark of a great genius, so we've got some breathing space."

"Are we sure it was a thief?" asked Beatrice. "Couldn't it just be grammasites?"

"I don't think so," replied Perkins, who had made book-zoology into something closely resembling a science. "Punctusauroids are pretty rare, and to make off with so many punctuations you would need a flock of several hundred. Also, I don't think they would have left the last full stop—that looks to me like a mischievous thief."

"Okay," said the Bellman, "so what are we to do?"

"The only ready market for stolen punctuation is in the Well."

"Hmm," mused the Bellman. "A Jurisfiction agent down there is about as conspicuous as a brass band at a funeral. We need someone to go undercover. Any volunteers?"

"It's my case," said Vernham Deane. "I'll go. That is—if no one thinks themselves better qualified."

There was silence.

"Looks like you're it!" enthused the Bellman, writing a note on his clipboard. "Item six. As you recall, David and Catriona Balfour were lost a few weeks back. Because there can't be much to *Kidnapped* and *Catriona* without them and Robert Louis Stevenson remains a popular author, the Council of Genres have licensed a pair of A-4 Generics to take their place. They'll be given unlimited access to all Stevenson's books, and I want you all to make them feel welcome."

There was a murmuring from the collected agents.

"Yes," said the Bellman with a resigned air, "I know they'll never be *exactly* the same, but with a bit of luck we should be okay; no one in the Outland noticed when David Copperfield was replaced, now did they?"

No one said anything.

"Good. Item seven. As you know, I am retiring in two weeks' time and the Council of Genres will need a replacement. All nominations are to be given direct to the Council for consideration.

He paused again.

"Item eight. As you all know, Text Grand Central have been working on an upgrade to the Book Operating System for the last fifty years—"

The assembled agents groaned. Clearly this was a matter of some contention. Snell had explained about the imaginotransference technology behind books in general, but I had no idea how it worked. Still don't, as a matter of fact.

"Do you know what happened when they tried to upgrade SCROLL?" said Bradshaw. "The system conflict wiped out the entire library at Alexandria—they had to torch the lot to stop it spreading."

"We knew a lot less about operating systems then, Commander," replied the Bellman in a soothing voice, "and you can rest assured that early upgrading problems have not been ignored. Many of us have reservations about the standard version of BOOK that all our beloved works are recorded in, and I think the latest upgrade to BOOK V9 is something that we should all welcome."

No one said anything. He had our attention.

"Good. Well, I could rabbit on all day but I really feel that it would be better to let WordMaster Libris, all the way from Text Grand Central, tell you the full story. Xavier?"

11.

Introducing UltraWord™

First there was OralTrad, upgraded ten thousand years later by the rhyming (for easier recall) OralTradPlus. For thousands of years this was the *only* Story Operating System and it is still in use today. The system branched in two about twenty thousand years ago; on one side with CaveDaubPro (forerunner of PaintPlus V2.3, GrecianUrn V1.2, Sculpt-Marble V1.4 and the latest, all-encompassing SuperArtisticExpression-5). The other strand, the Picto-Phonetic Storytelling Systems, started with ClayTablet V2.1 and went through several competing systems (Wax-Tablet, Papyrus, VellumPlus) before merging into the award-winning SCROLL, which was upgraded eight times to V3.5 before being swept aside by the all new and clearly superior BOOK V1. Stable, easy to store and transport, compact and with a workable index, BOOK has led the way for nearly eighteen hundred years.

WORDMASTER XAVIER LIBRIS,
Story Operating Systems—the Early Years

A SMALL AND RATHER pallid-looking man took his position on the dais; he could only just see over the lectern. He wore a white, short-sleeved shirt and was almost weighed down by the number of pens in his top pocket. We all took a seat and gazed at him with interest. UltraWord™ had been the talk of the Well for ages and everyone was keen to learn whether the rumors of its technical virtuosity were true.

"Good morning, everyone," began Libris in a nervous voice, "over the next thirty minutes I will try and explain a little about

our latest operating system: BOOK Version 9, which we have code-named UltraWord™."

There was silence as the agents mulled this over. I got the feeling that this was not just important but *really* important. Like being at the signing of a peace accord or something. Even Bradshaw, who was no fan of technology, was leaning forward and listening with interest, a frown etched on his forehead.

Libris pulled the first sheet off a flip chart. There was a picture of an old book.

"Well," he began, "when we first came up with the 'page' concept in BOOK V1, we thought we'd reached the zenith of story containment—compact, easy to read, and by using integrated PageNumber™ and SpineTitle™ technologies, we had a system of indexing far superior to anything SCROLL could offer. Over the years—"

Here he flipped the chart over to show us varying degrees of books through the ages.

"—we have been refining the BOOK system. Illustrations were the first upgrade at 1.1, standardized spelling at V3.1 and vowel and irregular verb stability in V4.2. Today we use BOOK V8.3, one of the most stable and complex imaginotransference technologies ever devised—the smooth transfer of the written word into the reader's imagination has never been faster."

He stopped for a moment. We all knew that BOOK V8.3 was excellent; apart from a few typos that crept in and the variable quality of stories—neither of which were the system's fault—it was good, very good indeed.

"Constructing the books down in the subbasements, although time-consuming, seems to work well even if it is a little chaotic."

There were murmurs of agreement from the assembled agents; it was clear that no one much liked it down there.

"But," went on Libris, "endlessly recycling old ideas might not hold the readers' attention for that much longer—the Council of Genres' own market research seems to indicate that readers are becoming bored with the sameness of plotlines."

"I think it's already happened," said the Bellman, then checked himself quickly, apologized for the interruption and let Libris carry on.

"But to understand the problem we need a bit of history. When we first devised the BOOK system eighteen hundred years ago, we designed it mainly to record events—we never thought there would be such a demand for *story*. By the tenth century story usage was so low that we still had enough new plots to last over a thousand years. By the time the seventeenth century arrived, this had lowered to six hundred—but there was still no real cause for worry. Then, something happened that stretched the Operating System to the limit."

"Mass literacy," put in Miss Havisham.

"Exactly," replied Libris. "Demand for written stories increased exponentially during the eighteenth and nineteenth centuries. Ten years before *Pamela* was published in 1740, we had enough new ideas to last four hundred years; by the time of Jane Austen this had dropped to thirty. By Dickens's time ideas were almost wholly recycled, something we have been doing on and off since the thirteenth century to stave off the inevitable. But by 1884, for all intents and purposes, we had depleted our stock of original ideas."

There was a muttering amongst the collected Jurisfiction agents.

"*Flatland*," said Bradshaw after pausing for a moment's reflection. "It was the last original idea, wasn't it?"

"Pretty much. The few leftover pieces were mopped up by the SF movement until the 1950s, but as far as *pure* ideas are concerned, 1884 was the end. We were expecting the worst—a meltdown of the whole BookWorld and a wholesale departure of readers. But that didn't happen. Against all expectations, recycled ideas were *working*."

"But isn't it the way they are told?" asked Havisham in her not-to-be-argued-with voice. "Surely the *permutations* of storytelling are endless!"

"Large perhaps, but not *infinite,* Miss Havisham. What I'm

trying to say is that once all the permutations are used up, there will be nowhere for us to go. The twentieth century has seen books being written and published at an unprecedented rate—even the introduction of the Procrastination 1.3 and Writer's-Block 2.4 Outlander viruses couldn't slow the authors down. Plagiarism lawsuits are rising in the Outland; authors are beginning to write the same books. The way I see it we've got a year—possibly eighteen months—before the well of fiction runs dry."

He paused to let this sink in.

"That's why we had to go back to the drawing board and rethink the whole system."

He flipped the chart again and there were audible gasps. On the chart was written *32-Plot Story Systems*.

"As you know," he went on, "every Book Operating System has at its heart the basic eight-plot architecture we inherited from OralTrad. As we used to say, 'No one will ever need more than eight plots.' "

"Nine if you count *Coming of Age*," piped up Beatrice.

"Isn't that *Journey of Discovery*?" said Tweed.

"What's *Macbeth* then? asked Benedict.

"*Bitter Rivalry/Revenge*, my dear," answered Havisham.

"I thought it was *Temptation*," mused Beatrice, who liked to contradict Benedict whenever possible.

"Please!" said the Bellman. "We could argue these points all night. And if you let Libris finish, you can."

The agents fell silent. I guessed this was a perennial argument.

"So the only way forward," continued Libris, "is to completely rebuild the Operating System. If we go for a thirty-two-plot basis for our stories, there will be more ideas than you or I will know what to do with. The BookWorld won't have seen such an advance since the invention of movable type."

"I'm always supportive of new technology, Mr. Libris," said Lady Cavendish kindly, "but isn't the popularity of books a fair indication of how good the current system actually is?"

"It depends what you mean by *popular*. Only thirty percent of the Outland read fiction on a regular basis—with UltraWord™

we aim to change all that. But I'm running ahead of myself—an abundance of new ideas is only half the story. Let me carry on and tell you what other benefits the new system will give us."

Libris flipped the chart again. This time it read, *Enhanced Features*.

"Firstly, UltraWord™ is wholly reverse compatible with all existing novels, plays and poetry. Furthermore, new books written with this system will offer bonus features that will enhance and delight."

"I say," asked Bradshaw slowly, "how do you hope to improve a book?"

"Let me give you an example," replied Libris enthusiastically. "In books that we know at present, dialogue has to be dedicated to the people who are talking as the reader has no idea who is speaking from the words alone. This can be tricky if we want a large scene with many people talking to one another—it's very easy to get bogged down in the 'said George,' 'replied Michael,' 'added Paul' and suchlike; with the UltraWord™ Enhanced Character Identification™, a reader will have no trouble placing who is speaking to whom without all those tedious dialogue markers. In addition, UltraWord™ will be bundled with PlotPotPlus™, which gives the reader a potted précis if they are lost or have put the book down unfinished for a few months or more. Other options will be ReadZip™, PageGlow™ and three music tracks."

"How will the reader get these new features to work?" asked Lady Cavendish.

"There will be a preferences page inserted just after the frontispiece."

"Touch sensitive?" I asked.

"No," replied Libris excitedly, "*read* sensitive. *Ultra* words that know when they are being read. On the preferences page you can also select WordClot™, which adjusts the vocabulary to the reader—no more difficult words, or, if you *like* difficult words, you can *increase* the vocabulary complexity."

There was silence as everyone took this in.

"But to get back to your point, Lady Cavendish, a lot of people reject fiction because they find reading tedious and slow. At present levels the fastest throughput we can manage is about six words per second. With UltraWord™ we will have the technology to quadruple the uptake—something that will be very attractive to new readers—or slow ones."

"Cards on the table and all that, Libris," said Bradshaw in a loud voice. "Technology is all very well but unless we get it *absolutely* right, it could turn out to be a debacle of the highest order."

"You didn't like the ISBN positioning system, either, Commander," replied Libris, "yet book navigation has never been easier."

They stared at one another until a loud belch rent the air. It was Falstaff.

"I have lived," he said, getting to his feet with a great deal of effort, "through much in my time; some good, some bad—I was witness to the great vowel shift and remember fond those better days when puns, fat people and foreigners were funny beyond all. I saw the novel rise and the epic poem fall, I remember when you could get blind drunk, eat yourself ill and still have change for a whore out of sixpence. I remember when water would kill you and spirits would save you; I remember—"

"Is there a point to all this?" asked Libris testily.

"Ah!" replied Falstaff, trying to figure out where he *was* going with all this. "Oh, yes. I was there for the much heralded Version-4 upgrade. 'Change the way we read forever,' quoth the Council of Genres. And what happened? The Deep Text Crash of 1842. Almost everything by Euripedes, Aeschylus and Sophocles gone forever—and we created grammasites."

"It was never proven that Version 4 created the grammasites, Sir John—"

"Come, come, Libris, have you dried your brain? I was there. I saw it. *I know.*"

Libris put up his hands. "I didn't come here to argue, Sir John—I just want to stick to the facts. Anyhow, UltraWord™ is incompatible with grammasites. Text will be locked—they'll have nothing to feed on."

"You hope, sir."

"We *know*," replied Libris firmly, adding more slowly, "Listen, Version-4 *was* a big mistake, we freely admit that—which is why we have taken so long to rigorously test UltraWord™. It is no small boast that we call it 'the ultimate reading experience.' " He paused for a moment. "It's here to stay, ladies and gentlemen—so get used to it."

He expected another attack from Falstaff, but King Hal's old friend had sat down and was shaking his head sadly. No one else added anything.

Libris took a step back and looked pointedly at the Bellman, who tingled his bell.

"Well, thank you all for listening to WordMaster Libris's presentation, and I would like to thank him for coming here today to tell us all about it."

The Bellman started to clap his hands and we joined in—with the notable exceptions of Falstaff and Bradshaw.

"Presentation booklets will be available shortly," said the Bellman, who had suddenly begun to fidget, "individual assignments will be given out in ten minutes. And remember, let's be careful out there. That's it. Session's over."

And he tingled his bell.

Libris stepped down from the dais and melted away before Bradshaw had a chance to question him further. Miss Havisham rested her hand on his shoulder. Bradshaw was the only man to whom I had ever seen Miss Havisham show any friendliness at all. Born of a long working association, I think.

"I'm too long in the tooth for this game, Havisham, old girl," he muttered.

"You and me both, Trafford. But who'd teach the young

ones?" She nodded in my direction. I hadn't been described as "young" for over a decade.

"I'm spent, Estella," said Bradshaw sadly. "No more new technology for me. I'm going back to my own book for good. At least I won't have to put up with all this nonsense in *Bradshaw of the Congo*. Good-bye, old girl."

"Good-bye, Commander—send my regards to Mrs. Bradshaw."

"Thank you. And to you, too. Miss—I'm sorry, what was your name again?"

"Thursday Next."

"Of course it is. Well, toodle-oo."

And he smiled, tipped his pith helmet and was gone.

"Dear old Bradshaw," mused Miss Havisham, "he's retired about twelve times a year since 1938. I expect we'll see him again next week."

"Ah!" muttered the Bellman as he approached. "Havisham and Next." He consulted his clipboard for a moment. "You weren't in the Outland on another speed attempt, were you?"

"Me?" replied Havisham. "Of course not!"

"Well," murmured the Bellman, not believing her for an instant, "the Council of Genres have told me that any Jurisfiction staff found abusing their privileges will be dealt with severely."

"How severely?"

"*Very* severely."

"They wouldn't dare," replied Havisham in the manner of an elderly duchess. "Now, what have you got for us?"

"You're chairing the *Wuthering Heights* rage-counseling session."

"I've done my six sessions. It's Falstaff's turn."

The Bellman raised an eyebrow. "Now that's not true, is it? You're only on your third. Changing counselors every week is not the best way to do it. Everyone has to take their turn, Miss Havisham, even you."

She sighed. "Very well."

"Good. Better not keep them waiting!"

The Bellman departed rapidly before Havisham could answer. She stood silently for a moment, a bit like a volcano deciding whether to erupt or not. After a few moments her eyes flicked to mine.

"Was that a smile?" she snapped.

"No, Miss Havisham," I replied, trying to hide my inner amusement that someone like her would try to counsel anyone about anything—especially rage.

"Please do tell me what you think is so very funny. I really am very keen to know."

"It was a smile," I said carefully, "of surprise."

"Was it now? Well, before you get the mistaken belief that I am somehow concerned about the feelings of such a pathetic bunch of characters, let's make it clear that I was *ordered* to do this job—same as being drafted on to Heathcliff Protection Duty. I'd sooner he were dead, personally speaking—but orders are orders. Fetch me a tea and meet me at my table."

There was a lot of excited chatter about the upgrade to Ultra-Word™ and I picked up snatches of conversation that ran the full gamut from condemnation to full support. Not that it mattered; Jurisfiction was only a policing agency and had little say in policy—that was all up to the higher powers at the Council of Genres. It was sort of like being back at SpecOps. I bumped into Vernham Deane at the table of refreshments.

"Well," said Vernham, helping himself to a pastry, "what do you think?"

"Bradshaw and Falstaff seem a bit put out."

"Caution is sometimes an undervalued commodity," Vernham said warily. "What does Havisham think?"

"I'm really not sure."

"Vern!" said Beatrice, who had just joined us along with Lady Cavendish. "Which plot does *Winnie-the-Pooh* have?"

"*Triumph of the Underdog?*" he suggested.

"Told you!" said Beatrice, turning to Cavendish. " 'Bear with little brain triumphs over adversity.' Happy?"

"No," she replied, "it's *Journey of Discovery* all the way."

"You think every story is *Journey of Discovery!*"

"It is."

They continued to bicker as I selected a cup and saucer.

"Have you met Mrs. Bradshaw yet?" asked Deane.

I told him that I hadn't.

"When you do, don't laugh or anything."

"Why?"

"You'll see."

I poured some tea for Miss Havisham, remembering to put the milk in first.

Deane ate a canapé and asked, "So how are things with you these days? Last time we met, you were having a little trouble in the Outland."

"I'm living in the Well now, as part of the Character Exchange Program."

"Really? What a lark. How's the latest Farquitt getting along?"

"Well, I *think*," I told him, always sensitive to Deane's slight shame at being a one-dimensional evil-squire figure, "the working title is *Shameless Love.*"

"Sounds like a Farquitt," sighed Deane. "There'll probably be a rustic serving girl who is ravaged by someone like me, cruelly cast from the house to have her baby in the poorhouse—only to have their revenge ten chapters later."

"Well, I don't know—"

"It's not fair, you know," he said, his mood changing. "Why should I be condemned, reading after reading, to drink myself to a sad and lonely death eight pages before the end?"

"Because you're the bad guy and they *always* get their comeuppance in Farquitt novels?"

"It's still not fair." He scowled. "I've applied for an Internal Plot Adjustment countless times but they keep turning me down. You wouldn't have a word with Miss Havisham, would you? She's on the Council of Genres Plot Adjustment subcommittee, I'm told."

"Would that be appropriate? Me talking to her, I mean?"

"Not really," he retorted, "but I'm willing to try anything. Speak to her, won't you?"

I told him I would try but decided on the face of it that I probably wouldn't. Deane seemed pleasant enough at Jurisfiction, but in *The Squire of High Potternews* he was a monster. Dying sad, lonely and forgotten was probably just right for him—in narrative terms, anyway.

I gave the tea to Miss Havisham, who abruptly broke off talking to Perkins as I approached. She gave me a grimace and vanished. I followed her to the second floor of the Great Library, where I found her in the Brontë section already with a copy of *Wuthering Heights* in her hand. I knew from Havisham's hatred of men that she probably *did* have a soft spot for Heathcliff—but I imagined it was only the treacherous marsh below Penistone crag.

"Did you meet the three witches, by the way?" she asked.

"Yes," I replied. "They told me—"

"Ignore *everything* they say. Look at the trouble they got Macbeth into."

"But they said—"

"I don't want to hear it. Claptrap and mumbo jumbo. They are troublemakers and nothing more. Understand?"

"Sure."

"Don't say 'Sure'—it's so slovenly! What's wrong with 'Yes, Miss Havisham'?"

"Yes, Miss Havisham."

"Better, I suppose. Come, we are Brontë bound!"

And so saying, we read ourselves into the pages of *Wuthering Heights*.

12.

Wuthering Heights

Wuthering Heights was the only novel written by Emily Brontë, which some say is just as well, and others, a crying shame. Quite what she would have written had she lived longer is a matter of some conjecture; given Emily's strong-willed and passionate character, probably more of the same. But one thing is certain; whatever feelings are aroused in the reader by *Heights*, whether sadness for the ill-matched lovers, irritability at Catherine's petulant ways or even profound rage at how stupid Heathcliff's victims can act as they meekly line up to be abused, one thing is for sure: the evocation of a wild and windswept place that so well reflects the destructive passion of the two central characters is captured here brilliantly—and some would say, it has not been surpassed.

MILLON DE FLOSS,
Wuthering Heights: Masterpiece or Turgid Rubbish?

IT WAS SNOWING when we arrived and the wind whipped the flakes into something akin to a large cloud of excitable winter midges. The house was a lot smaller than I imagined but no less shabby, even under the softening cloak of snow. The shutters hung askew and only the faintest glimmer of light showed from within. It was clear we were visiting the house not in the good days of old Mr. Earnshaw but in the tenure of Mr. Heathcliff, whose barbaric hold over the house seemed to be reflected in the dour and windswept abode that we approached.

Our feet crunched on the fresh snow as we approached the front door and rapped upon the gnarled wood. It was answered, after a very long pause, by an old and sinewy man who looked at us both in turn with a sour expression before recognition dawned across his tired features and he launched into an excited gabble:

"It's bonny behavior, lurking amang t' fields, after twelve o' t' night, wi' that fahl, flaysome divil of a gipsy, Heathcliff! They think I'm blind; but I'm noan: nowt ut t' soart!—I seed young Linton boath coming and going, and I seed *yah*—yah gooid fur nowt, slatternly witch!—nip up and bolt into th' house, t' minute yah heard t' maister's horse-fit clatter up t' road!"

"Never mind all that!" exclaimed Miss Havisham, to whom patience was an alien concept. "Let us in, Joseph, or you'll be feeling my boot upon your trousers!"

He grumbled but opened the door anyway. We stepped in amidst a swirl of snowflakes and tramped our feet upon the mat as the door was latched behind us.

"What did he say?" I asked as Joseph carried on muttering to himself under his breath.

"I have absolutely no idea," replied Miss Havisham, shaking the snow from her faded bridal veil, "in fact, *nobody* does. Come, you are to meet the others. For the rage-counseling session, we insist that every major character within *Heights* attends."

There was no introductory foyer or passage to the room. The front door opened into a large family sitting room where seven people were clustered around the hearth. One of the men rose politely and inclined his head in greeting. This, I learned later, was Edgar Linton, husband of Catherine Earnshaw, who sat next to him on the wooden settle and glowered meditatively into the fire. Next to them was a dissolute-looking man who appeared to be asleep, or drunk, or quite possibly both. It was clear that they were waiting for us, and equally clear from the lack of enthusiasm that counseling wasn't high on their list of priorities—or interests.

"Good evening, everyone," said Miss Havisham, "and I'd like to thank you all for attending this Jurisfiction Rage Counseling session."

She sounded almost friendly. It was quite out of character and I wondered how long she could keep it up.

"This is Miss Next, who will be observing this evening's session. Now, I want us all to join hands and create a circle of trust to welcome her to the group. Where's Heathcliff?"

"I have no idea where that scoundrel might be!" declaimed Linton angrily. "Facedown in a bog for all I care—the devil may take him and not before time!"

"Oh!" cried Catherine, withdrawing her hand from Edgar's. "Why do you hate him so? He, who loved me more than you ever could—!"

"Now now," interrupted Havisham in a soothing tone, "remember what we said last week about name-calling? Edgar, I think you should apologize to Catherine for calling Heathcliff a scoundrel, and Catherine, you did promise last week not to mention how much you were in love with Heathcliff in front of your husband."

They grumbled their apologies.

"Heathcliff is due here any moment," said another servant, who I assumed was Nelly Dean. "His agent said he had to do some publicity. Can we not start without him?"

Miss Havisham looked at her watch. "We could get past the introductions, I suppose," she replied, obviously keen to finish this up and go home. "Perhaps we could introduce ourselves to Miss Next and sum up our feelings at the same time. Edgar, would you mind?"

"Me? Oh, very well. My name is Edgar Linton, true owner of Thrushcross Grange, and I hate and despise Heathcliff because no matter what I do, my wife, Catherine, is still in love with him."

"My name is Hindley Earnshaw," slurred the drunk, "Old Mr. Earnshaw's eldest son. I hate and despise Heathcliff because my father preferred Heathcliff to me, and later, because that scoundrel cheated me out of my birthright."

"That was very good, Hindley," said Miss Havisham, "not one single swear word. I think we're making good progress. Who's next?"

"I am Hareton Earnshaw," said a sullen-looking youth who

stared at the table as he spoke and clearly resented these gatherings more than most, "son of Hindley and Frances. I hate and despise Heathcliff because he treats me as little more than a dog—and it's not as though I did anything against him, neither—he punishes me because my *father* treated him like a servant."

"I am Isabella," announced a good-looking woman, "sister of Edgar. I hate and despise Heathcliff because he lied to me, abused me, beat me and tried to kill me. Then, after I was dead, he stole our son and used him to gain control of the Linton inheritance."

"Lot of rage in *that* one," whispered Miss Havisham. "Do you see a pattern beginning to emerge?"

"That they don't much care for Heathcliff?" I whispered back.

"Does it show that badly?" she replied, a little crestfallen that her counseling didn't seem to be working as well as she'd hoped.

"I am Catherine Linton," said a confident and headstrong young girl of perhaps no more than sixteen, "daughter of Edgar and Catherine. I hate and despise Heathcliff because he kept me prisoner for five days away from my dying father to force me to marry Linton—solely to gain the title of Thrushcross Grange, the true Linton residence."

"I am Linton," announced a sickly looking child, coughing into a pocket handkerchief, "son of Heathcliff and Isabella. I hate and despise Heathcliff because he took away the only possible happiness I might have known and let me die a captive, a pawn in his struggle for ultimate revenge."

"Hear, hear," murmured Catherine Linton.

"I am Catherine Earnshaw," said the last woman, who looked around at the small group disdainfully, "and I *love* Heathcliff more than life itself!"

The group groaned audibly, several members shook their heads sadly and the younger Catherine did the "fingers down the throat" gesture.

"None of you know him the way I do, and if you had treated him with kindness instead of hatred, none of this would have happened!"

"Deceitful harlot!" yelled Hindley, leaping to his feet. "If you hadn't decided to marry Edgar for power and position, Heathcliff might have been half-reasonable—no, you brought all this on yourself, you selfish little minx!"

There was applause at this, despite Havisham's attempts to keep order.

"He is a *real* man," continued Catherine, amidst a barracking from the group, "a Byronic hero who transcends moral and social law; my love for Heathcliff resembles the eternal rocks. Group, I *am* Heathcliff! He's always, always in my mind: not as a pleasure, any more than I am always a pleasure to myself, but as my own being!"

Isabella thumped the table and waved her finger angrily at Catherine. "A *real* man would love and cherish the one he married," she shouted, "not use and abuse all those around him in a never-ending quest for ultimate revenge for some perceived slight of twenty years ago! So what if Hindley treated him badly? A good Christian man would forgive him and learn to live in peace!"

"Ah!" said the young Catherine, also jumping up and yelling to be heard above the uproar of accusations and pent-up frustrations. "There we have the nub of the problem. Heathcliff is as far from Christian as one can be; a devil in human form who seeks to ruin all those about him!"

"I agree with Catherine," said Linton weakly. "The man is wicked and rotten to the core!"

"Come outside and say that!" yelled the elder Catherine, brandishing a fist.

"You would have him catch a chill and die, I suppose?" replied the younger Catherine defiantly, glaring at the mother who had died giving birth to her. "It was your haughty spoilt airs that got us into this whole stupid mess in the first place! If you loved him as much as you claim, why didn't you just marry him and have done with it?"

"Can we have some order please!" yelled Miss Havisham so loudly that the whole group jumped. They looked a bit sheepish and sat down, grumbling slightly.

"Thank you. Now, all this yelling is *not* going to help, and if we are to do anything about the rage inside *Wuthering Heights,* we are going to have to act like civilized human beings and discuss our feelings sensibly."

"Hear, hear," said a voice from the shadows. The group fell silent and turned in the direction of the newcomer, who stepped into the light accompanied by two minders and someone who looked like his agent. The newcomer was dark, swarthy and extremely handsome. Up until meeting him I had never comprehended why the characters in *Wuthering Heights* behaved in the sometimes irrational ways that they did; but after witnessing the glowering good looks, the piercing dark eyes, I understood. Heathcliff had an almost electrifying charisma; he could have charmed a cobra into a knot.

"Heathcliff!" cried Catherine, leaping into his arms and hugging him tightly. "Oh, Heathcliff my darling, how much I've missed you!"

"Bah!" cried Edgar, swishing his cane through the air in anger. "Put down my wife immediately or I'll swear to God I shall—"

"Shall what?" inquired Heathcliff. "You gutless popinjay! My dog has more valor in its pizzle than you possess in your entire body! And, Linton, you weakling, what did you say about me being 'wicked and rotten'?"

"Nothing," said Linton quietly.

"Mr. Heathcliff," said Miss Havisham sternly, "it doesn't pay to be late for these sessions, nor to aggravate your cocharacters."

"The devil take your sessions, Miss Havisham," he said angrily. "Who is the star of this novel? Who do the readers expect to see when they pick up this book? Who has won the Most Troubled Romantic Lead at the BookWorld Awards seventy-seven times in a row? Me. All me. Without me, *Heights* is a tediously overlong, provincial potboiler of insignificant interest. I am the star of this book and I'll do as I please, my lady, and you can take that to the Bellman, the Council, or all the way to the Great Panjandrum for all I care!"

He pulled a signed glossy photo of himself from his breast pocket and passed it to me with a wink. The odd thing was, I actually *recognized* him. He had been acting with great success in Hollywood under the name Buck Stallion, which probably explained where he got his money from; he could have bought Thrushcross Grange and Wuthering Heights three times over on his salary.

"The Council of Genres has decreed that you *will* attend the sessions, Heathcliff," said Havisham coldly. "If this book is to survive, we have to control the emotions within it; as it is, the novel is three times more barbaric than when first penned—left to its own devices it won't be long before murder and mayhem start to take over completely—remember what happened to that once gentle comedy of manners *Titus Andronicus*? It's now the daftest, most cannibalistic blood fest in the whole of Shakespeare. *Heights* will go the same way unless you can all somehow contain your anger and resentment!"

"I don't want to be made into a pie!" moaned Linton.

"Brave speech," replied Heathcliff sardonically, "*very* brave." He leaned closer to Miss Havisham, who stood her ground defiantly. "Let me 'share' something with your little group. *Wuthering Heights* and all who live within her may go to the devil for all I care. It has served its purpose as I honed the delicate art of treachery and revenge—but I'm now bigger than this book and bigger than all of you. There are better novels waiting for me out there, that know how to properly service a character of my depth!"

The assembled characters gasped as this new intelligence sank in. Without Heathcliff there would be no book—and in consequence, none of them, either.

"You wouldn't make it into *Spot's Birthday* without the Council's permission," growled Havisham. "Try and leave *Heights* and we'll make make you wish you'd never been written!"

Heathcliff laughed. "Nonsense! The Council has urgent need of characters such as I; leaving me stuck in the classics where I am only ever read by bored English students is a waste of one of the finest romantic leads ever written. Mark my words, the Council will do whatever it takes to attract a greater readership—a transfer will not be opposed by them or anyone else, I can assure you of *that*!"

"What about us?" wailed Linton, coughing and on the verge of tears. "We'll be reduced to text!"

"Best thing for all of you!" growled Heathcliff. "And I'll be there at the shoreline, ready to rejoice at your last strangled cry as you dip beneath the waves!"

"And me?" asked Catherine.

"You will come with me." Heathcliff smiled, softening. "You and I will live again in a modern novel, without all these trappings of Victorian rectitude. I thought we could reside in a spy thriller somewhere, go shopping at Ikea and have a boxer puppy with one ear that goes down—"

There was a loud detonation and the front door exploded inwards in a cloud of wood splinters and dust. Havisham pushed Heathcliff to the ground and laid herself across him, yelling, "Take cover!"

She fired her small pistol at a masked man who jumped through the smoking doorway firing a machine gun. Havisham's bullet struck home and the figure crumpled in a heap. One of Heathcliff's two minders took rounds in the neck and chest from the first assailant, but the second minder pulled out his own submachine gun and pressed himself against the wall. Linton fainted on the spot, quickly followed by Isabella and Edgar. At least it stopped them screaming. I drew my gun and fired along with the minder and Havisham as another masked assassin came in the door; we got him, but one of his bullets caught the second bodyguard in the head, and he dropped lifeless to the flags.

I crawled across to Havisham and heard Heathcliff whimper, "Help me! Don't let them kill me! I don't want to die!"

"Shut up!" hissed Havisham, and Heathcliff was instantly quiet. I looked around. His agent was cowering under a briefcase, and the rest of the cast were hiding beneath the oak table. There was a pause.

"What's going on?" I hissed.

"ProCath attack," murmured Havisham, reloading her pistol in the sudden quiet, "support of the young Catherine and hatred of Heathcliff runs deep in the BookWorld; usually its only a lone gunman—I've never seen anything this well planned before. I'm going to jump out with Heathcliff; I'll be back for you straightaway."

She mumbled a few words but nothing happened. She tried them again but still nothing.

"The devil take them!" she muttered, pulling her mobilefootnoterphone from the folds of her wedding dress. "They must be using a textual sieve."

"What's a textual sieve?"

"I don't know—it's never fully explained."

She looked at the mobilefootnoterphone and tossed it aside. "Blast! No signal. Where's the nearest footnoterphone?"

"In the kitchen," replied Nelly Dean, "next to the breadbasket."

"We have to get word to the Bellman. Thursday, I want you to go to the kitchen—"

But she never got to finish her sentence because a barrage of machine-gun fire struck the house, decimating the windows and shutters. The curtains danced as they were shredded, the plaster erupting off the wall as the shots slammed into it. We kept our heads down as Catherine screamed, Linton woke up only to faint again, Hindley took a swig from a hip flask and Heathcliff convulsed with fear beneath us. After about five minutes the firing stopped. Dust hung lazily in the air and we were covered with plaster, shards of glass and wood chips.

"Havisham!" came a subdued voice on a bullhorn from outside. "We wish you no harm! Just surrender Heathcliff and we'll leave you alone!"

"No!" cried the older Catherine, who had crawled across to us and was trying to clasp Heathcliff's head in her hands. "Heathcliff, don't leave me!"

"I have no intention of doing any such thing," he said in a

muffled voice, nose pressed hard into the flags by Havisham's weight. "Havisham, I hope you remember your orders."

"Send out Heathcliff and we will spare you and your apprentice!" yelled the bullhorn again. "Stand in our way and you'll both be terminated!"

"Do they mean it?" I asked.

"Oh, yes," replied Havisham grimly. "A group of ProCaths attempted to hijack *Madame Bovary* last year to force the Council to relinquish Heathcliff."

"What happened?"

"The ones who survived were reduced to text, but it hasn't stopped the ProCath movement. Do you think you can get to the footnoterphone?"

"Sure—I mean, yes, Miss Havisham."

I crawled off towards the kitchen.

"We'll give you two minutes," said the voice into the bullhorn again. "After that, we're coming in."

"I have a better deal," yelled Havisham.

There was a pause.

"And that is?" came the voice on the bullhorn.

"Leave now and I will be merciful when I find you."

"I think," replied the voice on the bullhorn, "that we'll stick to *my* plan. You have one minute forty-five seconds."

I reached the doorway of the kitchen, which had been as devastated as the living room. Flour and beans from broken storage jars were strewn across the floor, and a flurry of snowflakes was blowing in through the windows. I found the footnoterphone; it had been riddled with machine-gun fire. I cursed and went to look out the pantry window. I could see two of them, sitting in the snow, weapons ready. I dashed back to Havisham.

"Well?"

"Footnoterphone destroyed, and two ProCaths at the back that I could see."

"And at least three at the front," she added, snapping her pistol shut. "I'm open to suggestions."

"How about giving them Heathcliff?" came a chorus of voices.

"*Other* than that?"

"I can try and get behind them," I muttered, "if you give me covering fire—"

I was interrupted by an unearthly cry of terror from outside, followed by a sort of crunching noise, then another cry and sporadic machine-gun fire. There was a large thump and another shot, then a shout, then the ProCaths at the back started to open fire. But not at the house—at some unseen menace. We heard two more cries of terror, a few more gunshots, a slow tearing noise, then silence.

I got up and peered cautiously from the door. There was nothing outside except the soft snow, disturbed occasionally by dinner-plate-sized footprints.

We found only one complete body, tossed onto the roof of the pigsty.

"Look at this," said Miss Havisham from where she was standing at the corner of the barn. It looked as though one of the ProCaths had been stationed there by the large quantity of spent cartridges, but what Havisham was actually pointing out were the four freshly dug grooves in the masonry, spaced about six inches apart.

"It looks like . . . *claw marks*," I murmured.

"Must have caught the corner of the barn midswipe," replied Miss Havisham thoughtfully, peering closer at the damaged stonework.

"It was Big Martin," I said with a shiver. "Some of his friends had me pegged for dinner down on the twenty-second floor yesterday."

"Then we should be glad Big Martin got to this bunch first. Mind you, I've heard rumors that the Big M was into classics—he might have been doing us a favor."

We turned and walked through the snow back to the house.

"Who is Big Martin?" I asked.

"Less of a *who* and more of a *what*," replied Miss Havisham, tramping her feet on the doorstep to get rid of the snow. "Even the Glatisant is nervous of Big Martin. He's a law unto himself. I'd watch your back and eat plenty of cashews."

"Cashews?"

"Big Martin *loathes* them. Unusually for a Book Fiend he has a sense of smell—one whiff and he's off."

"I'll remember that."

We returned to where the cast of *Wuthering Heights* were dusting themselves down. Joseph was muttering incomprehensibly to himself and trying to block the windows up with blankets.

"Well," said Miss Havisham, clapping her hands together, "that was an exciting session, wasn't it?"

"I am still leaving this appalling book," retorted Heathcliff, who was back on full obnoxious form again.

"No you're *not*," replied Havisham.

"You just try and stop—"

Havisham, who was fed up with pussyfooting around and hated men like Heathcliff with a vengeance, grasped him by the collar and pinned his head to the table with her pistol pressed painfully into his neck.

"Listen here," she said, her voice quavering with anger, "to me, you are worthless scum. Thank your lucky stars I am loyal to Jurisfiction. Many others in my place would have handed you over. I could kill you now and no one would be any the wiser."

Heathcliff looked at me imploringly.

"I was outside when I heard the shot," I told him.

"So were we!" exclaimed the rest of the cast eagerly, excepting Catherine Earnshaw, who simply scowled.

"Perhaps I *should* do it!" growled Havisham again. "Perhaps it would be a mercy. I could make it look like an accident!"

"No!" cried Heathcliff in a contrite tone. "I've changed my mind. I'm going to stay right here and just be plain old Mr. Heathcliff for ever and ever."

Havisham slowly released her grasp. "Right," she said, switching her pistol to *safe* and regaining her breath, "I think that pretty much concludes this session of Jurisfiction rage counseling. What did we learn?"

The cocharacters all stared at her, dumbstruck.

"Good. Same time next week, everyone?"

14.

Educating the Generics

Generics are the chameleons of the Well. In general they were trained to do specific jobs but could be upgraded if the need arose. Occasionally a Generic would jump up spontaneously within the grade, but to jump from one grade to another without external help, they said, was impossible. From what I would learn, *impossible* was a word that should not be bandied about the Well without due thought—imagination being what it is, anything could happen—and generally did.

THURSDAY NEXT,
The Jurisfiction Chronicles

BIG MARTIN HAD made a mess of the ProCath fanatics who had attacked us. The leader was identified by his dental records—why he had them on him, no one was quite sure. He had been a D-3 crew member in *On the Beach* and was replaced within twenty-four hours. *Wuthering Heights* was repaired within a few lines, and because Havisham had been holding the rage-counseling session *between* chapters, no one reading the book noticed anything. In fact, the only evidence of the attack now to be seen in the book was Hareton's shotgun, which exploded accidentally in chapter 32, most likely as a result of a ricocheting bullet damaging the latching mechanism.

"How was your day today?" asked Gran as I walked back on board the Sunderland.

"Very . . . *expositional* to begin with," I said, falling into a sofa and tickling Pickwick, who had come over all serious and matronly, "but it ended quite dramatically."

"Did you have to be rescued again?"

"Yes and no."

"The first few days in a new job are always a bit shaky," said Gran. "Why do you have to work for Jurisfiction anyway?"

"It was part of the Exchange Program deal."

"Oh, yes," she replied. "Would you like me to make you an omelette?"

"Anything."

"Right. I'll need you to crack the eggs and mix them and get me down the saucepan and . . ."

I heaved myself up and went through to the small galley, where the fridge was full of food, as always.

"Where's ibb and obb?" I asked.

"Out, I think," replied Gran. "Would you make us both a cup of tea while you're up?"

"Sure. I still can't remember Landen's second name, Gran—I've been trying all day."

Gran came into the galley and sat on a kitchen stool, which happened to be right in the way of everything. She smelt of sherry, but for the life of me I didn't know where she hid it.

"But you remember what he looks like?"

I stopped what I was doing and stared out of the kitchen porthole.

"Yes," I replied slowly, "every line, every mole, every expression—but I still remember him dying in the Crimea."

"That *never* happened, my dear. But the fact—I should use a bigger bowl if I were you—you can remember his features proves he's not gone any more than yesterday. I should use butter and not oil; and if you have any mushrooms, you could chop them up with a bit of onion and bacon—do you have any bacon?"

"Probably. You still didn't tell me how you managed to find your way here, Gran."

"That's easily explained. Tell me, did you manage to get a list of the dullest books you could find?"

Granny Next was 108 years old and was convinced that she couldn't die until she had read the ten most boring classics. On an earlier occasion I had suggested *Fairie Queene*, *Paradise Lost*, *Ivanhoe*, *Moby-Dick*, *A la recherche du temps perdu*, *Pamela* and *A Pilgrim's Progress*. She had read them all and many others but was still with us. Trouble is, "boring" is about as hard to quantify as "pretty," so I really had to think of the ten books that *she* would find most boring.

"What about *Silas Marner*?"

"Only boring in parts—like *Hard Times*. You're going to have to do a little better than that—and if I were you, I'd use a bigger pan—but on a lower heat."

"Right," I said, beginning to get annoyed, "perhaps you'd like to cook? You've done most of the work so far."

"No, no," replied Gran, completely unfazed, "you're doing fine."

There was a commotion at the door and Ibb came in, followed closely by Obb.

"Congratulations!" I called out.

"What for?" asked Ibb, who no longer looked identical to Obb. For a start, Obb was at least four inches taller and its hair was darker than Ibb's, which was beginning to go blond.

"For becoming capitalized."

"Oh, yes," enthused Ibb, "it's amazing what a day at St. Tabularasa's will do for one. Tomorrow we'll finish our gender training, and by the end of the week we'll be streamed into character groups."

"I want to be a male mentor figure," said Obb. "Our tutor said that sometimes we can have a choice of what we do and where we go. Are you making supper?"

"No," I replied, testing their sarcasm response, "I'm giving my pet egg heat therapy."

Ibb laughed—which was a good sign, I thought—and went

off with Obb to practice whimsical retorts in case either of them was given a posting as a humorous sidekick.

"Teenagers," said Granny Next. "Tch. I better make it a bigger omelette. Take over, would you? I'm going to have a rest."

We all sat down to eat twenty minutes later. Obb had brushed its hair into a parting and Ibb was wearing one of Gran's gingham dresses.

"Hoping to be female?" I asked, passing Ibb a plate.

"Yes," replied Ibb, "but not one like you. I'd like to be more feminine and a bit hopeless—the sort that screams a lot when they get into trouble and has to be rescued."

"Really?" I asked, handing Gran the salad. "Why?"

Ibb shrugged. "I don't know. I just like the idea of being rescued a lot, that's all—being carried off in big, strong arms sort of . . . *appeals.* I thought I could have the plot explained to me a lot, too—but I should have a few good lines of my own, be quite vulnerable, yet end up saving the day due to a sudden flash of idiot savant brilliance."

"I think you'll have no trouble getting a placement," I sighed, "but you seem quite specific—have you used someone in particular as a model?"

"Her!" exclaimed Ibb, drawing out a much thumbed Outland copy of *Silverscreen* from beneath the table. On the cover was none other than Lola Vavoom, being interviewed for the umpteenth time about her husbands, her denial of any cosmetic surgery and her latest film—usually in that order.

"Gran!" I said sternly. "Did you give Ibb that magazine?"

"Well—!"

"You *know* how impressionable Generics can be! Why didn't you give her a magazine with Jenny Gudgeon in it? She plays proper women—and can act, too."

"Have you seen Ms. Vavoom in *My Sister Kept Geese*?" replied Gran indignantly. "I think you'd be surprised—she shows considerable range."

I thought about Cordelia Flakk and her producer friend Harry Flex wanting Lola to play me in a film. The idea was too awful to contemplate.

"You were going to tell us about subtext," said Obb, helping itself to more salad.

"Oh, yes," I replied, a distraction from Vavoom a welcome break. "Subtext is the implied action behind the written word. Text tells the reader what the characters *say and do* but subtext tells us what they *mean and feel*. The wonderful thing about subtext is that it is common grammar, written in human experience—you can't understand it without a good working knowledge of people and how they interact. Got it?"

Ibb and Obb looked at one another. "No."

"Okay, let me give you a simple example. At a party, a man gives a woman a drink and she takes it without answering. What's going on?"

"She isn't very polite?" suggested Ibb.

"Perhaps," I replied, "but I was really looking for some sort of clue as to their relationship."

Obb scratched its head and said, "She can't speak because, er, she lost her tongue in an industrial accident due to his negligence?"

"You're trying too hard. For what reason would someone not *necessarily* say 'thank you' for something?"

"Because," said Ibb slowly, "they know one another?"

"Good. Being handed a drink at a party by your wife, husband, girlfriend or partner, you would as likely as not just take it; if it was from a host to a guest, then you would thank them. Here's another: there is a couple walking down the road—and she is walking eight paces behind him."

"He has longer legs?" suggested Ibb.

"No."

"They've broken down?"

"They've had an argument," said Obb excitedly, "and they live nearby or they would be taking their car."

"Could be," I responded. "Subtext tells you lots of things. Ibb, did you take the last piece of chocolate from the fridge?"

There was a pause. "No."

"Well, because you paused, I know pretty confidently that you did."

"Oh!" said Ibb. "I'll remember *that*."

There was a knock at the door.

I opened it to reveal Mary's ex-beau Arnold looking very dapper in a suit and holding a small bunch of flowers. Before he had time to open his mouth, I had closed the door again.

"Ah!" I said, turning to Ibb and Obb. "This is a good opportunity to study subtext. See if you can figure out what is going on *behind* our words—and Ibb, *please* don't feed Pickwick at the table."

I opened the door again, and Arnold, who had started to slink off, came running back.

"Oh!" he said with mock surprise. "Mary not back yet?"

"No. In fact, she probably won't be back for some time. Can I take a message?"

And I closed the door on his face again.

"Okay," I said to Ibb and Obb, "what do you think is going on?"

"He's looking for Mary?" suggested Ibb.

"But he *knows* she's gone away," said Obb. "He must be coming to speak to *you*, Thursday."

"Why?"

"For a date?"

"Good. What am I saying to him?"

Ibb and Obb thought hard. "If you didn't want to see him, you'd have told him to go away, so you might be the tiniest bit interested."

"Excellent!" I told them. "Let's see what happens next."

I opened the door again to a confused-looking Arnold, who broke into a wide smile.

"Well," he said, "no message for Mary—it's just—we had planned to see Willow Lodge and the Limes this evening . . ."

I turned to Ibb and Obb, who shook their heads. They didn't believe it, either.

"Well," said Arnold slowly, ". . . perhaps *you* might like to come with me to the concert?"

I shut the door again.

"He *pretended* to have the idea about going to see Willow Lodge tonight," said Ibb slowly and more confidently, "when in fact I think he had it planned all along that way. I think he fancies you big time."

I opened the door again.

"I'm sorry, no," I told him hastily, "happily married."

"It's not a date," exclaimed Arnold quickly, "just a lift to a concert. Here, take the ticket anyway. I've no one else to give it to; if you don't want to go, just bin it."

I shut the door again.

"Ibb's wrong," said Obb, "he *really* fancies you—but he's blown it by being *too* desperate—it would be hard for you to respect someone who would almost start begging."

"Not bad," I replied, "let's see how it turns out."

I opened the door again and stared into Arnold's earnest eyes.

"You miss her, don't you?"

"Miss who?" asked Arnold, seemingly nonchalant.

"Denial of love!" yelled Ibb and Obb from behind me. "He doesn't really fancy you at all—he's in love with Mary and wants a date on the rebound!"

Arnold looked suspicious. "What's going on?"

"Subtext classes," I explained, "sorry for being rude. Do you want to come in for a coffee?"

"Well, I should be going really—"

"Playing hard to get!" hooted Ibb, and Obb added quickly, "The balance of power has tipped in his favor because you've been rude to him with all that door nonsense, and now you're going to have to *insist* that he come in for coffee, even if that means being nicer to him than you originally intended!"

"Are they always like this?" inquired Arnold, stepping inside.

"They learn quick," I observed. "That's Ibb and that's Obb. Ibb and Obb, this is Arnold."

"Hullo!" said Arnold, thinking for a moment. "Do you Generics want to go and see Willow Lodge and the Limes?"

They looked at one another for a moment, realized they were sitting just that little bit too close and moved apart.

"Do you?" said Ibb.

"Well, only if you want to—"

"I'm easy—it's your decision."

"Well y-es, I'd really like to."

"Then let's go—unless you've made other plans—?"

"No, no, I haven't."

They got up, took the tickets from Arnold and were out the door in a flash.

I laughed and went though to the galley.

"Who's the elderly woman?" asked Arnold.

"It's my Gran," I replied, switching on the kettle and getting out the coffee.

"Is she—you know?"

"Goodness me, no! She's only asleep. She's one hundred and eight."

"Really? Why is she dressed in this dreadful blue gingham?"

"Has been for as long as I can remember. She came here to make sure I didn't forget my husband. Sorry. That makes me sound as though I'm laboring the point, doesn't it?"

"Listen, don't worry. I didn't mean to come over all romantic just then. But, Mary, well, she's quite something, you know—and I'm not just in love with her because I was written that way. This one's for real. Like Nelson and Emma, Bogart and Bacall—"

"Finch Hatton and Blixen. Yes, I know. I've been there."

"Denys was in love with Baron Blixen?"

"*Karen* Blixen."

"Oh."

He sat down and I placed a coffee in front of him.

"So, tell me about your husband."

"Hah!" I said, smiling. "You don't want me to bore you about Landen."

"It's not boring. You listen to me when I hark on about Mary."

I stirred my coffee absently, running through my memories of Landen to make sure they were all there. Gran mumbled something about lobsters in her sleep.

"It must have been a hard decision to come and hide out here," said Arnold quietly. "I don't imagine Thursdays generally do that sort of thing."

"You're right, they don't. But sometimes falling back and regrouping is not the same as running away."

"Tactical withdrawal?"

"Right. What would you do to get together with Mary again?"

"Anything."

"And I with Landen. I *will* get him back—just not quite yet. But the strange thing is," I added slightly wistfully, "when he comes back, he won't even know he'd been gone—it's not as though he's waiting for me to reactualize him."

We chatted for about an hour. Arnold told me about the Well and I talked about the Outland. He was just trying to get me to repeat "irrelevant benevolent elephant" when Gran woke up with a yell shouting, "The French! The French!" and had to be calmed down with a glass of warm whiskey before I put her to bed.

"I'd better be going," said Arnold. "Mind if I drop round again?"

"Not at all," I replied. "That would be nice."

I went to bed after that and was still awake when Ibb and Obb returned from the concert. They were giggling and made a noisy cup of tea before retiring. I lay back and tried to sleep, hoping that I would dream of being back at our house, the one that Landen and I shared when we were married. Failing that, on holiday somewhere. Failing *that,* when we first met—and if that wasn't available, an argument—and lastly, anything with Landen in it at all. Aornis had other ideas.

15.

Landen Parke-*Somebody*

Before Aornis Hades, the existence of mnemonomorphs was suspected only to SO-5, who, through deceit, idleness or forgetfulness, never told anyone else. The files on mnemonomorphs are kept in eight different locations and updated automatically between each location every week. An ability to control entropy does not necessarily go with the skill to alter memories; indeed, Aornis has been the only entity (thus far that we know about) who can do such a thing. As Miss Next demonstrated between 1986–87, mnemonomorphs are not without their Achilles' heel. There is one question we would all like answered about Aornis, however, since no physical evidence of her remains: Was she real, or just a bad memory?

BLAKE LAMME (EX-SO-5),
Remember Them? A Study of Mnemonomorphs

DEAR, SWEET THURSDAY!" muttered a patronizing voice that was chillingly familiar.

I opened my eyes. I was on the roof of Thornfield Hall, Rochester's house in *Jane Eyre*. It was the time and place of my final showdown with Acheron Hades. The old house was on fire and I could feel the roof growing hot beneath my feet. I coughed in the smoke and felt my eyes begin to smart. Next to me was Edward Rochester, cradling a badly wounded hand. Acheron had already thrown Rochester's poor wife, Bertha, over the parapet and was now preparing to finish us both off.

"*Sweet madness*, eh?" Acheron laughed. "Jane is with her cousins; the narrative is with her. And I have the manual!" He waved it at me, deposited it in his pocket and picked up his gun. "Who's first?"

I ignored Hades and looked around. The patronizing "Dear, sweet Thursday!" voice had not been his—it had belonged to Aornis. She was wearing the same designer clothes as when I last saw her—she was only my memory of her, after all.

"Hey!" said Acheron. "I'm talking to you!"

I turned and dutifully fired, and Hades caught the approaching bullet—as he had when this had happened for real. He opened his fist; the slug was flattened into a small lead disk. He smiled and a shower of sparks flew up behind him.

But I wasn't so interested in Acheron this time around.

"Aornis!" I shouted. "Show yourself, coward!"

"No coward, I!" said Aornis, stepping from behind a large chimney piece.

"What are you doing to me?" I demanded angrily, pointing my gun at her. She didn't seem to be in the least put out—in fact, she seemed more concerned with preventing the dirt from the roof soiling her suede shoes.

"Welcome"—she laughed—"to the museum of your mind!"

The roof at Thornfield vanished and was replaced by the interior of the abandoned church where Spike and I were about to do battle with the Supreme Evil Being that was stuck in his head. It had happened for real a few weeks ago; the memories were still fresh—it was all chillingly lifelike.

"I am the curator in this museum," said Aornis as we moved again, to the dining room at home when I was eight, a small girl with pigtails and as precocious as they come. My father—before his eradication, of course—was carving the roast and telling me that if I kept on being a nuisance, I would be made to go to my room.

"Familiar to you?" asked Aornis. "I can call on any exhibit I want. Do you remember this?"

And we were back on the banks of the Thames, during my father's abortive attempt to rescue the two-year-old Landen. I felt the fear, the hopelessness, squeezing my chest so tight I could barely breathe. I sobbed.

"I can run it again if you want to. I can run it for you every night *forever*. Or I can delete it completely. How about this one?"

Night came on and we were in the area of Swindon that young couples go with their cars to get a bit of privacy. I had come here with Darren, a *highly* unlikely infatuation kindled in the furnace of parental disapproval. He loomed close to me in an amorous embrace in the back of his Morris 8. I was seventeen and impulsive—Darren was eighteen and repulsive. I could smell his beery breath and a postadolescent odor that was so strong you could have grabbed the air and wrung the stench from it with your bare hands. I could see Aornis outside the car, grinning at me, and through the labored panting of Darren, I screamed.

"But this isn't the *worst* place we could go." Aornis grinned through the window. "We can go back to the Crimea and unlock memories that have been too terrifying even for you. The suppressed memories, the ones you block out to let you carry on the day."

"No, Aornis, not the charge—!"

But there we were, in the last place I wanted to be, driving my APC into the massed field artillery of the Russian army that August afternoon in 1973. Of the eighty-four APCs and light tanks that advanced into the Russian guns, only two vehicles returned. Out of the 534 soldiers involved, 51 survived.

It was the moment before the barrage began. My CO, Major Phelps, was riding on the outside as he liked to do, foolhardy idiot that he was, and to my left and right I could see the other armored vehicles throwing up large swathes of summer dust from the parched land. We could be seen for miles. The first salvo was so unexpected that I thought the munitions in a light tank had simply ignited by accident; the whine of a near miss made me realize that it hadn't. I changed direction instantly and started to zigzag. I looked to Phelps for orders, but he was slumped in the hatch; he had lost the lower part of his arm and was unconscious.

The barrage was so intense that it became a single rumbling growl, the pressure waves thumping the APC so hard that it was all I could do to keep my hands on the controls.

I read the official report two years later. Forty-two guns had been trained on us from a thousand yards, and they had expended 387 rounds of high-explosive shells—about four to each vehicle. It had been like shooting fish in a barrel.

Sergeant Tozer took command and ordered me to an APC that had lost its tracks and been thrown upside down. I parked behind the wrecked carrier as Tozer and the squad jumped out to retrieve the wounded.

"But what were you *really* thinking about?" asked Aornis, who was beside me in the carrier, looking disdainfully at the dust and oil.

"Escape," I said. "I was terrified. We all were."

"Next!" yelled Tozer. "Stop talking to Aornis and take us to the next APC!"

I pulled away as another explosion went off. I saw a turret whirling through the air, a pair of legs dangling from beneath it.

I drove to the next APC, the shrapnel hitting our carrier almost continuously like hail on a tin roof. The survivors were firing impotently back with their rifles; it wasn't looking good. The APC was filled with the wounded, and as I turned round, something hit the carrier a glancing blow. It was a dud; it had struck us obliquely and bounced off—I would see the yard-long gouge in the armor plate the following day. Within a hundred yards we were in relative safety as the dust and smoke screened our retreat; pretty soon we had passed the forward command post, where all the officers were shouting into their field telephones, and were on to the dressing areas beyond. Even though I knew this was a dream, the fear felt as real as it had on the day, and tears of frustration welled up inside me. I thought Aornis would carry on with this memory for the return run to the barrage, but there was clearly a technique behind her barbaric game. In a blink we were back on the roof at Thornfield Hall.

Acheron was looking at me with a triumphant expression and carried on where he had left off:

"It may come as some consolation that I planned to bestow upon you the honor of becoming Felix9— Who are you?"

He was looking at Aornis.

"Aornis," she said shyly.

Acheron gave a rare smile and lowered his gun.

"Aornis?" he echoed. "*Little* Aornis?" She nodded and ran across to give him a hug.

"My goodness!" he said, looking her over carefully. "How you have grown! Last time I saw you, you were this high and had barely even *started* torturing animals. Tell me, did you follow us into the family business or did you flunk out like that loser Styx?"

"I'm a mnemonomorph!" she said proudly, eager for her sibling's approval.

"Of course! I should have guessed. We're in that Next woman's memories right now, aren't we?"

She nodded enthusiastically.

"Attagirl! Tell me, did she actually kill me? I'm only here as the *memory* of me in her mind, after all."

"I'm afraid so," said Aornis glumly. "She killed you well and good."

"By using treachery? Did I die a Hades?"

"I'm afraid not—it was a noble victory."

"Bitch!"

"Seconded. But I'll have the revenge you deserve, dear brother, you can be sure of that."

A family reunion like this should have been heartwarming, but I can't say I was moved. Still, at least it kept us away from the Crimea.

"Mother's very upset with you," said Aornis, who had the Hades penchant for straight talking.

"Why?"

"Why do you think? You murdered Styx."

"Styx was a fool and he brought shame on the Hades family. If father was still alive, he would have done the job himself."

"Well, Mother was very upset about it and I think you should apologize."

"Okay, next time—wait a moment, I'm dead—I can't apologize to anyone. *You* apologize for me."

"I'm a mnemonomorph, remember—and this is only me as a mindworm; a sort of satellite persona, if you like. Listen, if I knew where Thursday was, she'd be dead already. No, when I can report back to Aornis proper, this is what we'll do—"

"*Psssst!*" said a voice close to my ear. It was Granny Next.

"Gran! Am I glad to see you!"

"C'mon, while Aornis is distracted."

Gran took my hand and led me across the roof to the window, where we entered the building. But instead of being in the burning remains of Thornfield Hall, we were on the sidelines of a croquet match. Not *any* croquet match; it was a Croquet Federation Final—a SuperHoop. I used to play croquet quite seriously until SpecOps work absorbed all my free time. The two teams were in their body armor, leaning on their willow mallets and discussing strategy during a time-out.

"Okay," said Aubrey Jambe, who was wearing the captain's sweater, "Biffo is going to take the red ball from the forty-yard line over the rhododendron bushes, past the Italian sunken garden and into a close position to hoop five. Spike, you'll take it from there and croquet their yellow—Stig will defend you. George, I want you to mark their number five. He's a neanderthal, so you're going to have to use any tricks you can. Smudger, you're going to foul the duchess—when the vicar gives you the red card, I'm calling in Thursday. Yes?"

They all looked at me. I was in body armor, too. I was a substitute. A croquet mallet was slung round my wrist with a lanyard and I was holding a helmet.

"Thursday?" repeated Aubrey. "Are you okay? You look like you're in a dreamworld!"

"I'm fine," I said slowly. "I'll wait for your command."

"Good."

A horn went off, indicating the time-out was over. I looked up at the scoreboard. Swindon was losing, 12 hoops to 21.

"Gran," I said slowly, watching the team run out to continue play, "I don't remember this."

"Of course not!" she said as though I were a fool. "This is one of *mine*. Aornis will never find us here."

"Wait a moment. How can I be dreaming with *your* memories?"

"Tch tch," she scolded, "so many questions! It will all be explained in due course. Now, do you want to go into some of that deep, dreamless sleep and get some rest?"

"Please!"

"Good. Aornis will not bother you again tonight—I shall watch over you."

Gran approached a burly croquet player who only had one ear. After saying a few words, she pointed at me. I looked around at the stadium. It was the Swindon croquet stadium, yet somehow different. Behind me at the dignitaries box I was surprised to see Yorrick Kaine speaking to one of his assistants. Next to him was President Formby, who gave me a smile and a wave. I turned away, my eyes looking into the crowd and falling upon the one person that I *did* want to see. It was Landen, and he was bouncing a young child on his lap.

"Landen!" I shouted, but a cheer went up from the crowd and I was drowned out. But he *did* see me and smiled. He held the infant's hand and made it wave, too. Gran tugged my shoulder pad to get my attention.

"Gran," I said, "it's Lan—"

And then the mallet struck my head. Blackness and oblivion. As usual, just when I got to the good bit.

16.

Captain Nemo

Wemmick's Stores: To enable Jurisfiction agents to travel easily and undetected within fiction, Wemmick's Stores was built within the lobby of the Great Library. The stores have an almost unlimited inventory as Mr. Wemmick is permitted to create whatever he needs using a small ImaginoTransferenceDevice licensed by Text Grand Central. To reduce pilfering by Jurisfiction staff, all items checked out must be checked in again, where they are promptly reduced to text.

CAT FORMERLY KNOWN AS CHESHIRE,
Guide to the Great Library

I WOKE LATE THE following morning. My bed was next to the porthole so I rolled over, doubled up a pillow and gazed out at the sun sparkling upon the surface of the lake. I could hear the gentle slap of the water against the flying boat's hull, and it gave me a sense of ease and inner peace that ten years of SpecOps' finest stressperts couldn't bully into you.

I got up slowly and felt woozy all of a sudden. The room spun around and I felt hot. After a brief and unpleasant visit to the loo, I felt a bit better and went downstairs.

I made myself some toast, as it helped the nausea, and caught sight of myself in the chrome toaster. I looked dreadful, and I was holding up the toaster and sticking my tongue out, trying to see what it looked like, when the Generics walked in.

"What on earth are you doing?" asked Ibb.

"Nothing," I replied, hurriedly replacing the toaster. "Off to college?"

They both nodded. I noticed that they'd not only made their own lunch but actually cleared away after themselves. A certain sensitivity to others is a good sign in a Generic. It shows personality.

"Do you know where Gran is?" I asked.

"She said she was off to the Medici court for a few days," replied Obb. "She left you that note."

I found the note on the counter and picked it up, studying the one-word message with slight confusion.

"We'll be back at five," announced Ibb. "Do you need anything?"

"What, er—no," I said, reading Gran's note again. "See you then."

I made some more toast and continued with the multiple-choice test. After a half hour battling through such questions as *Which book does Sam Weller the Bootboy reside in?* and *Who said, "When she appeared, it was as though spring had finally arrived after a miserable winter"?* I stopped and looked at Gran's note for the tenth time. It was confusing. Written in a small and shaky hand, the note consisted of a single word: REMEMBER!

"Remember *what*?" I muttered to myself, and went for a walk.

I strolled down the banks of the lake, taking a path through a grove of birches that grew by the water's edge. I ducked under the low branches and followed my nose towards the odd assortment of vessels that were moored next to the old Sunderland. The first was a converted naval pinnace, her decks covered in plastic and in a constant state of conservation. Beyond this was a Humber lighter, abandoned and sunk at its moorings. As I walked on, a sudden screech of demonic laughter was followed by a peal of thunder and the smell of brimstone borne on a gust of icy wind. I blinked and coughed as thick green smoke momentarily enveloped me; when it had cleared, I was no longer alone. Three old hags with hooked chins and mottled complexions danced and cackled in front of me, rubbing their dirty hands and dancing in the most clumsy and uncoordinated fashion. It was the worst piece of overacting I had ever seen.

"Thrice the blinded dog shall bark," said the first witch, producing a cauldron from the air and placing it on the path in front of me.

"Thrice and once the hedgepig ironed," said the second, who conjured up a fire by throwing some leaves beneath the cauldron.

"Passerby cries, ' 'Tis time, 'tis time!' " screeched the third, tossing something into the cauldron that started to bubble ominously.

"I really don't have time for this," I said crossly. "Why don't you go and bother someone else?"

"Fillet of a pickled hake," continued the second witch, *"in the cauldron broil and bake; lie of Stig and bark of dog, woolly hat and bowl of fog, Fadda loch and song by Bing, wizard's leg and Spitfire's wing. For a charm of powerful trouble, like a hell-broth boil and bubble!"*

"I'm sorry to interrupt," I said, "but I really am very busy—and none of your prophecies have come true—apart from the citizen of Swindon bit and anyone with a telephone directory could find that out—and listen, you knew I was an apprentice so I *had* to be taking my finals sooner or later!"

They stopped cackling and looked at one another. The first witch drew a large pocket watch from the folds of her tatty cloak and looked at it carefully.

"Give it ye time, imperfect waiter!" she cried. *"All hail MsNext! Beware, beware the thrice-read rule!"*

"All hail MsNext! Exempted from I before E except after C rule Reigate is!" cackled the second.

"All hail MsNext!" added the third, who clearly didn't want to be left out. *"Meet a king but not be one, read a King but not visit one—"*

"Shoo!" shouted a loud voice behind me. The three witches stopped and stared at the new visitor crossly. He was an old man whose weathered face looked as though it had been gnarled by years of adventuring across the globe. He wore a blue blazer over

a polo-neck Aran sweater, and on his head a captain's cap sat above his lined features, a few wisps of gray hair showing from underneath the sweatband. His eyes sparkled with life and a grimace cracked his craggy features as he walked along the path towards us. It could only be Captain Nemo.

"Away with you, crones!" he cried. "Peddle your wares elsewhere!"

He would probably have beaten them with the stout branch he was brandishing had the witches not taken fright and vanished in a thunderclap of sound, cauldron and all.

"Hah!" said Nemo, throwing the branch towards where they had been. "Next time I will make mincemeat of you, foul dissemblers of nature with your 'hail this' and your 'hail that'!"

He looked at me accusingly. "Did you give them any money?"

"No, sir."

"Truthfully now! Did you give them anything at all?"

"No."

"Good, *never* give them any money. It only encourages them. They'll coax you in with their fancy prophecies—suggest you'll have a new car, and as soon as you start thinking you might need one—*bang!*—they're offering you loans and insurance and other unwanted financial services. Poor old Macbeth took it a bit too seriously—all they were trying to do was sell him a mortgage and insurance on a bigger castle—when the Birnam wood and 'no woman born' stuff all came true, the witches were as surprised as anyone. So *never* fall for their little scams—it'll drain your wallet before you know it. Who are you, anyway?"

"Thursday Next. I'm standing in for—"

"Ah!" he muttered thoughtfully. "The *Outlander*. Tell me, how do escalators work? Do they have one long staircase that is wound up on a huge drum and then rewound every night, or are they a continuous belt that just goes round and round?"

"An—um—continuous belt."

"Really?" he replied reflectively. "I've always wondered that. Welcome to *Caversham Heights*. I am Captain Nemo. I have some coffee on the stove—I wonder whether you would do me the honor of your company?"

I thanked him and we continued to walk along the lake's edge.

"A beautiful morning, would you not agree?" he asked, sweeping a hand towards the lake and the puffy clouds.

"It usually is."

"For a terrestrial view it is *almost* passable," added Nemo quickly. "It is nothing but a passing fancy to the beauty of the deep, but in retirement, we all have to make sacrifices."

"I have read your book many times," I said as courteously as I could, "and have found much pleasure in its narrative."

"Jules Verne was not simply my author but also a good friend," said Nemo sadly. "I was sorrowful on his passing, an emotion I do not share with many others of my kind."

We had arrived at Nemo's home. No longer the sleek and dangerous craft from *20,000 Leagues Under the Sea*, the riveted iron submarine was a shabby wreck streaked with rust, a thick green line of algae growing on the glass of the two large viewing windows. She belonged to a redolent age of high technological expectation. She was the *Nautilus*.

We made our way up the gangplank and Nemo helped me aboard.

"Thank you," I said, walking down the outer casing to the small conning tower, where he had set up a chair and a table upon which stood a glass hookah. He pulled up another folding chair and bid me sit down.

"You are here, like me," he asked, "resting—between engagements?"

"Maternity leave—of a sort."

"Of these matters I know nothing," he said gravely, pouring out a cup of coffee; the porcelain was White Star Line.

I took a sip and accepted the proffered biscuit. The coffee was excellent.

"Good, is it not?" he asked, a smile upon his lips.

"Indeed! Better than I have ever tasted. What is it?"

"From the Guiana Basin, an area of sea scattered with subter-ranean mountains and hills every bit as beautiful as the Andes. In a deep valley in this region I discovered an aquatic plant whose seeds, when dried and ground, make a coffee to match any that land can offer."

His face fell for a moment and he looked into his cup, swirling the brown liquid around.

"As soon as this coffee is drunk, that will be the end of it. I have been moved around the Well of Lost Plots for almost a cen-tury now. I was to be in a sequel, you know—Jules Verne had written half of it when he died. The manuscript, alas, was thrown out after his death, and destroyed. I appealed to the Council of Genres against the enforced demolition order, and I—and the *Nautilus* of course—were reprieved."

He sighed. "We have survived numerous moves from book to book within the Well. Now, as you see, I am marooned here. The voltaic piles, the source of the *Nautilus*'s power, are almost worn out. The sodium, which I extract from seawater, is exhausted. For many years I have been the subject of a preservation order, but preservation without expenditure is worthless. The *Nautilus* needs only a few thousand words to be as good as new—yet I have no money, nor influence. I am only an eccentric loner await-ing a sequel that I fear will never be written."

"I—I wish I could do something," I replied, "but Jurisfic-tion only keeps fiction in order—it does not dictate policy nor choose which books are to be written. You have, I trust, adver-tised yourself?"

"For many years. Here, see for yourself."

He handed me a copy of *The Word*. The Situations Sought page took up half the newspaper and I read where Nemo pointed.

Eccentric and autocratic sea dog (ex-Verne) requires excit-ing and morally superior tale to exercise knowledge of the oceans and discuss man's place within his environment. French spoken, has own submarine. Apply: Captain Nemo, c/o *Caversham Heights,* Subbasement Six, WOLP.

"Every week for over a century," he grumbled, "but not one sensible offer."

I doubted that his idea of a sensible offer would be like anyone else's—*20,000 Leagues Under the Sea* was a tough act to follow.

"You have read *Caversham Heights*?" he asked.

I nodded.

"Then you will know that the scrapping is not only inevitable, but quite necessary. When the book goes to the breakers yard, I will not apply for a transfer. The *Nautilus*—and I, too—will be broken down into text—and long do I wish for it!"

He scowled at the floor and poured another cup of coffee.

"Unless," he added, suddenly perking up, "you thought I should have the advert in a box, with a picture? It costs extra but it might make it more eye-catching."

"It is worth a try, of course."

Nemo rose to his feet and went below without another word. I thought he might return, but after twenty minutes had elapsed I decided to go home. I was ambling back along the lakeside path when I got a call from Havisham on the footnoterphone.[1]

"As always, Miss Havisham."[2]

"Perkins must be annoyed about *that*," I said, thinking, what with grammasites, a Minotaur, Yahoos and a million or two rabbits, life in the bestiary must be something of a handful.[3]

"I'm on my way."

---

1. "Miss Next, are you there?"

2. "Good. Meet me at the Jurisfiction office as soon as possible. It's about Perkins—the Minotaur has escaped."

3. "Not really. You see, Perkins isn't responding to footnoterphone communications—we think something might have happened to him."

17.

Minotaur Trouble

TravelBook: Standard-issue equipment to all Jurisfiction agents, the dimensionally ambivalent TravelBook contains information, tips, maps, recipes and extracts from popular or troublesome novels to enable speedier transbook travel. It also contains numerous JurisTech gadgets for more specialized tasks such as an MV Mask, TextMarker and Eject-O-Hat. The TravelBook's cover is read-locked to each individual operative and contains as standard an emergency alert and autodestruct mechanism.

CAT FORMERLY KNOWN AS CHESHIRE,
Guide to the Great Library

I READ MYSELF INTO the Well and was soon in an elevator, heading up towards the library. I had bought a copy of *The Word*; the front page led with "Nursery Rhyme Characters to Go on Indefinite Strike." Farther down, the previous night's attack on Heathcliff had been reported. It added that a terror group calling itself the Great Danes had also threatened to kill him—they wanted Hamlet to win this year's Most Troubled Romantic Lead BookWorld Award and would do anything to achieve this. I turned to page two and found a large article extolling the virtues of UltraWord™ with an open letter from Text Grand Central explaining how nothing would change and all jobs and privileges would be protected.

The elevator stopped on the first floor; I quickly made my way to *Sense and Sensibility* and read myself in. The crowd were still outside the doors of Norland Park, this time with tents, a brass band and a metal brazier burning scrap wood. As soon as they saw me a chant went up:

"*We need a break, we need a break . . .*"

A tired-looking woman with an inordinate amount of children gave me a leaflet.

"Three hundred and twenty-five years I've been doing this job," she said, "without even so much as a weekend off!"

"I'm sorry."

"We don't want pity," said Solomon Grundy, who, what with it being a Saturday, wasn't looking too healthy, "we want *action*. Oral traditionalists should be allowed the same rights as any other fictioneers."

"Right," said a young lad carrying a bucket with his head wrapped in brown paper, "no amount of money can compensate the brotherhood for the inconvenience caused by repetitive retellings. However, we would like to make the following demands: One, that all nursery rhyme characters are given immediate leave of absence for a two-week period. Two, that—"

"Really," I interrupted him, "you're talking to the wrong person. I'm only an apprentice. Jurisfiction has no power to dictate policy anyway—you need to speak to the Council of Genres."

"The Council sent us to talk to TGC, who referred us to the Great Panjandrum," said Humpty-Dumpty to a chorus of vigorous head-nodding, "but no one seems to know if he—or she—even *exists*."

"If you've never seen him, he probably doesn't exist," said Little Jack Horner. "Pie anyone?"

"I've never seen Vincent Price," I observed, "but I know *he* exists."

"Who?"

"An actor," I explained, feeling somewhat foolish. "Back home."

Humpty-Dumpty narrowed his eyes suspiciously. "You're talking complete *Lear*, Miss Next."

"King?"

"No. Edward."

"Oh."

"Mongoose!" yelled Humpty, drawing a small revolver and throwing himself on to the ground where, unluckily for him, there just happened to be a muddy puddle.

"You're mistaken," explained Grundy wearily, "it's a guide dog. Put the gun away before you hurt yourself."

"A guide dog?" repeated Humpty, slowly getting to his feet. "You're sure?"

"Have you spoken to WordMaster Libris?" I asked. "We all know *he* exists."

"He won't speak to us," said Humpty-Dumpty, wiping his face with a large handkerchief. "The oral tradition is unaffected by the UltraWord™ upgrade, so he doesn't think we're that important. If we don't negotiate a few rights before the new system comes in, we won't *ever* get any!"

"Libris won't even speak to you?" I repeated.

"He sends us notes," squeaked the oldest of three mice, all of whom had no tails, held a white cane in one hand and a golden retriever in the other. "He says that he is very busy but will give our concerns his 'fullest attention.' "

"What's going on?" squeaked one of the other mice. "Is that Miss Next?"

"It's a brush-off," said Grundy again. "Unless we get an answer soon, there won't be a single nursery rhyme anywhere, either spoken *or* read! We're going on a forty-eight-hour stoppage from midnight. When parents can't remember the words to our rhymes, the fur will really fly, I can promise you that!"

"I'm sorry," I began again, "I have no authority—I can't do anything—"

"Then just take this to WordMaster Libris?"

Humpty-Dumpty handed me a list of demands, neatly written on a page of foolscap paper. The crowd grew suddenly silent. A sea of eyes, all blinking expectantly, were directed at me.

"I promise *nothing*," I said, taking the piece of paper, "but if I see Libris, I will give this to him—okay?"

"Thank you very much," said Humpty. "At last *someone* from Jurisfiction will listen!"

*   *   *

I turned away and overheard Humpty say to Grundy, "Well, I thought that went pretty well, don't you?"

I walked briskly up the front steps of Norland Park, where I was admitted by the same froglike footman I had seen on my first visit. I crossed the hall and entered the ballroom. Miss Havisham was at her desk with Akrid Snell, who was talking into the footnoterphone. Standing next to them was Bradshaw, who had *not* retired as promised, filling out a form with the Bellman, who appeared grave. The only other occupant of the room was Harris Tweed, who was reading a report. He looked up as I entered, said nothing and continued reading. Miss Havisham was studying some photographs as I approached.

"Damn and blast!" she said, looking at one before tossing it over her shoulder and staring at the next. "Pathetic!" she muttered, looking at another. "Derisive!"

"Perkins?" I asked, sitting down.

"Speed-camera pictures back from the labs," she said, handing them over. "I thought I would have topped one hundred and sixty, but look, well—it's *pitiful,* that's what it is!"

I looked. The speed camera had caught the Higham Special but recorded only a top speed of 152.76 mph—but what was worse, it showed Mr. Toad traveling at *over* 180—and he had even raised his hat at the speed camera as he went past.

"I managed a hundred and seventy when I tried it on the M4," she said sadly. "Trouble is, I need a longer stretch of road—or sand. Well, can't be helped now. The car has been sold. I'll have to go cap in hand to Sir Malcolm if I want to get a shot at beating Toad."

"Norland Park to Perkins," said Snell into the footnoterphone, "come in please. Over."

I looked at Havisham.

"No answer for almost six hours," she said. "Mathias isn't answering, either—we got a Yahoo once but you might as well talk to Mrs. Bennett. What's that?"

"It's a list of demands from the nurseries outside."

"Rabble," replied Havisham, "all of them replaceable. How hard can it be, appearing in a series of rhyming couplets? If they don't watch themselves, they'll be replaced by scab Generics from the Well. It happened when the Amalgamated Union of Gateway Guardians struck in 1932. They never learn."

"All they want is a holiday—"

"I shouldn't concern yourself with nursery politics, Miss Next," said Havisham so sharply I jumped.

"Good work on the ProCath attack," announced Tweed, who had walked over. "I've had a word with Plum over at JurisTech; he's going to extend the footnoterphone network to cover more of *Wuthering Heights*—we shouldn't have a problem with mobile-footnoterphones dropping out again."

"We'd better not," replied Miss Havisham coldly. "Lose Heathcliff and the Council of Genres will have our colons for garters. Now, to work. We don't know what to expect in the bestiary, so we have to be prepared."

"Like Boy Scouts?"

"Can't stand them, but that's beside the point. Turn to page seven hundred eighty-nine in your TravelBook."

I did as she bid. This was an area of the book where the pages contained gadgets in hollowed-out recesses deeper than the book was thick. One page contained a device similar to a flare gun that had *Mk IV TextMarker* written on its side. Another page had a glass panel covering a handle like a fire alarm. A note painted on the glass read, IN UNPRECEDENTED EMERGENCY, BREAK GLASS. The page Havisham had indicated was neither of these; page 789 contained a brown homburg hat. Hanging from the brim was a large red toggle with *In emergency pull down sharply* written on it. There was also a chin strap, something I've never seen on a homburg before—or even a fedora or trilby, come to that.

Havisham took the hat from my hands and gave me a brief induction course: "This is the Martin-Bacon Mk VII Eject-O-Hat, for high-speed evacuation from a book. Takes you straight out in an emergency."

"Where to?"

"A little-known novel entitled *The Middle of Next Week*. You can make your way out to the library at leisure. But be warned: the jump can be painful, even fatal—so it should only be used as a last resort. Remember to keep the chin strap tight or it'll take your ears off during the ejection sequence. I will say 'Jump!' twice—by the third I will have gone. Any questions?"

"How does it work?"

"I'll rephrase that—any questions I can possibly hope to answer?"

"Does this mean we'll see Bradshaw without his pith helmet?"

"Ha-ha!" laughed Bradshaw, releasing the toggle from the brim. "I have the smaller Mk XII version—it could be fitted into a beret or a veil, if we so wished."

I picked up the homburg from the table and put it on.

"What are you expecting?" I asked slightly nervously, adjusting the chin strap.

"We think the Minotaur has escaped," Havisham answered gravely. "If it has and we meet it, just pull the cord as quick as you can—it always takes at least ten to twelve words to initiate a jump—you could be Minotaur appetizer by that time."

I pulled out my automatic to check it, but Bradshaw shook his head. "Your Outlander lead will not be enough." He held up the box of cartridges he had signed for. "Boojum-tipped," he explained, tapping the large hunting rifle he was carrying, "for total annihilation. Back to text in under a second. We call them eraserheads. Snell? Are you ready?"

Snell had a fedora version of the Eject-O-Hat, which suited his trench coat a bit better. He grunted but didn't look up. This assignment was personal. Perkins was his partner—not just at Jurisfiction but in the Perkins & Snell series of detective novels. If Perkins was hurt in some way, the future could be bleak. Generics could be trained to take over a vacated part, but it's never the same.

"Okay," said Havisham, adjusting her own homburg, "we're out of here. Hold on to me, Next—if we are split up, we'll meet at the gatehouse—no one enters the castle without Bradshaw, okay?"

Everyone agreed and Havisham mumbled to herself the code word and some of the text of *The Sword of the Zenobians*.

Pretty soon Norland Park had vanished and the bright sun of Zenobia greeted us. The grass was springy underfoot and herds of unicorns grazed peacefully beside the river. Grammasites wheeled in the blue skies, riding the thermals that rose from the warm grassland.

"Everyone here?" asked Havisham.

Bradshaw, Snell, and I nodded our heads. We walked in silence, past the bridge, up to the old gatehouse and across the drawbridge. A dark shadow leaped from a corner of the deserted guardroom, but before Bradshaw could fire, Havisham yelled, "Wait!" and he stopped. It was a Yahoo—but he hadn't come to throw his shit about—he was running away in terror.

Bradshaw and Havisham exchanged nervous looks and we moved closer to where Perkins and Mathias had been doing their work. The door was broken and the hinges had vanished, replaced by two very light burn marks.

"Hold it!" said Bradshaw, pointing at the hinges. "Did Perkins hold any vyrus on the premises?"

For a moment I didn't understand why Bradshaw was asking this question, but realization slowly dawned upon me. He meant the mispeling vyrus. The hinges had become *singes*.

"Yes," I replied, "a small jar—well shielded by dictionaries."

There was a strange and pregnant pause. The danger was real and clear, and even seasoned PROs like Bradshaw and Havisham were thinking twice about entering Perkins's lab.

"What do you think?" asked Bradshaw.

"Vyrus *and* a Minotaur," sighed Havisham. "We need more than the four of us."

"I'm going in," said Snell, pulling the MV mask from his Travel-Book. The device was made of rubber and similar to the gas respirator I had worn in the Crimea—only with a dictionary on the side where the filter would have been. It wasn't just one dictionary, either—the *Lavinia-Webster* had been taped back to back with the *Oxford English Dictionary*.

"Don't forget your carrot," said Havisham, pinning a vegetable to the front of his jacket.

"I'll need the rifle," said Snell.

"No," replied Bradshaw, "I signed for it, so I'm keeping it."

"This is not the time for sticking to the rules, Bradshaw, my partner's in there!"

"This is *exactly* the time we should stick to the rules, Snell."

They stared at one another.

"Then I'll go alone," replied Snell with finality, pulling the mask down over his face and releasing the safety on his automatic.

Havisham caught his elbow as she rummaged in her Travel-Book for her own mask. "We go together or not at all, Akrid."

I found the correct page for the mask, pulled it out of its slot and put it on under the Eject-O-Hat. Miss Havisham pinned a carrot to my jacket, too.

"A carrot is the best litmus test for the mispeling vyrus," she said, helping Bradshaw on with his mask. "As soon as the carrot comes into contact with the vyrus, it will start to mispel into *parrot*. You need to be out before it can talk. We have a saying: 'When you can hear Polly, use the brolly.' " She tapped the toggle of the Eject-O-Hat. "Understand?"

I nodded.

"Good. Bradshaw, lead the way!"

We stepped carefully across the door with its mispeled hinges, and into the lab, which was in chaotic disorder. Mispeling was merely an annoyance to readers—but *inside* the Book-World it was a menace. The mispeling was the effect of sense distortion, not the cause—once the internal meaning of a word started to break down, then the mispeling arose merely as a result of this. Unmispeling the word at TGC might work if the vyrus hadn't taken a strong hold, but usually it was pointless; like making the beds in a burning house.

The interior of the laboratory was heavily disrupted. On the far wall the shelves were filled with a noisy company of *featherbound rooks;* we stepped forward onto the *fattened tarpit* only to see that the imposing table in the center of the room was now an enormous *label.* The glass apparatus had become *grass asparagus,* and worst of all, Mathias the talking horse was simply a large model *house*—like a doll's house but much more detailed. Miss Havisham looked at me and pointed to her carrot. Already it was starting to change color—I could see tinges of red, yellow and blue.

"Carefool," said Snell, "look!"

On the floor next to more shards of broken *grass* was a small layer of the same purple mist I had seen the last time I was here. The area of the floor touched by the vyrus was constantly changing meaning, texture, color and appearance.

"Where waz the Minotour kept?" asked Havisham, her carrot beginning to sprout a small beak.

I pointed the way and Bradshaw took the lead. I pulled out my gun, despite Bradshaw's assurances that it was a waste of time, and he gently pushed the door open to the vault beneath the old hall. Snell snapped on a torch and flicked it within the chamber. The door to the Minotaur's cage was open, but of the beast, there was no sign. I wish I could have said the same for Perkins. He—or what was left of him—was lying on the stone floor. The Minotaur had devoured him up to his chest. His spine had been picked clean and the lower part of a leg had been thrown to one side. I choked at the sight and felt a knot rise in my throat. Bradshaw cursed low and turned to cover the doorway. Snell dropped to his knees to close Perkins's eyes, which were staring off into space, a look of fear still etched upon his features. Miss Havisham laid a hand on Snell's shoulder.

"I'm so sory, Akrid. Perkins wos a good man."

"I can't beleive he wood have been sew stewpid," muttered Snell angrily.

"We shood be leaving," said Bradshaw, "now we kno there is *definitly* a Minotour loose, we must come bak beter armed and with more peeple!"

Snell got up. Behind his MV Mask I could see tears in his eyes. Miss Havisham looked at me and pointed to her carrot, which had started to sprout feathers. A proper cleanup gang would be needed. Snell placed his jacket over Perkins and joined us as Bradshaw led the way out.

"Bak to Norland, yes?"

"I've hunted Minotour befour," said Bradshaw, his instincts alerted, "Stalingrad, 1944. They neffer stray far from the kil."

"Bradshore—!" urged Miss Havisham, but the commander wasn't the sort to take orders from another, not even someone as forthright as Havisham.

"I don't git it," murmured Snell, stopping for a moment and staring at the chaos within the laboratory and the small glob of purple mist on the floor. "Their just isn't enuff vyrus here to corze the problims we've seen."

"Wot are U saying?" I asked.

Bradshaw looked carefully out of the open door, indicated all was clear and beckoned for us to leave.

"There mite be some *moor* vyrus around," continued Snell. "Wot's in this cuppboard?"

He strode towards a small wooden cabinet that had telephone directory pages pasted all over it.

"Wate!" cried Bradshaw, striding from the other side of the room. "Let me."

He grasped the handle as a thought struck me. They weren't telephone directory pages, they were from a dictionary. The door was *shielded*.

I shouted but it was too late. Bradshaw opened the cupboard and was bathed in a faint purple light. The cabinet contained two dozen or so broken jars, all of which leaked the pestilential vyrus.

"Ahh!" he cried, staggering backwards and dropping his *gum* as the carrot transformed into a loud *parrot*. Bradshaw, his actions instinctive after years of training, pulled the cord on his Eject-O-Hat and vanished with a loud *bang*.

The room mutated as the mispeling got a hold. The floor buckled and softened into *flour,* the walls changed into *balls.* I looked across at Havisham. Her carrot was a parrot, too—it had hopped to her other shoulder and was looking at me with its head cocked to one side.

"*Go, go!*" she yelled at me, pulling the cord and vanishing like Bradshaw before her. I grasped the handle and pulled—but it came off in my hand. I threw it to the ground, where it became a *candle*.

"Hear," said Snell, removing his own Eject-O-Hat, "use myne."

"Bat the vyruz!"

"Hange the vyruz, Neckts—jist go!"

He did not look at me again. He just walked towards the cupboard with the broken jars and slowly closed the door, his hands morphing into *lands*—complete with miniature trees, forests and hills—as he touched the raw power of the vyrus. I ran outside, casting off the now useless hat and attempting to clip on the chin strap of Snell's. It wasn't easy. I caught my foot on a piece of half-buried masonry and fell headlong—to land within three paces of two large cloven hooves.

I looked up. The Minotaur was semicrouched on his muscular haunches, ready to jump. His bull's head was large and sat heavily on his body—what neck he did have was hidden beneath taut muscle. Within his mouth two rows of fine-pointed teeth were shiny with saliva, and his sharpened horns pointed forward, ready to attack. Five years eating nothing but yogurt. You might as well feed a tiger on Ryvita.

"Nice Minotaur," I said soothingly, slowly reaching for my automatic, which had fallen on the grass beside me, "good Minotaur."

He took a step closer, his hooves making deep impressions in the grass. He stared at me and breathed out heavily through his nostrils, blowing tendrils of mucus into the air. He took another step, his deep-set yellow eyes staring into mine with an expression of loathing. My hand closed around the butt of my automatic as the Minotaur bent closer and put out a large clawed hand. I moved the gun slowly towards me as the Minotaur reached down and—picked up Snell's hat. He turned it over in his claws and licked the brim with a tongue the size of my forearm. I had seen enough. I leveled my automatic and pulled the trigger at the same time as the Minotaur's clawed hand caught in the toggle and activated the Eject-O-Hat. The mythological manbeast vanished with a loud detonation as my gun went off, the shot whistling harmlessly through the air.

I breathed a sigh of relief but quickly rolled aside because, with a loud whooshing noise, a packing case fell from the heavens and landed with a crash right where I had lain. The case had *Property of Jurisfiction* stenciled on it and had split open to reveal—*dictionaries.* Another case landed close by, then a third and a fourth. Before I had time to even begin to figure out what was happening, Bradshaw had reappeared.

"Why didn't you jump, you litle fool?"

"My hat failed!"

"And Snell?"

"Insyde."

Bradshaw pulled on his MV Mask and rushed off into the building as I took refuge from the packing cases of dictionaries that were falling with increased rapidity. Harris Tweed appeared and barked orders at the small army of Mrs. Danvers that had materialized with him. They were all wearing identical black dresses high-buttoned to the collar, which only served to make their pale skin seem even whiter, their hollow eyes more sinister. They moved slowly but purposefully, and began to stack, one by one, the dictionaries against the castle keep.

"Where's the Minotaur?" asked Havisham, who suddenly appeared close by.

I told her he had ejected with Snell's fedora and she vanished without another word.

Bradshaw reappeared from the keep, dragging Snell behind him. The rubber on Akrid's MV Mask had turned to *blubber,* his suit to *soot.* Bradshaw removed him from *Sword of the Zenobians* to the Jurisfiction sick bay just as Miss Havisham returned. We watched together as the stacked dictionaries rose around the remains of Perkins's laboratory, twenty feet thick at the base, rising to a dome like a sugarloaf over the castle keep. It might have taken a long time but there were many Mrs. Danvers, they were highly organized and they had an inexhaustible supply of dictionaries.

"Find the Minotaur?" I asked Havisham.

"Long gon. There will be hell to pay about this, I assure you!"

When our carrots had returned to being crunchy vegetables, and the last vestiges of parrotness had been removed, Havisham and I pulled off our vyrus masks and tossed them in a heap—the dictionary filters were almost worn out.

"What happens now?" I asked.

"It is torched," replied Tweed, who was close by, "it is the only way to destroy the vyrus."

"What about the evidence?" I asked.

"Evidence?" echoed Tweed. "Evidence of what?"

"Perkins," I replied. "We don't know the full details of his death."

"I think we can safely say he was killed and eaten by the Minotaur," said Tweed, borrowing Havisham's not-to-be-questioned voice. "It's too dangerous to go back in, even if we wanted to. I'd rather torch this now than risk spreading the vyrus and having to demolish the whole book and everything in it—do you know how many creatures live in here?"

He lit a flare.

"You'd better stand clear."

The DanverClones were leaving now, vanishing with a faint pop, back to wherever they had been pulled from. Bradshaw and I withdrew as Tweed threw the flare on the pile of dictionaries. They burst into flames and were soon so hot that we had to withdraw to the gatehouse, the black smoke that billowed into the sky taking with it the remnants of the vyrus—and the evidence of Perkins's murder. Because I was sure it *was* murder. When we had walked into the Minotaur's vault, I had noticed that the key was missing from its hook. *Someone had let the Minotaur out.*

18.

Snell Rest in Peece
and Lucy Deane

I didn't notice it straightaway but Vernham, Nelly and Lucy all had the same surname: Deane. They weren't related. In the Outland this happens all the time, but in fiction it is rare; the problem is aggressively attacked by the **echolocators** (qv), who insist that no two people in the same book have the same name. I learned years later that Hemingway once wrote a book that was demolished because he insisted that every single one of the eight characters was named Gordon.

THURSDAY NEXT,
The Jurisfiction Chronicles

THE MINOTAUR HAD given Havisham the slip and was last seen heading towards the works of Zane Grey; the semibovine wasn't stupid—he knew we'd have trouble finding him amidst a cattle drive. Snell lasted another three hours. He was kept in an isolation tent made of fine plastic sheeting that had been over-printed with pages from the *Oxford English Dictionary*. We were in the sick bay of the Anti-mispeling Fast Response Group. At the first sign of any deviant mispeling, thousands of these volumes were shipped to the infected book and set up as barrages either side of the chapter. The barrage was then moved in, paragraph by paragraph, until the vyrus was forced into a single sentence, then word, then smothered completely. Fire was not an option in a published work; they had tried it once in Samuel Pepys's *Diary* and burnt down half of London.

"Does he have any family?" I asked.

"Snell was a loner detective, Miss Next," explained the doctor. "Perkins was his only family."

"Is it safe to go up to him?"

"Yes—but be prepared for some mispelings."

I sat by his bed while Havisham stood and spoke quietly with the doctor. Snell lay on his back and was breathing with small, shallow gasps, the pulse on his neck racing—it wouldn't be long before the vyrus took him away and he knew it. I leaned closer and held his hand through the sheeting. His complexion was pail, his breething labored, his skein covered in painful and unsightly green pastilles. As I wotched, his dry slips tried to foam worlds but all he could torque was ninsense.

"Thirsty!" he squeeked. "Wode—Cone, udder whirled—doughnut Trieste—!"

He grisped my arm with his fungers, made one last stringled cry before feeling bakwards, his life force deported from his pathotic mispeled boddy.

"He was a fine operative," said Havisham as the doctor pulled a sheep over his head.

"What will happen to the Perkins and Snell series?"

"I'm not sure," she replied softly. "Demolished—saved with new Generics—I don't know."

"What ho!" exclaimed Bradshaw, appearing from nowhere. "Is he—?"

"I'm afraid so," replied Havisham.

"One of the best," murmured Bradshaw sadly. "When they made Snell, they threw away the mold."

"I hope not," added Havisham. "If we *do* replace him, it might make things a bit tricky."

"Figure of speech," countered Bradshaw. "Did he say anything before he died?"

"Nothing coherent."

"Hmm. The Bellman wanted a report on his death as soon as possible. What do you think?"

He handed Havisham a sheet of paper, and she read:

" 'Minotaur escapes, finds captor, eats captor, captor dies. Horse mispeled in struggle. Colleague dies attempting rescue. Minotaur escapes.' "

She turned over the piece of paper, but it was blank on the other side.

"That's it?"

"I didn't want it to get boring," replied Bradshaw, "and the Bellman wanted it as simple as possible. I think he's got Libris breathing down his neck. The investigation of a Jurisfiction agent so close to the launch of UltraWord™ will make the Council of Genres jittery as hell."

Miss Havisham handed the report back to Bradshaw. "Perhaps, Commander, you should lose that report in the pending tray for a bit."

"This sort of stuff happens in fiction all the time," he replied. "Do you have any evidence that it was *not* accidental?"

"The key to the padlock wasn't on its hook," I murmured.

"Well spotted," replied Miss Havisham.

"Skulduggery?" Bradshaw hissed excitedly.

"I fervently hope not," she returned. "Just delay the findings for a few days—we should see if Miss Next's observational skills hold up to scrutiny."

"Righty-o!" replied Bradshaw. "I'll see what I can do!"

And he vanished. We were left alone in the corridor, the bunk beds of the DanverClones stretching off to the distance in both directions.

"It might be nothing, Miss Havisham, but—"

She put her fingers to her lips. Havisham's eyes, usually resolute and fixed, had, for a brief moment, seemed troubled. I said nothing but inwardly I felt worried. Up until now I had thought Havisham feared nothing.

She looked at her watch. "Go to the bun shop in *Little Dorrit*, would you? I'll have a doughnut and a coffee. Put it on my tab and get something for yourself."

"Thank you. Where shall we meet?"

"*Mill on the Floss*, page five hundred twenty-three in twenty minutes."

"Assignment?"

"Yes," she replied, deep in thought. "Some damn meddling fool told Lucy Deane that Stephen and not Philip will be boating with Maggie—she may try to stop them. Twenty minutes and not the jam doughnuts, the ones with the pink icing, yes?"

Thirty-two minutes later I was inside *Mill on the Floss*, on the banks of a river next to Miss Havisham, who was observing a couple in a boat. The woman was dark-skinned with a jet-black coronet of hair. She was lying on a cloak with a parasol above her as a man rowed her gently downriver. He was of perhaps five-and-twenty years old, quite striking, and with short dark hair that stood erect, not unlike a crop of corn. They were talking earnestly to each other. I passed Miss Havisham a cup of coffee and a paper bag full of doughnuts.

"Stephen and Maggie?" I asked, indicating the couple as we walked along the path by the river.

"Yes," she replied. "As you know, Lucy and Stephen are a hairsbreadth from engagement. Stephen and Maggie's indiscretion in this boat causes Lucy Deane no end of distress. I told you to get the ones with pink icing."

"They'd run out."

"Ah."

We kept a wary eye on the couple in the boat as I tried to remember what actually happened in *Mill on the Floss*.

"They agree to elope, don't they?"

"Agree to—but don't. Stephen is being an idiot and Maggie should know better. Lucy is meant to be shopping in Lindum with her father and Aunt Tulliver, but she gave them the slip an hour ago."

We walked on for a few more minutes. The story seemed to be following the correct path with no intervention of Lucy's we could see. Although we couldn't make out the words, the sound of Maggie's and Stephen's voices carried across the water.

Miss Havisham took a bite of her doughnut.

"I noticed the missing key, too," she said after a pause. "It was pushed under a workbench. It was murder. Murder . . . by Minotaur."

She shivered.

"Why didn't you tell Bradshaw?" I asked. "Surely the murder of a Jurisfiction operative warrants an investigation?"

She stared at me hard and then looked at the couple in the boat again.

"You don't understand, do you? *The Sword of the Zenobians* is code-word-protected."

"Only Jurisfiction agents can get in and out," I murmured.

"Whoever killed Perkins and Mathias was Jurisfiction, and *that's* what frightens me. A rogue agent."

We walked in silence, digesting this information.

"But why would anyone want to kill Perkins and a talking horse?"

"I think Mathias just got in the way."

"And Perkins?"

"Not just Perkins. Whoever killed him tried to get someone else that day."

I thought for a moment and a sudden chill came over me.

"My Eject-O-Hat. It failed."

Miss Havisham produced the homburg from a carrier bag, slightly squashed from where several Mrs. Danvers had trodden on it. The frayed cord looked as though it might have been cut.

"Take this to Professor Plum at JurisTech and have him look at it. I'd like to be sure."

"But . . . but why am *I* a threat?"

"I don't know," admitted Miss Havisham. "You are the most junior member of Jurisfiction and arguably the least threatening—you can't even bookjump without moving your lips, for goodness' sake!"

I didn't need reminding, but I saw her point.

"So what happens now?" I asked at length.

"We have to assume whoever killed Snell might try again. You are to be on your guard. Wait—there she is!"

We had walked over a small rise and were slightly ahead of the boat. A young woman was lying on the ground in a most unladylike fashion, pointing a sniper's rifle towards the small skiff that had just come into view. I crept cautiously forward; she was so intent on her task that she didn't notice me until I was close enough to grab her. She was a slight thing, and her strugglings, whilst energetic, were soon overcome. I secured her in an armlock as Havisham unloaded the rifle. Maggie and Stephen, unaware of the danger, drifted softly past on their way to Mudport.

"Where did you get this?" asked Havisham, holding up the rifle.

"I don't have to say anything," replied the angelic-looking girl in a soft voice. "I was only going to knock a hole in the boat, honestly I was!"

"Sure you were. You can let go, Thursday."

I relaxed my grip and the girl stepped back, pulling at her clothes to straighten them after our brief tussle. I checked her for any other weapons but found nothing.

"Why should Maggie force a wedge between our happiness?" she demanded angrily. "Everything would be so *wonderful* between my darling Stephen and I—why am I the victim? I, who only wanted to do good and help everyone—especially Maggie!"

"It's called drama," replied Havisham wearily. "Are you going to tell us where you got the rifle or not?"

"Not. You can't stop me. Maybe they'll get away, but I can be here ready and waiting on the next reading—or even the one after that! Think you have enough Jurisfiction agents to put Maggie under constant protection?"

"I'm sorry you feel that way," replied Miss Havisham, looking her squarely in the eye. "Is that your final word?"

"It is."

"Then you are under arrest for attempted Fiction Infraction, contrary to Ordinance FMB/0608999 of the Narrative Continuity Code. By the power invested in me by the Council of Genres, I sentence you to banishment outside *Mill on the Floss*. Move."

Miss Havisham ordered me to cuff Lucy and, once I had, held on to me as we jumped into the Great Library. Lucy, for an arrested ad-libber, didn't seem too put out.

"You can't imprison me," she said as we walked along the corridor of the twenty-third floor. "I reappear in Maggie's dream seven pages from now. If I'm not there, you'll be in more trouble than you know what to do with. This could mean your job, Miss Havisham! Back to Satis House—for good."

"Would it mean that?" I asked, suddenly wondering whether Miss Havisham wasn't exceeding her authority.

"It would mean the same as it did the last time," replied Havisham, "absolutely *nothing*."

"Last time?" queried Lucy. "But this is the first time I've tried something like this!"

"No," replied Miss Havisham, "no, it most certainly is not."

Miss Havisham pointed out a book entitled *The curious experience of the Patterson Family on the island of Uffa* and told me to open it. We were soon inside, on the foreshore of a Scottish island in the late spring.

"What do you mean?" asked Lucy, looking around her as her earlier confidence evaporated to be replaced by growing panic. "What is this place?"

"It is a prison, Miss Deane."

"A prison? A prison for whom?"

"For them," said Havisham, indicating several identically youthful and fair-complexioned Lucy Deanes, who had broken cover and were staring in our direction. Our Lucy Deane looked at us, then at her identical sisters, then back to us again.

"I'm sorry!" she said, dropping to her knees. "Give me another chance—please!"

"Take heart in that this doesn't make you a bad person," said Miss Havisham. "You just have a repetitive character disorder. You are a serial ad-libber and the seven hundred and ninety-sixth

Lucy we have had to imprison here. In less civilized times you would have been reduced to text. Good day."

And we vanished back to the corridors of the Great Library.

"And to think she was the most pleasant person in *Floss!*" I said, shaking my head sadly.

"You'll find that the most righteous characters are the first ones to go loco down here. The average life of a Lucy Deane is about a thousand readings; self-righteous indignation kicks in after that. No one could believe it when David Copperfield killed his first wife, either. Good day, Chesh."

The Cheshire Cat had appeared on a high shelf, grinning to us, itself and anything else in view.

"Well!" said the Cat. "Next and Havisham! Problems with Lucy Deane?"

"The usual. Can you get the Well to send in the replacement as soon as possible?"

The Cat assured us he would, seemed crestfallen that I hadn't brought him any Moggilicious cat food and vanished again.

"We need to find out anything unusual about Perkins's death," said Miss Havisham. "Will you help?"

"Of course!" I enthused.

Miss Havisham smiled a rare smile. "You remind me of myself, all those years ago, before that rat Compeyson brought my happiness to an end."

She moved closer and narrowed her eyes. "We keep this to ourselves. Knowledge can be a dangerous thing. Start poking around in the workings of Jurisfiction and you may find more than you bargained for—just remember that."

She fell silent for a few moments.

"But first, we need to get you fully licensed as a Jurisfiction agent—there's a limit to what you can do as an apprentice. Did you finish the multiple choice?"

I nodded.

"Good. Then you can do your practical exam today. I'll go and organize it while you take your Eject-O-Hat to JurisTech."

She melted into the air about me and I walked off down the

library corridor towards the elevators. I passed Falstaff, who invited me to dance around his maypole. I told him to sod off, of course, and pressed the elevator call button. The doors opened a minute later and I stepped in. But it wasn't empty. With me were Emperor Zhark and Mrs. Tiggy-winkle.

"Which floor?" asked Zhark.

"First, please."

He pressed the button with a long and finely manicured finger and continued his conversation with Mrs. Tiggy-winkle.

". . . and that was when the rebels destroyed the third of my battle stations," said the emperor sorrowfully. "Have you any idea how much these things cost?"

"Tch," said Mrs. Tiggy-winkle, bristling her spines, "they always find some way of defeating you, don't they?"

Zhark sighed. "It's like one huge conspiracy," he muttered. "Just when I think I have the galaxy at my mercy, some hopelessly outnumbered young hothead destroys my most insidious death machine using some hitherto-undiscovered weakness. I'm suing the manufacturer after that last debacle."

He sighed again, sensed he was dominating the conversation and asked, "So how's the washing business?"

"Well, the price of starch is something terrible these days."

"Oh, I know," replied Zhark, thumbing his high collar, "look at this. My name alone strikes terror into billions, but can I get my collars done exactly how I want them?"

The elevator stopped at my floor and I stepped out.

I read myself into *Sense and Sensibility* and avoided the nursery rhyme characters who were still picketing the front door; I had Humpty's proposals in my back pocket but still hadn't given them to Libris—in truth I had only promised to do my best, but didn't particularly want to run the gauntlet again. I ran up the back stairs, nodded a greeting to Mrs. Henry Dashwood and bumped into Tweed in the lobby; he was talking to a lithe and adventurous-looking young man whose forehead was etched with an almost permanent frown.

Tweed quickly broke off when I appeared. "Ah! Thursday. Sorry to hear about Snell; he was a good man."

"I know—thank you."

"I've appointed the Gryphon as your new attorney," Tweed said. "Is that all right?"

"Sounds fine." I turned to the youth, who was pulling his hands nervously through his curly hair. "Hello! I'm Thursday Next."

"Sorry!" mumbled Tweed. "This is Uriah Hope from *David Copperfield*, an apprentice I have been asked to train."

"Pleased to meet you," replied Hope in a friendly tone. "Perhaps you and I could discuss apprenticeships together sometime?"

"The pleasure's mine, Mr. Hope. I'm a big fan of your work in *Copperfield*."

I thanked them both and left to find the JurisTech offices along Norland Park's seemingly endless corridors. I stopped at a door at random, knocked and looked in. Behind a desk was one of the many Greek heroes who could be seen wandering around the library; licensing their stories for remakes made a very reasonable living. He was on the footnoterphone.

"Okay," he said, "I'll be down to pick up Eurydice next Friday. Anything I can do for you in return?" He raised a finger at me to wait. "Don't look back? That's all? Okay, no problem. See you then. Bye."

He put down the horn and looked at me. "Thursday Next, isn't it?"

"Yes; do you know where the JurisTech office is?"

"Down the corridor, first on the right."

"Thanks."

I made to leave but he called me back, pointing at the footnoterphone. "I've forgotten already—what was I meant not to do?"

"I'm sorry, I wasn't listening."

I walked down the corridor, opened another door into a room that had nothing in it except a man with a frog growing out of his shiny bald head.

"Goodness!" I said. "How did that happen?"

"It all started with a pimple on my bum," said the frog. "Can I help you?"

"I'm looking for Professor Plum."

"You want JurisTech. This is Old Jokes. Try next door."

I thanked him and knocked on the next door. There was a very singsong "Come in!" and I entered. Although I had expected to see a strange laboratory full of odd inventions, there was nothing of the sort—just a man dressed in a check suit sitting behind a desk, reading some papers. He reminded me of Uncle Mycroft—just a little more perky.

"Ah!" he said, looking up. "Miss Next. Did you bring the hat with you?"

"Yes, but how—?"

"Miss Havisham told me," he said simply.

It seemed there weren't many people who didn't talk to Miss Havisham or who didn't have Miss Havisham talk to them.

I took out the battered Eject-O-Hat and placed it on the table. Plum picked up the broken activation handle, flicked a magnifying glass in front of his eye and stared at the frayed end minutely.[1]

---

1. "Sofya! Where were you? I have been calling forever! Tell me, the Karenins—they divorced?"

"No! Maybe if they *had* been divorced, events would have been different. I remember her attending the theater in Petersburg. What a disaster!"

"Why? Whatever happened? Did she make a fool of herself?"

"Yes, by appearing in the first place! How could she? Madame Kartasova, who was in the adjacent box with that fat, bald husband of hers, made a scene. She said something aloud, something insulting, and left the theater. We all saw it happen. Anna tried to ignore everything but she must have known."

"Why didn't they push for a divorce, the foolish pair!"

"Vronsky wanted her to but she kept putting it off. They moved to Moscow, but she was never happy. Vronsky spent his time involved in politics and she was convinced that he was with other women. A jealous, fallen disgrace of a woman she was. Then, at Znamanka station she could take it no longer—she flung herself upon the rails and was crushed by the 20:02 to Obiralovka!"

"Oh!" I said. "I'm getting it again!"

"What?"

"A crossed line on my footnoterphone!"

"I can get a trace if you want—here, put this galvanized bucket on your head."

"Not for a minute or two. I want to see how it all turns out."

"As you wish."

So as he examined the hat, I listened to Sofya and Vera prattle on.

"Well," he said finally, "it looks as though it has chafed through. The Mk VII is an old design—I'm surprised to see it still in use."

"So it was just a failure due to poor maintenance?" I asked, not without some relief.

"A failure that saved a life, yes."

"What do you mean?" I asked, my relief short-lived.

He showed me the hat. Inside an inspection cover were intricate wires and small flashing lights that looked impressive.

"Someone has wired the retextualizing inhibitor to the ISBN Code rectifiers. If the cord had been pulled, there would have been an overheat in the primary booster coils."

"Overheat? My head would have got hot?"

"More than hot. Enough energy would have been released to write about fourteen novels."

"I'm an apprentice, Plum, tell me in simple terms."

He looked at me seriously. "There wouldn't be much left of the hat—or the person wearing it. It happens occasionally on the Mk VII's—it would have been seen as an accident. Good thing there *was* a broken cord."

He whistled low. "Nifty piece of work, too. Someone who knew what they were doing."

"No!"

"Yes—but don't tell a soul—it is a secret between you and I! Come for dinner on Tuesday—we are having Turnips à l'Orange—I have a simply *adorable* new cook. Adieu, my good friend, adieu!"

"That's very interesting," I said slowly. "Can you give me a list of people who might have been able to do this sort of work?"

"Take a few days."

"Worth the wait. I'll call back."

I met up with Miss Havisham and the Bellman in the Jurisfiction offices.

The Bellman nodded a greeting and consulted his ever-present clipboard. "Looks like a dog day, ladies."

"Thurber again?"

"No, *Mansfield Park*. Lady Bertram's pet pug has been run over and needs to be replaced."

"Again?" replied Havisham. "That must be the sixth. I wish she'd be more careful."

"Seventh. You can pick it up from stores."

He turned his attention to me. "Miss Havisham says you are ready to take the practical test to bring you up from apprentice to restricted agent."

"I'm ready," I replied, thinking I was anything but.

"I'm sure you are," answered the Bellman thoughtfully, "but it *is* a bit soon—if it wasn't for the shortage caused by Mrs. Naka-jima's retirement, I think you would remain as an apprentice for a few more months. Well," he sighed, "can't be helped. I've had a look at the duty roster and I think I've found an assignment that should test your mettle. It's an Internal Plot Adjustment order from the Council of Genres."

Despite my natural feelings of caution, I was also, to my shame, *excited* by a practical test of my abilities. Dickens? Hardy? Perhaps even Shakespeare.

"*Shadow the Sheepdog*," announced the Bellman, "by Enid Blyton. It needs to have a happy ending."

"*Shadow . . . the Sheepdog*," I repeated slowly, hoping my disappointment didn't show. Blyton wasn't *exactly* high literature, but on reflection, perhaps that was just as well.

"Okay," I said more enthusiastically, "what do you want me to do?"

"Simple. As the story stands, Shadow is blinded by the barbed wire, so he can't be sold to the American film producer. Up ending because he isn't sold, down ending because he is blinded and useless. All we need to do is to have him miraculously regain his sight the next time he goes to the vet on page"—he consulted his clipboard—"two thirty-two."

"And," I said cautiously, not wanting the Bellman to realize how unprepared I was, "what plan are we going to use?"

"Swap dogs," replied the Bellman simply. "All collies look pretty much the same."

"What about Vestigial Plot Memory?" asked Havisham. "Do we have any smoothers?"

"It's all on the job sheet." The Bellman tore off a sheet of paper and handed it to me. "You do know all about smoothers, of course?"

"Of course!" I replied.

"Good. Any more questions?"

I shook my head.

"Excellent!" exclaimed the Bellman. "Just one more thing. Bradshaw is investigating the Perkins incident. Would you make sure he gets your reports as soon as possible?"

"Of course!"

"Er . . . Good."

He made a few "must get on" noises and left.

As soon as he had gone, I said to Havisham, "Do you think I'm ready for this, ma'am?"

"Thursday," she said in her most serious voice, "listen to me. Jurisfiction has need of agents who can be trusted to do the right thing." She looked around the room. "Sometimes it is difficult to know whom we can trust. Sometimes the sickeningly self-righteous—like you—are the last bastion of defense against those who would mean the BookWorld harm."

"Meaning?"

"Meaning you can stop asking so many questions and do as you're told—just pass this practical first time. Understand?"

"Yes, Miss Havisham."

"That's settled, then. Anything else?"

"Yes. What's a smoother?"

"Do you not read your TravelBook?"

"It's quite long," I pleaded. "I've been consulting it whenever possible but still got no further than the preface."

"Well," she began as we jumped to Wemmick's Stores in the lobby of the Great Library, "plots have a sort of inbuilt memory. They can *spring* back to how they originally ran with surprising ease."

"Like time," I murmured, thinking about my father.

"If you say so. On Internal Plot Adjustment duties we often have to have a smoother—a secondary device that reinforces the primary plot swing. We changed the end of Conrad's *Lord Jim*, you know. Originally, he runs away. A bit weak. We thought it would be better if Jim delivered himself to Chief Doramin as he had pledged following Brown's massacre."

"That didn't work?"

"No. The chief kept on forgiving him. We tried everything. Insulting the chief, tweaking his nose—after the forty-third attempt we were getting desperate; Bradshaw was almost pulling his hair out."

"So what did you do?"

"We retrospectively had the chief's son die in the massacre. It did the trick. The chief had no trouble shooting Jim after that."

I mused about this for a moment. "How did Jim take it? The decision for him to die, I mean?"

"He was the one that asked for the plot adjustment in the first place. He thought it was the only honorable thing to do—mind you, the chief's son wasn't exactly over the moon about it."

"Ah," I said, pondering that here in the BookWorld the pencil of life occasionally *did* have an eraser on the other end.

"So you'll send a check for a hundred pounds to the farmer and buy his pigs for double the market rate—that way, he won't need the cash and won't want to resell Shadow to the film producer. Get it? Good afternoon, Mr. Wemmick."

We had arrived at the stores. Wemmick himself was a short

man, a native of *Great Expectations,* aged about forty with a pock-marked face. He greeted us enthusiastically.

"Good afternoon, Miss Havisham, Miss Next—I trust all is well?"

"Quite well, Mr. Wemmick. I understand you have a few canines for us?"

"Indeed," replied the storekeeper, pointing to where two dogs were attached to a hook in the wall by their leads.

"Pug, Lady Bertram's, to be replaced, one. Shadow, sheepdog, sighted, to swap with existing dog, blind, one. Check for the farmer, value one hundred pounds sterling, one. Cash to buy pigs, forty-two pounds, ten shillings and fourpence. Sign here."

The two dogs panted and wagged their tails. The collie had his eyes bound with a bandage.

"Any questions?"

"Do we have a cover story for this check?" I asked.

"Use your imagination. I'm sure you'll think of something."

"Wait a moment," I said, alarm bells suddenly ringing, "aren't you coming with me to supervise?"

"Not at all!" Havisham grinned with a strange look in her eye. "Assessed work has to be done solo; I'll mark you on your report and the successful—or not—realigned story within the book. This is so simple even *you* can't mess it up."

"Couldn't I do Lady Bertram's pug?" I asked, trying to make it sound like something hard and of great consequence.

"Out of the question! Besides, I don't do children's books any-more—not after the incident with Larry the Lamb. But since *Shadow* is out of print, no one will notice if you make a pig's ear of it. Remember that Jurisfiction is an honorable establishment and you should reflect that in your bearing and countenance. Be resolute in your work and fair and just. Destroy grammasites with extreme prejudice—and shun any men with amorous intentions."

She thought for a moment. "Or *any* intentions, come to that. Have you got your TravelBook to enable you to jump back?"

I patted my breast pocket where the slim volume was kept

and she was gone, only to return a few moments later to swap dogs and vanish again. I read my way diligently to the second floor of the Library and picked *Shadow the Sheepdog* off the shelf. I paused. I was nervous and my palms had started to sweat. I scolded myself. How hard could a plot adjustment in an Enid Blyton be? I took a deep breath and, notwithstanding the simplistic nature of the novel, opened the slim volume with an air of serious trepidation—as though it were *War and Peace*.

19.

Shadow the Sheepdog

Shadow the Sheepdog, the story of a supremely loyal and intelligent sheepdog in a rural prewar countryside, was published by Collins in 1950. A compulsive scribbler from her early teens, Enid Blyton found escape from her own unhappy childhood in the simple tales she wove for children. She has been republished in revised forms to suit modern tastes and has consistently remained popular over five decades. The independently minded children of her stories live in an idealized world of eternal summer holidays, adventure, high tea, ginger beer, cake and grown-ups with so little intelligence that they need everything explained to them—something that is not so very far from the truth.

MILLON DE FLOSS,
Enid Blyton

I READ MYSELF INTO *Shadow's* featured town halfway down page 231. Johnny, the farmer's boy who was Shadow's owner and coprotagonist, would be having Shadow's eyes checked in a few days, so a brief reconnaissance of the locality seemed like a good idea. If I could *persuade* rather than order the vet to swap the dogs, then so much the better. I alighted in a town that looked like some sort of forties English rural idyll—a mix between Warwickshire and the Dales. All green grass, show-quality cattle, yellow-lichened stone walls, sunshine and healthy-looking, smiling people. Horses pulled carts laden high with hay down the main street, and the odd shiny motorcar puttered past. Pies cooled on windowsills and children played with hoops and tinplate steam engines. The smell in the breeze was of freshly mown grass, clean linen and cooking. Here was a world of high tea, tasty trifles, zero crime, eternal summers and boundless good health. I suspected living here might be quite enjoyable—for about a week.

I was nodded at by a passerby.

"Beautiful day!" she said politely.

"Yes. My—"

"Rain later?"

I looked up at the puffy clouds that stretched away to the horizon. "I shouldn't have thought so, but can you—"

"Well, be seeing you!" said the woman politely, and was gone.

I found an alleyway and tied the sheepdog to a downpipe; it was neither useful nor necessary to lead a dog around town for the next few hours. I walked carefully down the road, past a family butcher's, a tearoom and sweetshop selling nothing but gobstoppers, bull's-eyes, ginger beer, lemonade and licorice. A few doors farther on I found a newsagent and post office combined. The outside of the small shop was liberally covered with enamel signs advertising Fry's chocolates, Colman's starch, Wyncarnis tonic, Ovaltine and Lyons cakes. A small sign told me I could use the telephone, and a rack of postcards shared the pavement with boxes of fresh veg. There was also a display of newspapers, the headlines reflecting the interwar politics of the book.

Britain Voted Favorite Empire Tenth Year Running, said one. *Foreigners Untrustworthy, Study Shows*, said another. A third led with *"Spiffing"—New Buzzword Sweeps Nation*.

I posted the "smoother" check to Johnny's father with a covering letter explaining that it was an old loan repaid. Almost immediately a postman appeared on a bicycle and removed the letter—the only one in the postbox, I noted—with the utmost of reverence, taking it into the post office where I could hear cries of wonderment. There weren't many letters in *Shadow*, I assumed. I stood outside the shop for a moment, watching the townsfolk going about their business. Without warning one of the cart horses decided to drop a huge pile of dung in the middle of the road. In a trice a villager had run across with a bucket and shovel and removed the offending article almost as soon as it had happened. I watched for a while and then set off to find the local auctioneers.

"So let me get this straight," said the auctioneer, a heavyset and humorless man with a monocle screwed into his eye, "you want to buy pigs at treble the going rate? Why?"

"Not anyone's pigs," I replied wearily, having spent the last half hour trying to explain what I wanted, "Johnny's father's pigs."

"Quite out of the question," muttered the auctioneer, getting to his feet and walking to the window. He did it a lot, I could tell—there was a worn patch right through the carpet to the floorboards beneath, but only from his chair to the window. There was another worn patch from the door to a side table—the use of which I was yet to understand. Considering his limitations, I guessed the auctioneer was no more than a C-9 Generic—it explained the difficulty of persuading him to alter anything.

"We do things to a set formula here," added the auctioneer, "and we don't very much like change."

He walked back across the worn floorboards to his desk, turned to face me and wagged a reproachful finger.

"And believe me, if you try anything a bit rum at the auction, I can discount your bid."

We stared at each other. This wasn't working.

"Tea and cake?" asked the auctioneer, walking to the window again.

"Thank you."

"Splendid!" He rubbed his hands together and returned to his desk. "They tell me there is *nothing* quite so refreshing as a cup of tea!"

He flipped the switch on the intercom. "Miss Pittman, would you bring in some tea, please?"

The door opened instantaneously to reveal his secretary holding a tray of tea things. She was in her late twenties, and pretty in an English rose sort of way; she wore a floral summer dress under a fawn cardigan.

Miss Pittman followed the smoothly worn-down floorboards and carpet from the door to the side table. She curtsied and laid the tea things next to an identical tray left from an earlier occasion. She threw the old tea tray out the window and I heard the soft tinkle of broken crockery; I had seen a large pile of broken tea things outside the window when I arrived.

His secretary paused, hands pressed tightly together. "Shall— shall I pour you a cup?" she asked, a flush rising to her cheeks.

"Thank you!" exclaimed Mr. Phillips, walking excitedly to the window and back again. "Milk and—"

"One sugar." His secretary smiled shyly. "Yes, yes . . . I know."

"But of course you do!" He smiled back.

Then, the next stage of this odd charade took place. The auctioneer and secretary moved to the place where their two worn paths were closest, the outer limits that their existence and limited story line allowed them. Miss Pittman held the cup by its rim, placed her toes right on the edge where the worn carpet began and shiny floorboard ended, stretching out as far as she could. Mr. Phillips did the same on his side of the divide. The tips of his fingers could just touch the opposite rim of the cup, but try as he might, he could not reach far enough to grasp it.

"Allow me," I said, unable to watch the cruel spectacle any longer. I passed the cup from one to the other.

How many cups of tea had gone cold in the past thirty-five years, I wondered, how uncrossable the six feet of carpet that divided them! Whoever event-managed this book down in the Well had a cruel sense of humor.

Miss Pittman curtsied politely and departed while the auctioneer watched her go. He sat down at his desk, eyeing the teacup thirstily. He licked his lips and rubbed his fingertips in expectation, then took a sip and savored the moment lovingly.

"Oh my goodness!" he said deliriously, "Even better than I thought it would be!"

He took another sip and closed his eyes with the sheer delight of it.

"Where were we?" he asked.

I took a deep breath. "I want you to buy Johnny's father's pigs with an offer that purports to come from an unknown buyer— and as close to the top of page two hundred and thirty-two as you can."

"Utterly impossible! You are asking me to change the narrative! I will have to see higher authority."

I passed him my Jurisfiction ID card. It wasn't like me to pull rank, but I was getting desperate.

"I'm on official business sanctioned by the Council of Genres themselves through Text Grand Central." It was how I thought Miss Havisham might say it.

"You forget that we are out of print pending modernization," he replied shortly, tossing my ID back across the table. "You have no mandatory powers here, *Apprentice* Next. I think Jurisfiction will look very carefully before attempting a change on a book without internal approval. You can tell the Bellman that, from me."

We stared at each other, a diplomatic impasse having arrived.

I had an idea. "How long have you been an auctioneer in this book?"

"Thirty-six years."

"And how many cups of tea have you had in that time?"

"*Including* this one?"

I nodded.

"One."

I leaned forward. "I can fix it for you to have as many cups of tea as you want, Mr. Phillips."

He narrowed his eyes. "Oh, yes? And how would you manage that? As soon as you've got what you want, you'll be off and I'll never be able to reach Miss Pittman's proffered cup again!"

I stood up and went to the table on which the tea tray was lying. It was a small table made of oak and lightly decorated. It had a vase of flowers on it, but nothing else. As Mr. Phillips watched, I picked up the table and placed it next to the window. The auctioneer looked at me dumbfounded, got up, walked to the window and delicately touched the table and the tea things.

"An audacious move," he said, waving the sugar tongs at me, "but it won't work—she's a D-7—she won't be able to change what she does."

"D-7s never have names, Mr. Phillips."

"*I* gave her that name," he said quietly, "you're wasting your time."

"Let's see, shall we?" I spoke into the intercom to ask Miss Pittman to bring in more tea.

The door opened as before and a look of shock and surprise crossed the girl's face.

"The table!" she gasped, rattling the Royal Doulton tea things on the tray. "It's—!"

"You can do it, Miss Pittman," I told her, "just place the tea where you always do."

She moved forward, following the well-worn path, arrived at where the table used to be and then looked at its new position, two strides away. The smooth and unworn carpet was alien and fearful to her; it might as well have been a bottomless chasm. She stopped dead.

"I don't understand—!" she began, her face bewildered as her hands continued to shake.

"Tell her to put the tea things down," I told the auctioneer, who was becoming as distressed as Miss Pittman—perhaps more so. *"Tell her!"*

"Thank you, Miss Pittman," murmured Mr. Phillips, his voice croaking with emotion, "put the tea things down over here, would you?"

She bit her lip and closed her eyes, raised her foot and held it, quivering above the edge of the shiny floorboards. Then she moved it forward and rested it on the soft carpet. She opened her eyes, looked down and beamed at us both.

"Well done!" I said. "Just two more."

Brimming with confidence, she negotiated the two remaining steps with ease and placed the tray on the table. She and Mr. Phillips were closer now than they had ever been before. She put out a hand to touch his lapel, but checked herself quickly.

"Shall—shall I pour you a cup?"

"Thank you!" exclaimed Mr. Phillips. "Milk and—"

"One sugar," She smiled shyly. "Yes, yes, I know."

She poured the tea and handed the cup and saucer to him. He took it gratefully.

"Mr. Phillips?"

"Yes?"

"Do I have a first name?"

"Of course," he replied quietly and with great emotion, "I have had over thirty years to think about it. Your name is Aurora, as befits somebody as beautiful as the dawn."

She covered her nose and mouth to hide her smile and blushed deeply.

Mr. Phillips raised a shaking hand to touch her cheek but stopped as he remembered that I was still present. He nodded imperceptibly in my direction and said, "Thank you, Miss Pittman—perhaps later you might come in for some . . . *dictation*."

"I will look forward to it, Mr. Phillips!"

And she turned, trod softly on the carpet to the door, looked round once more and went out. When I looked back at Mr. Phillips, he had sat down, drained by the emotionally charged encounter.

"Do we have a deal? Or do I put the table back where it was?"

He looked shocked. "You wouldn't."

"I would."

He considered his position for a moment and then offered me his hand. "Pigs at treble the going rate?"

"Top of page two thirty-two."

"Deal."

Pleased with my actions so far, I collected the dog and jumped forward to the middle of page two thirty-two. By now the sale of Johnny's father's pigs was the talk of the town and had even made it into the headlines of the local papers: *Unprecedented Pig Prices Shock Town*. There was only one thing left to do—replace the blind collie for the sighted one.

"I'm looking for the vet," I asked a passerby.

"Are you?" replied the woman amiably. "Good for you!" and she hurried on.

"Could you tell me the way to the vet?" I asked the next person, a sallow man in a tweed suit.

He was no less literal: "Yes, I could." He attempted to walk on. I tried to grasp him by the sleeve but missed and momentarily clasped his hand. He gasped out loud. This was echoed by two women who had witnessed the incident. They started to gossip volubly. I pulled out my ID.

"Jurisfiction," I told him, adding, "on official business," just to make sure he got the picture.

But something had happened. The townsfolk, who up until that moment had seemed to wander the streets like automatons, were all of a sudden animated individuals, talking, whispering and pointing. I was a stranger in a strange land, and while the townsfolk didn't *seem* hostile, I was clearly an object of considerable interest.

"I need to get to the vet," I said loudly. "Now, can anyone tell me where he lives?"

The two ladies who had been chattering suddenly smiled and nodded to one another.

"We'll show you where he works."

I left the first man still staring at his hand and looking at me in an odd way. I didn't take offense. People looked at me oddly quite a lot.

I followed the ladies to a small building set back from the road. I thanked them both, one of whom I noticed remained at the gate while the other bustled away with a purposeful stride. I rang the doorbell.

"Hello?" said the vet, opening the door and looking surprised; he only had one client booked that day—Johnny and Shadow. The vet was meant to tell the young lad how Shadow would stay blind forever.

"This dog," said the vet automatically, "will never see again. I'm sorry, but that's the way it is."

"Jurisfiction," I told him, showing him my ID. "There's been a change of plan."

"What sort of change?" he asked as I gently forced my way in and closed the door. "Are you here to alter the less-than-savory references to stereotypical Gypsy folk in chapters thirteen to fifteen?"

"We'll get round to that, don't you worry."

I wasn't going to take any chances and go through the same rigmarole as I had with Mr. Phillips, so I looked around furtively and said in a conspiratorial whisper, "I shouldn't be telling you this, but . . . wicked men are planning to steal Shadow and sell him off for medical experiments!"

"No!" exclaimed the vet, eyes open wide.

"Indeed," I replied, adding in a hushed tone, "and what's more, we suspect that these men might not even be English."

"You mean . . . Johnny Foreigners?" asked the vet, visibly shocked.

"Probably French. Now, are you with me on this?"

"Absolutely!" he breathed. "What are we going to do?"

"Swap dogs. When Johnny arrives, you tell him to go outside for a moment, we swap the dogs, when he comes back, you unwrap the bandages, the dog can see—and you say this dialogue instead."

I handed him a scrap of paper. He looked at it thoughtfully.

"So Shadow stays here and the *swapped* Shadow is abducted by Johnny Foreigner and used for medical experiments?"

"Something like that. But not a word to anyone, you understand?"

"Word of honor!" replied the vet.

So I gave him the collie, and sure enough, when Johnny brought in the blinded Shadow, the vet told him to go and get some water, we swapped dogs and when Johnny returned, lo and behold, the dog could see again. The vet feigned complete surprise and Johnny, of course, was delighted. They left soon after.

I stepped from the office where I had been hiding.

"How did I do?" asked the vet, washing his hands.

"Perfect. There could be a medal in it for you."

It all seemed to have gone swimmingly well. I couldn't believe my luck. But more than that, I had the feeling that Havisham might actually be quite proud of her apprentice—at the very least this should make up for having to rescue me from the grammasites. Pleased, I opened the door to the street and was surprised to find that a lot of the locals had gathered, and they all seemed to be staring at me. My feeling of euphoria over the completed mission suddenly evaporated as unease welled up inside me.

"It's time! It's time!" announced one of the ladies I had seen earlier.

"Time for what?"

"Time for a wedding!"

"Whose?" I asked, not unreasonably.

"Why *yours*, of course!" she answered happily. "You touched Mr. Townsperson's hand. You are betrothed. *It is the law!*"

The crowd surged towards me and I reached, not for my gun, but for my TravelBook in order to get out quickly. It was the wrong choice. Within a few moments I had been overpowered. They took my book and gun, then held me tightly and propelled me towards a nearby house, where I was forced into a wedding dress that had seen a lot of previous use and was several sizes too big.

"You won't get away with this!" I told them as they hurriedly brushed and plaited my hair with two men holding my head. "Jurisfiction know where I am and will come after me, I swear!"

"You'll get used to married life," exclaimed one of the women, her mouth full of pins. "They *all* complain to begin with—but by the end of the afternoon they are as meek as lambs. Isn't that so, Mr. Rustic?"

"Aye, Mrs. Passerby," said one of the men holding my arms, "like lambs, meek."

"You mean there were others?"

"There is nothing like a good wedding," said one of the other men, "nothing except—"

Here Mr. Rustic nudged him and he was quiet.

"Nothing except *what*?" I asked, struggling again.

"Oh, hush!" said Mrs. Passerby. "You made me drop a stitch! Do you really want to look a mess on your wedding day?"

"Yes."

Ten minutes later, bruised and with my hands tied behind my back and a garland of flowers in my badly pinned hair, I was being escorted towards the small village church. I managed to grab the lych-gate on the way in but was soon pulled clear. A few moments later I was standing at the altar next to Mr. Townsperson, who was neatly dressed in a morning suit. He smiled at me happily and I scowled back.

"We are gathered here today in the eyes of God to bring together this woman and this man . . ."

I struggled but it was no good.

"This proceeding has no basis in law!" I shouted, attempting to drown out the vicar. He signaled to the verger, who placed a bit of sticking plaster over my mouth. I struggled again, but with four burly farmworkers holding me, it was useless. I watched with a sort of strange fascination as the wedding proceeded, the villagers sniveling with happiness in the small church. When it came to the vows, my head was vigorously nodded for me, and a ring pressed on my finger.

". . . I now pronounce you man and wife! You may kiss the bride."

Mr. Townsperson loomed closer. I tried to back away but was held tightly. Mr. Townsperson kissed me tenderly on the sticking plaster that covered my mouth. As he did so, an excited murmur went up from the congregation.

There was applause and I was dragged towards the main door, covered in confetti and made to pose for a wedding photograph. For the picture the sticking plaster was removed so I had time to make my protestations.

"No coerced wedding was ever recognized by law!" I bellowed. "Let me go *right now* and I may not report you!"

"Don't worry, Mrs. Townsperson," said Mrs. Passerby, addressing me, "in ten minutes it really won't matter. You see, we rarely get the opportunity to perform nuptials as no one in here ever gets married—the Well never went so far as to offer us that sort of luxury."

"What about the others you mentioned?" I asked, a sense of doom rising within me. "Where are the other brides who were forced into marriage?"

Everyone looked solemn, clasped their hands together and stared at the ground.

"What's going on? What will happen in ten minutes?"

I turned as the four men let go of me and saw the vicar again. But he wasn't cheery this time. He was solemn, and well he might be. Before him was a freshly dug grave. *Mine.*

"Oh my God!" I muttered.

"Dearly beloved, we are gathered . . . ," began the vicar as the same townsfolk began to sniffle into their hankies again. But this time the tears weren't of happiness—they were of *sorrow.*

I cursed myself for being so careless. Mr. Townsperson had my automatic and released the safety. I looked around desperately. Even if I had been able to get a message to Havisham, I doubted whether she could have made it in time.

"Mr. Townsperson," I said in a quiet voice, staring into his eyes, "my own husband! You would kill your bride?"

He trembled slightly and glanced at Mrs. Passerby. "I'm . . . I'm afraid so, my dear," he faltered.

"Why?" I asked, stalling for time.

"We need the . . . need the—"

"For Panjandrum's sake get on with it or I shall!" snapped Mrs. Passerby, who seemed to be the chief instigator of all this. "I need my emotional fix!"

"Wait!" I said. "You're after *emotion?*"

"They call us *sentiment junkies,*" said Mr. Townsperson sadly. "It's not our fault. We are all Generics rated between C-7 and D-3; we don't have many emotions of our own but are smart enough to know what we're missing."

"If you don't kill her, I shall!" mumbled Mr. Rustic, tapping my "husband" on the elbow.

He pulled away. "She has a right to know. She is my wife, after all." He looked nervously left and right.

"Go on."

"We started with humorous one-liners that offered a small kick. That kept us going for a few months, but soon we wanted more: laughter, joy, happiness in any way we could get it. Thrice-monthly garden fetes, weekly harvest festivals and tombola four times a day were not enough; we wanted . . . the *hard stuff*."

"Grief," murmured Mrs. Passerby, "grief, sadness, sorrow, loss—we wanted it but we wanted it *strong*. Ever read *On Her Majesty's Secret Service*?"

I nodded.

"We wanted that. Our hearts raised by the happiness of a wedding and then dashed by the sudden death of the bride!"

I stared at the slightly crazed Generics. Unable to generate emotions synthetically from within the confines of their happy rural idyll, they had embarked upon a systematic rampage of enforced weddings and funerals to give them the high they desired. I looked at the graves in the churchyard and wondered how many others had suffered this fate.

"We will all be devastated by your death, of course," whispered Mrs. Passerby, "but we will get over it—the slower the better!"

"Wait!" I said. "I have an idea!"

"We don't want ideas, my love," said Mr. Townsperson, pointing the gun at me again, "we want *emotion*."

"How long will this fix last?" I asked him. "A day? How sad can you be for someone you barely know?"

They all looked at one another. I was right. The fix they were getting by killing and burying me would last them until teatime if they were lucky.

"You have a better idea?"

"I can give you more emotion than you know how to handle, feelings so strong you won't know what to do with yourselves."

"She's lying!" cried Mrs. Passerby dispassionately. "Kill her now—I can't wait any longer! I need the sadness! Give it to me!"

"I'm Jurisfiction. I can bring more jeopardy and strife into this book than a thousand Blytons could give you in a lifetime!"

"You could?" echoed the townspeople excitedly, lapping up the expectation I was generating.

"Yes—and here's how I can prove it. Mrs. Passerby?"

"Yes?"

"Mr. Townsperson told me earlier he thought you had a fat arse."

"He said *what*?" she replied angrily, her face suffused with joy as she fed off the hurt feelings I had generated.

"I most certainly said no such thing!" blustered Mr. Townsperson, obviously getting a big hit himself from the indignation.

"Us, too!" yelled the townsfolk excitedly, eager to see what else I had in my bag of goodies.

"Nothing before you untie me!"

They did so with great haste; sorrow and happiness had kept them going for a long time, but they had grown bored—I was here like a dealer, offering new and different experiences.

I asked for my gun and was handed it, the townspeople watching me expectantly like a dodo waiting for marshmallows.

"For a start," I said, rubbing my wrists and throwing the wedding ring aside, "I can't remember who got me pregnant!"

There was a sudden silence.

"Shocking!" said the vicar. "Outrageous, morally repugnant—mmmm!"

"But better than that," I added, "if you had killed me, you would also have killed my unborn son—guilt like that could have lasted for months!"

"Yes!" yelled Mr. Rustic. "Kill her now!"

I pointed the gun at them and they stopped in their tracks.

"You'll always regret not having killed me," I murmured.

The townsfolk went quiet and mused upon this, the feeling of loss coursing through their veins.

"It feels wonderful!" said one of the farmworkers, taking a seat on the grass to focus his mind more carefully on the strange emotional potpourri of a missed opportunity of double murder.

But I wasn't done yet. "I'm going to report you to the Council of Genres and tell them how you tried to kill me—you could be shut down and reduced to text!"

I had them now. They all had their eyes closed and were rocking backwards and forwards, moaning quietly.

"Or perhaps," I added, beginning to back away, "I won't."

I pulled off the wedding dress at the lych-gate and looked back. The townspeople were laid out on the ground, eyes closed, surfing their inner feelings on a cocktail of mixed emotions. They wouldn't be down for days.

I picked up my jacket and TravelBook on the way to the vet's, where the blind Shadow was waiting for me. I had completed the mission, even if I had come a hairsbreadth from a sticky end. I could do better, and would, given time. I heard a low, growly voice close at hand.

"What happens to me? Am I reduced to text?"

It was Shadow.

"Officially, yes."

"I see. And unofficially?"

I thought for a moment.

"Do you like rabbits?"

"Rather."

I pulled out my TravelBook.

"Good. Give me your paw. We're off to Rabbit Grand Central."

20.

Ibb and Obb Named and *Heights* Again

BookStackers: To rid a book of the mispeling vyrus, many thousands of dictionaries are moved into the offending novel and stacked either side of the outbreak as a *mispeling barrage*. The wall of dictionaries is then moved in, paragraph by paragraph, until the vyrus is forced into a single sentence, then a word, then smothered completely. The job is done by BookStackers, usually D-grade Generics, although for many years the Anti-mispeling Fast Response Group (AFRG) has been manned by over five thousand WOLP-surplus Mrs. Danvers. (See *Danvers, Mrs., Over-production of.*)

CAT FORMERLY KNOWN AS CHESHIRE,
Guide to the Great Library

IT WAS THREE days later. I had just had my early-morning vomit and was lying back in bed, staring at Gran's note and trying to make sense of it. One word. *Remember.* What was I meant to remember? She hadn't yet returned from the Medici court, and although the note might have been the product of a Granny Next "fuzzy moment," I still felt uneasy. There was something else. Beside my bed was a sketch of an attractive man in his late thirties. I didn't know who he was—which was odd, because I had sketched it.

There was an excited knock at the door. It was Ibb. It had been looking more feminine all week and had even gone so far as to put on haughty airs all day Wednesday. Obb, on the other hand, had been insisting it was right about everything, knew everything, and had sulked when I proved it wrong, and we all knew where *that* was leading.

"Hello, Ibb," I said, placing the sketch aside, "how are you?"

Ibb replied by unzipping and opening the top of its overalls.

"Look!" she said excitedly, showing me her breasts.

"Congratulations," I said slowly, still feeling a bit groggy, "you're a *her*."

"I know!" said Ibb, hardly able to contain her excitement. "Do you want to see the rest?"

"No, thanks, I believe you."

"Can I borrow a bra?" she asked, moving her shoulders up and down. "These things aren't terribly comfortable."

"I don't think mine would fit you," I said hurriedly, "you're a lot bigger than I am."

"Oh," she answered, slightly crestfallen, then added, "How about a hair tie and a brush? I can't do a thing with this hair. Up, down—perhaps I should have it cut—and I *so* wish it were curly!"

"Ibb, it's fine, really."

"*Lola*," she corrected me, "I want you to call me Lola from now on."

"Very well, Lola, sit on the bed."

So Lola sat while I brushed her hair and she nattered on about a weight-loss idea she had had, which seemed to revolve around weighing yourself with one foot on the scale and one on the floor. Using this idea, she told me, she could lose as much weight as she wanted and not give up cakes. Then she started talking about this great new thing that she had discovered that was so much fun she thought she'd be doing it quite a lot—and she reckoned she'd have no trouble getting men to assist.

"Just be careful," I told her. "Think before you do what you do with whom." It was advice my mother had given me. I expected Lola would ignore it as much as I had.

"Oh, yes," Lola assured me, "I'll be very careful—I'll always ask them their name first."

When I had finished, she stared at herself in the mirror for a moment, gave me a big hug and skipped out the door. I dressed slowly and walked into the kitchen.

Obb was sitting at the table painting a Napoleonic cavalry officer the height of a pen top. He was gazing intently at the miniature horseman and glowering with concentration. He had developed into a dark-haired and handsome man of at least six foot three over the past few days, with a deep voice and measured speech; he also looked about fifty. I suspected *it* was now a *he* but hoped he wouldn't try to demonstrate it in the same way that Lola had.

"Morning, Obb," I said, "breakfast?"

He dropped the horseman on the floor.

"Now look what you've made me do!" he growled, adding, "Toast, please, and coffee—and it's *Randolph,* not Obb."

"Congratulations," I told him, but he only grunted in reply, found the cavalry officer and carried on with his painting.

Lola bounced into the living room, saw Randolph and stopped for a moment to stare at her nails demurely, hoping he would turn to look at her. He didn't. So she stood closer and said:

"Good morning, Randolph."

"Morning," he grunted without looking up, "how did you sleep?"

"Heavily."

"Well, you would, wouldn't you?"

She missed the insult and carried on jabbering. "Wouldn't yellow be prettier?"

Randolph stopped and stared at her. "*Blue* is the color of a Napoleonic cavalry officer, Lola. Yellow is the color of custard—and bananas."

She turned to me and pulled a face, mouthed *square* and then helped herself to coffee.

"Can we go shopping, then?" she asked me. "If we are buying underwear, we might as well get some makeup and some scent; we could try on clothes and generally do girl sort of things together—I could take you out to lunch and gossip a lot, have our hair done and then shop some more, talk about boyfriends and perhaps after that go to the gym."

"It's not *exactly* my sort of thing," I said slowly, trying to figure out what sort of book St. Tabularasa's had thought Lola might be most suitable for. I couldn't remember the last time I had a girls' day out—certainly not this decade. Most of my clothes came mail order—when did I ever have time for shopping?

"Oh, go *on*!" said Lola. "You could do with a day off. What were you doing yesterday?"

"Attending a course on bookjumping using the ISBN positioning system."

"And the day before?"

"Practical lessons in using textual sieves as PageRunner capturing devices."

"And before that?"

"Searching in vain for the Minotaur."

"*Exactly* why you need a break. We don't even have to leave the Well—the latest Grattan catalog is still under construction. We can get in because I know someone who's got a part-time job as a text-justifying engineer. Please say yes. It means so much to me!"

I sighed. "Well, all right—but after lunch. I've got to do my Mary Jones thing in *Caversham Heights* all morning."

Lola jumped up and down and clapped her hands with joy. I had to smile at her childish exuberance.

"You might move up a size, too," said Randolph.

She narrowed her eyes and turned to face him. "And *what* do you mean by that?" she asked angrily.

"Exactly what I said."

"That I'm fat?"

"You said it, not me," replied Randolph, concentrating on his metal soldier.

She picked up a glass of water and poured it into his lap.

"*What the hell did you do that for!*" he spluttered, getting up and grabbing a tea towel.

"To teach you," yelled Lola, wagging a finger at him, "that you can't say *whatever* you want, to *whoever* you want!"

And she walked out.

"What did I say?" said Randolph in an exasperated tone. "Did you see that? She did that for no reason at all!"

"I think you got off lightly," I told him. "I'd go and apologize if I were you."

He thought about this for a few seconds, lowered his shoulders and went off to find Lola, whom I could hear sobbing somewhere near the stern of the flying boat.

"Young love!" said a voice behind me. "Eighteen years of emotions packed into a single week—it can't be easy, now can it?"

"Gran!" I said, whirling round. "When did you get back?"

"Just now." She removed her gingham hat and gloves and passed me some cash.

"What's this?"

"D-3 Generics are annoyingly literal, but it can pay dividends—I asked the cabbie to drive backwards all the way here, and by the end of the trip he owed *me* money. How are things?"

"Well," I sighed, "it's like having a couple of teenagers in the house."

Look upon it as training for having your own children." Gran sat down on a chair and sipped at my coffee.

"Gran?"

"Yes?"

"How did you get here? I mean, you are here, aren't you? You're not just a memory, or something?"

"Oh, I'm real all right." She laughed. "You just need a bit of looking after until we sort out Aornis."

"Aornis?"

"Yes," sighed Gran. "Think carefully for a moment."

I mulled the name around in my mind, and sure enough, Aornis came out of the murk like a ship in fog. But the fog was deep, and other things were hidden within—I could feel it.

"Oh, yes," I murmured, "*her*. What else was I meant to remember?"

"Landen."

He came out of the fog, too. The man in the sketch. I sat down and put my head in my hands. I couldn't believe I'd forgotten him.

"I'd regard it a bit like measles," said Gran, patting my back. "We'll cure you of her, never fear."

"But then I have to go and battle with her again, in the real world?"

"Mnemonomorphs are always easier to contain on the physical plane. Once you have beaten her in your mind, the rest should be easy."

I looked up at her. "Tell me again about Landen."

And she did, for the next hour—until it was time for me to stand in for Mary Jones again.

I drove into Reading in Mary's car, past red minis, blue Morris Marinas and the ubiquitous Spongg Footcare trucks. I had visited the real Reading on many occasions in my life, and although the *Heights* Reading was a fair *impression,* the town was lacking in detail. A lot of roads were missing, the library was a supermarket, the Caversham district was a lot more like Beverly Hills than I remember and the very grotty downtown was more like New York in the seventies. I think I could guess where the author got his inspiration; I suppose it was artistic license—something to increase the drama.

I stopped in a traffic jam and drummed my fingers on the steering wheel. Our investigation of Perkins's death had not made much progress. Bradshaw had found the partially molten padlock and key in the remnants of the castle keep, but it didn't tell us any more. Havisham and I were not having much better luck ourselves: after three days of discreet investigation, only two pieces of information had come to light: Firstly, that only eight members of Jurisfiction had access to *The Sword of the Zenobians,* and that one of them was Vernham Deane. I mention this because he was posted as missing following an excursion into *Ulysses* to try to figure out what had happened to the stolen punctuation in the final chapter, and no one had seen him since. Successive sweeps of *Ulysses* had failed to show that he had been there at all.

In the absence of any more information, Havisham and I had started to discuss the possibility that Perkins might have removed the padlock himself—to clean out the cage or something, although this seemed doubtful. And what about my sabotaged Eject-O-Hat? Neither Havisham nor I had any more idea why I should be considered a threat; as Havisham delighted in pointing out, I was "completely unimportant."

But the big news that had emerged in the past few days was that the time of the UltraWord™ upgrade had been set. Text Grand Central had brought the date forwards a fortnight to coincide with the 923rd Annual BookWorld Awards. During the ceremony Libris would inaugurate the new system before an audience of seven million invited characters. The Bellman told us he had been up to Text Grand Central and seen the new UltraWord™ engines for himself. Sparkling new, each engine could process about a thousand simultaneous readings of each book—the old V8.3 engines were lucky to top a hundred.

I wound down the window and looked out. Traffic jams in Reading weren't uncommon, but they usually moved a *little* bit, and this one had been solid for twenty minutes. Exasperated, I got out of the car and went to have a look. Strangely, there appeared to have been an accident. I say strangely because all the drivers and pedestrians inside *Caversham Heights* were only Generic D-2s to D-9s, and anything as dramatic as an accident was quite outside their brief. As I walked past the eight blue Morris Marinas in front of me, I noticed that each one had an identically damaged front wing and shattered windscreen. By the time I reached the head of the queue, I could see that the incident involved one of the white Spongg Footcare trucks. But this truck was different from the others. Usually, they were unwashed Luton-bodied Fords with petrol streaks near the filler cap and a scratched rollershutter at the rear. This truck had none of these— it was pure white, very boxy and without a streak of dirt on it anywhere. The wheels, I noticed, weren't strictly round, either— they were more like a fifty-sided polygon, which gave an impression of a circle. I looked closer. The tires had no surface detail or texture. They were just flat black, without depth. The driver was no more detailed than the truck; he—or she or it—was pink and cubist with simple features and a pale blue boilersuit. The truck had been turning left and had hit one of the blue Morris Marinas, damaging all of them identically. The driver, a gray-haired man wearing herringbone tweed, was trying to remonstrate with the cubist driver but without much luck. The truck driver turned to face him, tried to speak but then gave up and looked straight ahead, going through the motions of driving the truck even though he was stationary.

"What's going on?" I asked the small crowd that had gathered.

"This idiot turned left when he shouldn't have," explained the gray-haired Morris Marina driver while his identical gray-haired Generic D-4 clones nodded their heads vigorously. "We could all have been killed!"

"Are you okay?" I said to the cubist driver, who looked blankly at me and attempted to change gear.

"I've been driving in *Caversham Heights* since the book was written and never had an accident," carried on the Morris Marina driver indignantly. "This will play hell with my no-claims bonus—and what's more, I can't get any sense out of *him* at all!"

"I saw it all," said another Spongg truck driver—a proper one this time. "Whoever he is he needs to go back to driving school and take a few lessons."

"Well, the show's over," I told them. "Mr. Morris Marina Driver, is your car drivable?"

"I think so," replied the eight identical middle-aged drivers in unison.

"Then get it out of here. Generic Truck Driver?"

"Yes?"

"Find a towrope and get this heap of junk off the road."

He left to do my bidding as the eight Morris Marina drivers drove off in their identically spluttering cars.

I was waving the cars around the stranded truck when there was a crackle in the air. The cubist truck vanished from the roadside, leaving nothing but the faint smell of cantaloupes. I stared at the space left by the truck. The drivers were more than happy that this obstacle to their ordered lives had been removed, and they sounded their horns at me to get out of the way. I examined the area of the road carefully but found nothing except a single bolt made in the same style as the truck—no texture, just the same cubic shape. I walked back to my car, placed it in my bag and drove on.

Jack was waiting for me outside Mickey Finn's Gym, situated above a couple of shops in Coley Avenue. We were there to question a boxing promoter about allegations of fight fixing. It was the best scene in *Caversham Heights*—gritty, realistic—and with good characterization and dialogue. I met Jack slightly earlier while the story was off on a subplot regarding a missing consignment of ketamine, so there was time for a brief word together. *Caversham Heights* wasn't first person—which was just as well, really, as I didn't think Jack had the depth of character to support it.

"Good morning, Jack," I said as I walked up, "how are things?"

He looked a lot happier than the last time I'd seen him and he smiled agreeably, handing me a coffee in a paper cup.

"Excellent, Mary—I should call you Mary, shouldn't I, just in case I have a slip of the tongue when we're being read? Listen, I went to see my wife, Madeleine, last night, and after a heated exchange of opinions we came to some sort of agreement."

"You're going back to her?"

"Not quite." Jack took a sip of coffee. "But we agreed that if I stopped drinking and never saw Agatha Diesel again, she would consider it!"

"Well, that's a start, isn't it?"

"Yes, but it might not be as simple as you think. I received this in the post this morning."

He handed me a letter. I unfolded it and read:

Dear Mr. Spratt,

It has come to our attention that you may be attempting to give up the booze and reconcile with your wife. While we approve of this as a plot device to generate more friction and inner conflicts, we most strongly advise you not to carry it through to a happy reconciliation, as this would put you in direct contravention of Rule 11c of the Union of Sad Loner Detectives' Code, as ratified by the Union of Literary Detectives, and it will ultimately result in your expulsion from the association with subsequent loss of benefits.

I trust you will do the decent thing and halt this damaging and abnormal behavior before it leads to your downfall.

P.S. Despite repeated demands, you have failed to drive a classic car or pursue an unusual hobby. Please do so at once or face the consequences.

"Hmm," I muttered, "it's signed Poi—"

"I know who it's signed by," replied Jack sadly, retrieving the letter. "The union is *very* powerful. They have influence that goes all the way up to the Great Panjandrum. This could hasten the demolition of *Caversham Heights*, not delay it. Father Brown wanted to renounce the priesthood umpteen times, but, well, the union—"

"Jack, what do *you* want?"

"Me?"

"Yes, you."

He sighed. "It's not as simple as that. I have a responsibility for the seven hundred eighty-six other characters in this book. Think of it—all those Generics sold off like post-Christmas turkeys or reduced to text. It makes me shudder just to think about it!"

"That might happen anyway, Jack. At least this way we have a fighting chance. Do your own thing. Break *away* from the norm."

He sighed again and ran his fingers through his hair. "But what about the *conflicts*? Isn't that the point of being a loner detective? The appalling self-destruction, the inner battles within ourselves that add spice to the proceedings and enable the story to advance more interestingly? We can't just have setup–murder–interview–interview–second murder–conjecture–interview–more conjecture–false ending–third murder–dramatic twist–resolution, can we? Where's the interest if a detective *doesn't* get romantically involved with someone who has something to do with the first murder? Why, I might never have to make a choice between justice and my own personal feelings ever again!"

"And what if you don't?" I persisted. "It needn't be like that. There's more than one way to make a story interesting."

"Okay, let's say I *do* live happily with Madeleine and the kids—what am I going to do for subplots? Conflict, for want of a better word, is good. Conflict is right. Conflict *works*."

He gazed at me angrily, but I knew he still believed in himself—that we were even having this conversation proved that.

"It doesn't have to be marital conflicts," I told him. "We could get a few subplots from the Well and sew them in—I agree the action can't always stay with you, but if we— Hello, I think we've got company."

A pink Triumph Herald had pulled up with a middle-aged woman in it. She got out, walked straight up to Jack and slapped him hard in the face.

"How dare you!" she screamed. "I waited three hours for you at the Sad and Single wine bar—what happened?"

"I told you, Agatha. I was with my wife."

"Sure you were," she spat, her voice rising. "Don't patronize me with your pathetic little lies—who are you screwing this time? One of those little tarts down at the station?"

"It's true," he replied in an even voice, more shocked than outraged. "I told you last night—it's all over, Agatha."

"Oh, yes? I suppose *you* put him up to this?" she said, looking at me, scorn and anger in her eyes. "You come down here on a character exchange with your Outlander airs and self-determination bullshit and think you can improve the story line? The supreme arrogance of you people!"

She stopped for a moment and narrowed her eyes. "You're sleeping together, aren't you?"

"No," I told her firmly, "and if there aren't some improvements round here soon, there won't be a book. If you want a transfer out of here, I'm sure I can arrange something—"

"It's all so easy for you, isn't it?" she said, her face convulsing with anger and then fear as her voice rose. "Think you can just make a few footnoterphone calls and everything will be just dandy?" She pointed a long bony finger at me. "Well, I'll tell you, Miss Outlander, I will *not* take this lying down!"

She glared at us both, marched back to her car and drove off with a squeal of tires.

"How about that for a conflictual subplot?" I asked, but Jack wasn't amused.

"Let's see what else you can dream up—I'm not sure I like that one. Did you find out when the Book Inspectorate are due to read us?"

"Not yet."

Jack looked at his watch. "Come on, we've got the fight-rigging scene to do. You'll like this one. Mary was sometimes a little late with the 'If you don't know, we can't help you' line when we did the old good-cop/bad-cop routine, but just stay on your toes and you'll be fine."

He seemed a lot happier having stood up to Agatha, and we walked across the road to where some rusty iron stairs led up to the gym.

Reading, Tuesday. It had been raining all night and the rain-washed streets reflected the dour sky. Mary and Jack walked up the steel steps that led to Mickey Finn's. A lugubrious gym that smelt of sweat and dreams, where hopefuls tried to spar their way out of Reading's underclass. Mickey Finn was an ex-boxer himself, with scarred eyes and a tremor to prove it. In latter days he was a trainer, then a manager. To-day he just ran the gym and dabbled in drugs on the side.

"Who are we here to see?" asked Mary as their feet rang out on the iron treads.

"Mickey Finn," replied Jack. "He got caught up in some trouble a few years ago and I put in a good word. He owes me."

They reached the top and opened the doo—

It was a good job the door opened outwards. If it had opened inwards, I would not be here to tell the tale. Jack teetered on the edge and I grabbed his shoulder and pulled him back. The only part of Mickey Finn's that remained were short floorboards that changed to descriptive prose less than a foot out, the ragged ends whipping and fluttering like pennants in the wind. Beyond these remnants was nothing but a dizzying drop to a bleak and wind-swept sea, whipped up into a frenzy by a typhoon. The waves rose and fell, carrying with them small ships that looked like trawlers, the sailors on board covered in oilskins. But the sea wasn't water as I knew it, the waves here were made of *letters*. Every now and then they would coalesce and a word or sentence would burst enthusiastically from the surface, where it would be caught by the sailors who held nets on long poles.

"Blast!" said Jack. "Damn and blast!"

"What is it?" I asked as a word that spelled *saxophone* came barreling towards us, changing to a *real* saxophone as it crossed the threshold and hit the ironwork of the staircase with a crash. The clouds of individual letters in the sky above the wave-tossed sea contained punctuation marks that swirled in ugly patterns. Now and then a bolt of lightning struck the sea and the let-ters swirled near the point of discharge, spontaneously creat-ing words.

"The Text Sea!" yelled Jack against the rush of wind. We attempted to close the door against the gale as a grammasite flew past with a loud "Gark!" and expertly speared a verb that had jumped from the sea at a badly chosen moment.

We pressed our weight against the door and it closed. The wind abated, the thunder now merely a distant rumble behind the half-glazed door. I picked up the bent saxophone.

"I had no idea the Text Sea looked like anything at all," I said, panting. "I thought it was just an abstract notion."

"Oh, it's real all right," replied Jack, picking up his hat, "as real as anything is down here. The LiteraSea is the basis for all prose written in roman script. It's connected to the Searyllic Ocean somewhere, but I don't know the details. You know what this means, don't you?"

"That scene stealers have been at work?"

"It looks more like a deletion to me," replied Jack grimly, "*excised*. The whole kerfuffle. Characters, setting, dialogue, subplot and the narrative-turning device regarding the fight-fixing that the writer had pinched from *On the Waterfront*."

"Where to?"

"Probably to another book by the same author," sighed Jack. "Kind of proves we won't be long for the Well. It's the next nail in the coffin."

"Can't we just jump into the next chapter and the discovery of the drug dealer shot dead when the undercover buy goes wrong?"

"It would never work," said Jack, shaking his head. "Let me see—I wouldn't have known about Hawkins's involvement with Davison's master plan. More importantly, Mickey Finn would have no reason to be killed if he didn't talk to me, so he would have been there to stop the fight before Johnson placed his three-hundred-thousand-pound bet—and the heartwarming scene in the last two pages of the book with the young lad will make no sense unless I meet him here first. Shit. There isn't a holesmith anywhere in the Well who can fill this one. We're finished, Thursday. As soon as the book figures the gym scene has gone, the plot will start to spontaneously unravel. We'll have to declare literary insolvency. If we do it quick, we might be able to get most of the major parts reassigned to another book."

"There must be *something* we can do!"

Jack thought for a moment. "No, Thursday. It's over. I'm calling it."

"Hang on. What if we come in again, but instead of us *both* walking up the stairs, you start at the top, meet me coming up and explain what you have just found out. We jump straight from there to chapter eight and . . . you're looking at me a bit oddly."

"Mary—"

"Thursday."

"Thursday. That would make chapter seven only a page long!"

"Better than nothing."

"It won't work."

"Vonnegut does it all the time."

He sighed. "Okay. Lead on, maestro."

I smiled and we jumped back three pages.

Reading, Tuesday. It had been raining all night and the rain-washed streets reflected the dour sky. Mary was late and she met Jack walking down the stairway from an upstairs gymnasium, his feet ringing on the iron treads.

"Sorry I'm late," said Mary, "I had a puncture. Did you meet up with your contact?"

"Y-es," replied Jack. "Had you visited the gym—which you haven't of course—you would have found it a lugubrious place that smells of sweat and dreams, where hopefuls try to spar their way out of Reading's underclass."

"Who were you seeing?" asked Mary as they walked back to her car.

"Mickey Finn, ex-boxer with scarred eyes and a tremor to match. He told me that Hawkins was involved with Davison's master plan. There is talk of a big shipment coming in on the fifth and he also let slip that he was going to see Jethro—the importance of which I won't understand until later."

"Anything else?" asked Mary, looking thoughtful.

"No."

"Are you sure?"

"Yes."

"Are you *sure* you're sure?"

"Er . . . No, wait. I've just remembered. There was this young kid there up for his first fight. It could make him. Mickey said he was the best he'd ever seen—he could be a contender."

"Sounds like you had a busy morning," said Mary, looking up at the gray sky.

"The busiest," answered Jack, pulling up his jacket around his shoulders. "Come on, I'll buy you lunch."

The chapter ended and Jack covered his face with his hands and groaned.

"I can't believe I said 'the importance of which I won't understand until later.' They'll never buy it. It's *rubbish!*"

"Listen," I said, "stop fretting. It'll be fine. We just have to hold the book together long enough to figure out a rescue plan."

"What have we to lose?" replied Jack with a good measure of stoicism. "You get up to Jurisfiction and see what you can find out about the Book Inspectorate. I'll hold a few auditions and try to rebuild the scene from memory."

He paused.

"And, Thursday?"

"Yes?"

"Thanks."

I drove back to the flying boat. Having said I wasn't going to get involved with any internal politics, I was surprised by how much of a kinship with *Caversham Heights* I was feeling. Admittedly, the book was pretty dreadful, but it was no worse than the average Farquitt—perhaps I felt this way because it was my home.

"Are we going shopping now?" asked Lola, who had been waiting for me. "I need something to wear for the BookWorld Awards the week after next."

"Are you invited?"

"We all are," she breathed excitedly. "It's going to be quite an event!"

"It certainly will," I said, going upstairs. Lola followed me and watched from my bed as I changed out of Mary's clothes.

"You're quite important at Jurisfiction, aren't you?"

"Not really," I replied, trying to do up my trouser button and realizing that it was tighter than normal. "Blast!" I said.

"What?"

"My trousers are too small."

"Shrunk?"

"No . . ." I stared into the mirror. There was no doubt about it. I was starting to put on a small amount of girth. I stared at it this way and that and Lola did the same, trying to figure out what I was looking at.

Catalog shopping from the inside was a lot more fun than I had thought. Lola squeaked with delight at all the clothes on offer and tried about thirty different types of perfume before deciding not to buy any at all—she, in common with nearly all bookpeople, had no sense of smell. Watching her was like letting a child loose in a toy store—and her energy to shop was almost unbelievable. It was while we were on the lingerie page that she asked me about Randolph.

"What do you think of him?"

"Oh, he's fine," I replied noncommittally, sitting on a chair and thinking of babies while Lola tried on one bra after another, each of which she seemed to love to bits until the next one. "Why do you ask?"

"Well, I rather like him in a funny kind of way."

"Does he like you?"

"I'm not sure. I think that's why he ignores me and makes jokes about my weight. Men always do that when they're interested. It's called subtext, Thursday—I'll tell you all about it someday."

"Okay," I said slowly, "so what's the problem?"

"He doesn't really have a lot of, well, *charisma*."

"There are lots of men out there, Lola, don't hurry. When I

220

was seventeen, I had the hots for this complete and utter flake named Darren. My mother disapproved, which made him into something of a magnet."

"Ah! What about this bra?"

"I thought the pink suited you better."

"Which pink? There were twelve."

"The sixth pink, just after the tenth black and nineteenth lacy."

"Okay, let's look at that one again." She rummaged through the pile, found what she wanted. "Thursday?"

"Yes?"

"Randolph calls me a tart because I like boys. Do you think that's fair?"

"It's one of the great injustices of life. If he did the same, he'd be toasted as a 'ladies' man.' But, Lola, have you met anyone who you *really* like, someone with whom you'd like to spend more *exclusive* time with?"

"You mean—a boyfriend?"

"Yes."

She paused and looked at herself in the mirror. "I don't think I'm written that way, Thurs. But you know, sometimes—just afterwards, you know—when there is that really nice moment and I'm in his big strong arms and feeling sleepy and warm and contented, I can feel there is something that I need just outside my grasp—something I want but can't have."

"You mean love?"

"No—a Mercedes."

She wasn't joking.[1]

It was my footnoterphone.

"Hang on, Lola—Thursday speaking."[2]

I looked at Lola, who was trying on a basque.

"Yes," I replied, "why?"[3]

---

1. "Thursday, are you there?"
2. "It's the Cheshire Cat. Do you know how to play the piano?"
3. "Oh, no reason; I just thought I'd ask to be on the safe side."

"The safe side of what?"[4]

"I see. What can I do for you apart from answering questions about pianos?"[5]

I wasn't busy. Apart from a Jurisfiction session tomorrow at midday, I was clear.

"Sure. Where and when?"[6]

"Okay."

Lola was looking at me mournfully. "Does this mean we'll have to miss out on the gym? We have to go to the gym—if I don't, I'll feel guilty about eating all those cakes."

"What cakes?"

"The ones I'm going to eat on the way to the gym."

"I think you get enough exercise, Lola. But we've got half an hour yet—c'mon, I'll buy you a coffee."

4. "Why the *piano*, of course!"

5. "You've got a hearing for your trial—remember the Fiction Infraction? Well, there have been some delays with Max De Winter's appeal, so they've applied for a continuance—can you come this afternoon if you're not too busy, say three o'clock?"

6. "*Alice in Wonderland*, just after the 'Alice's Evidence' chapter. The Gryphon will be representing you. Don't forget—three o'clock."

21.

Who Stole the Tarts?

My first adult foray into the BookWorld had not been without controversy. I had entered *Jane Eyre* and changed the ending. Originally, Jane goes off to India with the drippy St. John Rivers, but in the ending that I engineered, Jane and Rochester married. I made the decision from the heart, which I had not been trained to do but couldn't help myself. Everyone liked the new ending but my actions weren't without criticism. Technically I had committed a Fiction Infraction, and I would have to face the music. My first hearing in Kafka's *The Trial* had been inconclusive. The trial before the King and Queen of Hearts in *Alice in Wonderland* would not be as strange—it would be stranger.

THURSDAY NEXT,
The Jurisfiction Chronicles

THE GRYPHON WAS a creature with the head and wings of an eagle and the body of a lion. In his youth he must have been a frightening creature to behold, but in his later years he wore spectacles and a scarf, which somewhat dented his otherwise fearsome appearance.

He was, I was told, one of the finest legal eagles around, and after Snell's death he became head of the Jurisfiction legal team. It was the Gryphon who secured the record payout in the celebrated *Farmer's Wife v. Three Blind Mice* case, and he was instrumental in reducing Nemo's piracy charges to "accidental manslaughter."

The Gryphon was reading my notes when I arrived and made small and incomprehensible noises as he flicked through the pages, grunting here and there and staring at me over his spectacles with large eyes.

"Well!" he said. "We should be in for some fun now!"

"Fun?" I repeated. "Defending a Class II Fiction Infraction?"

"I'm prosecuting a class action for blindness against the Triffids this afternoon," said the Gryphon soberly, "and the Martians' war crimes trial in *War of the Worlds* just drags on and on. Believe me, a Fiction Infraction is fun. Do you want to see my caseload?"

"No, thanks."

"Okay. We'll see what their witnesses have to say and how Hopkins presents his case. I may decide not to put you on the stand. Please don't do anything stupid like grow—it nearly destroyed Alice's case there and then. And if the Queen orders your head to be cut off, ignore her."

"Okay," I sighed, "let's get on with it."

The King and Queen of Hearts were seated on their thrones when we arrived, but they were the only people in the courtroom who were seemingly composed—Alice's exit two pages earlier had caused a considerable amount of distress to the jury, who were back in their places but were bickering furiously with the foreman, a rabbit who stared back at them, nibbling a large carrot that he had somehow smuggled in.

The Knave of Hearts was being escorted back to the cells, and the tarts—exhibit A—were being taken away and replaced by the original manuscript of *Jane Eyre*. Seated before the King and Queen was prosecuting attorney Mathew Hopkins and a collection of severe-looking birds. He glared at me with barely concealed venom. He looked a lot less amused since we had last crossed swords in *The Trial*, and he hadn't looked particularly amused then. The King was obviously the judge because he wore a large wig, but quite which part the Queen of Hearts was to play in the proceedings, I had no idea.

The twelve jurors calmed down and all started writing busily on their slates.

"What are they doing?" I whispered to the Gryphon. "The trial hasn't even begun yet!"

"Silence in court!" yelled the White Rabbit in a shrill voice.

"Off with her head!" yelled the Queen.

The King put on his spectacles and looked anxiously round to find out who had been talking. The Queen nudged him and nodded in my direction.

"You there!" he said. "You will have your say soon enough, Miss, Miss . . ."

"Next," put in the White Rabbit after consulting his parchment.

"Really?" replied the King with some confusion. "Does that mean we're done?"

"No, Your Majesty," replied the White Rabbit patiently, "her name is Next. *Thursday* Next."

"I suppose you think that's funny?"

"No, indeed, Your Majesty," I replied. "It was the name I was born with."

The jurymen all frantically started to write "It was the name I was born with" on their slates.

"You're an Outlander, aren't you?" said the Queen, who had been staring at me for some time.

"Yes, Your Majesty."

"Then answer me this: When there are two people and one of them has left, who is left? The person who *is* left or the person who *has* left? I mean, they can't both be left, can they?"

"Herald, read the accusation!" said the King.

On this, the White Rabbit blew three blasts on the trumpet, then unrolled the parchment scroll and read as follows:

"Miss Thursday Next is hereby accused of a Fiction Infraction Class II against the Jurisfiction penal code FAL/0605937 and pursuant to the BookWorld general law regarding continuity of plotlines, as ratified to the Council of Genres, 1584."

"Consider your verdict," said the King to the jury.

"Objection!" cried the Gryphon. "There's a great deal to come before that!"

"Overruled!" shouted the King, adding, "Or do I mean 'sustained'? I always get the two mixed up—it's a bit like is it 'feed a cold and starve a fever' or 'starve a cold and feed a fever'? I never know. At any rate, you may call the first witness."

The White Rabbit blew three more blasts on the trumpet and called out, "First witness!"

The first witness was Mrs. Fairfax, the housekeeper at Thornfield Hall, Rochester's home. She blinked and looked around the court slowly, smiling at Hopkins and glaring at me. She was assisted into the witness box by an usher who was actually a large guinea pig.

"Do you promise to tell the whole truth and nothing but the truth?" asked the White Rabbit.

"I do."

"Write that down," the King said to the jury, and the jury eagerly all wrote "write that down" on their slates.

"Mrs. Fairfax," began Hopkins, rising to his feet, "I want you to tell me in your own words the events surrounding Miss Next's intrusion into *Jane Eyre*, starting at the beginning and not stopping until you get to the end."

"And then what?" asked the King.

"Then she may stop," said Hopkins with a trace of annoyance.

"Ah," said the King in the voice of someone who thinks he understands a great deal but is sadly mistaken, "proceed."

For the next two hours we listened to not only Mrs. Fairfax but Grace Poole, Blanche Ingram and St. John Rivers all giving evidence to explain the old ending and how by calling "Jane Jane Jane!" at Jane's bedroom I had changed the narrative completely. The jury tried to keep up with the proceedings, and they wrote as and when directed by the King until there was no more room on their slates and they tried to write on the benches in front of them, and failing that, on each other.

After every witness, the smallest dormouse in the jury was excused for a trip to the bathroom, which gave the Gryphon time to explain to the King—who probably wouldn't have been able to touch his head with his eyes shut—the procedure of the law. When the dormouse returned, the witness was given to the Gryphon for cross-examination, and every time he called, "No further questions." The afternoon wore on and it became hotter in the courtroom. The Queen grew more and more bored and seemed to demand the verdict on a more and more frequent basis, once even asking during a witness's testimony.

And all during this tedious performance, as the characters from *Jane Eyre* came and repeated the truth in front of me, a seemingly endless parade of guinea pigs interrupted the proceedings. Each one was immediately set upon and placed headfirst into a large canvas bag, then ejected from the court. Each time this happened, there followed a quite inordinate amount of confusion, cries and noise. As the din grew to a fever pitch, the Queen would scream "Off with his head! Off with his head!" as though she were somehow in direct competition with the tumult. By the time another guinea pig had been thrown from the court, Grace Poole had vanished in a cloud of alcoholic vapors, and no one knew where she was.

"Never mind!" said the King with an air of great relief. "Call the next witness." He added in an undertone to the Queen, "Really, my dear, *you* must cross-examine the next witness. It quite makes my forehead ache!"

I watched the White Rabbit as he fumbled over the list and read out at the top of his shrill little voice, "Thursday Next!"

"Excuse me," said the Gryphon, stirring himself from the lethargy he had shown throughout the trial, "but Miss Next will not be giving evidence against herself in this court of law."

"Is that allowed?" asked the King. The jury all looked at one another and shrugged.

"It proves she's guilty!" screamed the Queen. "Off with her head! Off with—"

"It proves nothing of the sort," interrupted the Gryphon. The Queen went scarlet and would probably have exploded had not the King laid his hand on her arm.

"Come come, my dear," he said softly, "you must stay calm. All these orders of execution are probably not good for your hearts."

He chuckled. "Hearts," he said again. "I say, I've made a joke that's rather good, don't you think?"

The jury all laughed dutifully and the brighter ones explained to the more stupid ones what the joke was, and the stupid ones explained to the even stupider ones what a joke actually *is*.

"Excuse me," said the dormouse again, "may I go to the bathroom?"

"Again?" bellowed the King. "You must have a bladder the size of a peanut."

"A grain of rice, so please Your Majesty," said the dormouse, knees knocking together.

"Very well," said the King, "but make it quick. Now, can we reach a verdict?"

"*Now* who wants a verdict?" asked the Queen triumphantly.

"There's more evidence to come yet, please Your Majesty," said the White Rabbit, jumping up in a great hurry. "We have to hear from the defense yet."

"The defense?" asked the King wearily. "Haven't we just heard from them?"

"No, Your Majesty," replied the White Rabbit, "that was the prosecution."

"The two always confuse me," replied the King, staring at his feet, "a bit like that 'Overruled' and 'Sustained' malarkey—which was which again?"

"The prosecution rests," said Hopkins, who could see that this trial might last for months if he didn't get a move on, "and I think we have conclusively proved that Miss Next not only changed the ending of *Jane Eyre* but was also premeditated in her actions. This is not a court of opinion, it is a court of law, and there is only one verdict which this court can reach—guilty."

"I told you she was guilty," muttered the King, getting up to leave.

"Please Your Majesty," said the White Rabbit, "that was just the prosecution summing up. You must listen to the defense now."

"Ah!" said the King, sitting down again.

The Gryphon stood up and walked to the jury box. They all recoiled in fear as he scratched his chin with a large paw. The dormouse put up his hand to be excused and was allowed to leave. When he had returned, the Gryphon began.

"The question here is not whether Miss Next took a few textual and narrative liberties with the end of *Jane Eyre*, as my learned friend the prosecution has made so abundantly clear. We admit that she did."

There was a gasp from the jury.

"No, I contend that whilst Miss Next broke the law in a technical sense, she did so for the best possible motives—love."

The Gryphon paused for dramatic effect.

"Love?" said the King, "Is that a defense?"

"Historically speaking," whispered the White Rabbit, "one of the best, Your Majesty."

"Ah!" said the King. "Proceed."

"And not for her own love, either," continued the Gryphon. "She did it so that two others who were in love might stay that way and not be parted. For such things are against the natural order, a court far higher than the court Miss Next faces today."

There was silence, so he continued:

"I contend that Miss Next is a very extraordinary person with a selfless streak that demands the highest leniency from this court. I have only one witness to call, who will prove the veracity of this defense. I call . . . *Edward Rochester!*"

There was a sharp intake of breath and the remaining guinea pig fainted clean away. The clerks of the court, unsure what to do, popped the guinea pig in a sack and sat on it.

"Call Edward Rochester!" cried the White Rabbit in his shrill voice, a demand that was echoed four times in a succession of voices each diminished further by the distance.

We heard his footfalls shuffle on the floor before we saw him, a slightly hesitant stride with the click of a cane for punctuation. He walked slowly into the courtroom with a fragile yet resolute air and scanned the room carefully to gauge, as well as he could, which of the shapes before him were judge and jury and counsel. The change I had wrought upon *Jane Eyre* had not been without its price. Rochester had lost a hand and only had the milkiest vision in one eye only. I put my hand to my mouth as I watched his form shuffle into the silenced courtroom. If I had known the outcome of my actions, would I still have taken them? Acheron's perfidy had been the author of Rochester's ills, but I had been the catalyst.

Edward's face was healed, although badly scarred, but it did no desperate harm to his looks. He took the oath, his features glowering beneath the dark hair that hung in front of his face.

"Excuse me," said the dormouse who was sitting closest to Rochester, "would you sign my slate, please?"

Rochester gave a dour half smile, took the stylus and said, "Name?"

"Geoffrey."

Rochester signed and returned the slate and was instantly handed eleven more, all wiped clean of their carefully written notes.

"Enough!" roared the King. "I will not have my court turned into a haven for autograph hunters! We pursue the truth here, not celebrities!"

There was dead silence.

"But if you wouldn't mind . . . ," said the King, passing down his notebook to Rochester and adding quietly, "It's for my daughter."

"And your daughter's name?" asked Rochester, pen poised.

"Rupert."

Rochester signed the book and passed it back.

"Mr. Rochester," said the Gryphon, "I wonder if you might expound in your own words what Miss Next's actions have done for you?"

The court fell silent. Even the King and Queen were interested to see what Mr. Rochester had to say.

"To me alone?" replied Rochester slowly. "Nothing. For *us,* my own dear sweet Jane and I—everything!"

He clenched the hand that carried his wedding ring, rubbing the band of gold with his thumb, trying to turn his feelings into words.

"What has Miss Next *not* done for us?" he intoned quietly. "She has given us everything we could want. She has released us both from a prison that was not of our making, a dungeon of depression from which we thought we should never be free. Miss Next gave us the opportunity to love and be loved—I can think of no greater gift anyone could have been given, no word in my head can express the thanks that is ours, for her."

There was silence in the courtroom. Even the Queen had fallen quiet and was staring—quite like a fish, I thought—at Rochester.

The Gryphon's voice broke the silence: "Your witness."

"Ah!" said Hopkins, gathering his thoughts. "Tell me, Mr. Rochester, just to confirm one point: Did Miss Next change the end of your novel?"

"Although I am now, as you see, maimed," replied Rochester, "no better than the old lightning-struck chestnut tree in Thornfield orchard, I am happier than I have ever been. Yes, sir, Miss Next changed the ending, and I thank her every evening for it!"

Hopkins smiled. "No further questions."

"Well," said the Gryphon after the court had been adjourned for the King to consider what form the sentence should take. The Queen, unusually for her, had called for acquittal. The word sounded alien on her lips and everyone stared at her with shock and surprise when she said it—Bill the lizard almost choked and had to be slapped on the back.

"The outcome was a foregone conclusion," said the Gryphon, nodding his respect to Hopkins, who was organizing some notes with the White Rabbit, "but I knew Rochester would put on a good show for you. The King and Queen of Hearts may be the stupidest couple to ever preside upon a court, but they are, after all, *Hearts,* and since you were undeniably guilty, we needed a court to show a bit of compassion when it came to sentencing."

"Compassion?" I echoed with some surprise. "With the Queen of 'Off with her head'?"

"It's just her little way," replied the Gryphon, "she never actually executes anyone. I was just worried for a moment that they might try to hold you on remand until the sentencing, but fortunately the King isn't very up on legal terminology."

"What do you think I'll get?"

"Do you know, I have absolutely no idea. Time will tell. I'll see you around, Next!"

I made my way slowly back to the Jurisfiction offices, where I found Miss Havisham.

"How did it go?" she asked.

"Guilty as charged."

"Bad luck. When's the sentencing?"

"Not a clue."

"Might not be for years, Thursday. I've got something for you."

She passed me across the report I had written for her regarding *Shadow the Sheepdog.* I read the mark on the cover, then read it again, then looked at Havisham.

"A-plus-plus Hons?" I echoed incredulously.

"Think I'm being overgenerous?"

"Well, yes," I said, feeling confused. "I was forcibly married and then nearly murdered!"

"Marriage by force is not recognized, Next. But bear this in mind: we've given that particular assignment to every new Jurisfiction apprentice for the past thirty-two years and every single one has failed."

I gaped at her.

"Even Harris Tweed."

"Tweed was married to Mr. Townsperson?"

"Apart from that bit. He didn't even manage to buy the pigs—let alone fool the vet. You did well, Next. Your cause-and-effect technique is good. Needs work, but good."

"Oh!" I said, kind of relieved, then added after a moment's reflection, "But I could have been killed!"

"You wouldn't have been killed. Jurisfiction has eyes and ears everywhere—we're not that reckless with our apprentices. Your multiple-choice mark was ninety-three percent. Congratulations. Pending final submissions to the Council of Genres, you're made."

I thought about this and felt some pride in it, despite knowing in my heart of hearts that this would not be a long appointment—as soon as I could return to the Outland, I would.

"Did you find out anything about Perkins?"

"Nothing," I replied. "Any news of Vernham Deane?"

"Vanished without trace. The Bellman's going to talk to us about it."

"Could the two be related?"

"Perhaps," she said slightly mysteriously. "I'll have to make further inquiries. Ask me again tomorrow."

22.

Crimean Nightmares

Echolocator: An artisan who will enter a book close to publication and locate and destroy echoed words in the work. As a general rule, identical words (with exceptions such as names, small words and modified repetitions) cannot be repeated within fifteen words as it interrupts the smooth transfer of images into the reader's mind. (See *ImaginoTransferenceDevice User's Manual*, page 782.) Although echoes can be jarring to the eye, they are more jarring when read out loud, which belies their origin from the first OralTrad Operating System. (See also *OralTradPlus, Operating Systems, History of.*)

CAT FORMERLY KNOWN AS CHESHIRE,
Guide to the Great Library

"AH!" SAID GRAN as I walked in the door. "There you are! How were things at work today?"

"Good and bad," I told her, sitting on a sofa and undoing the top button of my trousers. "The good news is I passed the Jurisfiction practical; the bad news is that I was found guilty of my Fiction Infraction."

"Did they tell you the sentence?"

"I'll have to wait for that."

"Waiting's the worst part," she murmured. "I was up for murder once and the worst part of it all was waiting for the jury to come back with their verdict. Longest eight hours of my life."

"I believe you. Did you go home today?"

She nodded. "I brought you a few bits and bobs. I notice there

234

is no chocolate here in the WOLP—nothing worth eating, anyway."

"Did you find out anything about Yorrick Kaine?"

"Not much," replied Gran, eating the chocolate she had brought for me, "but he's not in hiding or anything. He's bought another publishing house and at the same time trying to rebuild his political career after that *Cardenio* debacle."

"Ah. Where are Lola and Randolph?"

"At a party, I think. You look all done in—why don't you get an early night?"

"And have what's-her-name pester me?"

Gran looked at me seriously through her large-framed spectacles. "Aornis. It's Aornis. Remember?"

"Yes. Who was my husband again?"

"Landen. He was eradicated by the ChronoGuard, yes?"

I remembered and my heart sank. "Yes," I said in a quiet voice. I had been happy in my nonremembering state, but now I could feel the anger rising again.

"Sometimes I think it would be better if I just forgot, Gran."

"*Never* say that, Thursday!" said Gran so sharply I jumped, and she had to rest for a moment to get her breath back and eat a few more chocolates. "Aornis has no right to take that which does not belong to her, and you must be strong with her, and yourself—retake your memories!"

"Easier said than done, Gran." I tried to grab a chocolate as they were pulled out of my reach. "I want to dream about—"

"Landen."

"—Landen, yes—I want to dream about him again. He's there but we don't talk like we used to."

The door banged open and Randolph walked in. He ignored us both and hung up his coat.

"Randolph?" I said. "You okay?"

"Me?" he said, not looking at either of us. "I'm fine—it's that little tarty little bitchlet who's going to come to a sticky end—she can't talk to a man without wanting to add him to her collection!"

And he walked out.

"Is she all right?" I called after him, but all we heard was the door to their bedroom slam shut. We looked at each other and shrugged.

"Where were we?"

"I was telling you how I never dream about Landen the way I used to. We used to go to the really great memories we shared. We never got to—you know—but it was wonderful—at least I had *some* control of where I went when the 'Sable Goddess' laid down her cloak."

Gran looked at me and patted my hand reassuringly. "You need to make her feel she's winning, Thursday. Lull her into a trap. She might *think* she is in command, but she's only in your mind and *you* are the one that controls what you think. Our memories are precious and should never be sullied by an outside agent."

"Of course—but how?"

"Well," said Gran, passing me a chocolate she didn't like, "it isn't Aornis up there, my dear, it's only your *memory* of her. She's alone and afraid, too. Without the real Aornis here in the BookWorld she doesn't have so much power; all she can do is try and—"

The door burst open again. This time it was Lola. She looked as though she had been crying. She stopped dead when she saw us.

"Ah!" she said. "Is rat-face shit-for-brains in?"

"Do you mean Randolph?"

"Who else?"

"Then, yes, he is."

"Right!" she announced. "I'll go and sleep over at Nemo's." She started to leave.

"Wait!" I said. "What's going on?"

She stopped and put her hands on her hips. Her bag slid down and hung off her elbow, which spoiled the illusion, but Lola was past caring.

"I went to meet him for coffee after college, and blow me if he's not talking to that little D-2 runt—you know, the one with the squinty eyes and the stupid, snorty laugh?"

"Lola," I said quietly, "they were probably just talking."

She looked at her hands for a moment. "You're right. And what do I care anyway? They clearly deserve one another!"

"I heard that!" said a voice from the back of the flying boat. Randolph strode into the room and waved a finger at Lola, who glared back angrily.

"You've got a nerve accusing me of being with another woman when you've slept with almost everyone at school!"

"And so what if I have?" screamed Lola. "Who are you, my father? Have you been spying on me?"

"Even the worst spy in the genre couldn't fail to notice what you're up to—don't you know the meaning of the word *discretion*?"

"One-dimensional!"

"Cardboard!"

"Stereotype!"

"Predictable!"

"Jerkoff!"

"*Arsehole!*"

"Duck, Gran," I whispered as Lola picked up a vase and threw it at Randolph. It missed and went sailing over the top of our heads to shatter on the far wall.

"Okay," I said loudly, using my best and most assertive voice, "any more crap out of you two and you can live somewhere else. Randolph. You can sleep on the sofa. Lola, you can go to your room—and if I hear a peep out of either of you, I'll have you both allocated to knitting patterns—*get it?*"

They went quiet, mumbled something about being sorry and walked slowly from the room.

"Oh, that was good, balls-for-brains," muttered Lola as they moved off, "get us both into trouble, why don't you?"

"Me?" he returned angrily. "Your knickers are off so often I'm amazed you bother with them at all."

"*Did you hear me?*" I yelled after them, and there was quiet.

I sat down next to Gran again, who was picking bits of broken vase from the tabletop.

"Where were we?" she asked

"Er . . . retaking my memories?"

"Exactly so. She'll be wanting to try and break you down, so things are going to get worse before they get better—only when she thinks she has defeated you can we go on the offensive."

"What do you mean by getting worse? Hades? Landen's eradication? Darren? How far do I have to go?"

"Back to the worst time of all—the truth about what happened during the charge."

"Anton." I groaned and rubbed my face. "I don't want to go back there, Gran, I can't!"

"Then she'll pick away at your memory until there is nothing left; she doesn't want that—she's after revenge. You *have* to go back to the Crimea, Thursday. Face up to the worst and grow stronger from it."

"No, I won't go back there and you can't make me."

I got up without a word and went to have a bath, trying to soak away the worries. Aornis, Landen, Goliath, the Chrono-Guard and now Perkins's and Snell's murders here in the Book-World; I'd need a bath the size of Windermere to soak those away. I had come to *Caversham Heights* to stay away from crisis and conflict—but they seemed to follow me around like a stray dodo.

I stayed in the bath long enough to need to top it up with hot water twice and, when I came out, found Gran sitting on the laundry basket outside the door.

"Ready?" she asked softly.

"Yes, I'm ready."

I slept in my own bed—Gran said she would sit in the armchair and wake me if things looked as though they were getting out of hand. I stared at the ceiling, the gentle curve of the wooden paneling and the single domed ceiling light. I stayed awake for hours, long after Gran had fallen asleep and dropped her copy of *Tristram Shandy* on the floor. Night and sleep had once been a time of joyous reunion with Landen, a collection of moments that I treasured: tea and hot buttered crumpets, curled up in front of a crackling log fire, or golden moments on the beach, cavorting in slow motion as the sun went down. But no longer. With Aornis about, my memory was now a battleground. And with the whistle of an artillery shell, I was back where I least wanted to be—the Crimea.

"So there you are!" cried Aornis, grinning at me from her seat in the armored personnel carrier as the wounded were removed. I had returned from the lines to the forward dressing station where the disaster had generated a sustained and highly controlled panic. Cries of "Medic!" and swearing punctuated the air while less than three miles away we could still hear the sound of the Russian guns pummeling the remains of the Wessex Light Tank. Sergeant Tozer stepped from the back of the APC with his hand still inside the leg of a soldier as he tried to staunch the bleeding; another soldier blinded by splinters was jabbering on about some girl he had left back home in Bradford-on-Avon.

"You haven't dreamt for a few nights," said Aornis as we watched the casualties being unloaded. "Have you missed me?"

"Not even an atom," I replied, adding, "Are we done?" to the medics unloading the APC.

"We're done!" came back the reply, and with my foot I flicked the switch that raised the rear door.

"Where do you think you're going?" asked a red-faced officer I didn't recognize.

"To pick up the rest, sir!"

"The hell you are! We're sending in Red Cross trucks under a flag of truce!"

It would take too long and we both knew it. I dropped back into the carrier, revved the engine and was soon heading back into the fray. The amount of dust thrown up might screen me—as long as the guns kept firing. Even so, I still felt the whine of a near miss, and once an explosion went off close by, the concussion shattering the glass in the instrument panel.

"Disobeying a direct order, Thursday?" said Aornis scathingly. "They'll court-martial you!"

"But they didn't. They gave me a medal instead."

"But you didn't go back for a gong, did you?"

"It was my duty. What do you want me to say?"

The noise grew louder as I drove towards the front line. I felt something large pluck at my vehicle and the roof opened up, revealing a shaft of sunlight in the dust that was curiously beautiful. The same unseen hand picked up the carrier and threw it in the air. It ran along on one track for a few yards and then fell back upright. The engine was still functioning, the controls still felt right; I carried on, oblivious to the damage. Only when I reached up for the wireless switch did I realize the roof had been partially blown off, and only later did I discover an inch-long gash in my chin.

"It was your duty, all right, Thursday, but it was not for the army, regiment, brigade or platoon—certainly not English interests in the Crimea. You went back for Anton, didn't you?"

Everything stopped. The noise, the explosions, everything. My brother Anton. Why did she have to bring him up?

"Anton," I whispered.

"Your dear brother Anton," replied Aornis. "Yes. You worshiped him. From the time he built you a tree house in the back garden. You joined the army to be like him, didn't you?"

I said nothing. It was true, all true. Tears started to course down my cheeks. Anton had, quite simply, been the best elder brother a girl could have. He always had time for me and always included me in whatever he got up to. My anger at losing him had been driving me for longer than I cared to remember.

"I brought you here so you can remember what it's like to lose a brother. If you could find the man that killed Anton, what would you do to him?"

"Losing Anton was *not* the moral equivalent of killing Acheron," I shouted. "Hades deserved to die—Anton was just doing his misguided patriotic duty!"

We had arrived outside the remains of Anton's APC. The guns

were firing more sporadically now, picking their targets more carefully; I could hear the sound of small arms as the Russian infantry advanced to retake the lost ground. I released the rear door. It was jammed but it didn't matter; the side door had vanished with the roof and I rapidly packed twenty-two wounded soldiers into an APC designed to carry eight. I closed my eyes and started to cry. It was like seeing a car accident about to happen, the futility of knowing something is about to occur but being unable to do anything about it.

"Hey, Thuzzy!" said Anton in the voice I knew so well. Only he had ever called me that; it was the last word he would speak. I opened my eyes and there he was, as large as life and despite the obvious danger, smiling.

"No!" I shouted, knowing full well what was going to happen next. "Stop! Don't come over here!"

But he did, as he had done all those years before. He stepped out from behind cover and ran across to me. The side of my APC was blown open and I could see him clearly.

"Please no!" I shouted, my eyes full of tears. The memory of that day would fill my mind for years to come. I would immerse myself in work to get away from it.

"Come back for me, Thuz—!"

And then the shell hit him.

He didn't explode; he just sort of vanished in a red mist. I didn't remember driving back and I didn't remember being arrested when I tried to take another APC back into the fray to find him. I had to be forcibly restrained and confined to barracks. I didn't remember anything up until the moment Sergeant Tozer told me to have a shower and clean myself up. I remember treading on the small pieces of sharp bone that washed out of my hair in the shower.

"This is what you try and forget, isn't it?" said Aornis, smiling at me through the steam from the shower as I tugged my fingers through my matted hair, heart thumping, the fear and pain of loss tensing my every muscle and numbing my senses. I tried to grab her by the throat in the shower but my fingers collapsed on nothing and I barked my knuckles on the shower stall. I swore and thumped the wall.

"You all right, Thursday?" said Prudence, a WT operator from Lincoln in the next shower. "They said you went back. Is that true?"

"Yes, it's true," put in Aornis, "and she'll be going back again right now!"

The shower room vanished and we were back on the battlefield, heading towards the wrecked armor amidst the smoke and dust.

"Well!" said Aornis, clapping her hands happily. "We should be able to manage at least eight of these before dawn—don't you just hate reruns?"

I stopped the APC near the smashed tank and the wounded were heaved aboard.

"Hey, Thursday!" said a familiar male voice. I opened one eye and looked across at the soldier with his face bloodied and less than ten seconds of existence remaining on his slate. But it wasn't Anton—it was another officer, the one I had met earlier and with whom I had become involved.

"Thursday!" said Gran in a loud voice. "Thursday, wake up!"

I was back in my bed on the Sunderland, drenched in sweat. I wished it had all just been a bad dream; but it *was* a bad dream and that was the worst of it.

"Anton's not dead," I gabbled, "he didn't die in the Crimea it was that *other* guy and that's the reason he's not here now because he died and I've been telling myself it was because he was eradicated by the ChronoGuard but he wasn't and—"

"Thursday!" snapped Gran. "Thursday, that is *not* how it happened. Aornis is trying to fool with your mind. Anton died in the charge."

"No, it was the other guy—"

"Landen?"

But the name meant little to me. Gran explained about Aornis and Landen and mnemonomorphs, and although I *understood* what she was saying, I didn't fully believe her. After all, I had seen the Landen fellow die in front of my own eyes, hadn't I?

"Gran, are you having one of your fuzzy moments?"

"No, far from it."

But her voice didn't have the same sort of confidence it usually did. She wrote *Landen* on my hand with a felt pen and I went back to sleep wondering what Anton was up to, and thinking about the short and passionate fling I had enjoyed in the Crimea with that lieutenant, the one who's name I couldn't remember— the one who died in the charge.

23.

Jurisfiction Session
No. 40320

Snell was buried in the Text Sea. It was invited guests only, so although Havisham went, I did not. Both Perkins's and Snell's places were to be taken by B-2 Generics who had been playing them for a while in tribute books—the copies you usually find in cheaply printed book-of-the-month choices. As they lowered Snell's body into the sea to be reduced to letters, the Bellman tingled his bell and spoke a short eulogy for both of them. Havisham said it was very moving—but the most ironic part of it was that the entire Perkins & Snell detective series was finally to be offered as a boxed set, and neither of them ever knew.

THURSDAY NEXT,
The Jurisfiction Chronicles

I FELT TIRED AND washed-out the following morning. Gran was still fast asleep, snoring loudly with Pickwick on her lap when I got up. I made a cup of coffee and was sitting at the kitchen table flicking through a copy of *Movable Type* and feeling grotty when there was a gentle rap at the door. I looked up too quickly and my head throbbed.

"Yes?" I called.

"It's Dr. Fnorp. I teach Lola and Randolph."

I opened the door, checked his ID and let him in. A tall man, he seemed quite short and was dark-haired, although on occasion seemed blond. He spoke with a notable accent from nowhere at all, and he had a limp—or perhaps not. He was a Generic's Generic—all things to all people.

"Coffee?"

"Thank you," he said, adding, "Aha!" when he saw the article I had been reading. "Every year there are more categories!"

He was referring to the BookWorld Awards, which had, I noted, been sponsored by UltraWord™.

" 'Dopiest Shakespearean Character,' " he read. "Othello should win that one hands down. Are you going to the Bookies?"

"I've been asked to present one. Being the newest Jurisfiction member affords one that privilege, apparently."

"Oh? It's the first year all the Generics will be going—we've had to give them a day off college."

"What can I do for you?"

"Well, Lola has been late every day this week, constantly talks in class, leads the other girls astray, smokes, swears and was caught operating a distillery in the science block. She has little respect for authority and has slept with most of her male classmates."

"That's terrible! What shall we do?"

"Do?" replied Fnorp. "We aren't going to do anything—Lola has turned out admirably—so much so that we've got her a leading role in *Girls Make All the Moves*, a thirty-something romantic comedy novel. No, I'm really here because I'm worried about Randolph."

"I . . . see. What's the problem?"

"Well, he's just not taking his studies very seriously. He's not stupid; I could make him an A-4 if only he'd pay a little more attention. Those good looks of his are probably his downfall. Aged fifty-something and what we call a 'distinguished gray' archetype, I think he feels he doesn't need any depth—that he can get away with a good descriptive passage at introduction and then do very little."

"And this is a problem because . . . ?"

"I just want something a bit better for him," sighed Dr. Fnorp, who clearly had the best interests of his students at heart. "He's failed his B-grade exams twice; once more and he'll be nothing but an incidental character with a line or two—if he's lucky."

"Perhaps that's what he wants. There isn't enough room for all characters to be A-grade."

"That's what's wrong with the system," said Fnorp bitterly. "If incidental characters had more depth, the whole of fiction would be a lot richer—I want my students to enliven even the C-grade parts."

I got the point. Even from my relative ignorance I could see the importance of fully rounded characters—trouble was, for budgetary reasons, the Council of Genres had pursued a policy of minimum characterization requirements for Generics for more than thirty years.

"They fear rebellion," he said quietly. "The C of G want Generics to stay stupid; an unsophisticated population is a compliant one—but it's at the cost of the BookWorld."

"So what do you want me to do?"

"Well," sighed Fnorp, finishing his coffee, "have a word with Randolph and see what you can do—try to find out why he is being so intransigent."

I told him I would and saw him out the door.

I found Randolph asleep back in his own bed. He was clutching his pillow. Lola had gone out early to meet some friends. A photo of her was on the bedside table next to him and he snored quietly to himself. I crept back to the door and banged on it.

"Wshenifyduh," said a sleepy voice.

"I need to run one of the engines," I told him, "can you give me a hand?"

There was a thump as he fell out of bed. I smiled to myself and took my coffee up to the flight deck.

Mary had told me to run the number three engine periodically and left instructions on how to do so in the form of a checklist. I didn't know how to fly but did know a thing or two about engines—and needed an excuse to talk to Randolph. I sat in the pilot's seat and looked along the wing to the engine. The cowlings were off and the large radial was streaked with oil and grime. It never rained here, which was just as well, although things didn't actually age either, so it didn't matter if it did. I consulted the checklist in front of me. The engine would have to be turned by hand to begin with and I didn't really fancy this, so got a slightly annoyed Randolph out on the wing.

"How many times?" he asked, turning the engine by way of a crank inserted through the cowling.

"Twice should do," I called back, and ten minutes later he returned, hot and sweaty with the exertion.

"What do we do now?" he asked, suddenly a lot more interested. Starting big radial engines was quite a boy thing, after all.

"You read it out," I said, handing him the checklist.

" 'Master fuel on, ignition switches off,' " he read.

"Done."

" 'Prop controls fully up and throttle one inch open.' "

I wrestled with the appropriate levers from a small nest that sprouted from the center console.

"Done. I had Dr. Fnorp round this morning."

" 'Gills set to open and mixture at idle cutoff.' What did that old fart have to say for himself?"

I set the gills and pulled back the mixture lever. "He said he thought you could do a lot better than you had been. What's next?"

" 'Switch on the fuel booster pump until the warning light goes out.' "

"Where do you think that is?"

We found the fuel controls in an awkward position above our heads and to the rear of the flight deck. Randolph switched on the booster pumps.

"I don't want to be a featured character," he said. "I'll be quite happy working as a mature elder-male mentor figure or something; there is call for one in *Girls Make All the Moves*."

"Isn't that the novel Lola will be working in?"

"Is it?" he said, feigning ignorance badly. "I had no idea."

"Okay," I said as the fuel pressure warning light went out, "now what?"

" 'Set the selector switch to the required engine and operate the priming pump until the delivery pipes are full.' "

I pumped slowly, the faint smell of aviation spirit filling the air.

"What's this love/hate thing between you and Lola?"

"Oh, that's all well over," he said dismissively. "She's seeing some guy over at the Heroes Advanced Classes."

I stopped pumping as the handle met with some resistance. "We have fuel pressure. What's next?"

" 'Ignition and booster coil both on.' "

"Check."

" 'Press starter and when engine is turning, operate the primer.' Does that make sense?"

"Let's see."

I pressed the starter button and the prop slowly started to move. Randolph pumped the primer, and there was a cough as the engine fired; then another, this time accompanied by a large puff of black smoke from the exhaust. A few waders who were poking around in the shallows took flight as the engine appeared to die, then caught again and started to fire more regularly, the loud detonations transmitting through the airframe as a series of rumbles, growls and squeaks. I released the start button and Randolph stopped priming. The engine smoothed out, I switched to *Auto-Rich* and the oil pressure started to rise. I throttled back and smiled at Randolph, who grinned at me.

"Are you seeing anyone?" I asked him.

"No."

He looked at me with his large eyes. When we had first met, he had been an empty husk, a blank face with no personality or features to call his own. Now he was a man of fifty but with the emotional insecurity of a fifteen-year-old.

"I can't imagine life without her, Thursday!" he suddenly burst out. "I think about her every second of every minute of every day!"

"So tell her."

"And make myself look an idiot? She'd tell everyone at Tabularasa's—I'd be the laughingstock of them all!"

"Who cares? Dr. Fnorp tells me it's affecting your work; do you want to end up as a walk-on part somewhere?"

"I really don't care," he said sadly. "Without Lola there *isn't* much of a future."

"There'll be other Generics!"

"Not like her. Always laughing and joking. When she's around, the sun shines and the birds sing." He stopped and coughed, embarrassed at his admission. "You won't tell anyone I said all that stuff, will you?"

He was smitten good and proper.

"Randolph," I said slowly, "you have to tell her your feelings, even for your own sake. This will prey on your mind for years!"

"What if she laughs at me?"

"What if she doesn't? There's a good chance she actually quite likes you!"

Randolph's shoulders slumped. "I'll speak to her as soon as she gets back."

"Good." I looked at my watch. "I've got roll call in twenty minutes. Let the engine run for ten minutes and then shut her down. I'll see you tonight."

"Who are we waiting for?" asked the Bellman.

"Godot," replied Benedict.

"Absent *again*. Anybody know where he is?"

There was a mass shaking of heads.

The Bellman made a note in his book, tingled his bell and cleared his throat.

"Jurisfiction session number 40320 is now in session," he said in a voice tinged with emotion.

"Item one. Perkins and Snell. Fine operatives who made the ultimate sacrifice for duty. Their names will be carved into the Boojumorial to live forever as inspiration for those who come after us. I call now for two minutes silence. Perkins and Snell!"

"Perkins and Snell," we all repeated, and stood in silent memory of those lost.

"Thank you," said the Bellman after two minutes had ticked by. "Commander Bradshaw will be taking over the bestiary.

Mathias's mare has been contacted and asked me to say thank you to all those who sent tributes. The Perkins and Snell detective series will be taken over by B-2 clones from the tribute book, and I know you will join me in wishing them the very best on their new venture."

He paused and took a deep breath.

"These losses are a great shock to us all, and the lessons to be learned must not be ignored. We can *never* be too careful. Okay, item two."

He turned over a page on his clipboard.

"Investigation of Perkins's death. Commander Bradshaw, doesn't this come under your remit?"

"Investigations are proceeding," replied Bradshaw slowly. "There is no reason to suppose that their deaths were anything other than an accident."

"So what stops you closing the case?"

"Because," replied Bradshaw, trying to think up an excuse quickly, "because, um, we still want to speak to Vernham Deane."

"Deane is somehow involved?" asked the Bellman.

"Yes—perhaps."

"Interesting turn of events," said the Bellman, "which brings us neatly on to item three. I'm sorry to announce that Vernham Deane has been placed on the PageRunner's list."

There was a sharp intake of breath. Classed as a PageRunner meant only one thing: illegal activities.

"We've known Vern since he was written, guys, and hard as it might be, we think he's done something pretty bad. Tweed, haven't you got something to say about this?"

Harris Tweed stood up and cleared his throat. "Vernham Deane is familiar to all of us. As the resident cad in *The Squire of High Potternews*, he was well-known for his cruelty towards the maidservant, who he ravages and then casts from the house. The maid returns ten chapters later, but three days ago—the morning following Perkins's death, I might add—she didn't."

He placed a picture of an attractive dark-haired woman on the board.

"She's a C-3 Generic by the name of Mimi. Twenty years old, identification code CDT/2511922."

"What did Deane say about her disappearance?"

"That's just it," replied Tweed grimly, "he vanished at the same time. *The Squire of High Potternews* has been suspended pending further inquiries. It's been removed to the Well and will stay there until Deane returns. *If* he returns."

"Aren't you leaping to conclusions just a little bit early?" asked Havisham, obviously concerned by the lack of objectivity in Tweed's report. "Do we even have a motive?"

"We all liked Vern," said Tweed, "me included. Despite being a villain in *Potternews*, he never gave us any cause for alarm. I was surprised by what I found, and you might be, too."

He pulled a piece of paper from his top pocket and unfolded it.

"This is a copy of a refusal by the Council of Genres narrative realignment subcommittee to agree to Deane's application for an Internal Plot Adjustment."

He pinned it on the board next to the picture of the maidservant.

"In it he requests for the maidservant to die in childbirth, thus saving his character from the traumatic scene at the end of chapter twenty-eight when the maidservant turns up with the infant, now aged six, to his wedding to Ellen O'Shaugnessy, the wealthy mill owner's daughter. With the maidservant out of the way he can marry O'Shaugnessy and not suffer the degrading slide into alcoholism and death that awaits him in chapter thirty-two. I'm sorry to say that he had motive, Miss Havisham. He also had the opportunity—and the Jurisfiction skills to cover his tracks."

There was silence as everyone took in the awful possibility of a Jurisfiction agent gone bad. The only time it had happened before was when David Copperfield murdered Dora Spenlow so he could marry Agnes Wickfield.

"Did you search his book?" asked Falstaff.

"Yes. We subjected *The Squire of High Potternews* to a word-by-word search and we only found one person who was not meant to be there—a stowaway from Farquitt's previous book, *Canon of Love*, hiding in a cupboard in Potternews Hall. She was evicted back to her book."

"Have you tried the bookhounds?" inquired the Red Queen, running a cleaner through the barrel of her pistol. "Once they get onto a scent, there's no stopping them."

"We lost them at the fence-painting sequence in *The Adventures of Tom Sawyer.*"

"Tell them about the Perkins connection, Harris."

"I think that *is* assumption, Bellman, if you please," answered Tweed.

"Tell them," repeated the Bellman, his shoulders sagging. "I think everyone needs to know the full facts if we are to hunt Deane down."

"Very well." Tweed upended a box and deposited a huge quantity of full stops, commas and semicolons onto the table.

"We found these hidden at the back of Deane's locker. We had them analyzed and found traces of Guinness."

"*Ulysses!*" gasped Benedict.

"So it would appear," replied Tweed gravely. "Perkins mentioned something about a *surprising discovery* in a report filed the day before he died. We're working on the theory that Deane was involved in stealing or handling stolen punctuation. Perkins finds out, so Deane releases the Minotaur and vyrus to cover his tracks. Flushed with success and knowing he will have to vanish, he kills the maidservant, something he has been wanting to do since first publication."

"Isn't Perkins my investigation?" asked Bradshaw.

"My apologies," replied Tweed, "I will give you a full copy of my report."

He stopped and sat down.

"I hate to say this," began the Bellman sadly, "but it seems as though we have underestimated Deane. Until I am shown otherwise, I have no choice but to declare him a PageRunner. He is to be arrested on sight—and exercise extreme caution. If he has killed twice, he will not hesitate to kill again."

We exchanged anxious glances. Being declared a PageRunner was serious—few were captured alive.

"Item four," continued the Bellman. "The Minotaur. We've got an APB out on him at present, but until he turns up or does something stupid, we won't know where he is. There was a report he had crossed over into nonfiction, which I would love to believe. Until we know otherwise, everyone should keep a good lookout."

He consulted his clipboard again.

"Item five. The 923rd Annual BookWorld Awards. Because we are launching UltraWord™ at the same time, all serving members of the BookWorld have been invited. Obviously we can't leave books unmanned, so skeleton staff will be left in charge. The venue will be the Starlight Room again, although with a displacement field technology we've borrowed from the SF boys so everyone can attend. This will mean extra security and I have allocated Falstaff to look after it. Any questions?"

There weren't, so he moved on.

"Item six. Thursday Next has been made a probationary Jurisfiction member. Where are you?"

I put up my hand.

"Good. Let me be the first to welcome you to the service—and not before time; we need all the extra hands we can get. Ladies and gentlemen, Thursday Next!"

I smiled modestly as there was a round of applause; the people nearest me patted me on the arm.

"Well done!" said Tweed, who was close by, grinning.

"Miss Next will be afforded full rights and privileges, although she will remain under Miss Havisham's watchful eye for twenty chapters or a year, whichever be the longer. Will you take her up to the Council of Genres and have her sworn in?"

"Happily," replied Miss Havisham.

"Good. Item seven. The *had had* and *that that* problem. Lady Cavendish, weren't you working on this?"

Lady Cavendish stood up and gathered her thoughts. "Indeed. The uses of *had had* and *that that* have to be strictly controlled;

they can interrupt the imaginotransference quite dramatically, causing readers to go back over the sentence in confusion, something we try to avoid."

"Go on."

"It's mostly an unlicensed-usage problem. At the last count *David Copperfield* alone had had *had had* sixty-three times, all but ten unapproved. *Pilgrim's Progress* may also be a problem due to its *had had/that that* ratio."

"So what's the problem in *Progress*?"

"That that had *that that* ten times but had had *had had* only thrice. Increased *had had* usage had had to be overlooked, but not if the number exceeds that *that that* usage."

"Hmm," said the Bellman, "I thought *had had* had had TGC's approval for use in Dickens? What's the problem?"

"Take the first *had had* and *that that* in the book by way of example," explained Lady Cavendish. "You would have thought that that first *had had* had had good occasion to be seen as *had*, had you not? *Had* had had approval but *had had* had not; equally it is true to say that that *that that* had had approval but that that other *that that* had not."

"So the problem with that other *that that* was that . . . ?"

"That that other-other *that that* had had approval."

"Okay," said the Bellman, whose head was in danger of falling apart like a chocolate orange, "let me get this straight: *David Copperfield*, unlike *Pilgrim's Progress*, had had *had*, had had *had had*. *Had had* had had TGC's approval?"

There was a very long pause.

"Right," said the Bellman with a sigh, "that's it for the moment. I'll be giving out assignments in ten minutes. Session's over—and let's be careful out there."

"Never would have thought it of Vernham, by George!" exclaimed Bradshaw as he walked up. "He was like a son to me!"

"I didn't know you had a son."

"I don't. But if I did, he would be just like Vern."

"His character in *Potternews* wasn't that pleasant," I observed.

"We usually try and keep our book personalities separate from our Jurisfiction ones," said Havisham. "Think yourself lucky I don't carry over any of my personality from *Great Expectations*—if I did, I'd be pretty intolerable!"

"Yes," I said diplomatically, "I'm very grateful for it."

"Ah!" said the Bellman as he joined us. "Miss Havisham. You're to go and swear in Agent Next at the C of G, then get yourself to the Well and see if you can find any clues inside *The Squire of High Potternews*. If possible, I want him alive. But—take no risks."

"Understood," replied Miss Havisham.

"Good!" The Bellman clapped his hands together and departed to talk to the Red Queen.

Havisham beckoned me over to her desk and indicated for me to sit.

"Firstly, congratulations on becoming a full Jurisfiction agent."

"I'm not ready for this!" I hissed. "I'm probably going to fall flat on my face!"

"*Probably* has nothing to do with it; you shall. Failure concentrates the mind wonderfully. If you don't make mistakes, you're not trying hard enough."

I started to thank her for her faint praise, but she interrupted, "This is for you."

From the bottom drawer of her desk she had withdrawn a small, green leather box of the sort that might contain a wedding ring. She passed it over and I opened it. As I did, I felt a flash of inspiration move through me. I knew what it was. No bigger than a grain of rice, it had value far in excess of its size.

"From the Last Original Idea," murmured Havisham, "a small shard from when the whole was cleaved in 1884, but a part nonetheless. Use it wisely."

"I can't accept this," I said, shutting the case.

"Rubbish. Accept with good grace that which is given with good grace."

"Thank you very much, Miss Havisham."

"Don't mention it. Why do you have *Landen* written on your hand?"

I looked at my hand but had no idea why. Gran had put it there—she must have been having one of her fuzzy moments.

"I'm not sure, Miss Havisham."

"Then wash it off—it looks so vulgar. Come, let us adjourn to the Council of Genres—you are to sign the pledge!"

24.

Pledges, the Council of Genres
and Searching for Deane

Bookhound/Booktracker: Name given to a breed of bloodhound peculiar to the Well. With a keen sense of smell and boundless energy, a bookhound can track a PageRunner not only from page to page but from book to book. The finest bookhounds, diligently trained, have also been known to track transgenre PageRunners and, on occasion, to the Outland. They drool and slobber a lot. Not recommended as pets.

CAT FORMERLY KNOWN AS CHESHIRE,
Guide to the Great Library

E TOOK THE elevator. Miss Havisham told me that it was considered the height of poor breeding and vulgarity to jump all the way to the lobby at the Council of Genres—and it was impossible to jump straight into the Council chambers for security purposes. The chambers were situated on the twenty-sixth floor of the Great Library. Like the seventeenth floor it was almost deserted; authors whose names begin with Q and Z are not that abundant. The doors opened and we stepped out. But it wasn't like the previous library floors I had visited, all somber dark wood, molded plaster ceilings and busts of long-dead writers—the twenty-sixth floor had a glazed roof. Curved spans of wrought iron arched high above our heads supporting the glass, through which we could see clouds and a blue sky beyond. I had always thought that the library was created *conceptually* to contain the books and had no use or existence outside that. Miss Havisham noticed me staring up at the sky and drew me towards a large window. Although it was the twenty-sixth floor, it seemed a lot higher—and the library, inwardly shaped like a fine cross many miles in length, was far squatter when seen from the outside. I looked down the rain-streaked exterior and beyond the stone gargoyles to a tropical forest far below us, where wispy clouds flecked the tops of the lush foliage.

"Anything is possible in the BookWorld," murmured Miss Havisham. "The only barriers are those of the human imagination. See the other libraries?"

Not more than five miles distant, just visible in the aerial haze, was another tower like ours, and beyond that, another—and over to my right, six more. We were just one towering library of hundreds—or perhaps thousands.

"The nearest one to us is German," said Miss Havisham, "beyond that French and Spanish. Arabic is just beyond them—and that one over there is Welsh."

"What are they standing on?" I asked, looking at the jungle far below. "Where *exactly* are we?"

"Getting all philosophical, are we?" murmured Miss Havisham. "The long and short answer is we really don't know. Some people claim we are just part of a bigger story that we can't see. Others maintain that we were created by the Great Panjandrum, and still others that we are merely in the *mind* of the Great Panjandrum."

"Who," I asked, my curiosity finally getting the better of me, "is the Great Panjandrum?"

"Come and see the statue."

We turned from the window and walked along the corridor to where a large lump of marble rested on a plinth in the middle of the lobby. The marble was roped off, and below it was a large and highly polished plaque proclaiming *Our Glorious Leader.*

"That's the Great Panjandrum?" I asked, looking at the crude block of stone.

"No, that's only the statue of the Great P—or at least it will be when we figure out what he or she looks like. Good afternoon, Mr. Price."

Mr. Price was a stonemason but he wasn't doing anything; in

fact, I don't think he had *ever* done anything—his tools were brightly polished, unmarked, and lying in a neat row next to where he was sitting, reading a copy of *The Word*.

"Good afternoon, Miss Havisham," he said, politely raising his hat.

Havisham indicated the surroundings. "The Great Panjandrum is meant to be the architect of all this and controls everything we do. I'm a little skeptical myself; no one controls *my* movements."

"They wouldn't dare," I whispered.

"What did you say?"

"I said, *they couldn't care*. Not a great deal, given the violence in books."

She looked at me and raised an eyebrow. "Perhaps. Come along and see the Council at work."

She steered me down the corridor to a door that opened into a viewing gallery above the vast Council chamber with desks arranged in concentric circles.

"The main genres are seated at the front," whispered Miss Havisham. "The subgenres are seated behind and make up a voting group that can be carried forward to the elected head of each genre, although they do have a veto. Behind the subgenres are elected representatives from the Congress of Derivatives, who bring information forward to the subgenres inspectorate—and behind them are the subcommittees who decide on day-to-day issues such as the Book Inspectorate, new words, letter supply and licensing the reworkings of old ideas. The Book Inspectorate also license plot devices, Jurisfiction agents and the supply and training schedules for Generics."

"Who's that talking now?" I asked.

"The Thriller delegate. She's arguing against Detective having a genre all of its own—at present Detective is under Crime, but if they break away, the genres at Thriller will want to split themselves three ways into Adventure, Spy and Thriller."

"Is it always this boring?" I asked, watching the Thriller delegate drone on.

"Always. We try to avoid any entanglements and let Text Grand Central take all the flak. This way."

We left the viewing gallery and padded down the corridor to a door that led into the smallest room I had ever seen. It seemed to be mostly filing cabinet and desk. An equally small man was eating biscuits—and most of them were falling down his front.

"Thursday Next to take the pledge," announced Miss Havisham. "I have the documents all signed and sealed by the Bellman."

"Work, work, work," said the small man, taking a swig of tea and looking up at me with small yet oddly intense eyes. "I rarely get any peace—you're the second pledge this year." He sighed and wiped his mouth on his tie. "Who seconds the application?"

"Commander Bradshaw."

"And who vouches for Miss Next?"

"I do."

"Good. Stand up and repeat the oath of the BookWorld."

I stood up and, primed by Miss Havisham, repeated:

"I swear by the Great Panjandrum that I shall uphold the rules of Jurisfiction, protect the BookWorld and defend every fictioneer, no matter how poorly written, against oppression. I shall not shirk from my duty, nor use my knowledge or position for personal gain. Secrets entrusted to me by the Council of Genres or Text Grand Central must remain secret within the service, and I will do all I can to maintain the power of storytelling within the minds and hearts of the readers."

"That'll do," said the small man, after another bite of his biscuit. "Sign here, here, and, er, *here*. And you have to witness it, Miss Havisham."

I signed where he indicated in the large ledger, noting as I did so that the last Jurisfiction agent to have signed was Beatrice. He snapped the book shut after Miss Havisham had witnessed my signature.

"Good. Here's your badge."

He handed over a shiny Jurisfiction badge with my name and number engraved below the colorful logo. It could get me into any book I wanted without question—even Poe if I so chose, although it wasn't recommended.

"Now if you'll excuse me," said the bureaucrat, looking at his watch, "I'm very busy. These forms have to be processed in under a month."

We returned to the elevator and Miss Havisham pressed the twenty-sixth subbasement button. We were going back into the Well.

"Good," she said, "now that's out of the way we can get on. Perkins and Mathias we can safely say were murdered; Snell might as well have been. We are still waiting for Godot and someone tried to kill you with an exploding hat. As an apprentice you have limited powers; as a full member of Jurisfiction you can do a lot more. You must be on your guard!"

"But why?"

"Because I don't want you dead, and if you know what's good for you, neither do you."

"No, I mean why is someone trying to kill me?"

"I wish I knew."

"Let's suppose," I said, "that Deane isn't just missing—that he might have been murdered. Is there a link between Perkins, Deane, Mathias, and myself?"

"None that I can think of," said Miss Havisham after a great deal of thought, "but if we consider that Mathias might have been killed because he was a witness, and that one of your Outlander friends might be trying to kill *you,* then that narrows the list to Perkins and Deane. And there *is* a link between those two."

"Yes?"

"Harris Tweed, myself, Perkins and Deane were all given an UltraWord™ book to test."

"I didn't know this."

"No one did. I can only tell you now because you are a full agent—didn't you hear what was in the pledge?"

"I see," I said slowly. "What's UltraWord™ like?"

"As Libris states: 'the ultimate reading experience.' The first thing that hits you is the music and color."

"What about the new plots?"

"I didn't see that," confessed Miss Havisham as the elevator doors opened. "We were all given a copy of *The Little Prince* updated with the new operating system—but PageGlow™, WordBuddy™, PlotPotPlus™ and ReadZip™ are all quite dazzling in their simplicity."

"That's good."

"But something just doesn't seem right."

"That's not so good."

The doors of the elevator opened and we walked along the corridor to where the Text Sea opened out in front of us, the roof of the corridor lifting higher and higher until it had no discernible end, just swirling patterns of punctuation forming into angry storm clouds. Scrawltrawlers rode gently at their moorings at the dockside while the day's wordcatch was auctioned off.

"Like what? A problem with the system?"

"I wish I knew," said Miss Havisham, "but try as I might I couldn't make the book do anything it shouldn't. In BOOK V7.2 you could force an uncommanded translation into Esperanto by subjecting the book to a high-g maneuver. In BOOK V6.3 the verb *to eat* conflicted with any description of a pangolin and caused utter mayhem with the tenses. I've tried everything to get UltraWord™ to fail, but it's steady as a rock."

We walked beyond the harbor to where large pipes spewed jumbled letters back into the Text Sea amidst a strong smell of rubber.[1]

---

1. ". . . Dear Friend, I am a fifty-year-old lady from the Republic of Gondal. I got your details from the Council of Genres and decided to contact you to see if you could help. My husband, Reginald Jackson, was the rebel leader in *Gondal in Turmoil* (RRP: £4.99), and just before he was assassinated, he gave me twelve million dollars and I departed the book to be a refugee in the Well of Lost Plots with my two children. On arrival, I decided to deposit this money in a security company for safekeeping. Right now, I am seeking assistance from you so that I can transfer the funds from the Well to your

"This is where the words end up when you erase them in the Outland," mentioned Miss Havisham as we strolled past. "Anything the matter?"

"Junkfootnoterphones again," I muttered, trying to screen the rubbish out, "a scam of some sort, I think. What makes you believe anything *is* the trouble with UltraWord™?"

"Well," said Havisham slowly, "Perkins called me the night before he died. He said he had a surprising discovery but didn't want to talk over the footnoterphone."

"Was it about UltraWord™?"

Havisham shrugged. "To be truthful, I don't know. It's possible—but it could have been about Deane just as easily."

The road petered out into a beach formed by shards of broken letters. This was where novels met their end. Beneath the leaden skies the books—here taking the appearance of seven-story buildings—were cast high upon the shore, any plot devices and settings of any use torn out to be sold as salvage. The remaining hulks were then pulled to pieces by Generics working in teams with nothing more high-tech than crowbars, cutting torches and chains, stripping the old novels back into words, which were tipped into the sea by wheelbarrow gangs, the words dissolving back into letters, their meaning burning off into a slight bluish haze that collected at the foreshore.

We arrived at the copy of *The Squire of High Potternews*. It looked dark and somber here on the shore of the Text Sea. Anyone trying to find a copy in the Outland would have a great deal of trouble; when Text Grand Central withdraw a book, they really mean it.

The book was resting on its end and was slightly open. A large tape had been run round the outside that read *Jurisfiction, Do Not Cross.*

"Looking for something?"

Outland account. If this offer meets your approval, you could reach me on my footnoterphone. Thank you, Mrs. R. Jackson . . ."

It was Harris Tweed and Uriah Hope; they jumped down from the book and looked at us curiously.

"Good evening, Harris," said Miss Havisham. "We were trying to find Deane."

"Me, too. Have a look around if you wish, but I'm damned if I can find a single clue as to his whereabouts."

"Has anyone tried to kill you recently?" I asked.

"Me?" replied Harris. "No. Why, should they?"

I told him about the UltraWord™ connection.

"It's possible that there might be a link," he mused, "but I gave UltraWord™ the fullest test; it seemed to work extremely well no matter *what* I did! Do you have any idea what Perkins had discovered?"

"We don't know he found anything wrong at all," said Havisham.

Harris thought for a moment. "I think we should definitely keep this to ourselves," he said at last, "and take great care what we do. If Deane is about and had anything to do with Perkins's death, he might be after you or I next."

Havisham agreed, told me to go see Professor Plum to see if he could shed any more light on the failed Eject-O-Hat and vanished after telling me she had an urgent appointment to keep.

When she had gone, Harris said to me, "Keep an eye on the old girl, won't you?"

I promised I would and made my way back towards the elevators, deep in thought.

25.

Havisham—the Final Bow

///.//.////.......////...././.......//.././././//..////.......///.///.////
/////.........//////......///////.......//..
///////......////..././.......//.././././///..////.......///.///.////////
..........///////......///////..........//////......///////.......//..
///////......////..././.......///////./////..........//////......///////
/.......//..   ///////......///....///////......///////.......//..
///////......////..././.......//.././././///..////.......///.///./////////
..........///////......./

Macbeth for Yeast, translated by ..////..///..

"A"H!" SAID PLUM as I walked into his office. "Miss Next—good news and bad news."

"Better give me the bad news first."

Plum took off his spectacles and polished them.

"The Eject-O-Hat. I've pulled the records and traced the manufacturing process all the way back to the original milliner; it seems that over a hundred people have been involved in it's manufacture, modification and overhaul schedules. Fifteen years is a long service life for an Eject-O-Hat. Add the people with the know-how and we've got a shortlist of about six hundred."

"A broad net."

"I'm afraid so."

I went to the window and looked out. Two peacocks were strutting across the lawn.

"What was the good news?"

"You know Miss Scarlett at records?"

"Yes?"

"We're getting married on Tuesday."

"Congratulations."

"Thank you. Was there anything else?"

"I don't think so," I replied, walking to the door. "Thanks for your help."

"My pleasure!" he replied kindly. "Tell Miss Havisham she should get a new Eject-O-Hat—this one is quite beyond repair."

"It wasn't Havisham's, it was mine."

He raised his eyebrows. "You're mistaken," he said after a pause. "Look."

He pulled the battered homburg from his desk and showed me Havisham's name etched on the sweatband with a number, manufacturing details and size.

"But," I said slowly, "I was wearing this hat in—"

The awful truth dawned. There must have been a mix-up with the hats. They hadn't been trying to kill me that day—*they had been after Miss Havisham!*

"Problems?" said Plum.

"Of the worst sort," I muttered. "Can I use your footnoter-phone?"

I didn't wait for a reply; I picked up the brass horn and asked for Miss Havisham. She wasn't in the Well, nor *Great Expectations*. I replaced the speaking horn and jumped to the lobby of the Great Library, where the general stores were situated; if anyone knew what Havisham was up to, it would be Wemmick.

Mr. Wemmick wasn't busy; he was reading a newspaper with his feet on the counter.

"Miss Next!" he said happily, getting up to shake my hand warmly. "What can I do for you?"

"Miss Havisham," I blurted out, "do you know where she is?"

Wemmick squirmed inwardly. "I'm not sure she'd like me to tell—"

"Wemmick!" I cried. "Someone tried to kill Miss Havisham and they may try again!"

He looked shocked and bit his lip. "I don't know *where* she is," he said slowly, "but I know what she's doing."

My heart sank. "It's another land speed attempt, isn't it?"

He nodded miserably.

"Where?"

"I don't know. She said the Higham wasn't powerful enough. She signed out the Bluebird, a twin-engined, twenty-five-hundred horsepower brute of a car—it almost didn't fit in the storeroom."

"Do you have any idea where she's going to drive it?"

"None at all."

"Damn!" I yelled, slamming my hand against the counter. "Think, Thursday, think!"

I had an idea. I grasped the footnoterphone and asked to be put through to Mr. Toad from *Wind in the Willows*. He wasn't in but Ratty was; and after I had explained who I was and what I wanted, he gave me the information I needed. Havisham and Mr. Toad were racing on Pendine sands, in the Socialist Republic of Wales.

I ran up the stairs and to the works of Dylan Thomas, picked up a slim volume of poetry and concentrated on my exit point in the Outland. To my delight it worked and I was catapulted out of fiction and into an untidy heap in a small bookshop in Laugharne, Thomas's old village in the south of Wales. Now a shrine for Welsh and non-Welsh visitors alike, the bookshop was one of eight in the village selling nothing but Welsh literature and Thomas memorabilia.

There was a scream from a startled book buyer as I appeared, and I stepped backwards in alarm only to fall over a pile of Welsh cookery books. I got up and ran from the shop as a car screeched to a halt in front of me. Pendine sands with its ten miles of flat beach was down the coast from Laugharne and I would need transport to get me there.

I showed the driver my Jurisfiction badge, which *looked*

official even if it meant nothing, and said, in my very best Welsh, "Esgipysgod fi ond ble mae bws i Pendine?"

She got the message and drove me along the road towards Pendine. Before we arrived I could see the Bluebird on the sands, together with Mr. Toad's car and a small group of people. The tide was out and a broad expanse of inviting smooth sand greeted Miss Havisham. As I watched, my pulse racing, two plumes of black smoke erupted from the back of the record-breaker as the engines fired up. Even through the window I could hear the guttural cry of the engines.

"Dewch ymlaen!" I urged the driver, and we swerved onto the car park just near the statue of John Parry Thomas. I ran down onto the beach, arms waving and yelling, but no one heard me above the roar of the engines, and even if they had, there was little reason for them to take any notice.

"Hi!" I shouted. "Miss Havisham!"

I ran as fast as I could but only exhausted myself so that I ran slower with every passing step.

"Stop!" I yelled, getting weaker and breathless. "For pity's sake—!"

But it was too late. With another deep growl the car moved off and started to gather speed across the sand. I stopped and dropped to my knees, trying to gulp deep lungfuls of air, my heart racing. The car hurtled away from me, the engine roar fading as she tore along the hard sand. I watched it go at medium speed to the far end of the beach, then turn in a large arc for the first of her two runs. The engine growled again, rising to a high scream as the car gathered speed, the driving wheels throwing a shower of sand and pebbles far behind it. I willed her to be safe and for nothing to happen, and indeed, nothing did until she was decelerating after the first run. I was breathing a sigh of relief when one of the front wheels broke loose and was dragged beneath the car, throwing it up into the air. The front edge of the bodywork dug into the sand and the car swerved violently sideways. I heard a cry of fear from the small crowd and a series of sickening thuds as the car rolled end over end down the beach, the engine screaming out of control as the wheels gripped nothing but air. It came to rest right way up not five hundred yards from me, and I ran towards it. I was three hundred yards away when the petrol tank ignited in a mushroom of fire that lifted the three-ton car from the sand. When I got there, I jumped onto the front of the car and pulled Miss Havisham from the burning wreck, dragged her clear and rolled her on the sand to extinguish the flames.

"Water!" I cried. "Water for her burns!"

The small crowd of onlookers were hopeless and could do nothing but stare at us in shock as I used my pocketknife to cut away the burnt remnants of her wedding veil. I winced as I worked—she was horribly burned.

"Thursday?" she murmured, although she couldn't see me. "Please—please take me home."

I'd never jumped dual, taking someone with me, but I did it now. I jumped clean out of Pendine and into *Great Expectations*, right into Miss Havisham's room at Satis House, next to the rotting wedding party that never was, the darkened room, the clocks stopped at twenty to nine. It was the place where I had first seen her all those weeks ago, and it would be the place I saw her last. I laid her on the bed and tried to make her comfortable.

"Cat!"[1]

"There's been a code-12. Fictional vehicle left on Pendine sands in the Outland. I need a fixed perimeter and a cleanup gang ASAP!"[2]

"Not good, Chesh. I'll get back to you."[3]

"Dear Thursday," said Miss Havisham, clasping my hand in hers, "was it an accident?"

"I don't know, Miss Havisham. But the Eject-O-Hat was not mine—it was intended for you."

She sighed. "Then, then . . . they got to me."

---

1. "Speaking!"
2. "I'm on it. How is she?"
3. "Okay. A cleanup gang of Danvers are on their way now."

"Who?"

"I don't know. This is the BookWorld so it's got to be someone close and whom we don't suspect. Someone we thought was a friend."

"Bradshaw?"

She shook her head and started to cough. For a moment, I didn't think she would stop. The Jurisfiction medic jumped into the darkened room, followed by several nurses, who pushed me out of the way as they tried to cool and dress her wounds. But I couldn't get away. Havisham still had hold of my hand and pulled me closer.

"I will not come through this," she whispered.

"You'll be fine! In *Great Expectations* you survive until the end—can't let Dickens or the readers down, hey?"

"Then it looks like we will both be guilty of a Fiction Infraction, my dear."

She tried to smile but couldn't make her swollen features do as she bid.

"I have enough strength to make a good exit. I will make my peace with Pip and Estella—a far better ending for me, I think."

"Miss Havisham!" I pleaded. "Please don't talk this way!"

"You are close to me, my dear," she hissed, "they will come for you next!"

"But why?"

"The formulaic, Thursday. It is our enemy. Uphold fiction's independence, beware of Big Martin and shun the frumious bandersnatch . . ."

"She's becoming delirious," said the medic as I felt her clasp loosen from mine, and with it, I felt my eyes start to stream. More medics arrived and I moved towards the back of the room where Pip, Estella, and Mr. Pumblechook had all arrived to look on helplessly as the medics attempted to save her life.

"You did what you could," said Pip slowly, "and we are very grateful to you."

"It wasn't enough," I said quietly, "but she wants to improvise a new ending with you."

"Then I will stay here," said Pip softly, "until she regains consciousness."

We waited there, Pip and I, until Miss Havisham was well enough to make her final appearance in *Great Expectations*. She had bade farewell to the Bellman and Bradshaw. The Council of Genres had even interrupted their busy schedule to rubber-stamp an Internal Plot Adjustment to allow her to improvise her own fiery ending. An A-2 generic was being trained to take her place even as we were saying our good-byes. She took my arm even though she couldn't see me and pressed the UltraWord™ copy of *The Little Prince* into my hand.

"The formulaic," she said again, "is our one true enemy. Defend the BookWorld against it, promise me?"

"I promise."

"You know, Thursday, you're going to be pretty good at all this."

I thanked her.

"One more thing."

I leaned closer.

"Don't tell anyone I said this, but I don't think men are *quite* so bad as I make out."

I smiled. "You might be right."

She coughed again and signaled for me to leave. I had many questions I needed to ask, but she didn't have long and we both knew it. I nodded to Pip as we passed each other at the door, and I gently closed it behind me. I waited outside with a heavy heart and tensed as I heard a shriek and a flickering orange light shone beneath the door. I heard Pip curse, then more thumps and shouts as he smothered the fire with his cape. Jaw clenched, I turned away, my heart heavy with loss. She had been bossy and obnoxious, but she had protected me, rescued me and taught me well. I have yet to meet a more extraordinary woman, either real or imagined, and she would always have a place in my heart.

26.
Post-Havisham Blues

The Bellman lived in a grace-and-favor apartment at Norland Park when he wasn't working in *The Hunting of the Snark*. He had been head of Jurisfiction for twenty years and was required, under Council of Genres mandate, to stand down. The Bellman, oddly enough, had always been called the Bellman—it was no more than coincidence that he had actually been a Bellman himself. The previous Bellman had been Bradshaw, and before him, Virginia Woolf. Under Woolf, Jurisfiction roll calls tended to last several hours.

THE BELLMAN,
Hardest Job in Fiction

I WALKED INTO THE Jurisfiction offices an hour later. The Bellman, Bradshaw and Harris Tweed were staring at two pieces of broken and scorched metal lying on a desk.

"I can't say how sorry we all are," said the Bellman, "we all thought the world of her. Did she tell you about the time the Martians escaped and tried to force the Council of Genres into ordering a sequel—one where they were triumphant?"

"No," I said quietly, "she rarely talked about her past work. What's this?" I pointed at the broken pieces of metal.

"It's the stub axle from the Bluebird. It looks as though it failed through metal fatigue."

"An accident?"

The Bellman nodded his head. They hadn't got to her after all. Earlier, Bradshaw had shown me the UltraWord™ reports written by Perkins, Deane and Miss Havisham. They'd all given it the thumbs-up. If Perkins *was* murdered, it wasn't over UltraWord™. Despite all that had happened, I still only had a doctored Eject-O-Hat to point to anything suspicious about Havisham's death, and only a misplaced key for Perkins's. Motor racing has its own share of dangers, and Havisham knew it.

"You're off the active list for a few days, Miss Next," said the Bellman. "Take it easy at home and come back in when you're ready."

Tweed said, "She was one of the best."

"One in a million," added Bradshaw, "won't see the likes of her again, I'll be bound."

"We want to offer you a permanent job," said the Bellman. "A modern system like UltraWord™ needs people like you to police it. I want you to consider a post here within Fiction. Good retirement plan and plenty of perks."

I looked up at him. This seemed to me like rather a good idea. After all, there was no one waiting for me back at Swindon. What did I need the real world for?

"Sounds good, Mr. Bellman. Can I sleep on it?"

He smiled. "Take as long as you want."

I got back to Mary's flying boat and sat on the jetty until the sun had gone down, mulling over everything that Miss Havisham and I had done together. When it grew chilly, I moved myself indoors and read over what Miss Havisham had done with her final scene. A professional to the last, she had enacted her own death with a sensitivity I had never seen her exhibit in life. I found a bottle of wine, poured myself a large glass and drank it gratefully. Oddly, I thought there was a reason perhaps I *shouldn't* be drinking, but couldn't think what it was. I looked at my hand where there had been a name written that morning. Havisham had instructed me to scrub it out, and I had—but even so I was intrigued and tried to figure out from the small marks visible what had been written there.

"Lisbon," I muttered. "Why would I write *Lisbon* on my hand?"

I shrugged. The delicate red was a welcome friend and I poured another glass. I found the copy of *The Little Prince* that Havisham had given me and opened the cover. The paper felt like a sort of thin plastic, the letters a harsh black against the milky white pages. The text glowed in the dim light of the kitchen, and intrigued, I took the book into the darkness of the utility cupboard where I could still read it as clear as day. I returned to my place at the table and tried the "read sensitive" preferences page, the words changing from red to blue as I read them, then back again as I reread them. In this manner I turned the PageGlow™ feature on and off, and then I played with the levels of the background and music tracks.

I started to read the book, and as the first words entered my head, a huge panoply of new emotions opened up. As I read the sequence in the desert, I could hear the sound of the wind on the dunes and even feel the heat and taste the scorched sands. The voice of the narrator was different to that of the Prince, and no dialogue tags were needed to differentiate them. It was, as Libris had asserted, an extraordinary piece of technology. I shut the book, leaned back on my chair and closed my eyes.

There was a tap at the door.

"Hullo!" Arnold said. "Can I come in?"

"Make yourself at home. Drink?"

"Thank you."

He sat down and smiled at me. I'd never really noticed it before but he was quite a handsome man.

"Where's everyone else?" he asked, looking around.

"Out somewhere," I replied, waving a hand in the direction of the boat and feeling a bit dizzy. "Lola's probably under her latest beau, Randolph is doubtless complaining to someone about it—and I've no idea where Gran is. Have a drink?"

"You've already poured one."

"So I have. What brings you here, Arnie?"

"Just passing. How are things at work?"

"Shit. Miss Havisham died, and something maybe, perhaps,

possibly, is *wrong*—I just don't know what—if at all. Does that make sense?"

"Kind of. I've heard Outlanders sometimes go through a period of 'imagination free fall' where they start trying to create plotlines out of nothing. You'll settle down to it, I shouldn't worry. Congratulations, by the way, I read about your appointment in the paper."

I held up my glass in salute, and we both drank.

"So what's the deal with you and Mary?" I asked.

"Over for a long time. She thinks I'm a loser and—"

"—tells you to go to hell. Yes, I've heard. What about Lola? Have you slept with her yet?"

"No!"

"You must be the only bloke in *Caversham Heights* who hasn't. Do you want another drink?"

"Okay."

"What about you? Tell me about your husband in the Outland."

"I don't have a husband, never did."

"You told me—"

"Probably one of those 'push off' comments we girls sometimes use. There was this guy named Snood in the ChronoGuard, but that was a long time ago. He suffered a time aggre. Agg-era. Aggreg—"

"A what?"

"He got old before his time. He died."

I felt confused all of a sudden and looked at the wineglass and the half-empty bottle of wine.

"What's the matter, Thursday?"

"Oh—nothing. You know when you suddenly have a memory of something and you don't know why—a sort of *flashback*?"

He smiled. "I don't have many memories, Thursday, I'm a Generic. I could have had a backstory but I wasn't considered important enough."

"Is that a cat? I mean, is that a *fact*? Well, I just thought about the White Horse in Uffington back home. Soft, warm grassland and blue skies, warm sun on my face. Why would I have done that?"

"I have no idea. Don't you think you've had enough to drink?"

"I'm fine. Right as rain. Never better. What's it like being a Generic?"

"It's not bad." He took another swig of wine. "Promotion to a better or new part is always there if you are diligent enough and hang out at the Character Exchange. I miss having a family—that must be good."

"My mum is a hoot, and Dad doesn't exist—he's a time-traveling knight-errant—don't laugh—and I have two brothers. They both live in Swindon. One's a priest and the other . . ."

"Is what?"

I felt confused again. It was probably the wine. I looked at my hand. "I don't know what he does. We haven't spoken in years."

There was another flashback, this time of the Crimea.

"This bottle's empty," I muttered, trying to pour it.

"You have to take the cork out first. Allow me."

Arnold fumbled with the corkscrew and drew the cork after a lot of effort. I think he was drunk. Some people have no restraint.

"What do you think of the Well?" he asked.

"It's all right. Life here is pretty good for an Outlander. No bills to pay, the weather is always good and best of all—no Goliath, SpecOps or my mother's cooking."

"SpecOps can cook?"

I giggled stupidly and so did he. Within a few seconds we had both collapsed in hysterics. I hadn't laughed like this for ages.

The laughter stopped.

"What were we giggling about?" asked Arnold.

"I don't know."

And we collapsed in hysterics again.

I recovered and took another swig of wine. "Do you dance?"

Arnie looked startled for a moment. "Of course."

I took him by the hand and led him through into the living

room, found a record and put it on the turntable. I placed my hands on his shoulders and he placed his hands on my waist. It felt odd and somehow wrong, but I was past caring. I had lost a good friend that day and deserved a little unwinding.

The music began and we swayed to the rhythm. I had danced a lot in the past, which must have been with Filbert Snood, I supposed.

"You dance well for someone with one leg, Arnie."

"I have two legs, Thursday."

And we burst out laughing again. I steadied myself on him and he steadied himself on the sofa. Pickwick looked on and ruffled her feathers in disgust.

"Do you have a girl in the Well, Arnie?"

"Nobody," he said slowly, and I moved my cheek against his, found his mouth and kissed him, gently and without ceremony. He began to pull away, then stopped and returned the kiss. It felt dangerously welcome; I didn't know why I had been single for so long. I wondered whether Arnie would stay the night.

He stopped kissing me and took a step back.

"Thursday, this is all *wrong*."

"What could be wrong?" I asked, staring at him unsteadily. "Do you want to come and see my bedroom? It has a great view of the ceiling."

I stumbled slightly and held the back of the sofa.

"What are you staring at?" I asked Pickwick, who was glaring at me.

"My head's thumping," muttered Arnold.

"So's mine."

Arnold cocked his head and listened. "It's not our heads—it's the door."

"The door of perception," I noted, "of heaven and hell."

He opened the door and a very old woman dressed in blue gingham walked in. I started to giggle but stopped when she strode up to me and took away my wineglass.

"How many glasses have you had?"

"Two?" I replied, leaning against the table for support.

"Bottles," corrected Arnie.

"Crates," I added, giggling, although nothing actually seemed that funny all of a sudden. "Listen here, Gingham Woman," I added, wagging my finger, "give me my glass back."

"What about the baby?" she demanded, staring at me dangerously.

"What baby? Who's having a baby? Arnie, are you having a baby?"

"It's worse than I thought," she muttered. "Do the names Aornis and Landen mean anything to you?"

"Not a thing, but I'll drink to them, if you want. Hello, Randolph."

Randolph and Lola had arrived at the doorstep and were staring at me in shock.

"What?" I asked them. "Have I grown a second head or something?"

"Lola, fetch a spoon," said Gingham Woman. "Randolph, take Thursday to the bathroom."

"Why?" I collapsed in a heap. "I can walk. And why is there a carpet on the wall?"

The next thing I saw was the view down the back of Randolph's legs and the living room floor, then the stairs, as I was carried up over his shoulder. I started to giggle but the rest was a bit blurry. I remember choking and throwing up in the loo, then being deposited in bed, then starting to cry.

"She died. Burned. I tried to help her. It was her hat, you know."

"I know, darling. I'm your grandmother, do you remember?"

"Gran?" I sobbed, realizing who she was all of a sudden. "I'm sorry I called you Gingham Woman!"

"It's okay. Perhaps being drunk is for the best. You're going to sleep now, and dream—and in that dream you'll do battle to win back your memories. Do you understand?"

"No."

She sighed and wiped my forehead with her small, pink hand. It felt reassuring and I stopped crying.

"Be vigilant, my dear. Keep your wits about you and be stronger than you have ever been. We'll see you on the other side, come the morning."

But she was starting to fade as slumber swept over me, her voice ringing in my ears as my mind relaxed and transported me deep into my subconscious.

27.

The Lighthouse at the Edge
of My Mind

The Hades family when I knew them comprised, in order of age, Acheron, Styx, Phlegethon, Cocytus, Lethe, and the only girl, Aornis. Their father had died many years previously, leaving their mother in charge of the youthful and diabolical family all on her own. Described once by Vlad the Impaler as "unspeakably repellent," the Hades family drew strength from deviancy and committing every sort of horror that they could. Some with panache, some with halfhearted seriousness, others with a sort of relaxed insouciance about the whole thing. Lethe, the "white sheep" of the family, was hardly cruel at all—but the others more than made up for him. In time, I was to defeat three of them.

THURSDAY NEXT,
Hades: Family from Hell

A WAVE BURST ON the rocks behind me, showering me with cold water and flecks of foam. I shivered. I was on a rocky outcrop in the darkest gale-torn night, and before me stood a lighthouse. The wind whistled and moaned around the tower, and a flash of lightning struck the apex. The bolt coursed down the earthing cable and trailed a shower of sparks, leaving behind the acrid stench of brimstone. The lighthouse was as black as obsidian, and as I looked up, it seemed as though the arc lamp rotating within the vast lenses was floating in midair. The light swept through the inky blackness illuminating nothing but a heaving, angry sea. I looked backwards in my mind but could see nothing—I was without memory or past experiences. This was the loneliest outpost of my subconscious, a memoryless island where nothing existed other than that which I could feel and see and smell at this moment in time. But I still had emotions, and I had a sense of danger, and purpose. Somehow I understood I was here to vanquish—or be vanquished.

Another wave burst behind me, and with beating heart I pulled on the locking lever of the steel front door and was soon inside, safe from the gale. The door securely fastened, I looked around. There was a central spiral staircase but nothing else—not a stick of furniture, a book, a packing case, nothing.

I shivered again and pulled out my gun.

"A lighthouse," I murmured, "a lighthouse in the middle of nowhere."

I walked slowly up the concrete steps keeping a careful watch as they curved away out of sight. The first floor was empty and I moved on up, each circular room I reached devoid of any signs of habitation. In this way I slowly climbed the tower, gun arm outstretched and trembling with a dread of impending loss that I could not control or understand. On the top floor the spiral staircase ended; a steel ladder was the only means by which to climb any higher. I could hear the electric motors that drove the rotating lamp whine above me, the bright white light shining through the open roof hatch as the beam swept slowly about. But this room was not empty. Sitting in an armchair was a young woman powdering her nose with the help of a small handmirror.

"Who are you?" I asked, pointing my gun at her.

She lowered the mirror, smiled and looked at the pistol.

"Dear me!" she exclaimed. "Always the woman of action, aren't you?"

"What am I doing here?"

"You really don't know, do you?"

"No." I lowered the gun. I couldn't remember any facts but I could feel love and loss and frustration and fear. The woman was linked to one of these but I didn't know which.

"My name is—" The young woman stopped and smiled again. "No, I think even that is too much."

She rose and walked towards me. "All you need to know is that you killed my brother."

"I'm a murderer?" I whispered, searching in my heart for guilt of such a crime and finding none. "I . . . I don't believe you."

"Oh, it's true, and I will have my revenge. Let me show you something."

She took me to the window and pointed. There was another flash of lightning and the view was illuminated outside. We were on the edge of a massive waterfall that curved away from us into the darkness. The ocean was emptying over the edge; millions of gallons every second, falling into the abyss. But that wasn't all. In another flash of lightning I could see that the waterfall was rapidly eroding the small island on which the lighthouse was built—as I watched, the first piece of the rocky outcrop fell away noiselessly and disappeared into space.

"What's happening?" I demanded.

"You are forgetting everything," she said simply, sweeping her hands in the direction of the room. "These are a just a few of your memories I have cobbled together—a last stand, if you like. The storm, the lighthouse, the waterfall, the night, the wind—none of them are real." She walked closer to me until I could smell her perfume. "All this is merely a representation of your mind. The lighthouse is you; your consciousness. The sea around us your experience, your memories—everything that makes you the person you are. They are all draining away like water from a bath. Soon the lighthouse will topple into the void and then . . ."

"And then?"

"And then I will have won. You will remember nothing—not even this. You will relearn, of course—in ten years you might be able to tie your own shoelaces. But for the first few years the only decision you will have to make is which side of your mouth to drool out of."

I turned to leave but she called out, "You can't run. Where will you go? For you, there's nowhere else but here."

I stopped at the door and turned back, raised my gun and

fired a single shot. The bullet whistled through the young woman and impacted harmlessly on the wall behind.

"It will take more than that, Thursday."

"Thursday? That's my name?"

"It doesn't matter, there is no one you can remember who will help you."

"Doesn't this make your victory hollow?" I demanded, lowering my gun and rubbing my temple, trying to recall even a single fact.

"Ridding your mind of that which you value most was the hard bit. All I had to do then was to invoke your *dread,* the memory that you feared the most. After that, it was easy."

"My greatest fear?"

She smiled again and showed me the handmirror. There was no reflection, only images that flashed past anonymously. I took the mirror and peered at it, trying to make sense of what I saw.

"These are the images of your life, your memories, the people you love, everything you held dear—but also everything that you've ever feared. I can modify and change them at will—or even delete them completely. But before I do, I'm going to make you view the worst once more. Gaze upon it, Thursday, gaze upon it and feel the death of your brother one last time!"

The mirror showed me the image of a war long ago, the violent death of a soldier who seemed familiar, and I felt the pain of loss tearing through me. The woman laughed as the images repeated themselves, this time clearer, and more graphic. I shut my eyes to block the horror, but opened them again quickly in shock. I had seen something else, right at the edge of my mind, dark and menacing, waiting to engulf me. I gasped, and the woman felt my fear.

"What is it?" she cried. "There is something I have missed? Worse than the Crimea? Let me see!"

She tried to grasp the mirror but I let it drop. It shattered on the concrete floor as we heard a muffled thump of something striking the steel door five stories below.

"What was that?" she demanded.

I realized what I had seen. Its presence, unwelcome for so many years in the back of my mind, might be just what I needed to defeat her.

"My worst nightmare," I told her, "and now yours."

"But it can't be! Your worst nightmare was the Crimea, your brother's death—I know, I've searched your mind!"

"Then," I replied slowly, my strength returning as the woman's confidence trickled away, "you should have searched harder!"

"But it's still too late to help you," she said, her voice quavering, "it will not gain entry, I assure you of that!"

There was another loud crash; the steel door on the ground floor had been torn from its hinges.

"Wrong again," I said quietly. "You asked for my worse fear, my dread, to appear—and it came."

She ran to the stairs and yelled, "Who is there? Who are you? *What* are you?"

But there was no reply; only a soft sigh and the sound of footfalls on the stairs as it climbed slowly upwards. I looked from the window as another section of the rocky island fell away. The lighthouse was now poised on top of the abyss and I could see straight down into the dizzying depths. There was a tremor as the foundations shifted; the lighthouse flexed and a section of plaster fell from the wall.

"Thursday!" she yelled out pitifully. "You can control it! Make it stop!"

She slammed the door to the staircase, her hands shaking as she hurriedly threw the bolt.

"I could hide it if I chose," I said, staring at the terrified woman, "but I choose not. You asked me to gaze upon my fears— now you may join me."

The lighthouse shifted again and a crack opened in the wall revealing the storm-tossed sea beyond; the arc light stopped rotating with a growl of twisted metal. There was a thump at the door.

"There are always bigger fish, Aornis," I said slowly, suddenly realizing who she was as my past began to reveal itself from the fog. "Like all Hadeses, you were lazy. You thought Anton's demise was the worst thing you could dredge up. You never looked further. Hardly looked into my subconscious at all. The old stuff, the terrifying stuff, the stuff that keeps us awake as children, the nightmares we can only half glimpse on waking, the fear we sweep to the back of our minds but which is always there, gloating from a distance."

The door collapsed inwards as the lighthouse swayed and part of the wall fell away. An icy gust blew in, the ceiling dropped two feet and electricity sparked from a severed cable. Aornis stared at the form lurking in the doorway, making quiet slavering noises to itself.

"No!" she whined. "I'm sorry, I didn't mean to disturb you, I—"

I watched as Aornis's hair turned snow-white, but no scream came from her dry throat. I lowered my eyes and turned to the door, seeing only a vague shape out of the corner of my eye advancing towards Aornis. She had dropped to her knees and was sobbing uncontrollably. I walked past the shattered door and down the stairs two at a time. As I stepped outside, the outcrop shivered again and the conical roof of the lighthouse came wheeling down amidst masonry and scraps of rusty iron. Aornis found her voice, finally, and screamed.

I didn't pause or break my pace. I could still hear her yelling for mercy as I climbed into the small jolly boat she had kept for her escape and rowed away across the oily black water, her cries only drowned out as the lighthouse collapsed into the abyss, taking the malevolent spirit of Aornis with it.

I paused for a moment, then put my back into rowing, the oars rattling in the rowlocks.

"That was impressive," said a quiet voice behind me. I turned and found Landen sitting in the bow. He was every bit as I remembered him. Tall and good-looking with hair graying slightly at the temples. My memories, which had been blunted for so long, now made him more alive than he had been for weeks. I dropped the oars and nearly upset the small boat in my hurry to fling my arms around him, to feel his warmth. I hugged him until I could barely breath, tears coursing down my cheeks.

"Is it you?" I cried. "*Really* you, not one of Aornis's little games?"

"No, it's me all right." He kissed me tenderly. "Or at least, your memory of me."

"You'll be back for real, I promise!"

"Have I missed much? It's not nice being forgotten by the one you love."

"Well," I began as we made ourselves more comfortable in the boat, lying down to look up at the stars, "there's this upgrade called UltraWord™, see, and . . ."

We stayed in each other's arms for a long time, the small rowing boat adrift in the museum of my mind, the sea calming before us as we headed towards the gathering dawn.

28.

Lola Departs and *Heights* Again

Daphne Farquitt wrote her first book in 1936 and had by 1988 written three hundred others exactly like it. *The Squire of High Potternews* was arguably the least worst, although the best you could say about it was that it was a "different shade of terrible." Astute readers have complained that *Potternews* originally ended quite differently, an observation also made about *Jane Eyre*. It is all they have in common.

THURSDAY NEXT,
The Jurisfiction Chronicles

THE FOLLOWING MORNING my head felt as if it had a road drill in it. I lay awake in bed, the sun streaming through the porthole. I smiled as I remembered the defeat of Aornis the night before and mouthed out loud:

"Landen Parke-Laine, Landen Parke-Laine!"

Then I remembered the loss of Miss Havisham and sighed, staring up at the ceiling. After a few minutes of introspection I sat up slowly and stretched. It was almost ten. I staggered to the bathroom and drank three glasses of water, brought it all up again and brushed my teeth, drank more water, sat with my head between my knees, then tiptoed back to bed to avoid waking Gran. She was fast asleep in the chair with a copy of *Finnegans Wake* on her lap. I knew I was going to have to apologize to Arnie and thank him for not taking advantage of the situation. I couldn't believe I had made such a fool of myself but felt that I could, at a pinch, lay most of the blame at Aornis's door.

I got up half an hour later and went downstairs, where I

found Randolph and Lola at the breakfast table. They weren't talking to each other and I noticed Lola's small suitcase at the door.

"Thursday!" said Randolph, offering me a chair. "Are you okay?"

"Groggy," I replied as Lola placed a steaming mug of coffee in front of me that I inhaled gratefully. "Groggy but happy—I got Landen back. Thanks for helping me out last night—and I'm sorry if I made a complete idiot of myself. Arnie must think I'm the worst tease in the Well."

"No, that's me," said Lola innocently. "Your Gran explained to us all about Aornis and Landen. We had no idea what was going on. Arnie understood and he said he'd drop around later and see how you were."

I looked at Lola's suitcase and then at the two of them, who were studiously ignoring each other.

"What's going on?"

"I'm leaving to start work on *Girls Make All the Moves*."

"That's excellent news, Lola," I said, genuinely impressed. "Randolph?"

"Yes, very good. All the clothes and boyfriends she wants."

"You're sour because you didn't get that male-mentor part you wanted," retorted Lola.

"Not at all," replied Randolph, resentment bubbling under the surface. "I've been offered a small part in an upcoming Amis—a proper novel. A *literary* one."

"Well, good luck to you," replied Lola. "Send me a postcard if you can be troubled to talk to anyone in chicklit."

"Guys," I said, "don't part like this!"

Lola looked at Randolph, who turned away. She sighed, stared at me for a moment and then got up.

"Well," she said, picking up her case, "I've got to go. Fittings all morning, then rehearsals until six. Busy busy busy. I'll keep in touch, don't worry."

I got up, held my head for a moment as it thumped badly, then hugged Lola, who hugged me back happily.

"Thanks for all the help, Thursday," she said, tears in her eyes. "I wouldn't have made it up to B-3 without you."

She went to the door and stopped for a moment, looked across at Randolph, who was staring resolutely out the window at nothing in particular.

"Good-bye, Randolph."

"Good-bye," he said without looking up.

Lola looked at me, bit her lip and went across to him and kissed him on the back of the head. She returned to the door, said good-bye to me again and went out.

I sat down next to him. A large tear had rolled down his nose and dropped onto the table. I laid a hand on his.

"Randolph—!"

"I'm fine!" he growled. "I've just got a bit of grit in my eye!"

"Did you tell her how you felt?"

"No, I didn't!" he snapped. "And what's more, I don't want you dictating to me what I should and shouldn't do!"

He got up and stormed off to his bedroom, the door slamming shut behind him.

"Hellooo!" said a Granny Next sort of voice. "Are you well enough to come upstairs?"

"Yes."

"Then you can come and help me down."

I assisted her down the stairs and sat her at the table, fetching a cushion or two from the living room.

"Thanks for your help, Gran. I made a complete fool of myself last night."

"What's life for? Don't mention it. And by the way, it was Lola and me who undressed you, not the boys."

"I think I was past caring."

"All the same. Aornis will have a lot more trouble getting at you in the Outland, my dear—my experience of mnemono-morphs tends to be that once you dispose of a mindworm, the rest is easy. You won't forget her in a hurry, I assure you."

We chatted for an hour, Gran and I, about Miss Havisham, Landen, babies, Anton and all other things besides. She told me about her own husband's eradication and his eventual return. I knew he *had* returned because without him there would be no me, but it was interesting to talk to her nonetheless. I felt well enough to go into *Caversham Heights* at midday to see how Jack was getting on.

"Ah!" said Jack as I arrived. "Just in time. I've been thinking about a full *Caversham Heights* makeover—do you want to have a look?"

"Go on, then."

"Is anything the matter? You look a bit unwell."

"I got myself pickled to the gills last night. I'll be fine. What have you in mind?"

"Get in. I want you to meet someone."

I climbed into the Allegro and he handed me a coffee. We were parked opposite a large redbrick semi in the north of the town. In the book we stake out this house for two days, eventually sighting the mayor emerging with crime boss Angel DeFablio. With the mayor character excised from the manuscript for an unspecified reason, it would be a long wait.

"This is Nathan Snudd," said Jack, indicating a young man sitting in the backseat. "Nathan is a plotsmith who's just graduated in the Well and has kindly agreed to help us. He has some ideas about the book that I wanted you to hear. Mr. Snudd, this is Thursday Next."

"Hi," I said, shaking his hand.

"The *Outlander* Thursday Next?"

"Yes."

"Fascinating! Tell me, why doesn't glue stick to the inside of the bottle?"

"I don't know. What are your ideas for the book?"

"Well," said Nathan, affecting the manner of someone who knows a great deal, "I've being looking at what you have left and I've put together a rescue plan that uses the available budget, characters and remaining high points of the novel to best effect."

"Is it still a murder inquiry?"

"Oh, yes; and the fight-rigging bit I think we can keep, too. I've bought a few cut-price plot devices from a bargain warehouse in the Well and sewn them in. For instance, I thought that instead of having one scene where Jack is suspended by DCI Briggs, you could have six."

"Will that work?"

"Sure. Then there will be a bad-cop routine where an officer close to you is taking bribes and betrays you to the Mob. I've got this middle-aged, creepy housekeeper Generic we can adapt. In fact, I've got seventeen middle-aged, creepy housekeepers we can pepper about the book."

"Mrs. Danvers, by any chance?" I asked.

"We're working on a tight budget," replied Snudd coldly, "let's not forget that."

"What else?"

"I thought there could be several gangster's molls or a prostitute who wants to go straight and helps you out."

"A 'tart with a heart'?"

"In one. They're ten a penny in the Well at the moment—we should be able to get five for a ha'penny."

"Then what happens?"

"This is the good bit. Someone tries to kill you with a car bomb. I've bought this great little scene for you where you go to your car, are about to start it but find a small piece of wire on the floor mat. It's a cinch and cheap, too. I can buy it wholesale from my cousin; he said he would throw in a missing consignment of Nazi bullion and a sad-loser-detective-drunk-at-a-bar-with-whiskey-and-a-cigarette scene. You are a sad, loner, loser maverick detective with a drink problem, yes?"

Jack looked at me and smiled. "No, not anymore. I live with my wife and have four amusing children."

"Not on this budget." Snudd laughed. "Humorous sidekicks—kids or otherwise—cost bundles."

There was a tap on the window.

"Hello, Prometheus," said Jack, "have you met Thursday Next? She's from the Outland."

Prometheus looked at me and put out a hand. He was an olive-skinned man of perhaps thirty, with tightly curled black hair close to his head. He had deep black eyes and a strong Grecian nose that was so straight you could have laid a set square on it.

"Outland, eh? What did you think of Byron's retelling of my story?"

"I thought it excellent."

"Me, too. When are we going to get the Elgin marbles back?"

"No idea."

Prometheus, more generally known as the fire-giver, was a Titan who had stolen fire from the gods and given it to mankind, a good move or a terrible one, depending on which papers you read. As punishment, Zeus had him chained to a rock in the Caucasus, where his liver was picked out every night by eagles, only to regrow during the day. He looked quite healthy, in spite of it. What he was doing in *Caversham Heights*, I had no idea.

"I heard you had a spot of bother," he said to Jack, "something about the plot falling to pieces?"

"My attempts to keep it secret don't appear to be working," muttered Jack. "I don't want a panic. Most Generics have a heart of gold, but if there is the sniff of a problem with the narrative, they'll abandon *Heights* like rats from a ship—and an influx of Generics seeking employment to the Well could set the Book Inspectorate off like a rocket."

"Ah," replied the Titan, "tricky indeed. I was wondering if I could offer my services in any way?"

"As a Greek drug dealer or something?" asked Nathan.

"No," replied Prometheus slightly testily, "as Prometheus."

"Oh, yeah?" Snudd laughed. "What are you going to do? Steal fire from the DeFablio family and give it to Mickey Finn?"

Prometheus stared at him as though he were a twit—which he was, I suppose.

"No, I thought I could be here awaiting extradition back to the Caucasus by Zeus' lawyers or something—and Jack could be in charge of witness protection, trying to protect me against Zeus' hit men—sort of like *The Client* but with gods instead of the Mob."

"If you want to cross-genre we have to build from the ground up," replied Snudd disparagingly, "and that takes more money and expertise than you guys will *ever* possess."

"What did you say?" asked Prometheus in a threatening manner.

"You heard me. Everyone thinks it's easy to be a plotsmith."

"What you've described," continued the Titan, showing great restraint, "isn't a crime thriller—it's a mess."

Snudd prodded Prometheus on the tie and sneered, "Well, let me tell you, Mr. Smart-Aleck-Greek-Titan-fire-giver, I didn't spend four years at Plotschool to be told my job by an ex-convict!"

The Titan's lip quivered. "Okay," he snarled, pulling up his shirtsleeves, "you and me. Right now, here on the sidewalk."

"C'mon," said Jack in a soothing manner, "this isn't going to get us anywhere. Snudd, I think perhaps you should listen to what Prometheus has to say. He might have a point."

"A point?" cried Snudd, getting out of the car but avoiding Prometheus. "I'll tell you the point. You came to me wanting my help and I gave it—now I have to listen to dumb ideas from any myth that happens to wander along. This was a *favor,* Jack—my time isn't cheap. And since this is an ideas free-for-all, let me tell you a home truth: the Great Panjandrum himself couldn't sort out the problems in this book. And you know why? Because it was shit to begin with. Now, if you'll excuse me, I've got two sub-plots to write for proper, paying clients!"

And without another word, Snudd vanished.

"Well," said Prometheus, getting into the backseat, "who needs cretins like him?"

"Me," sighed Jack, "I need all the help I can get. What do you care what happens to us anyway?"

"Well," said the Titan slowly, "I kind of like it here, and all that mail redirection is a pain in the arse. What shall we do now?"

"Lunch?" I suggested.

"Good idea," said Prometheus. "I wait tables at Zorba's in the high street—I can get us a discount."

29.

Mrs. Bradshaw and Solomon (Judgments) Inc.

The "police officer being suspended by reluctant boss" plot device was pretty common in the crime genre. It usually happened just before a down-ending second act, when the author sets things up so the reader thinks that there is no way the hero can extricate himself. A down-ending second usually heralds an up-ending third, but not always; you can finish a third down, but it usually works better if the end of the second is up—which means the end of the first should be up, not down.

JEREMY FNORP,
The Ups and Downs of Act Breaks

I WENT TO WORK as normal the following morning, my head cleared and feeling better than I had for some time. Randolph, however, was inconsolable without Lola and had moped all the previous evening, becoming quite angry that I believed him when he said that nothing was the matter. Gran was out and I slept well for the first time in weeks. I even dreamt of Landen— and wasn't interrupted during the good parts, either.

"I share your grief for Miss Havisham," murmured Beatrice when I arrived at Norland Park.

"Thank you."

"Rotten luck," said Falstaff as I walked past. "There were the remains of a fine woman about Havisham."

"Thank you."

"Miss Next?" It was the Bellman. "Can I have a word?"

I walked over with him to his office and he shut the door.

"So, tell me, how do you feel about joining us permanently?"

"I can stay for a year, but I have a husband back in the real world who doesn't exist and needs me."

"Ah. Well, I'm sorry to hear that. Shame." He scratched his nose nervously. Something was going on that I didn't know about. "Anyway, irrespective of your plans, I will be moving you to less demanding duties. Miss Havisham's death shook us all up and I'm not risking your future health by hurrying you back onto the active list."

"I'm fine, really."

"I'm sure you are—but since you have only recently qualified and are without a mentor, we felt it was better if you were taken off the active list for a while."

" 'We'?"

He picked up his clipboard, which had beeped at him. Havisham had told me that he never actually placed any papers in the all-important clipboard—the words were beamed directly there from Text Grand Central.

"The Council of Genres have taken a personal interest in your case," he said after reading the clipboard. "I think they felt you were too valuable to lose through stress—an Outlander in Jurisfiction is quite a coup, as you know. You have powers of self-determination that we can only dream of. Take it in the good spirit it is meant, won't you?"

"So I don't get to take Havisham's place at Jurisfiction?"

"I'm afraid not. Perhaps when the dust has settled. Who knows? In the BookWorld, anything is possible."

He handed me a scrap of paper. "Report to Solomon on the twenty-sixth floor. Good luck!"

I got up, thanked the Bellman and left his office. There was silence as I walked back past the other agents, who looked at me apologetically. I had been canned through no fault of my own, and everyone knew it. I sat down at Havisham's desk and looked at all her stuff. She had been replaced by a Generic in *Expectations*, and although they would look almost identical, it could never be the same person. The Havisham that I had known had been lost at Pendine sands. I sighed. Perhaps demotion was a good thing. After all, I did have a lot to learn, and working with the C of G for a bit probably had its merits.

"Miss Next?"

It was Commander Bradshaw.

"Hello, sir."

He smiled and raised his hat. "Would you care to have tea with me on the veranda?"

"I'd be delighted."

He smiled, took me by the arm and jumped us both into *Bradshaw Hunts Big Game*. I had never been to East Africa, either in our world or this, but it was as beautiful as I had imagined it from the many images I had grown up with. Bradshaw's house was a low colonial building with a veranda facing the setting sun; the land around the house was wild scrub and whistling thorns. Herds of wildebeests and zebras wandered across in a desultory manner, their hooves kicking up red dust as they moved.

"Quite beautiful, wouldn't you say?"

"Extraordinary," I replied, staring at the scenery.

"Isn't it just?" He grinned. "Appreciate a woman who knows beauty when she sees it."

His voice lowered a tone. "Havisham was one of the finest, a little too fast for me, but a good egg in a scrap. She was very fond of you."

"And I of her. Mr. Bradshaw—"

"Trafford. Call me Trafford."

"Trafford, do you think it *was* an accident?"

"Well, it looked like one," he said after thinking for a moment, "but then a real one and a written one are pretty similar, even to an expert eye. Mr. Toad was pretty cut up about it and got into a helluva pickle for visiting the Outland without permission. Why, are you still suspicious?"

I shrugged. "It's in my nature. Someone wants me off the active list and it isn't the Bellman. Did Havisham confide in you about Perkins?"

"Only that she thought he'd been murdered."

"Had he?"

"Who knows?" Bradshaw took off his hat and fanned himself with it. "The office think it's Deane, but we'll never know for sure until we arrest him. Have you met the memsahib? My darling, this is Thursday Next—a colleague from work."

I looked up and jumped slightly because Mrs. Bradshaw was, in fact, a gorilla. She was large and hairy and was dressed only in a floral-patterned pinafore.

"Good evening," I said, slightly taken aback, "a pleasure to meet you, Mrs. Bradshaw."

"Good evening," replied the gorilla politely, "would you like some cake with your tea? Alphonse has made an excellent lemon sponge."

"That would be nice, thank you," I spluttered as Mrs. Bradshaw stared at me with her dark, deep-set eyes.

"Excellent! I'll be out in a jiffy to join you. Feet, Trafford."

"What? Oh!" said Bradshaw, taking his boots off the chair opposite. When Mrs. Bradshaw had left, he turned and said to me in a serious whisper, "Tell me, did you notice anything odd about the memsahib?"

"Er," I began, not wanting to hurt his feelings, "not really."

"Think, it's important. Is there anything about her that strikes you as a little out of the ordinary?"

"Well, she's only wearing a pinafore," I managed to say.

"Does that bother you?" he asked in all seriousness. "Whenever male visitors attend, I always have her cover up. She's a fine-looking gal, wouldn't you agree? Drive any man wild, wouldn't you say?"

"Very fine."

He shuffled in his chair and drew closer. "Anything else?" he said, staring at me intently. "Anything at all. I won't be upset."

"Well," I began slowly, "I couldn't help noticing that she was . . ."

"Yes?"

". . . a gorilla."

"Hmm," he said, leaning back, "our little subterfuge didn't fool you, then?"

"I'm afraid not."

"Melanie!" he shouted. "Please come and join us."

Mrs. Bradshaw lumbered back onto the veranda and sat in one of the club armchairs, which creaked under her weight.

"She knows, my love."

"Oh!" said Mrs. Bradshaw, producing a fan and hiding her face. "However did you find out?"

A servant appeared with a tray of teas, left them on the table, bowed and withdrew.

"Is it the hair?" she asked, delicately pouring the tea with her feet.

"Partly," I admitted.

"I told you the powder wouldn't cover it up," she said to Bradshaw in a scolding tone, "and I'm *not* shaving. It makes one itch so. One lump or two?"

"One please," I replied. "Is it a problem?"

"It's no problem *here*," said Mrs. Bradshaw. "I often feature in my husband's books and nowhere does it specify precisely that I am anything but human."

"We've been married for over fifty years," added Bradshaw. "The problem is that we've had an invitation to the Bookies next week and Melanie here is a little awkward in public."

"To hell with them all," I replied. "Anyone who can't accept that the woman you love is a gorilla isn't worth counting as a friend!"

"Do you know," said Mrs. Bradshaw, "I think she's right. Trafford?"

"Right also!" He grinned. "Appreciate a woman who knows when to call a wife a gorilla. Hoorah! Lemon sponge, anyone?"

I took the elevator to the twenty-sixth floor and walked out into the lobby of the Council of Genres, clasping the orders that the Bellman had given me.

"Excuse me," I said to the receptionist, who was busy fielding calls on a footnoterphone, "I have to report to Mr. Solomon."

"Seventh door on the left," she said without looking up. I

walked down the corridor amongst the thronging mass of bureaucrats walking briskly hither and thither clasping buff files as though their lives and existence depended on it, which they probably did.

I found the correct door. It opened onto a large waiting room full of bored people who all clutched numbered tickets and stared vacantly at the ceiling. At a door at the far end was a desk manned by a single receptionist. He stared at my sheet when I presented it, sniffed and said, "How did you know I was single?"

"When?"

"Just then, in your description of me."

"I meant *single* as in *solitary*."

"Ah. You're late. I'll wait ten minutes for you and 'His Lordship' to get acquainted, then send the first lot in. Okay?"

"I guess."

I opened the door to reveal another long room, this time with a single table at the far end of it. Sitting at the desk was an elderly, bewhiskered man dressed in long robes, who was dictating a letter to a stenographer. The walls of the room were covered with copies of letters from satisfied clients; he obviously took himself very seriously.

"Thank you for your letter dated the seventh of this month," said the elderly man as I walked closer. "I am sorry to inform you that this office no longer deals with problems arising with or appertaining to junkfootnoterphones. I suggest you direct your anger towards the FNP's complaints department. Yours very cordially, Solomon. That should do it. Yes?"

"Thursday Next reporting for duty."

"Ah!" he said, rising and giving me a hand to shake. "The *Outlander*. Is it true that—out there—two or more people can talk *at the same time*?"

"In the Outland it happens all the time."

"And do cats do anything else but sleep?"

"Not really."

"I see. And what do you make of this?"

He lifted a small traffic cone onto his desk and presented it with a dramatic flourish.

"It's . . . it's a traffic cone."

"Something of a rarity, yes?"

I chose my words carefully. "In many areas of the Outland they are completely unknown."

"I collect Outlandish objects," he said with a great deal of pride. "You must come and see my novelty-teapot collection."

"I'd be delighted."

He sat down and indicated for me to take a chair. "I was sorry to hear about Miss Havisham; she was one of the best operatives Jurisfiction ever had. Will there be a memorial?"

"Tuesday."

"I'll be sure to send flowers. Welcome to The Judgment of Solomon®. It's arbitration, mainly, a bit of licensing. We need someone to look after the crowds outside. It can get a bit impassioned sometimes."

"You're King Solomon?"

The old man laughed. "Me? You must be joking! There aren't enough minutes in the day for one Solomon—as soon as he did that 'divide the baby in two' thing, everyone and his uncle wanted him to arbitrate—from corporate takeovers to playground disputes. So he did what any right-thinking businessman would do: he franchised. How else do you think he could afford the temple and the chariots and the navy and whatnot? The land he sold to Hiram of Tyre? Give me a break! My real name's Kenneth."

I looked a little doubtful.

"I know what you're thinking. 'The Judgment of Kenneth' *does* sound a bit daft—that's why we are licensed to give judgments under his name. All aboveboard, I assure you. You have to purchase the cloak and grow a beard and go on the training course, but it works out very well. The *real* Solomon works from home, but he sticks only to the ultimate riddles of existence these days."

"What if a franchisee makes a dishonest judgment?"

"Very simple." Kenneth smiled. "The offender will be smitten from on high and forced to spend a painful eternity being tortured mercilessly by sadistic demons from the fieriest depths of hell. Solomon's very strict about *that*."

"I see."

"Good. Let's see the first punter."

I went to the door and asked for ticket holder number 32. A small man with a briefcase walked with me up to Kenneth's table. His knees became quite weak by the time he arrived, but he managed to contain himself.

"Name?"

"Mr. Toves from Text Grand Central, Your Eminence."

"Reason?"

"I need to ask for more exemptions from the '*I* before *E* except after *C*' rule."

"More?"

"It's part of the upgrade to UltraWord™, Your Honor."

"Very well, go ahead."

"*Feisty.*"

"Approved."

"*Feigned.*"

"Approved."

"*Weighty.*"

"Approved."

"*Believe.*"

"*Not* approved."

"*Reigate.*"

"Approved."

"That's it for the moment," said the small man, passing his papers across for Kenneth to sign.

"It is The Judgment of Solomon®," said Kenneth slowly, "that these words be exempt from Rule 7b of the arbitrary spelling code as ratified by the Council of Genres."

He stamped the paper and the small man scurried off.

"What's next?"

But I was thinking. Although I had been told repeatedly to ignore the three witches, their premonition about *Reigate* being exempted from the "*I* before *E* except after *C*" rule had just come true. Come to think of it, they had *all* come true. The "blinded dog"—the real Shadow—*had* barked, the "hedgepig"—Mrs. Tiggy-winkle—*had* ironed, and Mrs. Passerby from *Shadow the Sheepdog had* cried, " 'Tis time, 'tis time!" There must be something in it. But there were two *other* prophecies. One, I was to be the Bellman, which seemed unlikely in the extreme, and two, I was to beware the "thrice-read rule." What the hell did that mean?

"I'm a busy man," said Kenneth, glaring at me, "I don't need daydreamers!"

"I'm sorry, I was thinking of something the three witches told me."

"Charlatans! And worse—the *competition*."

"Sorry. What do you know of the *thrice-read* rule?"

"Is this a professional consultation?" he asked, sitting back and twiddling his thumbs.

"Staff freebie?" I asked hopefully.

Solomon laughed. "Never heard of any thrice-read rule. Now, you can do me a favor: if you see the three witches again, try and pinch their mailing list. In the meantime, can we have the next customer?"

I ushered them in. It was several characters from *Wuthering Heights* and they were all glaring at one another so much they didn't even recognize me. Heathcliff was wearing dark glasses and saying nothing; he was accompanied by his agent and a lawyer.

"Proceed!"

"*Wuthering Heights* first-person narrative dispute," said the lawyer, placing a sheet of paper on the table.

"Let me see," said Kenneth slowly, studying the report. "Mr. Lockwood, Catherine Earnshaw, Heathcliff, Nelly Dean, Isabella and Catherine Linton. Are you all here?"

They nodded their heads. Heathcliff looked over his sunglasses at me and winked.

"Well," murmured Kenneth at length, "you all believe that you should have the first-person narrative, is that it?"

"No, Your Worshipfulness," said Nelly Dean, " 'tis the other-ways. None of us want it. It's a curse to any honest Generic—and some *not* so honest."

"Hold your tongue, serving girl!" yelled Heathcliff.

"Murderer!"

"Say that again!"

"You heard me!"

And they all started to yell at one another until Kenneth banged his gavel on the desk and they were all instantly quiet. The Judgment of Solomon® was the last form of arbitration; there was no appeal from here and they all knew it.

"It is The Judgment of Solomon® that . . . you should *all* have the first-person narrative."

"What?!" yelled Mr. Lockwood. "What kind of loopy idea is that? How can we all be the first person?"

"It is fair and just," replied Kenneth, placing his fingertips together and staring at them all serenely.

"What will we do?" asked Catherine sarcastically. "Talk at the same time?"

"No," replied Kenneth. "Mr. Lockwood, you will introduce the story, and you, Nelly, will tell the major part of it in deep retrospection; the others will have your say in the following ratios."

Kenneth scribbled on the back of an envelope, signed it and handed it over. They all grumbled for a bit, Nelly Dean the most.

"Mrs. Dean," said Kenneth, "you are, for better or worse, the single linking factor for all the families. Consider yourself lucky I did not give the whole book to you. It is The Judgment of Solomon®—now go!"

And they all filed out, Nelly complaining bitterly while Heathcliff strode ahead, ignoring all the others.

"That was quite good," I said as soon as they had left.

"Do you think so?" asked Kenneth, genuinely pleased by my praise. "Judgmenting is not for everyone, but I quite like it. The trick is to be scrupulously fair and just—you could do with a few Solomon franchises in the Outland. Tell me, do you think Lola will be going to the Bookie Awards next week?"

"You know Lola?"

"Let's just say I have made her acquaintance in the course of my duties."

"I'm sure she'll be there—on the chicklit table, I should imagine—she's starring in *Girls Make All the Moves*."

"Is she really?" he said slowly. "Who's next?"

"I don't know; it depends on the choice available. Sometimes she goes through them alphabetically, other times in order of height."

"Not Lola, next for *me*."

"Sorry," I said, flushing slightly, "I'll go and get them."

It was Emperor Zhark. He seemed surprised to see me and told me what a great agent Miss Havisham had been. I walked him in, and he and Kenneth both stopped when they saw each other. They had clearly met before—but not for some time.

"Zhark!" cried Kenneth, walking around to the front of the desk and offering the emperor a Havana cigar. "You old trouble-maker! Haven't seen you for ages! What are you up to?"

"Tyrannical ruler of the known galaxy," he replied modestly.

"Get away! Old 'Slippery Zharky,' the class sneak of form 5C at St. Tabularasa's? Who'd have thought it!"

"It's *Emperor* Zhark, now, old chum," he said through gritted teeth.

"Glad to hear it. Whatever happened to Captain Ahab? Haven't seen him since we left school."

"Ahab?" queried the emperor, brow furrowed.

"You remember. One leg and madder than the March Hare. Set fire to his own trousers for a bet and stocked the school pond with piranhas."

"Oh, *him*. Last I heard he was convinced a white whale was after him—but that was years ago. We should have a reunion; one falls out of touch so easily in the BookWorld."

"Don't I know it," returned Kenneth sadly.

They sat in silence for a moment, recalling various school-friends, I imagine.

"So, Zharky old stick, how can I help you?"

"It's the Rambosians," he said at last, "they just refuse to cede power to me."

"How awkward for you. Is there any reason why they should?"

"Stability, old man, stability. The Rambosians have been responsible for numerous acts of savage satire in the Galactic Federation's daily tabloid *Stars My Destination*. They lampoon me constantly and the cartoons are shockingly insulting."

"So you want to invade?"

"Of course not; that would be wasteful of resources—no, I want them to open their arms and worship me as their one true God. They will give ultimate executive power to me, and in return, I will protect them with the might of the Zharkian Empire."

"Hmm," replied Kenneth thoughtfully, "that wouldn't be because the planet Rambosia is composed of eighteen trillon tons of valuable A-grade nutmeg, now would it?"

"Not in the least," replied the emperor unconvincingly.

"Very well. It is The Judgment of Solomon® that you make peace with the Rambosians."

"What?!"

The emperor jumped to his feet and went as dark as a thundercloud. He jabbed a long, slender finger in Kenneth's direction. Anywhere in the Zharkian Empire books such an action would have spelt instant death. Kenneth merely raised an eyebrow.

"You'll never play golf at the Old White Male Club again," yelled Zhark. "I'll have you blackballed so far out you won't be able to get your hat checked even if you come in the company of the Great Panjandrum himself!"

And so saying, he threw his cloak behind him, made a large huff noise, turned on his heels and strode to the door.

"Well," said Kenneth, "tyrants are all the same—shocking temper when they don't get their own way! Who's next?"

30.

Revelations

Commander Bradshaw did much of the booksploring in the early years, before the outlying Rebel Book Categories were brought within the controlling sphere of the Council of Genres. Inexplicably, novels can only be visited when someone has found a way in—and a way out. Bradshaw's mapping of the known BookWorld (1927–49) was an extraordinary feat, and until the advent of the ISBN Positioning System (1962), Bradshaw's maps were the *only* travel guide to fiction. Not all booksploring ends so happily. Ambrose Bierce was lost trying to access Poe. His name, along with many others, is carved on the Boojumorial, situated in the lobby of the Great Library.

RONAN EMPYRE,
A History of Gibbons

I COULDN'T FIND THE three witches, no matter how hard I looked. Their prophecies bothered me but not enough to keep me from sleeping soundly that night. It was two days later that I came home from a long day of Solomon's judgments to find Arnie waiting for me. He and Randolph were drinking some beers in the kitchen and talking about the correct time to use a long dash to designate interrupted speech.

"You can use it any—"

"Arnie, I owe you an apology," I said, blushing and forgetting my manners, "you must think me the worst tease in the Well."

"No, that would be Lola. Forget it. Gran explained everything. How are you? Memories returned?"

"All present and correct."

"Good. Dinner sometime—as good friends, of course?" he added hastily.

"I'd love to, Arnie. And thanks for being . . . so . . . well, decent."

He smiled and looked away.

"Beer?" said Randolph, who seemed to have recovered from his Lola-induced trauma.

"Anything nonalcoholic?"

He passed me a carton of orange juice and I poured myself a glass.

"Are you going to tell her?" said Arnie.

"Tell me what?"

"I didn't get the Amis part," began Randolph, "but I've been shortlisted for a minor speaking appearance in the next Wolfe."

"That's excellent news!" I responded happily. "When?"

"Sometime in the next couple of years. I'm going to do some standing-in work until then; the C of G has opened up travel writing as holiday destinations for Generics—no more away-day breaks in Barsetshire. I'm to cover for Count Smorltork while he goes on holiday for two weeks in Wainwright's *A Pictorial Guide to the Lakeland Fells*."

"Congratulations."

Randolph thanked me but was still somehow distant. He stared out of the porthole at the lake, deep in thought.

"What about you?" asked Arnie. "What will you do? Your demotion is all over the Well!"

"It's not a demotion. Well, perhaps it is."

"Word is that Harris Tweed is up to be the next Bellman," murmured Arnie, "despite his low experience. Jurisfiction favors an Outlander."

"What's so special about Outlanders?" asked Randolph.

"I think the C of G like our independence. We are not bound to our narrative, nor—in theory—do we favor one genre over another."

"And memories," murmured Arnie wistfully. "Love to be able to remember a childhood. *Any* childhood."

"Sense of smell, too," I added.

Randolph picked up the copy of *The Little Prince* that had been lying on the table and placed it on his nose.

"*Under* your nose," I told him, "and inhale deeply."

Randolph inhaled deeply and then exhaled. He looked confused. "What's meant to happen?"

"You kind of taste it in your head. Here."

I took the book and sniffed at it delicately. I had expected the odor of leather, but instead I could smell sweet melons— *cantaloupes*. I was transported back to the last time I had come across this particular scent: the odd boxy truck in *Caversham Heights*. The truck without texture, the automaton driver without personality. Something clicked.

"It was an UltraWord™ truck," I murmured, searching through my bag for the angular and textureless bolt I had picked up after the truck had departed. I found it and sniffed at it cautiously, my mind racing as I tried to think of a connection.

"If this is anything to go by," said Arnie, flicking through the pages of *The Little Prince*, "then the readers are in for a treat."

"They are indeed," I replied as Randolph tried to open the cover—but couldn't.

I took it from him and the book opened easily. I handed it back but the cover was still stuck fast.

"Odd," I muttered as Arnie opened it again without any problem.

"It's Havisham's copy," I said slowly, "she's read it, and me, and now you."

"A book which only three people can read!" observed Randolph scornfully. "A bit mean, I must say!"

"Only three readers," I murmured, my heart going cold as I recalled the three witches' prophecy: *Beware the thrice-read rule!* Perhaps the new operating system was not quite the egalitarian advance it claimed—if it was really the case that UltraWord™ books could only be opened by three people, then libraries would be a thing of the past. Secondhand bookshops closed overnight. You could only lend a book twice. I thought of the increased revenue that might be generated from such a commercially useful attribute and shook my head sadly. I had been right. There *was* something rotten in the state of fiction!

"Thursday?" asked Arnie. "Are you okay?"

I put *The Little Prince* down. "Yes—just one of those epiphanic moments that fiction seems to be littered with."

"Ah!" said Randolph knowledgeably. "We learnt all about *those* at Tabularasa's."

I got up and walked about the kitchen, thinking hard. The angular truck, the strange bolt? What did that all mean? I shivered. If something was so insidiously wrong with the new upgrade that they would kill to keep it quiet, then the "thrice-read rule" was just the beginning—after all, a timed readblock would only affect readers in the Outland—it wouldn't affect the BookWorld at all. There *had* to be more.

"Problems?" asked Arnie, sensing my disquiet.

"It's the UltraWord™ upgrade."

"Bad?"

"The worst. I was removed from Jurisfiction for a reason—who other than the grieving apprentice to ask awkward questions? Miss Havisham was sure there was something wrong with UltraWord™. Her death proves it."

"I think at best it only *suggests* it," declared Randolph, who had obviously been studying law as part of his Amis bit part. "Without any evidence it will be hard to prove. Did she or any of the others say *anything* to you about it?"

I thought hard. "From Havisham and Perkins—nothing. And all I got from Snell was gobbledygook on his deathbed. He might have told me everything, but it was so badly spelled I didn't understand a word."

"What did he say?"

"He said, 'Thirsty! Wode—Cone, udder whirled—doughnut Trieste—!' or something quite like it."

Arnie exchanged looks with Randolph.

"The *Thirsty* must be *Thursday*," murmured Arnie.

"I figured that," I returned, "but what about the rest?"

"Do you suppose," said Randolph thoughtfully, "that if you were to recite those words near a source of mispeling, they would revert back again?"

There was one of those long pauses that usually accompany a flash of brilliance.

"It's worth a try," I replied, thinking hard. I checked the clip of my automatic and opened my TravelBook.

"Where are you going?" asked Arnie.

"To visit the Anti-mispeling Fast Response Group on the seventeenth floor. I think they might be able to help."

"Will they want to?"

I shrugged. "Asking wasn't part of the plan."

The elevator doors opened on the seventeenth floor. This held all the books whose authors began with Q, and since there weren't that many of them, the remainder of the space had been given over to the Jurisfiction Anti-mispeling Fast Response Group. If any live mispeling vyrus was at Jurisfiction, this would be the place to find it.

This floor of the Great Library was more dimly lit than the others, and the rows of bunk beds containing the DanverClones began soon after the Quiller-Couch novels ended. The Danvers were all sitting bolt upright, their eyes following me silently as I walked slowly down the corridor. It was disquieting to be sure, but I could think of no other place to look.

I reached the central core of the library, a circular void surrounded by a wrought-iron rail at the center of the four corridors. The way I had come was all Danvers, and so were two of the others. The fourth corridor was lined with packing cases of dictionaries, and beyond them, the medical area in which I had last seen Snell. I walked closer, my feet making no noise on the padded carpet. Perhaps Snell had known as much as Perkins? They were partners, after all. I cursed myself for not thinking of this before.

I arrived at the small medical unit that was ready and waiting to deal with any infected person. The shielded curtains, the bandages overprinted with dictionary entries. They could soothe and contain but rarely cure—Snell was doomed as soon as he was soaked in the vyrus and he knew it.

I opened a few drawers here and there but found nothing. Then, I noticed a large pile of dictionaries stacked by themselves in a roped-off area. I walked closer, repeating the word *ambidextrous* as I did so.

"Ambidextrous . . . ambidextrous . . . ambidextrous . . . ambidextruos."

Bingo. I'd found it.

"Miss Next? What in heaven's name are you doing here?"

I nearly jumped out of my skin. If it had been Libris, I would have been worried; but it wasn't—it was Harris Tweed.

"You nearly scared me half to death!" I told him.

"Sorry!" He grinned. "What are you up to?"

"There's something wrong with UltraWord™."

Tweed looked up and down the corridor and lowered his voice. "I think so, too," he hissed, "but I'm not sure what—I've a feeling that it uses a faster 'memory fade' utility than Version 8.3 so the readers will want to reread the book more often. The Council of Genres are interested in upping their published ReadRates—the battle with nonfiction is hotting up; more than they care to tell *us* about."

It was the sort of thing I had suspected.

"What have *you* discovered?" he asked.

I leaned closer. "UltraWord™ has a 'thrice only' read capability."

"Good Lord!" exclaimed Tweed. "Find anything else?"

"Not yet. I was hoping to discover what Snell said before he died. It was badly mispeled but I thought perhaps I could *unmispel* it by repeating it close to a mispeling source."

"Good thought, but we must take care." Tweed donned a pair of dictosafe gloves. "Sit here and repeat Snell's words." He placed a chair not a yard from the pile of dictionaries. "I'll remove one OED at a time and we'll see what happens."

"Wode—Cone, udder whirled—doughnut Trieste," I recited as Tweed pulled a single dictionary from the large pile that covered the vyrus. *"Wode—Cone, ulder whirled—dougnut Trieste."*

"Who else knows about this?" he asked. "If what you say is true, this knowledge is dangerous enough to have killed three times—I hate to say it, but I think we have a rotten apple at Jurisfiction."

"I told no wun at Jurizfaction. *Wede—Caine, ulder whorled—dogn'ut Triuste.*"

Harris carefully removed another dictionary. I could see the faint purple glow from within the stacked books.

"We don't know who we can trust," he said somberly. "Who *did* you tell, precisely? It's important, I need to know."

He removed another dictionary.

"Twede—Caine, ulter whorled—dogn't Truste."

My heart went cold. *Twede.* Could that be *Tweed?* I tried to look normal and glanced across at him, attempting to figure out if he had heard me. I had good reason to be concerned; if he removed one too many dictionaries, I could be fatally mispeled into a *Thirsty Neck* or something—and nobody knew I was here.

"I cane right you a liszt if it wood yelp," I said, trying to sound as normal as I could.

"Why not just tell me," he said, still smiling. "Who was it? Some of those Generics at *Caversham Heights?*"

"I tolled the bell, man."

The smile dropped from his face. "Now I know you're lying."

We stared at one another. Tweed was no fool; he knew his cover was blown.

"Tweed," I said, the unmispeling now complete, *"Kaine—UltraWord—Don't trust!"*

I jumped aside as soon as I had said it. I was only just in time—Tweed yanked out three dictionaries near the bottom and the dictosafe partially collapsed.

I sprawled on the ground as the heavy glow, emanating in one direction from the disrupted pile of dictionaries, instantly turned the hospital bed behind me into an *hospitable ted,* a furry stuffed bear who waved his paw cheerfully and told me to pop round for dinner any day of the week—and to bring a friend.

I threw myself at Tweed, who was not as quick as I, my speech returning to normal almost immediately.

"Snell and Perkins?!" I yelled pinning him to the ground. "Who else? Havisham?"

"It's not important," he cried as I took his gun and forced his chin into the carpet.

"You're wrong!" I told him angrily. "What's the problem with UltraWord™?"

"Nothing's wrong with it," he replied, trying to sound reasonable. "In fact, everything's *right* with it! Control of the BookWorld will have never been easier. And with modern and freethinking Outlanders like you and I, we can take fiction to new and dizzying heights!"

I pushed my knee harder into the back of his neck and he yelped.

"And where does Kaine come into this?"

"UltraWord™ benefits everyone, Next. Us in here and publishers out there. It's the perfect system!"

"Perfect? You need to resort to murder to keep it on track? How can it be perfect?"

"You don't understand, Next. In the Outland murder is morally reprehensible, but in here it as a narrative necessity—without it and the jeopardy it generates, we'd have lost a million readers long ago!"

"She was my friend, Tweed!" I yelled. "Not some cannon fodder for a cheap thriller!"

"You're making a big mistake," he replied, face still pressed into the carpet. "I can offer you an important position at Text Grand Central. With UltraWord™ under our control we will have the power to change anything we please within fiction. You gave *Jane Eyre* a happy ending—we can do the same with countless others and give the reading public what they want. We will dictate terms to that moth-eaten bunch of bureaucrats at the

Council of Genres and forge a new, stronger fiction that will catapult the novel to new heights—no longer will we be looked down upon by the academic press and marginalized by nonfiction!"

I had heard enough. "You're finished, Tweed. When the Bellman hears what you've been up to—!"

"The Bellman is only a tool of Text Grand Central, Next. He does what we tell him. Release me and take your place at my side. Untold adventures and riches await you—we can even write your husband back."

"Not a chance. I want the real Landen or none at all."

"You won't know the difference. Take my hand—I won't offer it again."

"No deal."

"Then," he said slowly, "it is good-bye."

I saw something out of the corner of my eye and moved quickly to my right. A pickax handle glanced off my shoulder and struck the carpet. It was Uriah Hope. No wonder Tweed hadn't seemed that worried. I rolled off Tweed and dodged Uriah's next blow, pushing myself backwards along the carpet in my haste to get away. He swung again and shattered a desk, wedging the handle in the wood and struggling with it long enough for me to get to my feet and raise my gun. I wasn't quick enough and he knocked it from my grasp; I ducked the next blow and ran back towards Tweed, who was starting to get up. He hooked my ankle and I came crashing down. I rolled onto my back as Uriah jumped towards me with a wild cry. I put out a foot, caught him on the chest and heaved. His momentum carried him over onto the pile of dictionaries—and the mispeling vyrus. Tweed tried to grab me but I was off and running down the corridor as the DanverClones began to stir.

"Kill her!" screamed Tweed, and the Danvers started to move off their bunk beds and walk slowly towards me. I took my Travel-Book from my pocket, opened it at the right page and stopped, right in the middle of the corridor. I couldn't outrun them but I could *outread* them. As I jumped out, I could just feel the bony fingers of the Danvers clutching my rapidly vanishing form.

*   *   *

I jumped clean into Norland Park. Past the striking nursery characters and the frog-faced doorman to appear a little too suddenly in the Jurisfiction offices. I ran straight into the Red Queen, who collapsed and in turn knocked over Benedict and the Bellman. I quickly grabbed Benedict's pistol in case Tweed or Hope arrived ready for action and was consequently attacked from an unexpected quarter. Mistaking my intentions, the Red Queen grabbed my gun arm and twisted it around behind me while Benedict tackled me round the waist and pulled me down yelling, "Gun! Protect the Bellman!"

"Wait!" I shouted. "There's a problem with UltraWord™!"

"What do you mean?" demanded the Bellman when I had surrendered the gun. "Is this some sort of joke?"

"No joke. It's Tweed—"

"Don't listen to her!" shouted Tweed, who had just appeared. "She is an ambitious murderer who will stop at nothing to get what she wants!"

The Bellman looked at us both in turn. "You have proof of this, Harris?"

"Oh, yes—more proof than you'll ever need. Heep, bring it in."

Uriah Hope—or *Heep* as he was now—had survived the mispeling but had been changed irrevocably. Whilst before he had been *adventurous,* he was, thanks to the vyrus, *cadaverous; thin* instead of *lithe, fawning* instead of *frowning.* But that was, for the moment, by the by. Uriah was holding the stained pillowcase that contained Snell's head. Not his own, of course—the plot device Snell had paid so much for in the Well.

"We found this in Thursday's home," announced Tweed, "hidden in the broom cupboard. Heep, would you?"

The thin and sallow youth, whose hair was now *oily* rather than *curly,* laid the bag on a table and lifted the head out by its hair. A gasp came from Benedict's lips and the Red Queen crossed herself.

"Heavens above," murmured the Bellman, "it's Godot!"

31.

Tables Turned

Insider Trading: Slang term for Internal Narrative Manipulation. Illegal since 1932 and contrary to item B17(g) of the Narrative Continuity Code, this self-engineered plot fluctuation is so widespread within the BookWorld that it is dealt with on a discretionary basis to enable it to be enforced at all. Small manipulation such as dialogue violations are generally ignored, but larger unlicensed plot adjustments are aggressively investigated. The most publicized flaunting of these rules was by Heathcliff when he burned down Wuthering Heights. Fined and sentenced to 150 hours community service within *Green Eggs and Ham*, Heathcliff was just one of many high-profile cases that Jurisfiction were prosecuting at that time.

CAT FORMERLY KNOWN AS CHESHIRE,
Guide to the Great Library (glossary)

I HAD UNDERESTIMATED TWEED or the power he wielded in the BookWorld. Until then I don't think I'd realized just how far they would warp the narrative to realize their ambitions. I was still standing there gaping like an idiot when Heep grasped me painfully by the arm and twisted it around, pushing me into a bookcase as he did so.

"I be ever so humbly sorry about this, Miss Next," he whined, the mispeling having gone deeper than his skin and rotted his very soul. "Imagine me, an A-7 arresting a pretty Outlander such as yourself!"

His breath smelt rotten; I breathed through my mouth to avoid gagging. He reached in for my TravelBook and took the opportunity to slide his hand across my breast; I struggled harder—but to no avail.

"That head's not mine!" I shouted, realizing how stupid it sounded straightaway.

"That is one thing we *are* certain of," replied Tweed quietly. "Why did you kill him?"

"I didn't. It's Snell's," I said somewhat uselessly, "he bought it for use in his next book and asked me to keep it for him."

"Snell, insider trading? Any other ills you'd like to heap on the dead? I don't think that's very likely—and how did it turn out to be Godot's? Coincidence?"

"I'm being framed," I replied, "Godot's head in a bag in my closet? Isn't that a chapter ending too slick to be anything but an engineered dramatic moment?"

I stopped. I had been told many times by my SpecOps instructors that the biggest mistake anyone can make in a high-stress situation is to act too fast and say too much before thinking. I needed time—a commodity that was fast becoming a rarity.

"We have evidence of her involvement in at least three other murders, Mr. Bellman," said Tweed.

The Bellman sighed and shook his head sadly as I was relieved of my TravelBook and handcuffed to three anvils to stop me jumping out.

"Havisham?" he asked with a tremor in his voice.

"We believe so," replied Tweed.

"They're fooling you, Mr. Bellman, sir," I said, trying to sound as normal as I could. "Something is badly wrong with UltraWord™."

"That something is you, Next," spat Tweed. "Four Jurisfiction agents dead in the line of duty—and Deane nowhere to be found. I can't believe it—you'd kill your own mentor?"

"Steady, Tweed," said the Bellman, drawing up a chair and looking at me sadly. "Havisham vouched for her and that counts for something."

"Then let me educate you, Mr. Bellman," said Tweed, sitting on the corner of a table. "I've been making a few inquiries. Even discounting Godot, there is more than enough evidence of Next's perfidy."

"Evidence?" I scoffed. "Such as what?"

"Does the code word *sapphire* mean anything to you?"

"Of course."

"Only eight Jurisfiction agents had access to *The Sword of the Zenobians,*" said Tweed, "and four of them are dead."

"It's hardly a smoking gun, is it?"

"Not on its own," replied Tweed carefully, "but when we add other facts, it starts to make sense. Bradshaw and Havisham eject from *Zenobians* leaving you alone with Snell—they arrive a few minutes later and he is mortally mispeled. Very neat, very clever."

"Why?" I asked. "Why would I kill Miss Havisham? Why would I want to kill *any* of these people?"

"Ambition."

"What ambition? All I want to do is to have my child and go home."

"The Bellman's job," announced Tweed like a hidden trump. "As an Outlander you have seniority, but only after Bradshaw, Havisham, Perkins, Deane—and me. Bradshaw has been the Bellman already, so that rules him out. Were you going to kill me next?"

"I have no ambition to be the Bellman and didn't kill Miss Havisham," I muttered, trying to think of a plan of action.

Tweed leaned closer. "You've been using Jurisfiction as a springboard to feed your own burning ambition. It's a dangerous thing to possess. Ambition will sustain for a while—and then it kills indiscriminately."

The Bellman, who up until this moment had been quiet, suddenly said, "I'll need more proof than your say-so, Mr. Tweed."

"Indeed," replied Tweed triumphantly, "as you know, the three witches have to log all their prophecies. They don't like to do it, but they have to—no paperwork, no license to read chicken entrails. Simple as that."

He pulled a sheet of paper from his pocket. "The day after Miss Next arrived, they filed this report." He handed the paper to the Bellman. "Read the third on the list."

"Prophecy three," read the Bellman slowly, *"Thou shalt be Bellman thereafter."*

Tweed retrieved the sheet of paper and slid it across the table to me. "Do you deny this?"

"No," I said glumly.

"We call it *Macbeth's syndrome,*" said the Bellman sadly, "an insane desire to fulfill your own prophecies. It's nearly always fatal. Sadly, not only for the sufferer."

"I'm not a Macbeth sufferer, Mr. Bellman, and even if I am, shouldn't even the smallest error in UltraWord™ be looked at?"

"There aren't any errors," put in Tweed, "UltraWord™ is the finest piece of technology we have ever devised—foolproof, stable and totally without error. Tell me the problem—I'm sure there is a satisfactory explanation."

"Well—" I stopped myself. I knew the Bellman was still an honest man. Should I tell him about the thrice-read problem and risk Tweed covering his tracks even more? On reflection, probably not. The more I dug, the more would be found against me. I needed breathing space—I needed to *escape.*

"What's to become of me?"

"Permanent expulsion from the BookWorld," replied Tweed. "We don't have enough evidence to convict but we do have enough to have you banned from fiction forever. There is no appeals procedure. I only have to ratify it with the Bellman."

"Well," said the Bellman, tingling his bell sadly, "I must concur with Tweed's recommendation. Search her for any Book-World accessories before we send her back."

"You're making a mistake, Mr. Bellman," I said angrily, "a very—"

"Oooh!" said Heep, who had been rummaging in my pockets and taking the opportunity to try to touch my breasts again. "Look what I've found!"

It was the Suddenly, a Shot Rang Out! plot device Snell had given me at the Slaughtered Lamb.

"A plot device, Miss Next?" said Tweed, taking the small glass globe from Heep. "Do you have any paperwork for this?"

"No. It's evidence. I just forgot to sign it in."

"Illegal carriage of all Narrative Turning Devices is strictly illegal. Are you a dealer? Who's your source? Peddle this sort of garbage in teenage fiction?"

"Blow it out of your arse, Tweed."

"What did you say?"

"You heard me."

He went crimson and might have hit me, but all I wanted was for him to move close enough for me to kick him—or his hand, at least.

"You piece of crap," he sneered. "I've known you were no good from the moment I saw you. Think you're something special, Miss SpecOps Outlander supremo?"

"At least I don't work for the Skyrail, Tweed. Inside fiction you're a big cheese, but out in the real world you're less than a nobody!"

It had the desired effect. He took a step closer and I kicked out, connected with his hand and the small glass globe went sailing into the air, high above our heads. Heep, coward that he now was, dived for cover, but Tweed and the Red Queen, wary of a Narrative Turning Device going off in a confined area, tried to catch it. They might have been successful if just one of them had attempted it. As it was, they collided with a grunt and the small glass globe fell to the floor and shattered as they looked on helplessly.

Suddenly, a shot rang out. I didn't see where it came from but felt its full effect; the bullet hit the chain that was holding me to the anvils, shattering it neatly. I didn't pause for breath. I was off and running towards the door. I didn't know where I was heading; without my TravelBook I was trapped and *Sense and Sensibility* was not that big. Tweed and Heep were soon on their feet, only to hit the floor again as a second volley followed the first. I ducked through the door and came upon . . . Vernham Deane, pistol in hand. Heep and Tweed returned fire as Deane holstered his pistol and took both my hands.

"Hold tight," he said, "and empty your mind. We're going to go *abstract*."

I cleared my mind as much as I could and—[1]

"How odd!" said Tweed, walking to the place he had last seen Thursday. He knew she couldn't jump without her book, but something was wrong. She had *vanished*—not with the fade out of a standard bookjump, but an instantaneous departure.

Heep and the Bellman joined him, Heep with a bookhound on a leash, who sniffed the ground and whimpered and yelped noisily, chops slobbering.

1. The Jurisfiction office vanished and was replaced by a large and shiny underground tube. It was big enough to stand up in, but even so I had to keep pressed against the wall as a constant stream of words flashed past in both directions. Above us, another pipe was leading upwards, and every now and then a short stream of words were diverted into this small conduit.

"Where are we?" I asked, my voice echoing about the steel walls.

"Somewhere quite safe," replied Deane. "They'll be wondering where you went."

"We're in the Outland—I mean, home?"

Deane laughed. "No, silly, we're in the footnoterphone conduits."

I looked at the stream of messages again. "We are?"

"Sure."

"Come on, let me show you something."

We walked along the pipe until it opened out into a bigger room—a hub where messages went from one genre to another. The exits closest to me were marked *Crime, Romance, Thriller* and *Comedy*, but there were plenty more, all routing the footnoterphone messages towards some subgenre or other.

"It's incredible!" I breathed.

"Oh, this is just a small hub," replied Deane, "you should see the bigger ones. It all works on the ISBN number system, you know—and the best thing about it is that neither Text Grand Central nor the Council of Genres know that you can get down here. It's sanctuary, Thursday. Sanctuary away from the prying eyes of Jurisfiction and the rigidity of the narrative."

I caught his eye. "Tweed thinks you killed Perkins, Snell and that serving girl."

"No scent?" said the Bellman in a puzzled tone. "No destination signature? Harris, what's going on?"

"I don't know, sir. With your permission I'd like to set up textual sieves on every floor of the Great Library. Heep will be your personal bodyguard from now on; Next is quite clearly insane and will try to kill you—I have no doubt about that. Do I have your permission to apply for an Extremely Prejudicial Termination order from the Council of Genres?"

"No, that is one step I am not prepared to take. Order the death of an Outlander? Not I."

Tweed made to move off but the Bellman called him back. "Tweed, Thursday said there was a problem with Ultra-

---

He stopped walking and sighed. "Tweed is working with Text Grand Central to make sure UltraWord™ is launched without any hitches. He knew I wanted to conduct more tests. He offered me a plot realignment in *The Squire of High Potternews* to 'garner my support.'"

"He tried to buy you?"

"When I refused, he threatened to kill me—that's why we escaped."

"We?"

"Of course. The maidservant that I ravage in chapter eight and then cruelly cast into the night. She dies of tuberculosis and I drink myself to death. Do you think we could allow that?"

"But isn't that what happens in most Farquitt novels? Maidservant ravaged by cruel squire?"

"You don't understand, Thursday. Mimi and I are in love."

"Ah!" I replied slowly, thinking of Landen. "That can change things."

"Come," said Deane, beckoning me through the hub and dodging the footnoterphone messages, "we have made our home in a disused branch line—after Woolf wrote *To the Lighthouse* and *Mrs. Dalloway*, the Council of Genres thought Stream of Consciousness would be the next Detective— they built a large hub to support the rackloads of novels that never appeared."

We turned into a large tunnel about the size of the underground back in Swindon, and the messages whizzed back and forth, almost filling the tube to capacity.

After a few hundred yards we came to another hub and took the least used—barely two or three messages a minute buzzed languidly past, and these seemed to be lost; they moved around vaguely for a moment and then

Word™; do you think we should contact Text Grand Central and delay its release?"

"You mean you take all this seriously, sir?" exclaimed Tweed in a shocked tone. "Excuse me for being so blunt, but Next is a murderer and a liar—how many more people does she have to kill before she is stopped?"

"UltraWord™ is bigger than all of us," said the Bellman slowly, "even if she *is* a murderer, she still might have found something wrong. I cannot afford to take any risks over the new upgrade."

"Well, we can delay," said Tweed slowly, "but that would take the inauguration of the new Operating System out of your term as Bellman. If you think that is the best course of action, perhaps we should take it. But whichever Bellman

---

evaporated. The sides of the tube were less shiny, rubbish had collected at the bottom and water leaked in from the roof. Every now and then we passed small unused offshoots, built to support books that were planned but never written.

"Why did you come for me, Vern?"

"Because I don't believe you would kill Miss Havisham, and I love stories as much as anyone. UltraWord™ is flawed, and I'm not going to see it dominate the BookWorld if I can help it."

The tunnel opened out into a large chamber where a settlement of sorts had been built from rubbish and scrap wood—items that could be removed from the BookWorld without anyone noticing. The buildings were little more than tents with the orange flicker of oil lamps from within.

"Vern!" A dark-haired young woman waved at him from the nearest tent. She was heavily pregnant and Deane rushed up to hug her affectionately. I watched them with a certain degree of jealousy. I noticed I had placed my hand on my own tum quite subconsciously. I sighed and pushed it to the back of my mind.

"Mimi, this is Thursday," said Vern. I shook her hand and she led us into their tent, offering me a small wooden box to sit on that I noticed had once been used to held past tenses.

"So what's wrong with UltraWord™?" I asked, my curiosity overcoming me.

"Flawed by the need for control," he said slowly. "Think the BookWorld

signs UltraWord™ into law might be looked on favorably by history, do you not think?"

The Bellman rubbed his chin thoughtfully.

"What more tests could we do?" he asked at length.

Tweed smiled. "I'm not sure, sir. We fixed the flight manual conflict and debugged AutoPageTurnDeluxe™. The raciness overheat problem has been fixed, and the Esperanto translation module is now working one hundred percent. All these faults have been dealt with openly and transparently. We need to upgrade and upgrade now—the popularity of non-fiction is creeping up and we have to be vigilant."

Heep ran up and whispered in Tweed's ear.

"That was one of our intelligence sources, sir. It seems that Next has been suffering from a mnemonomorph recently."

"Great Scott!" gasped the Bellman. "She might not even know she had done it!"

—————————————

is overregulated? Believe me, it's an anarchist's dreamworld compared to the future seen by TGC!"

And so, as quickly as possible, he told me exactly what he had discovered. The problem was, I needed something more than his theories. To do battle with Tweed and TGC, I needed *proof*.

"Proof," said Deane, "yes, that was always the problem. Let me show you what Perkins left us."

He returned with a birdcage containing a skylark and set it upon the table.

I looked at the bird and the bird looked back.

"This is the proof?"

"So Perkins said."

"Do you have any idea what he meant?"

"None at all." Deane sighed. "He was Minotaur shit long before he tried to explain it to any of us."

I leaned forward for a closer look and smelt—*cantaloupes*.

"It's UltraWord™," I breathed.

"It is?" echoed Deane in surprise. "How can you tell?"

"It's an Outlander thing. I have a plan, but to do it I have to be at liberty—and free from the Bellman's suspicions."

"I can arrange that." Deane smiled. "Come on, let's do this thing before it gets any worse."

"It would explain that convincing act," added Tweed. "A woman with no memory of her evil has no guilt. Now, do I have your permission to apply for an Extremely Prejudicial Termination order?"

"Yes," sighed the Bellman, taking a seat, "yes, you better had—and UltraWord™ is to go ahead, as planned. We have dithered enough."

We jumped back into the Jurisfiction offices. Tweed and Heep were alone with the Bellman, overseeing a document that I found out later was my termination warrant. I had Deane's gun pointed—at Deane. He had his hands up. Heep and Tweed exchanged nervous glances.

"I've brought you Deane, Bellman," I announced. "I had no other way of proving my innocence. Vern, tell them what you told me."

"Go to hell!"

I whacked him hard on the back of the head with the butt of his pistol and he fell to the ground, momentarily stunned. Blood welled up in his hairline and I winced; luckily, no one saw me.

"That's for Miss Havisham," I told him.

"Miss Havisham?" echoed the Bellman.

"Oh, yes," I replied. "Bastard."

Deane touched the back of his head and looked at his hand.

"Bitch!" he muttered. "I'd have killed you, too!"

He turned and leaped at me with surprising speed, grasped me by the throat before I could stop him, and we both crashed to the floor, knocking over a table as we went. It was an impressive charade.

"The little slut serving wench deserved to die!" he screamed. "How dare she spoil the happy life that could have been mine!"

I couldn't breath and started to black out. I had wanted it to look realistic—and so, I suppose, did he.

Tweed placed a gun under Deane's chin and forced him off. He spat in my face as I lay there, trying to get my breath back. Deane was then set upon by Heep, who took an unhealthy delight in beating him despite apologizing superciliously every time he struck him.

"Stop!" yelled the Bellman. "Calm down, all of you!"

They propped the now bleeding Deane in a chair and Heep bound his hands.

"Did you kill Perkins?" asked the Bellman, and Deane nodded sullenly.

"He was going to blow the whistle on me—Havisham, too. Snell and Mathias just got in the way. Happiness should have been mine!" he sobbed. "Why did the slut have to turn up with that little bastard—I should have married Miss O'Shaugnessy—all I wanted was something no evil squire in Farquitt ever gets!"

"And what was that?" asked the Bellman sternly.

"A happy ending."

"Pitiful, wouldn't you say, Tweed?"

"Pitiful, yes, sir," he replied stonily, staring at me as I picked myself off the floor.

The Bellman tore up my termination order. "It looks like we have underestimated you," he said happily. "I knew Havisham couldn't be wrong. Tweed, I think you owe Miss Next an apology."

"I apologize unreservedly," replied Tweed through gritted teeth.

"Good," said the Bellman. "Now, Thursday, what's the problem with UltraWord™?"

It was a sticky moment. We had to take this higher than the Bellman. With Libris and the whole of Text Grand Central involved, there was no knowing what they would do. I remembered an error from an early UltraWord™ test version.

"Well," I began, "I think there is a flight manual conflict. If you read an UltraWord™ book on an airship, it can play havoc with the flight manuals."

"That's been cured," said the Bellman kindly, "but thank you for being so diligent."

"That's a relief. May I have some leave?"

"Of course. And if you find any other irregularities in Ultra-Word™, I want them brought to me and me alone."

"Yes, sir. May I?" I indicated my TravelBook.

"Of course! Very impressive job capturing Deane, don't you think, Tweed?"

"Yes," replied Tweed grimly, "very impressive—well done, Next."

I opened my TravelBook and read myself to Solomon's outer office. Tweed wouldn't try anything at the C of G, and the following three days were crucial. Everything I needed to say to the Bellman would have to wait until I had seven million witnesses.

32.

The 923rd Annual BookWorld Awards

The Annual BookWorld Awards (or Bookies) were instigated in 1063 C.E. and for the first two hundred years were dominated by Aeschylus and Homer, who won most of the awards in the thirty or so categories. Following the expansion in fiction and the inclusion of the oral tradition, categories totaled two hundred by 1423. Technical awards were introduced twenty years later and included Most Used English Word and the Most Widely Mispelt Word, witch has remained a contentious subject ever since. By 1879 there were over six hundred categories, but neither the length of the awards nor the vote-rigging scandal in 1964 has dented the popularity of this glittering occasion—it will remain one of the BookWorld's most popular fixtures for years to come.

COMMANDER TRAFFORD BRADSHAW, CBE,
Bradshaw's Guide to the BookWorld

I STOOD OFFSTAGE AT the Starlight Room, one in a long line of equally minor celebrities, all awaiting our turn to go and read the nominations. The hospitality lounge where we had all been mustered was about the size of a football pitch, and the massed babble of excited voices sounded like rushing water. I had been trying to avoid Tweed all evening. But whenever I lost him, Heep would take over. There were others about, too. Bradshaw had pointed out Orlick and Legree, two other assistants of Tweed's that he thought I should be wary of.

Of them all, Heep was the most amateur. His skills at unobserved observation were woefully inadequate.

"Well!" he said when I caught him staring at me. "You and me both waiting for awards!" He rubbed his hands and tapped his long fingers together. "I ask you, me all humble and you an Outlander. Thanks to you and the mispeling incident I'm up for Most Creepy Character in a Dickens Novel. What would you be up for?"

"I'm giving one, not accepting one, Uriah—and why are you following me?"

"Apologies, ma'am," he said, squirming slightly and clasping his hands together to try to stop them from moving, "Mr. Tweed asked me to keep a particular close eye on you in case of an attack, ma'am."

"Oh, yes?" I replied, unimpressed by the lame cover story. "From whom?"

"Those who would wish you harm, of course. ProCaths, bowdlerizers—even the townspeople from *Shadow*. It was them what tried to kill you at Solomon's, I'll be bound."

Sadly, it was true. There had been two attempts on my life since Deane's arrest. The first had been a tiger released in Kenneth's office. I thought at first it was Big Martin catching up with me—but it wasn't. Bradshaw had dealt with the creature; he sent it on a one-way trip to *Zenobians*. The second had been a contract killing. Fortunately for me, Heep's handwriting was pretty poor and Thursby from *The Maltese Falcon* was shot instead. It was only because I was an Outlander that I was still alive—if I'd been a Generic, Text Grand Central could have erased me at source long ago.

"Mr. Tweed said that Outlanders have to stick together," carried on Heep, "and look after each other. Outlanders have a duty—"

"This is all really very sweet of him," I interrupted, "but I can look after myself. Good luck with your award; I'm sure you'll win."

"Thank you!" he said, fidgeting for a moment before moving off a little way and continuing to stare at me in an unsubtle manner.

I was summoned towards the stage where I could see the master of ceremonies winding up the previous award. He reminded me of Adrian Lush—all smiles, insincerity and bouffant hair.

"So," he carried on, " 'teleportation' a clear winner for the Most Implausible Premise in an SF Novel, which was hard luck on 'And they lived happily after,' which won last year. If I could thank all the nominees and especially Ginger Hebblethwaite for presenting it."

There was applause; a freckled youth in a flying jacket waved to the crowd and winked at me as he trotted offstage.

The emcee took a deep breath and consulted his list. Unlike awards at home, there was no TV coverage as no one in the Book-World had a TV. You didn't need one. The Generics who had re-mained in the books as a skeleton staff to keep the stories in order were kept up-to-date with a live footnoterphone link from the Starlight Room. With all the usual characters away at the awards, fiction wasn't *quite* so good, but no one generally no-ticed. This was often the reason people in the Outland argued over the quality of a recommended book. They had read it during the Bookies.

"The next award, ladies, gentleman and, er, *things,* is to be given by the newest Jurisfiction agent to join the ranks of the BookWorld's own policing agency. Fresh from a glittering career in the Outland and engineer of the improved ending to *Jane Eyre*, may I present—Thursday Next!"

There was applause and I walked on, smiling dutifully. I shook the hand of the emcee and looked out into the auditorium.

It was vast. *Really* vast. The Starlight Room was the largest single-function room ever described in any book. A lit cande-labra graced each of the hundred thousand tables, and as I looked into the room, all I could see was a never-ending field of white lights, flickering in the distance like stars. Seven million charac-ters were here tonight, but by using a convenient temporal-field displacement technology borrowed from the boys in the SF genre, everyone in the room had a table right next to the stage and could hear and see us with no problems at all.

"Good evening," I said, staring out at the sea of faces, "I am here to read the nominations and announce the winner of the Best Chapter Opening in the English Language category."

I started to feel hot under the lights. I composed myself and read the back of the envelope.

"The nominations are *The Fall of the House of Usher* by Edgar Allan Poe, *Brideshead Revisited* by Evelyn Waugh, and *A Tale of Two Cities* by Charles Dickens."

I waited until the applause had died down and then opened the envelope.

"And the winner is . . . *Brideshead Revisited*!"

There was thunderous applause and I smiled dutifully as the emcee bent closer to the microphone.

"Wonderful!" he said enthusiastically as the applause subsided. "Let's hear the winning paragraph, shall we?"

He placed the short section of writing into the ImaginoTransferenceDevice that had been installed on the stage. But this wasn't a recording ITD like the ones they used to create books in the Well—it was a transmitter. The words of Waugh's story were read by the machine and projected directly into the crowd's imagination.

". . . I have been here before," I said; I had been there before; first with Sebastian more than twenty years ago on a cloudless day in June, when the ditches were creamy with meadowsweet and the air heavy with the scents of summer; it was a day of peculiar splendour, and although I had been there so often, in so many moods, it was to that first visit that my heart returned on this, my latest . . ."

There was more applause from the guests, and when finally it stopped, the emcee announced, "Mr. Waugh can't be with us tonight, so I would like to ask Sebastian to accept the award on his behalf."

There was a drumroll and a brief alarum of music as Sebastian walked from his table, up the steps to the podium and after kissing me on the cheek shook the emcee's hand warmly.

"Goodness!" he said, taking a swig from the glass he had brought with him. "It's a great honor to accept the award on behalf of Mr. Waugh. I know he would want me to thank Charles, from whose mouth all the words spring, and also Lord Marchmain for his excellent death scene, my mother, of course, and Julia, Cords—"

"What about me?" said a small voice from the *Brideshead* table.

"I was getting to you, Aloysius." Sebastian cleared his throat and took another swig. "Of course, I would also like to say that we in *Brideshead* could not have done it all on our own. I'd like to thank all the other characters in previous works who have done so much to lay the groundwork. I'd particularly like to mention Captain Grimes, Margot Metroland, and Lord Copper. In addition . . ."

He droned on like this for almost twenty minutes, thanking everyone he could think of before finally taking the Bookie statuette and returning to his table. I was thanked by the emcee and walked off the stage feeling really quite relieved, the voice of the emcee echoing behind me:

"And for the next category, Most Incomprehensible Plot in Any Genre, we are very pleased to welcome someone who has kindly taken a few hours' leave of his grueling schedule of sadistic galactic domination. Ladies, gentlemen and things, his Supreme Holiness Emperor Zhark!"

"You're on," I whispered to the emperor, who was trying to calm his nerves with a quick cigarette in the wings.

"How do I look? Enough to strike terror into the hearts of millions of merciless life-forms?"

"Terrifying. Have you got the envelope?"

He patted his thick black cloak until he found it and held it up, gave a wan smile, took a deep breath and strode purposefully onto the stage to screams of terror and boos.

I reentered the Starlight Room as the Most Incomprehensible Plot was awarded for the fifth year running to *The Magus*. I glanced at my watch. There was an hour to go until the last and most prestigious award was due to be announced—the Most Troubled Romantic Lead (Male). It was a hot contest and the odds had been fluctuating all day. Heathcliff was the clear favorite at 7–2. He had won it seventy-seven times in a row, and ever conscious of someone trying to steal his thunder, he had been altering his words and actions subtly to keep the crown firmly on his head, something the opposition had also been attempting. Jude Fawley had been trying to spike his own plot to add drama, and even Hamlet was not averse to a subtle amount of plot-shifting; he had hammed up his madness so much he had to be sent on a cruise to calm him down.

I passed a table populated entirely by rabbits.

"Waiter!" called one of them, thumping his rear paw to get attention. "More dandelion leaves for table eight, if you please, sir!"

"Good evening, Miss Next."

It was the Bradshaws; I was glad to see that they had not been swayed by convention—Mrs. Bradshaw had decided to attend after all.

"Good evening, Commander, good evening, Mrs. Bradshaw—nice dress you're wearing."

"Do you think so?" asked Mrs. Bradshaw slightly nervously. "Trafford wanted me to wear something full length, but I think this little Coco Chanel cocktail number is rather fetching, don't you?"

"Black suits your eyes," I told her, and she smiled demurely.

"I've got the *thing* you wanted me to keep for you," whispered Bradshaw under his breath. "Appreciate a girl who knows how to delegate—say the word and it's yours!"

"I'm waiting for the announcement of UltraWord™," I hissed. "Tweed is on my back; don't let him get it no matter what!"

"Don't worry your little head about *that*," he said, nodding towards Mrs. Bradshaw. "The memsahib's in the loop—she may look a delicate thing, but by Saint George she's a fearful lass when riled."

He gave me a wink and I moved on, heart pounding. I hoped the nervousness didn't show. Heep was on the stage, but Legree had taken his place and was keeping a surreptitious eye on me from seven hundred tables away—the temporal-field displacement technology worked in his favor—every table was next to every other.

All of a sudden there was a strong smell of beer.

"Miss Next!"

"Sir John, good evening."

Falstaff looked me up and down. I didn't wear a dress that often and I crossed my arms defensively.

"Resplendent, my dear, resplendent!" he exclaimed, pretending to be something of an expert.

"Thank you."

Usually I avoided Falstaff, but if I was being watched, it made sense to talk to as many people as possible; if Tweed and TGC thought I could throw a spanner in the works, I would not help them by drawing attention to my genuine confederates.

"I know of a side room, Mistress Next, a small place of an acquainting manner—a *niche d'amour*. What say you and I retire to that place where you might learn there how I came by the name 'Falstaff.' "

"Another time."

"Really?" he asked, surprised by my—albeit accidental—acquiescence.

"No, not really, Sir John," I said hurriedly.

"Phew!" he said, mopping his brow. " 'T'would not be half the sport if you were to lie with me—resistance, Mistress Next, is rich allurement indeed!"

"If resistance is all you seek," I told him, smiling, "then you will never have a keener woman to woo!"

"I'll drink to that!" He laughed heartily—the word might have been written for him.

"I have to leave you, Sir John, no more than a gallon of beer an hour, remember?"

I patted his large tum, which was as hard and unyielding as a beer barrel.

"On my word!" he replied, wiping the froth from his beard.

I reached the Jurisfiction table. Beatrice and Benedict were arguing, as usual.

"Ah!" said Benedict as soon as I sat down. " 'Tis beauty that dost oft make women proud, but God he knows Beatrice's share thereof is small!"

"How so?" replied Beatrice. "That face of yours that hungry cannibals would not have touch'd!"

"Have either of you seen the Bellman?" I asked.

They said they hadn't and I left them to their arguing as Foyle sat down next to me. I had seen him at Norland Park from time to time. He was Jurisfiction, too.

"Hello, we haven't been introduced. Gully Foyle is my name, terra is my nation; deep space is my dwelling place and death's my destination—I police Science Fiction."

I shook his hand. "Thursday Next. Call me Thursday. How are you liking the awards?"

"Pretty good. I was disappointed that Hamlet won the Shakespearean Character You'd Most Like to Slap Award—my money was on Othello."

"Well, Othello won Dopiest Shakespearean Lead, and they don't like them to win more than one each."

"Is that how it works?" Foyle mused. "The voting system makes no sense to me."

"They say you'll be partnered at Jurisfiction with Emperor Zhark," I said, more by way of conversation than anything else.

"I hope not. We've been trying to raise the intellectual and philosophical status of science fiction for some time now; people like him don't help the cause one iota."

"Why's that?"

"Well," mused Foyle, "how can I put it? Zhark belongs to what we describe as Lesser Science Fiction or Winsome or maybe even Classic."

"How about crap?"

"Yes, I'm afraid so."

There was a burst of applause as the emcee announced the next award.

"Ladies, gentlemen and things," he declared, "we had asked Dorothy to present the next award, but she was, sadly, kidnapped by flying monkeys just before the show. I will therefore read the nominations myself."

The emcee sighed. Dorothy's absence was just the latest in a number of small problems that usually interrupted the smooth running of the show. Earlier, Rumplestiltskin had gone berserk and attacked someone who guessed his name, Mary Elliot from *Persuasion* had declared herself "too unwell" to collect the Most Tiresome Austen Character Award, and Boo Radley couldn't be persuaded to come out of his dressing room.

"So," carried on the emcee, "the nominations for the Best Dead Person in Fiction Award are as follows." He looked at the back of the envelope. "First nomination: Count Dracula."

There was a brief burst of applause, mixed with a few jeers.

"Yes, indeed," exclaimed the emcee, "the supreme Dark Lord himself, father of an entire subgenre. From his castle in the Carpathians he embarked upon the world and darkened shadows forever. Let's read a little bit."

He placed a short extract under the ImaginoTransferance-Device and I felt a cold shadow on my neck as the Dark Lord's description entered my imagination.

There, in one of the great boxes, of which there were fifty in all, on a pile of newly dug earth, lay the Count! He was either dead or asleep, I could not say which—for the eyes were open and stony, but without the glassiness of death—and the cheeks had the warmth of life through all their pallor, and the lips were as red as ever. But there was no sign of movement, no pulse, no breath, no beating of the heart. I bent over him, to find any sign of life, but in vain . . .

There was applause and the lights came up again.

"From the undead to the very dead, the second nomination is for a man who returns selflessly from the grave to warn his erstwhile business partner the terrors which await him if he does not change his ways. All the way from *A Christmas Carol*—Jacob Marley!"

The same face: the very same. Marley in his pigtail, usual waistcoat, tights and boots; the tassels on the latter bristling, like his pigtail, and his coat-skirts, and the hair upon his head. The chain he drew was clasped about his middle. It was long, and wound about him like a tail; and it was made (for Scrooge observed it closely) of cash-boxes, keys, padlocks, ledgers, deeds, and heavy purses wrought in steel. His body was transparent; so that Scrooge, observing him, and looking through his waistcoat, could see the two buttons on his coat behind . . .

I glanced across at Marley at the *Christmas Carol* table. Through his semitransparent form I could see Scrooge pulling a large Christmas cracker with Tiny Tim.

When the applause died down, the emcee announced the third nomination:

"Banquo's ghost from *Macbeth*. A slain friend and bloody revenge are on the menu in this Scottish play of power and obsession in the eleventh century. Is Macbeth the master of his own destiny, or the other way round? Let's have a look."

Enter Ghost.

MACBETH
　　Avaunt, and quit my sight! Let the earth hide thee!
　　Thy bones are marrowless, thy blood is cold;
　　Thou hast no speculation in those eyes
　　Which thou dost glare with.
LADY MACBETH　　　　　　　　　Think of this, good peers,

But as a thing of custom. 'Tis no other,
Only it spoils the pleasure of the time.
MACBETH
What man dare, I dare.
Approach thou like the rugged Russian bear,
The arm'd rhinoceros, or th' Hyrcan tiger;
Take any shape but that, and my firm nerves
Shall never tremble. Or be alive again
And dare me to the desert with thy sword.
If trembling I inhabit then, protest me
The baby of a girl. Hence, horrible shadow!
Unreal mock'ry, hence!
Exit Ghost.

"And the winner is," announced the emcee, opening the envelope, ". . . Count Dracula."

The applause was deafening as the Count walked up to receive his award. He shook hands with the emcee and took the statuette before turning to the audience. He was white and cadaverous and I shivered involuntarily.

"First," said the Count in a soft voice with a slight lisp, "my thanks go to Bram for his admirable reporting of my activities. I would also like to thank Lucy, Mr. Harker and Van Helsing—"

"I hope he's not going to start crying like he did last year," said a voice close to my ear. I turned to find the Cheshire Cat sitting precariously on a seat back. "It's so embarrassing."

But he did. The Count was soon choking back floods of tears, thanking everyone he could think of and generally making a complete fool of himself.

"How are you enjoying the awards?" I said to the Cat, glad to see a friendly face.

"Not bad. I think Orlando was a bit miffed to lose out to Puss in Boots for the Best Talking Cat award."

"My money was on you."

"Was it really?" said the Cat, smiling even more broadly. "You *are* nice. Do you want some advice?"

"Indeed I do." The Cheshire Cat had always remained totally impartial at Jurisfiction. A hundred Bellmans could come and go, but the Cat would always be there—and his knowledge was vast. I leaned closer.

"Okay," he announced grandly, "here's the advice. Are you ready?"

"Yes."

"Don't get off a bus while it's still moving."

"That's very good advice," I said slowly. "Thank you very much."

"Don't mention it," said the Cat, and vanished.

"Hello, Thursday."

"Hi, Randolph. How are things?"

"Okay," he said slightly doubtfully. "Have you seen Lola?"

"No."

"Unlike her to miss a party," he muttered. "Do you think she's okay?"

"I think Lola can look after herself. Why are you so interested?"

"I'm going to tell her that I quite like her!" he answered resolutely.

"Why stop there?"

"You mean tell her I *really* like her?"

"And more—but it's a good place to start."

"Thanks. If you see her, tell her I'm on the Unplaced Generics table."

I wished him good luck and he left. I got up and walked to a curtained-off area where several bookies were taking bets. I placed a hundred on Jay Gatsby to win the Most Troubled Romantic Lead (Male) Award. I didn't think he would win; I just wanted Tweed to waste time trying to figure out what I was up to. I joined the *Caversham Heights* table soon afterwards and sat down next to Mary, who had returned for the awards.

"What's going on in the book?" she demanded indignantly. "Jack tells me he's been changing a few things whilst I've been away!"

"Just a few," I said, "but don't worry, we wouldn't write anything embarrassing for you without consultation."

Her eyes flicked across to Arnie, who was sharing a joke with Captain Nemo and Agatha Diesel.

"Just as well," she replied.

The evening drew on, the celebrities announcing the nominations becoming more important as the categories became more highly regarded. Best Romantic Male went to Darcy and Best Female in a Coming-of-Age Book went to Scout Finch. I looked at the clock. Only ten minutes to go before the prestigious Most Troubled Romantic Lead (Male) was due to be announced; the female version of this award had been well represented by Thomas Hardy; Bathsheba Everdene and Tess Durbeyfield had both made it to the nominations only to be pipped at the post by the surprise winner, Lady Macbeth. Sylvia Plath was shortlisted but was disqualified for being real.

I got up and walked to the Jurisfiction table as a drumroll announced the final category. The Bellman nodded politely to me and I looked around the room. It was time to act. UltraWord™ was not the savior of the BookWorld—it would be the end, and I hoped that Mimi down in the footnoterphone conduits was ready.[1]

---

1. Mimi was standing outside the footnoterphone tube entrance to Text Grand Central and looking at her watch. The words sped backwards and forwards, darting inside the tunnel, which had a sturdy grate across it streaked with rust. Every now and then messages were deflected off. It was a textual sieve—used here for deleting unwanted junkfootnoterphone messages.

She gestured to the man accompanying her and stepped back.

Quasimodo—who had found sanctuary, finally—grunted in reply and gently placed *Das Kapital* next to *Mein Kampf*, separating them only by a thin metal sheet. The "book sandwich" was held together by rubber bands, and a string was attached to the metal sheet. Quasimodo tied the books to the grate, then retired down the conduit, paying out the string as he went. He joined Mimi at a little-used subgenre pipe entitled Squid Action/Adventure and waited for Thursday's signal.

"And now, ladies, gentlemen and things, for the high point of the evening, the 923rd Annual BookWorld Award for Most Troubled Romantic Lead (Male). To read the nominations we have none other than WordMaster Xavier Libris, all the way from Text Grand Central!"

There was loud applause, which I hadn't expected—TGC wasn't that popular. I had a sudden attack of doubt. Could Deane be wrong? I thought again about Perkins, Snell and Havisham and my resolve returned. I grabbed my bag and got up. I saw Legree stiffen and rise from the *Uncle Tom's Cabin* table, speaking into his cuff as he did so. I headed towards the exit with him tailing me.

"Thank you very much!" said Libris, raising his hands to quell the applause as Hamlet, Jude Fawley and Heathcliff stood close by, each wishing that Libris would hurry up so they could collect the statuette. "I have a few words to say about the new Operating System and then we can all get back to the awards."

He took a deep breath. "Many good words have been written about UltraWord™, and I have to tell you, they are all true. The benefits to everyone will be felt throughout the BookWorld, from the lowliest D-10 in the trashiest paperback to the finest A-1 in high literature."

I walked to the side of the stage, towards the swing doors that led through to the hospitality lounge. Legree followed but was tripped up by Mathias's widow. She placed a hoof on his chest and held him firm while Mrs. Hubbard grabbed one arm and Miss Muffet the other. It had been done so quietly no one had noticed.

"Nonfiction is gaining in popularity, and this invasion into areas historically part of fiction must be cut off at the root. To this end, myself and the technicians at Text Grand Central have created UltraWord™, the Book Operating System that gives us more choice, more plots, more ideas and more ways in which to work. With these tools you and I will forge a new fiction, a fiction so varied that the readers will flock to us in droves. The future is bright—the future is UltraWord™."

"Going somewhere, missy?" asked Heep, blocking my path.

"Get out of my way, Uriah."

He pulled a gun from his pocket but stopped dead when a voice said:

"Do you know what an eraserhead can do to an A-7 like you, Heep?"

Bradshaw emerged from behind a potted Triffid. He was carrying his trusty hunting rifle.

"You'd *never* kill a featured Dickens character, Mr. Bradshaw!" said Heep, attempting to call his bluff.

Bradshaw pulled back the hammer on his rifle. "Poltroon! Ever wondered what happened to Edwin Drood?"

Heep's eyes nearly popped out of his skull, and coward that he was, he dropped his pistol and started pleading for his life.

Mrs. Bradshaw tied Heep's thumbs together and, after gagging him, hid him under the *Summer Lightning* table.

"Drood?" I asked Bradshaw with some surprise. "Was that you?"

"Not at all!" He laughed. "I only asked him if he had ever *wondered* what happened to Drood. Now get out of here, girly—there's work to be done!"

I pushed the swing doors to the hospitality lounge and pulled out my mobilefootnoterphone. The room was deserted, but I met Tweed at the entrance to the stage. I could see Libris talking, and beyond him, the audience hanging on his every word.

"Of course," he went on, "the new system will need new work procedures, and all of you have had ample time to study our detailed seventeen-hundred-page prospectus; all jobs will be protected, the status of all Generics will be maintained. In a few minutes I will ask for a vote to carry the new system, as required by the Council of Genres. But before we do, let us go over the main points again. Firstly, UltraWord™ will support the possibility of a 'No Frills' range of books with only forty-three different words, none of them longer than six letters. Designed for the hard-of-reading, these . . ."

I leaned forward and spoke to Tweed as Libris carried on.

"Is that why you invited all the C- and D-class Generics, Tweed?"

"What do you mean?"

"So you could force the vote? Your lies have the greatest effect on those with little influence in the Well—give them the power to change something and they'll meekly follow you. After Libris has finished, I'll give a rebuttal. When I'm done, you and Libris and UltraWord™ will be history."

Tweed glared at me as Libris went on to his third point. "UltraWord™ is too important to be loused up by you," said Tweed with a sneer. "I agree there might be certain downsides, but overall the benefits far outweigh the drawbacks."

"Benefits to who, Tweed? You and Kaine?"

"Of course. And you, too, if only you'd stop meddling."

"What did Kaine buy you with?"

"He didn't buy me, Next. We *merged*. His contacts in the Outland and my position at Jurisfiction. A fictional person in the real world and a real person in fiction. A better partnership it would be hard to imagine!"

"When they hear what I have to say," I replied calmly, "they'll *never* give you the vote."

Tweed smiled that supercilious smile of his and stepped aside. "You want to have your say, Thursday? Go ahead. Make a fool of yourself. But remember this: Anything you say, we can refute. We can modify the rules, change the facts, deny the truth, with *written proof*. That's the beauty of UltraWord™—everything can be keyed in direct from Text Grand Central, and as you've so correctly gathered, everything there is controlled by Kaine, Libris and I. It's as easy to change the facts as it is to write a stub axle failure on the Bluebird—or unlock a padlock, put Godot in a bag or create an outbreak of mispeling vyrus. Merely keystrokes, Next. We have the Great Library within our control— with the source text at our fingertips we can do anything. History will be good to us because we are the ones who shall write it!"

Tweed laughed. "Battle against UltraWord™ and you might as well try and canoe up a waterfall."

He patted me patronizingly on the shoulder. "But just in case you've got something up your sleeve, six thousand highly trained Mrs. Danvers are on call, ready to move in on my word. We can even write a BookWorld rebellion if we want—the Council won't be able to tell the difference between a real one and a written one. We *will* have this vote, Thursday."

"Yes, you might," I conceded. "All I want is for the characters to have their say with *all* the facts, not just yours."

I looked at Libris on the stage. "Point ten," he went on as Heathcliff looked at his watch impatiently, "all characters wherever they reside will be given four weeks' holiday a year in whichever book they choose."

There was a roar of applause. He was offering everything they wanted to hear, buying the inhabitants of the BookWorld with hollow promises.

Tweed spoke into his mobilefootnoterphone. "Miss Next wants to have her say."

I saw Libris touch his ear and turn round to stare at me contemptuously.

"But before the vote," he added, "before you say the word and we move upwards into broad, sunlit pastures, I understand we have a Jurisfiction agent who wants to offer a counterpoint to my statement. This is her right. It is *your* right to ask for proof if you wish—and I most strongly request that you do so. Ladies and gentlemen—things—Miss Thursday Next!"

I murmured into my mobilefootnoterphone, "Go, Mimi, go!"[2]

---

2. Mimi nodded to Quasimodo, who pulled the string. The steel plate shot out and *Das Kapital* and *Mein Kampf* came together, their conflicting ideologies starting to generate heat. The books turned brown, smoldered for a moment and then, as Mimi and Quasimodo scurried away up their retreat, the two volumes reached critical mass, turned white-hot and exploded. The

Everyone in the Starlight Room reacted slightly to the distant explosion.

Tweed steadied himself and spun round to glare at me. "What was that?"

I patted him patronizingly on the shoulder. "It's called leveling the playing field, Harris."

---

detonation echoed down the footnoterphone pipes, followed by a deathly silence. They had done it. The footnoterphone conduit was destroyed— Libris and Tweed were cut off from Text Grand Central.

33.

UltraWord™

Storycode Engine: The name given to the imaginotransference machines used by Text Grand Central to throughput the books in the Great Library to the readers in the Outland. On a single machine floor at TGC there are five hundred of these complex, cast-iron colossi. A single engine can cope with up to fifty thousand simultaneous readings of the same book at up to six words per second per reader. With a hundred similar floors, TGC is able to handle two and a half billion different readings, although the lowest ten floors are generally used only when a long-awaited bestseller is published. Using the UltraWord™ system, only twelve engines would be needed to handle the same number of readings— but at speeds of up to twenty words per second.

XAVIER LIBRIS,
UltraWord™—the Ultimate Reading Experience

AMLET AND JUDE Fawley exchanged glances and shrugged their shoulders as I walked up the steps and looked out at the crowd. Heathcliff, to whom all of this was merely delaying his moment of honor, glowered at me angrily. Oddly, I didn't feel at all nervous—only a sort of numb elation. I would do some serious throwing up in the loo later, but for now, I was fine.

"Good evening," I began to the utterly silent audience. "No one would deny that we need more plots, but there are one or two things about UltraWord™ that you should know."

"Grand Central?!" barked Tweed uselessly into his mobile-footnoterphone. "Tweed to Text Grand Central, come in please!"

I didn't have long. As soon as TGC knew what had happened, they could write themselves another footnoterphone link.

"Firstly, there are no new plots. In all the testing that has been done, not one has been described or hinted at. Libris, would you care to outline a 'new' plot now?"

"They won't be available until UltraWord™ is on-line," he said, glaring at Tweed, who was still trying to contact Text Grand Central.

"Then they are untested. Secondly," I went on, "UltraWord™ carries a thrice-read-only feature."

There was a gasp from the audience.

"This means no more book lending. Libraries will close down overnight, secondhand bookshops will be a thing of the past. Words can educate and liberate—but TGC want to make them a salable commodity and nothing more."

The crowd started to murmur to one another. Not one of those murmurs, which is just a descriptive term, you usually get in the BookWorld, but a *real* murmur—seven million people all discussing what I had just said.

"Orlick!" I heard Tweed shout. "Get to TGC—run if you have to—and get the footnoterphone repaired!"

"This is preposterous!" yelled Libris, almost apoplectic with rage. "Lies, damnable lies!"

"Here," I said, tossing Deane's copy of *The Little Prince* onto the table right at the front. The displacement-field technology worked perfectly—a single book landed on each of the hundred thousand tables.

"This is an UltraWord™ book," I explained. "Read the first page and pass it on. See how long it takes before you can't open it."

"Tweed!?" yelled Libris, who was still next to me on the stage and becoming more agitated by the second. "Do something!"

I pointed at Xavier. "WordMaster Libris could refute my arguments with ease, simply by rewriting the facts. He could have unblocked the book already but for one thing—all the lines are down to Text Grand Central. As soon as they are up again, each of these books will be unblocked. Perkins was murdered when he found out what they were up to. He told Snell and he was killed, too. Miss Havisham didn't know, but TGC *suspected* that she did, so she had to be silenced."

The Bellman had risen to his feet and was walking to the front of the stage. "Is this true?" he asked, eyes blazing.

"No, Your Bellship," replied Libris, "on my honor. As soon as we get back on-line, we will refute every single claim the misinformed Miss Next has made!"

The Bellman looked at me. "Better get a move on, young lady. You have the crowd, but for how long, I have no idea."

"Thirdly and more importantly, all books written using the UltraWord™ system can be fixed direct using the source storycode from Text Grand Central—there will be no need for Jurisfiction. Everything we do can be achieved by low-skilled technicians at TGC."

"Ah!" said Libris, interrupting. "Now we get to your *real* point—fearful of your job, perhaps?"

"Not my job, Libris—my real home is in the Outland. I would applaud a BookWorld in which we had no need of a policing agency—but not one where we lose the Well of Lost Plots!"

There was a gasp from the crowd, seven million people all drawing breath at the same time.

"Under UltraWord™ there will be no need for plotsmiths, echolocators, imaginators, holesmiths, grammatacists and spellcheckers. No need for Generics to be trained because characters will be constructed with the minimum of description necessary to do the job. I'm talking about the wholesale destruction of everything that is intuitive in writing—to be replaced by the formulaic. The Well would be dismantled and run instead by a few technicians at TGC who will construct books with no input from any of you."

"Then what will happen to us?" said a voice from the front.

"Replaced," I said simply, "replaced by a string of nouns and verbs. No hopes, no dreams, no future. No more holidays because you won't need or want one—you will all be reduced to nothing more than words on a page, lifeless as ink and paper."

There was silence.

"Proof!" cried Libris. "All you have demonstrated so far is that you can spin a yarn as good as any plotsmith! Where is your proof?"

"Very well," I said slowly. "Mrs. Bradshaw? The skylark, if you please."

Mrs. Bradshaw produced the small cage from beneath the table and handed it up to me.

"I have seen an UltraWord™ character with my own eyes, and they are empty husks. If an old book is read in UltraWord™, it is very good—but if it is *written* in UltraWord™, it will be flat and trite, devoid of feeling—the SmileyBurger of the storytelling world. The Well may be wasteful and long-winded, but every book read in the Outland was built there—even the greats."

I took the skylark from the cage. "This was the proof that Perkins died for."

I placed the small songbird beneath the ImaginoTransference-Device and the skylark's description was transmitted into the audience.

> O Lark so quick of wing,
> Dive down from up on high,
> Perch proud upon the post,
> Melt darkness with thy cry.
>
> Come make my spirits soar,
> Dance here and hover long,
> Tempt summer with your trill,
> Sweet stream of endless song.

The audience reacted favorably to the words and there was a smattering of applause, despite their nervousness.

"What's wrong with that?" insisted Libris. "UltraWord™

takes language and uses it in ways more wonderful than you can imagine!"

The Bellman looked at me. "Miss Next," he demanded, "explain yourself."

"Well," I said slowly, "that *wasn't* an UltraWord™ skylark. I picked it up from the library this morning."

There was an expectant hush as Mrs. Bradshaw produced a *second* bird seemingly identical to the first and handed it up to me.

"This is the UltraWord™ version. Shall we compare?"

"That's not necessary!" said Libris quickly. "We get the point." He turned to the Bellman. "Sir, we need a few more weeks to sort out a few minor kinks—"

"Go ahead, Thursday," said the Bellman, "let's see how Ultra-Word™ compares."

I placed the bird in the ITD, and it transmitted the cold and clinical description into the audience.

> With a short tail and large wings, a skylark is easily recognized in flight. There is a distinctive streaking pattern to the brown plumage on the breast, and a black-and-white pattern beneath the tail. Nests in hollow on ground. Can sing a bit.

"I call a vote right now!" exclaimed the Bellman, climbing onto the stage.[1]

I looked across at Tweed, who was tapping his mobilefootnoterphone and smiling.

"What's the problem?" I asked.[2]

"Eh?" asked the Bellman.

"The vote!" I urged. "Hurry!"

"Of course," he replied, knowing full well that Text Grand

1. "Thursday! It's Mimi, are you there?"
2. "They are rerouting messages through the auxiliary ducts past Spy Thrillers and through Horror. If you haven't got a vote, get one now!"

Central were not defeated until the vote had been taken. The Council of Genres weren't involved—but would be if TGC tried to go against a BookWorld referendum. That was something they could *never* rewrite.

"Good!" said Tweed into his mobilefootnoterphone. "Communications have been restored."

He smiled at me and signaled to Libris, who calmed dramatically as only the supremely confident can do.

"Very well," said Libris slowly, "the Bellman has called for a vote, and as the rules state, I am allowed to answer any criticism laid before me."

"A rebuttal of a rebuttal?" I cried. "The rules don't state that!"

"But they do!" said Libris kindly. "Perhaps you'd like to look at the BookWorld constitution?"

He pulled the slim volume from his coat and I could smell the cantaloupes from where I stood. It would say whatever they wanted it to say.

Libris walked over to us and said to the Bellman in a quiet voice, "We can do this the easy way or the hard way. We make the rules, we can change the rules, we can modify the rules. We can do anything we want. You are due to step down. Go with me on this one and you can have an easy retirement. Go against me and I'll crush you."

Libris turned to me. "What do you care? No one in the Outland will notice the difference. You'll have a week to pack up and move out—you have my word on that."

The Bellman glared at Libris. "How much did they pay you?"

"They didn't need to. Money doesn't mean anything down here. No, it's the technology that I really love. It's too perfect to be sidelined by people like you. I get one hundred percent control. Everything will go through TGC. No more Well of Lost Plots, no more Generics, no more Council, no more strikes by disgruntled nursery rhyme workers. But do you know the best bit? No more authors. No more missed deadlines. No more variable-quality second books—each one in the series will be the same as the last.

When a publisher needs a bestseller, all they need do is contact our sole representative in the Outland!"

"Yorrick Kaine," I murmured.

"Indeed. It's all for the best, my dear."

Incredibly, it was *worse* than I thought. It was as if the paint factories had decided to deal direct with the art galleries.

"But the books!" I cried. "They'll be terrible!"

"Within a few years no one will notice," replied Libris. "Mr. Bellman, do you go with us on this or not?"

"I would sooner die!" he exclaimed, trembling with rage.

"As you wish," replied Libris.

There was a short crackling noise and I saw the Bellman stiffen slightly.

"Now," said Libris, "let's finish this all up. Bellman, would you refute Miss Next's points one by one?"

"I should be delighted," he said slowly and without emotion. I turned to him in shock and could see how his features were less defined than before—sort of like a wire-framed, three-dimensional model clothed in realistic skintone. I could see it easily but I was up close—the audience hadn't noticed anything at all. The smell of melons once more drifted across the stage.

"Friends!" began the Bellman. "Miss Next is entirely mistaken . . ."

I turned to Libris and he smiled triumphantly. I reached into my bag for my gun, but it had been changed to marmalade.

"Tch, tch," said Libris in a whisper, "that's a BookWorld gun and under *our* control. What a shame you lost your Outlander Browning in the struggle with Tweed!"

I had only one card left. I pulled out my TravelBook and opened it, flicking past the TextMarker and Eject-O-Hat and on towards the glass panel covering a red-painted handle. A note painted on the glass read, IN UNPRECEDENTED EMERGENCY, BREAK GLASS. If this wasn't an unprecedented emergency, I didn't know what was. I smashed the glass, grabbed the handle and pulled it down with all my strength.

34.

Loose Ends

Contrary to Text Grand Central's claims, there were no new plots using UltraWord™. Ex-WordMaster Libris had become so obsessed with the perfection of his Operating System that nothing else had mattered to him and he lied repeatedly to cover up its failings. BOOK V8.3 remained the Operating System for many years to come, although one of the Ultra-Word™ copies of *The Little Prince* can be viewed in the Jurisfiction museum. To avoid a repeat of this near disaster, the Council of Genres took the only course of action open to them to ensure TGC would be too inefficient and unimaginative to pose a threat. They appointed a committee to run it.

MILLON DE FLOSS,
UltraWord™—the Aftermath

IT WAS NEARLY morning when the BookWorld Awards party finished. Heathcliff was furious that in all the excitement the final award of the night had been forgotten; I saw him talking angrily to his personal imaginator an hour after the appearance of the Great Panjandrum. There would be next year of course, but his seventy-seven-year record had been broken and he didn't like it. I thought he might take it out on Linton and Catherine when he got home, and he did.

No one had been more surprised than me by the arrival of the Great Panjandrum when I pulled the emergency handle. For the nonbelievers it was something of a shock, but not any less than for the faithful. She had been so long a figure of speech that seeing her in the flesh was something of a shock. I thought she had seemed quite plain and in her midthirties, but Humpty-Dumpty told me later he had been shaped like an egg. In any event, the marble statue that now stands in the lobby of the Council of Genres depicts the Great Panjandrum as Mr. Price the stonemason saw him—with a leather apron and carrying a mallet and stone chisel.

When she arrived, the Great Panjandrum read the situation perfectly. She froze all the text within the room, locked the doors and decreed that a vote be taken there and then. She summoned the head of the Council of Genres, and the vote against Ultra-Word™ was carried unanimously. She spoke to me three times: once to tell me I had *The Write Stuff*, second to ask me if I would take on the job of the Bellman, and lastly to ask if disco mirror-balls in the Outland had a motor to make them go round or whether they did it by the action of the lights. I answered "Thank you," "Yes" and "I don't know" in that order.

After the party was over, I walked back through the slowly stirring Well of Lost Plots to the shelf that held *Caversham Heights* and read myself back inside, tired but happy. The Bellman's job would, I hoped, keep me busy, but purely in administration—I wouldn't have to go jumping around in books—just the thing to allow my ankles to swell in peace and quiet, and to plan my return to the Outland when the infant Next and its mother were strong enough. Together we would face the tribulations of Landen's return, because the little one *would* have a father, I had promised it that much already. I opened the door to the Sunderland and felt the old flying boat rock slightly as I entered. When I'd first come here, it had unnerved me, but now I wouldn't have had it any other way. Small wavelets slapped against the hull, and somewhere an owl hooted as it returned to roost. It felt as much like home as home had ever done. I kicked off my shoes and flopped on the sofa next to Gran, who had fallen asleep over a sock she was knitting. It was already a good twelve feet long because, she said, she had "yet to build up enough courage to turn the heel."

I closed my eyes for a moment and fell fast asleep without the nagging fear of Aornis, and it was nearly ten the next morning when I awoke. But I didn't wake naturally—Pickwick was tugging at the corner of my dress.

"Not now, Pickers," I mumbled sleepily, trying to turn over and nearly impaling myself on a knitting needle. She carried on tugging until I sat up, rubbed the sleep from my eyes and stretched noisily. She seemed insistent so I followed her upstairs to my bedroom. Sitting on the bed and surrounded by broken eggshell was something that I could only describe as a ball of fluff with two eyes and a beak.

"Plock-*plock*," said Pickwick.

"You're right," I told her, "she's very beautiful. Congratulations."

The small dodo blinked at us both, opened its beak wide and said, in a shrill voice, *"Plunk!"*

Pickwick started and looked at me anxiously.

"Well!" I told her. "A rebellious teenager already?"

Pickwick nudged the chick with her beak and it *plunked* indignantly before settling down.

I thought for a moment and said, "You aren't going to feed her doing that disgusting regurgitation seabird thing are you?"

The door burst open downstairs.

"Thursday!" yelled Randolph anxiously. "Are you in here?"

"I'm here," I shouted, leaving Pickwick with her offspring and coming downstairs to find a highly agitated Randolph, pacing up and down the living room.

"What's up?"

"It's Lola."

"Some unsuitable young man again? Really, Randolph, you've got to learn not to be so jealous—"

"No," he said quickly, "it's not that. *Girls Make All the Moves* didn't find a publisher and the author burnt the only manuscript in a drunken rage! That's why she wasn't at the awards last night!"

I stopped. If a book had been destroyed in the Outland, then all the characters and situations would be up for salvage—

"Yes," said Randolph, reading my thoughts, "they're going to auction off Lola!"

I quickly changed out of my dress and we arrived as the sale was winding up. Most of the descriptive scenes had already gone, the one-liners packaged and sold as a single lot, and all the cars and most of the wardrobe and furniture were disposed of. I pushed through to the front of the crowd and found Lola looking dejected, sitting on her suitcase.

"Lola!" said Randolph, as they hugged. "I brought Thursday to help you!"

She jumped up and smiled, but it was a despairing half smile at best and it spoke volumes.

"Come on," I said, grabbing her by the hand, "we're out of here."

"Not so fast!" said a tall man in an immaculate suit. "No goods are to be removed until paid for!"

"She's with me," I told him as several hulking great bouncers appeared from nowhere.

"No, she's not. She's lot ninety-seven. You can bid if you want to."

"I'm Thursday Next, the Bellman-elect, and Lola is with me."

"I know who you are and you did good, but I have a business to run. I haven't done anything wrong. You can take the Generic home with you in ten minutes—*after* you have won the bidding."

I glared at him. "I'm going to close down this foul trade and enjoy it every step of the way!"

"Really? I'm quaking in my boots. Now, are you going to bid or do I withdraw the lot and put it up for private tender?"

"She's not an *it*," snarled Randolph angrily, "she's a Lola—and I love her!"

"You're breaking my heart. Bid or bugger off, the choice is yours."

Randolph made to plant a punch on the dealer's chin, but he was caught by one of the bouncers and held tightly.

"Control your Generic or I'll throw you both out! Get it?"

Randolph nodded and he was released. We stood together at the front watching Lola, who was weeping silently into her handkerchief.

"Gentlemen. Lot ninety-seven. Fine female B-3 Generic, ident: TSI-1404912-A, attractive and personable. An opportunity to secure this sort of highly entertaining and pneumatic young lady does not come often. Her high appetite for sexual congress, slight dopiness and winsome innocence mated to indefatigable energy makes her especially suitable for 'racy' novels. What am I bid?"

It was bad. *Very* bad. I turned to Randolph. "Do you have any money?"

"About a tenner."

The bidding had already reached a thousand. I didn't have a tenth of that either here or back home—nor anything to sell to raise such a sum. The bidding rose higher, and Lola grew more depressed. For the amount that was being bid, she was probably in for a series of books—and the movie rights. I shuddered.

"With you, sir, at six thousand!" announced the auctioneer as the bidding bounced backwards and forwards between two well-known dealers. "Any more bids?"

"Seven thousand!"

"Eight!"

"Nine!"

"I can't watch," said Randolph, tears streaming down his face. He turned and left as Lola stared after him, trying to see him as he pushed his way to the back.

"Any more bids?" asked the auctioneer. "With you, sir, at nine thousand . . . going once . . . going twice . . ."

"I bid one original idea!" I shouted, digging in my bag for the small nugget of originality and marching up to the auctioneer's table. There was a deathly hush as I held the glowing fragment aloft, then placed it on his desk with a flourish.

"A nugget of originality for a trollop like that?" muttered a man at the front. "The Bellman-elect's got a screw loose."

"Lola is that important to me," I said somberly. Miss Havisham had told me to use the nugget wisely—I think I did.

"Is it enough?"

"It's enough," said the vendor, picking up the nugget and staring at it avariciously through an eyeglass. "This lot is withdrawn from the sale. Miss Next, you are the proud owner of a Generic."

Lola nearly wet herself, poor girl, and she hugged me tightly during the five minutes it took to complete the paperwork.

We found Randolph sitting on a bollard down by the docks, staring off into the Text Sea with a sad and vacant look in his eyes. Lola leaned down and whispered in his ear.

Randolph jumped and turned round, flung his arms around her and cried for joy.

"Yes," he said, "yes, I did mean it! Every bit of it!"

"Come on, lovebirds," I told them, "I think it's time to leave this cattle market."

We walked back to *Caversham Heights*, Randolph and Lola holding hands, making plans to start a home for Generics who had fallen on hard times, and trying to think up ways to raise funding. Neither of them had the resources to undertake such a project, but it got me thinking.

The following week and soon after the Bellman inauguration, I gave my proposal to the Council of Genres—*Caversham Heights* should be bought by the Council and used as a sanctuary for characters who needed a break from the sometimes arduous and repetitive course that fictional people are forced to tread. A sort of textual summer camp. To my delight the Council approved the measure, as it had the added bonus of a solution to the nursery rhyme problem. Jack Spratt was overjoyed at the news and didn't seem in the least put out by the massive changes that would be necessary to embrace the visitors.

"The drug plot is out, I'm afraid," I told him as we discussed it over lunch a few days later.

"What the hell," he exclaimed, "I was never in love with it anyway. Do we have a replacement boxer?"

"The boxing plot is out, too."

"Ah. How about the money-laundering subplot where I discover the mayor has been taking kickbacks? That's still in, yes?"

"Not . . . as such," I said slowly.

"It's gone, too? Do we even have a murder?"

"*That* we have." I passed him the new outline I had been thrashing out with a freelance imaginator the previous day.

"Ah!" he said, scanning the words eagerly. "It's Easter in Reading—a bad time for eggs—and Humpty-Dumpty is found shattered beneath a wall in a shabby area of town. . . ."

He flicked a few more pages. "What about Dr. Singh, Madeleine, Unidentified Police Officers 1 and 2 and all the others?"

"All still there. We've had to reassign a few parts, but it should hold together. The only person who wouldn't move was Agatha Diesel—I think she might give you a few problems."

"I can handle her," replied Jack, flicking to the back of the outline to see how it all turned out. "Looks good to me. What do the nurseries say about it?"

"I'm talking to them next."

I left Jack with the outline and jumped to Norland Park, where I took the news to Humpty-Dumpty; he and his army of pickets were still camped outside the doors of the house—they had been joined by characters from nursery stories, too.

"Ah!" said Humpty as I approached. "The Bellman. The three witches were right after all."

"They generally are," I replied. "I have a proposal for you."

Humpty's eyes grew bigger and bigger as I explained what I had in mind.

"Sanctuary?" he asked.

"Of sorts," I told him. "I'll need you to coordinate all the nurseries who will find narrative a little bit alien after doing couplets for so long, so you'll be dead when the story opens."

"Not . . . the *wall* thing?"

"I'm afraid so. What do you think?"

"Well," said Humpty, reading the outline carefully and smiling, "I'll take it to the membership, but I think I can safely say that there is nothing here that we can find any great issue with. Pending a ballot, I think you've got yourself a deal."

It took the C of G almost a year to scrap the pristine and unused UltraWord™ engines, and many more arrests followed, although sadly, none in the Outland. Vernham Deane was released, and he and Mimi were awarded the Gold Star for Reading as well as the plot realignment they had wanted for so many years. They married and—quite unprecedented for a Farquitt baddy—lived happily ever after, something that caused a severe drop in sales for *The Squire of High Potternews*. Harris Tweed, Xavier Libris and twenty-four others at Text Grand Central were tried and found guilty of "crimes against the BookWorld." Harris Tweed was expelled permanently from fiction and returned to Swindon. Heep, Orlick and Legree were all sent back to their books, and the rest were reduced to text.

It was the first day of the influx of nursery rhyme refugees, and Lola and I were sitting on a park bench in *Caversham Heights*— soon to be renamed *Nursery Crime*. We were watching Humpty-Dumpty welcome the long line of guests as Randolph allocated parts. Everyone was happy with the arrangements, but I wasn't overwhelmed with joy myself. I still missed Landen and I was reminded of this every time I tried—and failed—to get my old trousers to button up over my rapidly expanding waistline.

"What are you thinking about?"

"Landen."

"Oh," said Lola, staring at me with her big brown eyes. "You will get him back, I am sure of it—please don't be downhearted!"

I patted her hand and thanked her for her kind words.

"I never did say thank you for what you did," she said slowly. "I missed Randolph more than anything—if only he'd told me what he felt I would have stayed in *Heights* or sought a dual placement—even as a C-grade."

"Men are like that. I'm just glad you're both happy."

"I'll miss being the main protagonist," she said wistfully. "*Girls Make All the Moves* was a good role but in a crap book. Do you think I'll ever be the heroine again?"

"Well, Lola, some would say that the hero of any story is the one who changes the most. If we take the moment when we first met as the beginning of the story and right now as the end, I think that makes you and Randolph the heroes by a long straw."

"It does, doesn't it?"

She smiled and we sat in silence for a moment.

"Thursday?"

"Yes?"

"So who did kill Godot?"

34a.

Heavy Weather

(Bonus chapter exclusive to the U.S. edition)

BookWorld Meteorology: Aside from the rain, snow and wind that often feature within the pages of novels for dramatic effect, another weather system works within the BookWorld; a sort of transgenre wind that is not a moving mass of air but one of text, sense distortion and snippets of ideas. It is usually only a mild zephyr whose welcome breeze brings with it a useful cross-fertilization of ideas within the genres and usually has no greater vice than the spread of the mispeling vyrus. On occasion, however, the wind has been known to whip itself up into a WordStorm that can dislodge whole sentences and plot devices and deposit them several genres away. It's not a common phenomenon, but it's wise to keep an eye on it. In my second week as Bellman, a WordStorm of unprecedented ferocity hit the library. It was the first real test of my Bellmanship. I think I did okay.

THURSDAY NEXT,
Private Diaries

I WAS ASLEEP IN my room in the Sunderland not long after my inauguration as Bellman. Everything had been pretty quiet that week. A few PageRunners and a sighting of the Minotaur, but nothing too serious. Text Grand Central was still coming to grips with the new management regime, and all the storycode engines had been shut down and rebooted to rid them of the Ultra-Word™ Operating System. So a lull was not only welcome, but necessary.

I was awoken from my slumber by a loud purring and was

shocked to find the Cat formerly known as Cheshire about an inch from my nose.

"Hullo!" he purred, grinning fit to burst. "Were you dreaming about oysters?"

"No," I confessed. "In fact," I added, rubbing my eyes and attempting to sit up, "I don't think I've *ever* dreamt about oysters."

"Really? I dream about them all the time. Sometimes on the half shell and other times in an oyster bed. Sometimes I dream about them playing the piano."

"How can an oyster play the piano?"

"No, I dream about them when *I'm* playing the piano."

I looked at the clock. It was three in the morning.

"Did you wake me up to tell me about your oyster dreams?"

"Not at all. I can't think for a moment why you are interested. Something has come up over at Text Grand Central and we thought you should be informed."

I was suddenly a great deal wider awake. I moved to get up and the Cat politely faded from view as I stepped from the bed.

"So what's up?" I asked, slipping on a T-shirt.

"It's the TextWind," said the Cat from the corridor. "We've been monitoring it all day and there is a possibility it could whip itself up into a WordStorm."

Weather inside fiction is much like weather at home, only usually more extreme. Book rain generally comes down in stair rods, and book snow always has flakes the size of farthings. But these all exist *within* books for narrative purposes. The Book-World itself has less easily recognized weather patterns but has them, just the same—a particularly bad storm in '34 swept through Horror and rained detritus on Drama for weeks, the most notable result being the grisly spontaneous-combustion sequence in Dickens's *Bleak House*.

I pulled on my trousers and shoes and walked out of the door, leaving Pickwick and her chick asleep in an untidy snoring mass on the rug. The Cat was waiting for me and together we jumped to Text Grand Central.

TGC was the technical nerve center of the BookWorld. Modified from an unpublished Gothic horror novel, the one hundred floors of TGC were lit by flickering gas mantles that only faintly illuminated the vaulted ceilings high above the polished marble floors. We entered near the corner of floor sixty-nine and I followed the Cat as we walked past the humming storycode engines, each one a colossi of cast iron, shiny brass and polished mahogany. Just one of five hundred on this floor alone, the bus-sized machine could cope with up to fifty thousand simultaneous readings of the same book—or one reading apiece of fifty thousand different books, as demand saw fit. I had only visited TGC once before as part of my induction to the Bellman's job and was amazed not only on how impossible the concept was to my flat Outlander mind, but the supreme scale of it all. The technicians scurried like tireless ants over the clanking machinery, checking dials, oiling moving parts and venting steam while keeping a close lookout for any narrative anomalies to report to the collators upstairs. It was from these collators that reports of Fiction Infractions, PageRunners and all the other BookWorld misdemeanors filtered through to us at the Jurisfiction offices. The whole system was hopelessly antiquated and manpower intensive—but it worked.

We left the engine floor and walked into a large anteroom where the BookWorld Meteorological Department worked. It was here the ten-strong team spent their days busily searching for patterns in the seemingly random textual anomalies that occur throughout fiction. The department was run by Dr. Howard. I had met him briefly once before and knew that a century or two ago he had been real, like me. TGC had commissioned a biography of the original Luke Howard solely so a Generic could be trained and then employed part-time in this office.

"Ah!" he said as we walked in. "Glad you're here, Bellman. Heavy weather moving in from the Western genre. This is Senator Jobsworth from the Council of Genres, here as part of the C of G committee for observation of anomalies."

Jobsworth, a small and weedy-looking man, didn't look comfortable nor regal in his senatorial robes. As part of the regime change after the UltraWord™ debacle, it was deemed that a senator should be present at any unusual event. He looked shifty and I took an instant dislike to him.

"Senator," I said, bowing slightly as protocol dictated.

"Miss Next," he said dryly, "I must tell you right now that I didn't vote for you. I will be keeping a close eye on your behavior."

"Good," I replied noncommittally, then added, "What's up, Dr. Howard?"

He motioned us towards the center of the room where beneath us in a recessed pit there was a large map of the Book-World.

"We plot everything," he explained as the staff below moved marker tags with long sticks to the orders of the controllers above, "from the largest unconstrained narrative flexation to the smallest tense distortion. Then, by plotting the size of the changes and their positions, a rough map of the BookWorld's weather can be constructed."

I looked down at the sea of small markers, which seemed, indeed, to have a sort of swirling pattern to them. He pointed to a mass of reports.

"About two hours ago an outbreak of anomalous plot flexations began in *Riders of the Purple Sage*."

"The Minotaur was reported in Zane Grey last week," I commented.

"That's what we thought at first," replied Dr. Howard, "but the slight flexations were moving too fast to be a PageRunner. Within twenty minutes a cloud of grammatical oddities had joined the weather front, and together they left the Western genre. The front brushed the southeast corner of Erotica and vanished ten minutes later into Stream of Consciousness."

"Vanished?"

"Difficult to spot, perhaps. It's been quiet in SOC ever since. But that's not all. At pretty much the same time a cloud of mispunctuation arose in Horror, circled twice and then developed into a pretty stiff breeze of split infinitives and jumbled words before traveling through Fantasy into Romance. Unchallenged, it hit the Farquitt series and split in two. One storm front headed north into Steel, the other along the Collins ridge just east of Krantz. We expect the two fronts to merge just past Cooper in a few minutes."

"So we can safely say it's over then?" asked the senator, staring at the plotting table with more than a little confusion.

"Up to a point, Senator," replied Dr. Howard diplomatically. "As you so expertly point out, it just *might* dissipate into the Taylor Bradford canon harmlessly."

"Oh, good!" said the senator with relief.

"However," continued Dr. Howard, "and far be it from me to contradict Your Grace, it's equally probable they will strengthen and then career off on a destructive course towards Drama."

"Boss!" said a technician who had been staring at a list of recent anomalies. "I think you better see this."

Below us on the plotting table we could see a small bulge emerge on the western flanks of Stream of Consciousness.

"How fast?" asked Dr. Howard.

"About three pages a second."

"Give me a projected route."

The technician picked up a slide rule and scribbled some notes on a pad of paper. Unluckily for us, the front that had begun in Western had traversed Stream of Consciousness and emerged four times as strong.

"I knew we hadn't seen the last of it," muttered Howard. "Damn and blast!"

But that wasn't all. In the next two minutes we watched nervously as the split storm fronts coursing through Romance rejoined, grew stronger and diverted off towards Drama, as feared.

"And that's why we called you," said Dr. Howard, gazing at me intently. "In under ten minutes the Romance and Stream of Consciousness frontal systems will merge and strengthen. We've got a WordStorm brewing of magnitude five-point-four or more heading straight for Drama."

"Five-point-four?" echoed the senator. "That's good, right?"

"In storm terms, it's very good," replied Dr. Howard grimly, "make no mistake about that. A two-point-three might only scramble text and change tenses; a three-point-five can muddle chapters and remove entire words. Anything above a five has enough power to tear whole ideas and paragraphs out of a book and dump them several shelves away."

"O-kay," I said slowly as Commander Bradshaw appeared, looking a bit bleary-eyed.

"Glad you could make it, Trafford. We've got a potential WordStorm brewing."

"WordStorm, eh?" he mused. "Reminds me of a typhoon that struck *The French Lieutenant's Woman* ten years back. By gad, we were picking superfluous adjectives out of the book for a month!"

"And that had been a small one," added Dr. Howard, "barely a two-point-one."

"Cat," I said, "issue a storm warning to the residents of all books on the storm's path. Trafford, we need every single Danver-Clone we have on thirty-second readiness. I want textual sieves ready and standing by."

"Well," said Senator Jobsworth, "this is all quite exciting, isn't it? And what is a textual sieve, anyway?"

We all ignored him and moved to a table in Dr. Howard's office where one of his team had unrolled a more detailed map of the threatened area of Drama. It was essentially one of Bradshaw's booksploring charts overlaid with the footnoterphone conduits in red ink. The map looked like a giant spiderweb of interconnections, the books that remained unexplored standing alone and unprotected. If we couldn't get in to warn them, they certainly wouldn't be able to see it coming.

We waited patiently as the minutes ticked by, the plotters updating the course of the two storm fronts on the chart as they merged, gathered speed and hurtled across the emptiness of intergenre space, directly towards Drama. Bradshaw had relayed my orders to the DanverClones; all we needed was the title of the books most likely to be hit by the coming storm.

"Why don't we set up those textual sieves across this area here?" suggested Senator Jobsworth, waving a hand at the chart.

"We mustn't spread our sieves too thin," I explained. "We need them concentrated at the place the storm hits to do any good at all."

As if to confirm its waywardness, the storm changed direction. It had been heading almost straight for the Satire end of Drama when it veered away and headed instead for Novel.

"Which one do you think, old girl?" asked Bradshaw, footnoterphone in hand. It was one of those moments where leadership has a lonely, hollow emptiness to it. The wrong decision now and we could be mopping up the mess for years. Give my order too early and the storm might veer again and cut an ugly swath through Trollope; give the order too late and the textual sieves might not be up in time to stop the storm in its tracks. A half-unfurled sieve would be broken like matchwood and carried with the storm to who knows where.

"What shall we do, Bellman?" asked the Cat. He wasn't smiling.

A technician updated the plot. The storm had moved slightly to the west and was now four minutes from hitting Drama. Would it hold that course or veer off again?

"Dr. Howard," I said, "I need your best estimate."

"It's almost impossible to say—!"

"I know that!" I snapped. "Like it or not, you are the best guesser and I'm going to go with your hunch—that's my decision. Now, where do you think it will hit?"

He sighed resignedly and stabbed a finger on the map. "I think about here. Page two hundred fourteen of *The Scarlet Letter*, give or take a chapter or two."

"Hawthorne," I murmured, "not good."

No one had ever traveled into any of his books before, so the DanverClones would be working on the books closest to it—never a satisfactory alternative.

"Right," I said, drawing a deep breath, "do we have an updated report on the size of this WordStorm?"

"It's now a five-point-seven," replied the technician in a voice tinged with fear, "and it's heavy with ideas and plot devices picked up on its journey so far."

"Compact?"

"I'd say," replied the technician, reading the latest weather report, "barely three paragraphs wide but with a density over six-point-four. It's currently moving at eight pages a second."

"It could tear a hole straight through *The Scarlet Letter* at that rate," exploded Bradshaw, "and litter the whole book with dramatic events!"

The consequence of this was terrible to consider—a new version of *The Scarlet Letter* where things actually happen.

"Impact time?"

"Three minutes."

I had an idea. "How many people are reading *Scarlet Letter* at present?"

"Six hundred and twenty-two," replied the Cat, who as librarian had these figures at his paws twenty-four hours a day.

"Pleasure readers?"

"Mostly," replied the Cat, thinking hard, "except for a class of thirty-two English students at Frobisher High School in Michigan who are studying it."

"Good. Bradshaw? I want you to set up textual sieves in every book ever written by Hemingway—even the bad ones. Sieves are to be set to *coarse* in all short stories, letters, *Winner Take Nothing* and *In Our Time*, *medium* in *The Sun Also Rises* and *The Green Hills of Africa*. I want to channel the storm, slowing it down as it passes. By *A Farewell to Arms* and *For Whom the Bell Tolls*, sieves should be set to *fine*. The storm will bounce between all the works, moving west towards the void between Hemingway and Fitzgerald. If it makes it that far, we'll reset the sieves and attack it again."

There was a pause.

"But, Thursday," said Bradshaw slowly, "the storm isn't going to hit Hemingway."

"It will if we shut *The Scarlet Letter* down."

"Out of the question!" exploded Senator Jobsworth, spontaneously and automatically rejecting any possible infringements of his sacred regulations. "The rules do not permit any book to be shut down without a vote at the Council of Genres—I can quote the rule number if you wish!"

Technically, he was right. Even with a vote, nobody had tried anything so audacious before. It usually took an hour to shut down a book, more to bring it up to full readability again.

"Is that wise?" asked Dr. Howard.

"Not in the least," I replied, "but I'm out of time and ideas right now."

"Isn't anyone listening to me?" continued the senator, more outraged at our lack of respect than at losing *The Scarlet Letter*.

"Oh, we're listening all right," purred the Cat, "we just don't agree with you."

"Rules are there for a good reason, Miss Next. We have ordered the demolition of bigger books than *The Scarlet Letter*. I personally—"

"Listen," I said, "classics have been lost before but never during my tenure as Bellman. Tomorrow morning you can have my badge if I'm wrong and send me packing. Right now you can sit down and shut up. Cat and Bradshaw, are you with me on this?"

"Appreciate a woman who can make bold decisions!" muttered Bradshaw, repeating my orders to the DanverClones. Senator Jobsworth had gone red with impotent fury, and his mouth was twitching as he sought to find words to adequately express his anger at my insubordination.

"Two minutes to impact."

I picked up the footnoterphone and asked to be put through to the storycode engine floor.

"Bradshaw, I want you to take a trip to the Outland and set the fire alarm off at Frobisher High in exactly seventy-eight seconds. That will give us a few minutes breathing space. The pleasure readers will just think they've got bored and lost concentration when the book shuts down. Hello, storycode floor? This is the Bellman. I want you to divert Hawthorne's *Scarlet Letter* to an empty storycode engine and shut it down. . . . Yes, that's quite correct. Shut it down. I don't have time to issue a written order so you're going to have to take my word for it. You are to do it in exactly sixty-three seconds."

"Sieves are going up as requested, Thursday," reported Bradshaw. "Think they'll hold?"

I shrugged. There was nothing else we could do. The storm plot ran towards *The Scarlet Letter* and struck it just as the storycode engine shut down. The book closed. The characters stopped in their tracks as an all-pervading darkness swept over every descriptive passage, every line of dialogue, every nuance, every concept. Where a moment ago there had been a fascinating treatise on morality, there was now only a lifeless hulk of dark reading matter. It was as if *The Scarlet Letter* had never been written. The storm bounced off, then attracted to the brighter lights of the Hemingway canon next door, struck off on a new course. I breathed a sigh of relief but then held my breath once more as the storm struck *In Our Time*—and glanced off. The sieve had held. Over the next few minutes the WordStorm ran between the books as planned, the textual sieves slowing it down as it brushed past the collected works of Hemingway.

"Damage report?"

"Slight grammatical warpage in *A Farewell to Arms*, but nothing serious," said the Cat. "*The Sun Also Rises* is reporting isolated bursts of narrative flexations, but nothing we can't handle. All other books report no damage."

"Good. Bring *The Scarlet Letter* back on-line."

We watched nervously as the storm slowly subsided. It had littered the Hemingway canon with words and ideas, but nothing violent enough to embed them and change the narrative. As likely as not the residents of the novels would just pick them up and sell them to traveling scrap merchants. But the WordStorm wasn't quite finished with us yet. After brushing past the preface to *For Whom the Bell Tolls*, the storm suddenly sped up and, in its last dying throes, embedded a Bride Shot at the Altar plot device right at the end of Blackmore's *Lorna Doone*, where it remains to this day. Aside from that minor flexation, no real harm was done by the WordStorm. The senator berated me for a good ten minutes and filed a report on my behavior the following day, which was summarily rejected by the other members of the Jurisfiction oversight committee.

I left the Cat and Bradshaw to log the damage reports and thanked Dr. Howard and his staff for their slavish attention. I decided to walk back home, across the storycode engine floor and down the empty corridors of the Great Library to the Well of Lost Plots and back to bed. I was feeling quite good about myself. I had run a team of highly skilled technicians and saved *The Scarlet Letter* from almost certain devastation. It would be one of my easier tasks as Bellman, but I didn't know that yet. The evening had gone well. Landen would have been proud of me.

Credits

Falstaff, the three witches, Banquo's ghost, Beatrice and Benedict—all kindly supplied by Shakespeare (William) Inc.

Our thanks to Mr. Heathcliff for graciously agreeing to appear in this novel.

Uriah Heep kindly loaned by Wickfield & Heep, attorneys-at-law.

My thanks to ScarletBea, Yan, Ben, Carla, Jon, Magda, AllAmericanCutie and Dave at the Fforde Fforum for their nominations in the Bookie Awards.

Hedgepig research, *Anna Karenina* footnoterphone gossip and "dodo egg" sarcasm furnished by Mari Roberts.

Solomon's Judgments © The Council of Genres, 1986.

"Chocolate orange" joke used with the kind permission of John Birmingham.

UltraWord—the Ultimate Reading Experience™ remains a trademark of Text Grand Central.

Bookie category Best Dead Person in Fiction courtesy of C. J. Avery.

Fictionaut wordsmithed by Jon Brierley.

Evilness consultant: Ernst Blofeld.

Mrs. Bradshaw's gowns by Coco Chanel.

Aornis little-sister idea courtesy of Rosie Fforde.

Our grateful thanks to the Great Panjandrum for help and guidance in the making of this novel.

No unicorns were written expressly for this book, and no animals or Yahoos (other than grammasites) were harmed in its construction.

This novel was written in BOOK V8.3 and was sequenced using an Mk XXIV Imagino-TransferenceDevice. Peggy Malone was the imaginator. Plot Devices and Inciting Incidents supplied by Billy Budd's Bargain Basement and the WOLP Plot Salvage and Recycling Corporation. Generics supplied and trained by St. Tabularasa's. Holes were filled by apprentices at the Holesmiths' Guild, and echolocation and grammatization were undertaken by Outland contractors at Hodder and Viking.

The "galactic cleansing" policy undertaken by Emperor Zhark is a personal vision of the emperor's, and its inclusion in this work does not constitute tacit approval by the author or the publisher for any such projects, howsoever undertaken. Warning: The author may have eaten nuts while writing this book.

Made wholly on location within the Well of Lost Plots.

A Fforde/Hodder/Viking production. All rights reserved.

Ever wanted to be in books?

Jurisfiction

needs enthusiastic staff
and is recruiting now!

Volunteers needed for an exciting and challenging job. Please apply,
in person, to Norland Park, *Sense and Sensibility*, anytime after chapter 5.
Duties can be hazardous and might involve painful and prolonged death.
No timewasters, please.

WANTED
For Murder and PageRunning

Jurisfiction

Minotaur   Height: 7'4"   Weight: 420 lb   Eyes: Yellow
Color: Light   Build: Heavy   Genre: Mythological

Jurisfiction are anxious to hear from anyone with information regarding the whereabouts of the Minotaur. He may be traveling under the alias "Norman Johnson" and be in disguise. A substantial reward has been offered but members of the BookWorld are advised that this creature is extremely dangerous and should not be approached.

This poster is published in the interests of character safety and narrative stability. TTD/33983

Why not visit –

Tara

for your character exchange program holiday break!

Rhett and Scarlett offer you a traditional Southern welcome to this beautiful Georgian home. Good food and accredited CofG 5-star accommodation in magnificently described surroundings. Parties catered for but sorry, no fantasy or sci-fi. Book early to avoid disappointment. Atlanta burned twice daily at 3:00 p.m. and 1:00 a.m. Warning: Mandatory dress code will be enforced.

Note to Trans-Genre book travelers: *Gone with the Wind* has been designated a book of outstanding historical description and special rules apply to visitors. For more details, contact your in-book exchange program officer or nearest travel agent. Tara is licensed holiday destination number TKD/1608976.

Jurisfiction

Thursday Next returns in March 2005.